I0629572

Instead of
the Thorn

Start Publishing PD LLC
Copyright © 2024 by Start Publishing PD LLC

All rights reserved, including the right to reproduce this book or portions thereof in any form whatsoever.

Start Publishing PD is a registered trademark of Start Publishing PD LLC
Manufactured in the United States of America

Cover art: Shutterstock/Taisiya Kozorez

Cover design: Jennifer Do

10 9 8 7 6 5 4 3 2 1

ISBN 979-8-8809-0615-4

Instead of the Thorn

by Georgette Heyer

To Joanna Cannan

My dear Joanna,

There was once a Sealyham whom you named Elizabeth. The rest you know, and why I dedicate this book to you who so strangely inspired it.

But there are other reasons for my dedication which I think your humility will not let you see. You and I have discussed the fortunes of Elizabeth Arden not once but many times, and good counsel have you given me, and sympathy in moments of depression. Step by step you have followed the book's growth until at last I put it into your hands, all in cold type, and you read it, and gave me a criticism that was careful, and shrewd, and very kind.

So because of these things, and because of the pleasant hours I have spent in your garden, and the delight I have felt in reading your work, I send you my book, such as it is, in admiration of your pen-craft, and with my love.

"Instead of the thorn shall come up the fir-tree. . ." Isaiah; 55, 13

Chapter One

When she was seven Elizabeth asked Mr. Hengist to come and play with her in her bath, and Miss Arden, who was Elizabeth's aunt, said:

"That'll do, Elizabeth."

Elizabeth knew by the way Miss Arden kept her eyes on her crochet that she ought not to have asked Mr. Hengist to come and see her in her bath, and quite suddenly, and for no tangible reason she felt that she had been naughty, and was ashamed. Only Mr. Hengist, who was Father's friend, did not seem to think that she ought not to have said it. He smiled in a friendly, comfortable way, and said that he was much honoured. Only he did not come to the bathroom after all. Elizabeth thought that he would have come if Aunt Anne had not looked so forbidding.

Later on, when she was older, Elizabeth discovered that a great many of the things one did, like cutting one's toe-nails and wearing a thicker vest in winter, must never be mentioned, except to Aunt Anne. Elizabeth could not understand this, and it seemed that Aunt Anne was unable to explain. She only said that you must not ask questions, and that nice little girls did not want to talk about underclothes and things like that. Elizabeth tried to tell her that she didn't exactly want to talk about them, they were not interesting, but they were so ordinary and they formed such a large part of your life that it seemed strange not to be able to speak of them if the conversation turned that way. Aunt Anne just said that she hoped the conversation never would turn that way, and that Elizabeth had better run along and play with her doll.

Elizabeth was tired of her doll, but she did not tell Aunt Anne that. She still loved the doll—in a way—but she was growing too old for it. She would rather have a puppy, only Aunt Anne was not fond of dogs. Then, too, Aunt Anne was never pleased when you grew out of your toys and thought them babyish. It was just as if she expected you always to be the same age and to like the same things. She wanted you to enjoy all the things she had enjoyed when she was little, and when you rebelled, as you had done at Cromer when you said you thought digging sand-castles was dull, she did not see that it was because you were growing up, or because you were "different" but said either

5

that you were showing-off, or that she did not know what present-day children were coming to. It was useless to explain to her that instead of playing with a doll or digging sand-castles, you would prefer to read a book. She seemed to think that you ought not to feel like that; it worried her, and she disapproved.

She was never unkind; she loved Elizabeth more than anyone else in all the world, because Elizabeth was the only thing in the world that was really her own. Her brother was Elizabeth's father, but Elizabeth did not belong to him. He kissed her before he went to business each morning, and when he came home he kissed her again and asked her what she had been doing with herself all day. That was all: he was not interested in Elizabeth, she was not interested in him. Miss Arden was glad that this was so, very secretly, but she would have been shocked if Elizabeth had told her that she did not love her father. She did not even realise that she did not want Elizabeth to care for Lawrence; it would not have been nice to face this fact, so she put it behind her and pretended that Elizabeth was just as fond of Lawrence as she should be. On the only occasion when Elizabeth had ventured to criticise her father, Miss Arden had told her that it was wrong, and that she was a silly little girl. Elizabeth never tried to discuss her father again; she had discovered that whatever you thought must be kept secret, because most of your really interesting thoughts were shocking and precocious. Only it didn't make matters better between her and Lawrence.

Too many things hurt Elizabeth: Aunt Anne's disapproval, consciousness of wrong-doing, and the cat's kittens being drowned. If you fell short of Aunt Anne's ideal of you, she was grieved and worried, and her annoyance made you feel worm-like and unhappy. It was better to pretend always, even to yourself, that you liked the things Aunt Anne wanted you to like. She was convinced that skipping was a pastime that should appeal to you. If you thought it dull, then you were extraordinary, and unchildlike, and you had to bring your brain down from the heights to which it had climbed, and force it to enjoy an amusement it had outgrown three years ago.

So to please Aunt Anne Elizabeth did this, and all the other things that were expected of her, and she did not allow herself to think that they were silly, or that she disliked them, because it was evident that she ought not to think that.

She did not go to school; she had a governess who taught her that Alfred burned the cakes, and that if one straight line stands on another straight line so that the adjacent angles are equal, they are both right angles. Her knowledge of literature was always defective, because there were so many writers of whom Aunt Anne disapproved. Shelley was banned because his private life did not bear inspection; Swinburne was a modern, and therefore unreadable; Byron had written a very disgusting poem called "Don Juan" (Miss Arden had not read any of Byron's poems, but she had heard that this was so) and therefore Elizabeth was forbidden to read his works. Wordsworth and Tennyson were given to Elizabeth, and the copy of Tennyson was well-worn and had the more trite passages underlined in pencil.

When Miss Arden was a girl everyone was rapturous in praise of Dickens, though of course it was a pity he had written such a horrid book as "Pickwick Papers." Elizabeth was given the "Old Curiosity Shop" to read, with assurances that it was a sweet tale and one that would make her cry. Elizabeth did not cry, because she did not think that little Nell was at all pathetic. She preferred Dick Swiveller, but as Miss Arden evidently expected her to rave over the tragedy and the general sugariness of little Nell, she said that she thought it was lovely. Gradually she cheated herself into believing this, so that when she read "Dombey and Son" she managed to feel quite a lump at the back of her throat at the death of Paul. If she had not felt this lump Miss Arden would have said that she didn't know how Elizabeth could read those passages without a tear, and further, that she shuddered to think what the younger generation was coming to.

Thackeray was no more than a name to Elizabeth; he had written a book called "Vanity Fair," which was not at all a nice book, but Scott rivalled Dickens in desirableness. Then there was Louisa Alcott and Charlotte Yonge, and L. T. Meade, and a host of well-meaning women who wrote books for girls especially designed, it seemed, to induce a morbidly sentimental frame of mind. Miss Arden labelled them all "pretty tales."

Mr. Hengist gave Elizabeth the "History of Henry Esmond" on her fourteenth birthday, but Miss Arden intercepted it and said gently:

"I think there's plenty of time yet for that, Mr. Hengist."

Mr. Hengist said, Stuff and nonsense! very gruffly, but Elizabeth was not allowed to read "Esmond."

She had friends, not many because most other girls were at school and had other interests, but a few, of whom Miss Arden approved, and Mr. Hengist.

She thought how she had loved Mr. Hengist when she was seven years old. She only liked him now, and she thought him queer sometimes and brusque. Aunt Anne was not fond of Mr. Hengist; she was polite to him because he was Father's friend, but she remarked occasionally to Elizabeth that he was a very strange man. He called Elizabeth Prunes and Prisms, which hurt her dignity, and he advised her not to be a little humbug when she told him how miserable the death of Paul had made her feel.

"My dear good child," he said, polishing his eyeglasses on a large silk handkerchief, "for heaven's sake cultivate some independence of thought! Don't repeat your aunt's views; let's hear your own. They're the only ones that are worth having from you."

Elizabeth thought he could not have heard Aunt Anne say that it was unbecoming for a child of her age to air her opinions. Either you were silent, or you agreed with what your elders said. She looked at Mr. Hengist and wondered why he said such funny things.

"Tell me what you really think," he said. "What about Dick Swiveller and the Marchioness?"

"Oh, they're very clever, aren't they?" she answered at once. "Of course they're not sad, like Nell and her grandfather."

"Why should they be?" he retorted, which was quite incomprehensible.

To Lawrence he said more, forcibly and often, but Lawrence wore a superior smile and replied that it was very easy for a bachelor to propound theories on a girl's education.

"And it's easy for a married man to shelve his responsibilities on to a

8

spinster's shoulders": Mr. Hengist said quickly.

Nothing disturbed Lawrence. He raised his eyebrows and still smiled.

"My dear Hengist, are you insinuating that Anne is incapable of bringing up Elizabeth?" he asked banteringly.

"Yes—no, I'm not insinuating, I'm saying it point-blank. Good God, Lawrence, don't you know that Elizabeth is being hopelessly mismanaged?"

"No, I can't say that I do." Lawrence was maddeningly amused. "Anne is a woman; she ought to know."

"She may be a woman, but she didn't bear Elizabeth," Mr. Hengist snapped. "Only an exceptional spinster ought to have sole charge of a child. I don't want to be rude about your sister, but she's not at all exceptional."

"I hope not," Lawrence said, more gravely. "I detest your exceptional woman. Anne is a good woman. I have no qualms."

"Evidently not. You don't realise that there's nothing more dangerous on this earth than your really good old maid."

Lawrence looked at him very much as Elizabeth had looked, and thought what a queer chap he was.

"What an extraordinary thing to say!" he remarked. "No one could call Anne dangerous, poor old thing!"

Mr. Hengist got quite excited, and banged the arm of his chair with his fist.

"Of course she's dangerous!" he said loudly. "All the more so because she's Mid-Victorian! Already she's taught Elizabeth to be careful that her skirt doesn't get above her knees."

"Well, I don't see anything wrong in that," said Lawrence, pondering it. "I don't approve of this modern tendency to show your knees."

"I'm not talking about her knees!" shouted Mr. Hengist.

"But you said—"

"Don't be so damned literal, Lawrence! That's only an example. Not that there's anything wrong with Elizabeth's knees. Far from it. That covering of them up is illustrative of the whole system. Cover 'em up if you like, but don't be for ever morbidly anxious that they should be covered. It's heading straight for a covered up mind. Mid-Victorianism. If a thing's true it's beastly,

9

so don't face it. Cover it up! Pretend it isn't there!"

Lawrence became pompous, and crossed his legs.

"I consider that there's too much license permitted these days in speech. When I was a boy girls didn't—"

"Shut up. Don't talk drivel. Supposing they didn't? We're progressing, aren't we? You didn't do the same as your father in his youth, did you?"

This was difficult to answer. Lawrence uncrossed his legs.

"Well, I still maintain that all this freedom of speech doesn't lead to any good. I should be very sorry to think that Elizabeth was setting herself up against her elders, or talking immodestly."

"You're no better than a decayed turnip," said Mr. Hengist flatly. "If a girl of Elizabeth's age is always careful not to mention something that might be considered improper it's a fairly sure sign that her mind'll be a sink by the time she's thirty—unless some man marries her and knocks the nonsense out of her."

"Really, Hengist, I can't see that—"

"No, because you don't want to see it. Probably you don't know that Elizabeth is fast becoming a humbug. She hasn't got a mind of her own; she echoes her aunt. She pretends to like things her aunt thinks she ought to like, she can't develop because her aunt won't let her. She isn't even allowed to read what she likes."

"You can't seriously be advocating an unrestricted library for Elizabeth!" said Lawrence, very sarcastically.

"No," Mr. Hengist had paused, and considered, frowning. "No. But surely it's easy enough to keep the books she isn't old enough to read out of her way? There are jolly few, anyway."

"My dear Hengist, some of these moderns—!"

"She wouldn't understand 'em. Better let her read modern realism than morbid sentimentality. For God's sake teach her to face facts!"

Lawrence thought that it was time to put a stop to the discussion. Hengist was talking nonsense, of course, but it was rather disturbing.

"As I said before," he smiled, "we all know that you bachelors have eccentric notions on the upbringing of children. I think we can trust Anne to look after Elizabeth,"

Chapter Two

Elizabeth at sixteen made a great discovery, that Men were fascinating, much more so than girls. Hitherto she had known no Men, only Father and Mr. Hengist, and people like the doctor and the dentist and shop-assistants. Somehow they did not seem to be Men, at least, not with a capital M. They were creatures who wore trousers; there was nothing exciting about them.

But Marjorie Drew's brother Tony was something entirely new and thrilling. He was twenty-two and had just come down from Cambridge. He thought Elizabeth was pretty, like a wild-rose. Marjorie laughed, and said, no, a prim-rose, and Tony was quite angry with her. He said Elizabeth was a little shy violet, or perhaps a snowdrop, until Marjorie grew tired of hearing horticultural similes, and left him.

Until he met Elizabeth Tony had rather thought that he was passionately in love with an attractive lady of thirty-three, living at Bedford, but now he began to think that he had mistaken his heart. The lady, one Mrs. Lambert, treated him as a boy and made him run errands for her; Elizabeth looked shyly up at him and was all admiration. It was rather refreshing, but of course Elizabeth was only a kid.

So Elizabeth, who had never known a school-girl's passion for one of her own sex, plunged into her first love-affair, and hugged it to her, and sighed, despaired, rejoiced and fluttered.

Luckily for her peace of mind Miss Arden knew nothing of the tumult that raged in her niece's bosom for six short weeks—Tony went to Scotland then, and by the time he came back the fickle flame had gone out. Miss Arden would have been shocked beyond measure if she had known of Elizabeth's passion. She was not altogether pleased when Elizabeth, in an expansive moment, confided that she liked men. To be sure, there wasn't anything exactly wrong in liking men, but it was not at all the thing that Miss Arden would have said when she was a girl. On the contrary, she had always affirmed and would still affirm if directly questioned that she disliked men. It was a poor compliment to her father and brother, and it was naturally untrue, but she did not know that. She would have found it hard to believe that men did not like her, and if anyone had had the courage to suggest it she would have been indignant at the impertinence of the male.

She knew nothing about men, but she was fond of generalising. Elizabeth learned that woman was superior to man always. Men had to be snubbed and kept in their places; they lived strange lives, and were a nuisance about the house. Even Father caused a deal of trouble, dropping cigar ash on the carpet, and never standing the cork-mat in the bathroom up on end.

Aunt Anne was very excitable on the subject of women's rights. She wanted to be in Parliament and to sit on juries, and even Mr. Hengist could not argue with her because she became so angry and so illogical, and said that she had not patience with him or with anyone else. And when Elizabeth, wrinkling her pretty brow, said that she thought women would be rather silly on juries, Aunt Anne told her that she was only a child and didn't know what she was talking about. So the Rights of Women were not spoken of at home; it was safer that way.

Elizabeth became a flapper and tied her hair back in a large bow at the back of her neck. Lawrence began to notice her and said, By Jove, what a beautiful girl she was going to be! He called her his pretty little daughter, and Elizabeth went at once to study herself in the mirror. She had always thought that she was nice-looking, but until Lawrence called her pretty she had not realised to the full the beauty of her great brown eyes with their long lashes like shadows about them, or the fascination of her short upper lip and little straight nose. She fingered the masses of her dusky hair, and discovered breathlessly that her shoulders sloped slightly and were milk-white.

Lawrence began to talk of her coming out as soon as the War was over, but Miss Arden begged him not to think of that yet.

"I want to keep the baby as long as possible," she sighed.

Lawrence thought this was absurd, but he supposed all women felt like that.

"Well, I don't know." he said. "Personally I don't see that there'd be any harm in it."

"It's such a pity to let her grow up so soon," Miss Arden answered. "I don't want to see the bloom knocked off yet."

This sounded rather alarming; Lawrence had an idea that he had heard the expression before.

"Oh, but she'd be chaperoned!" he said vaguely.

Miss Arden shook her head and became melancholy.

"It can never be the same again," she said.

"The same as what?" Lawrence was dense, so like a man.

Miss Arden knew quite well what she meant, but unfortunately it was difficult to explain. She sought refuge in a well-used formula.

"Ah, you can't understand, Lawrence! You're only a man."

It was conclusive; Lawrence had no pretensions towards understanding his daughter. He did not say any more.

Since the War had broken out Mr. Hengist had fallen very low in Miss Arden's estimation. He made munitions, which was most worthy, of course, and he would talk about the War in front of Elizabeth. Miss Arden found him impervious to hints; she was forced to speak plainly. She said:—

"Mr. Hengist, I wonder if you would mind not talking 'War' here? Atrocities and things. We know they happen, but I don't think there's any need to speak about them."

"*You* know they happen," he answered. "Does Elizabeth?"

"I hope not," she said gravely. "I don't approve of young girls reading about all these horrors."

"Most girls of Elizabeth's age are doing War-work, and facing facts."

"Elizabeth is only seventeen," she reminded him frigidly.

"She's old enough to know that life isn't always romantically rose-coloured."

Miss Arden rose, and put a stop to a possible discussion.

"I think I am the best judge of what is best for Elizabeth, Mr. Hengist."

Mr. Hengist checked a groan. It was hopeless to argue with Miss Arden; she defeated you at every point.

But the War ended and there was no need to talk about it any more. Elizabeth began to attend classes, and went on a sketching tour, with Miss Arden in the background, to Brittany. She enjoyed herself immensely, and when she came back her father cried, By Jove, she was taller than ever and quite a young lady!

He began to picture himself in the role of proud father. It would be rather jolly to take Elizabeth out to parties. He cast a surreptitious glance at the mirror and imagined his friends' surprise at finding that he possessed a grown-up daughter. Really, Elizabeth was quite lovely; moreover she was quiet and docile, unlike these terrible modern girls who wore short skirts, swore, and bobbed their hair. He thought how delightful it would be to display her, virginally shy, at the Opera, when people would surely wonder who that distinguished-looking couple were. Probably he would be taken for an elder brother, or perhaps a youthful uncle. Except for an almost imperceptible silveriness at the temples he had worn well, remarkably well, and kept his neat figure. So many men, notably poor old Hengist, seemed to have become baggy and stout.

Miss Arden did not fit in with the picture at all, which was annoying. Poor Anne, she had become woefully thin, and she could never wear her clothes as though they belonged to her. He reflected, conscious all the time of disloyalty, that Anne had never had the dress-sense. She followed the fashions of five years ago, or more, and somehow she seemed unable to wear the right clothes for the right occasion.

Lawrence admitted that he knew very little about women's clothes, but he rather thought that he had an eye for colour. Anne was too fond of mixing her colours: she would wear black shoes with a brown frock, and perhaps a grey golf-jersey, and always powdered her nose inadequately.

Secretly he decided that Anne would have to be left out of a good many parties. Probably she would prefer to stay at home. When one came to think of it it would be positively unfair to expect Anne to chaperon Elizabeth everywhere. He would do that; it was his duty, and certainly he would not shelve it on to Anne's shoulders. Besides, it was no longer the custom to chaperon debutantes, and although he by no means approved of this laxity, he thought it would make Elizabeth less conspicuous if he performed the rite. No one would think that he was Elizabeth's father.

He became affectionate towards Elizabeth, and thought that it was not every man who possessed so beautiful a daughter. He said:—

"What has my little girl been doing with herself all day?" and stroked her hair.

Elizabeth looked at him, rather puzzled, and answered that she had been doing the usual things. She wished that he would not stroke her hair; she hated to be touched.

"We shall have to think about bringing you out, eh?" he said, smiling. "What about putting this hair up?"

Elizabeth glanced at her aunt.

"Can I, Auntie?"

"Oh, it's very early days yet, darling! Lawrence, I thought perhaps when she's nineteen—"

"Oh, nonsense!" he said. "You're quite old enough now, aren't you, Elizabeth?"

"Yes, of course I am. Do let me, Aunt Anne!"

"You must do as your father wishes," Miss Arden replied in a tone that warned Lawrence that if harm came of it the blame was his.

He was relieved to find how easily he had won his point, and rubbed his hands together, nodding at Elizabeth.

"And my little girl will have to have some frocks, won't she? I've been thinking of making you a dress-allowance for some time. What do you think of that?"

Elizabeth thought it a delightful idea, but she wished her father would not talk to her as though she were a child.

"Thanks awfully, Father," she said dutifully. "I'd love it."

"And will yon let your old Daddy come and help you choose your pretty dance-frocks?"

Elizabeth had never called her father Daddy, and she looked at him now in undisguised astonishment. So did Miss Arden, but her look said frankly that she thought Lawrence was mad. This new attitude he had adopted was wholly unnecessary. It was almost as though he were trying to draw Elizabeth away from her.

"And is Auntie to be shut out of all these exciting plans?" she asked brightly.

"Oh, Auntie!" Elizabeth cried, embracing her. "How can you!" But even as she said it she was conscious of a wicked little hope that Aunt Anne would not always want to be one of the party. She didn't care for Father much —at least, she loved him, of course, because he was her father—but going to dances with him sounded more attractive than going to them with Aunt Anne. And very desperately she hoped that she might be allowed to choose her own frocks, and—more desperately still—her own lingeries. Aunt Anne said that the modern lingerie was almost indecent, and that it was most unsuitable to have everything made in silk; she inclined to stout materials with high necks, and buttons down the front. Elizabeth always agreed that they were far more sensible, but secretly she hated them, and longed for a set of silk underclothing, in primrose, she thought, just to see what it was like. Perhaps this new, playful Father would understand, only it would be rather difficult to broach such a delicate subject to him.

Lawrence paid her allowance into the bank, and gave Elizabeth a cheque-book, which made her feel most emancipated and important. He criticised her efforts at hairdressing, and for a whole hour, under the hostile eye of Miss Arden, taught her how to put it up so that the wave in it showed to the best advantage.

He was cunning when he took Elizabeth to choose her evening frocks. He came home from the office at midday, quite unexpectedly, and said that he was going to take Elizabeth to Bond Street. He pretended that he had forgotten it was the afternoon set apart by Miss Arden for the Mothers' Meeting.

"Can't you put it off?" Miss Arden said, rather snappily. "You really can't go and choose Elizabeth's frocks. It's hardly a man's sphere."

Lawrence began to feel very guilty, but he brazened it out.

"Rubbish, Anne! After all, I am her father. But I'm sorry you can't come. Too stupid of me. I can't think how I could have forgotten this was your Mothers' day. I suppose you couldn't desert the meeting for once?"

"It's most annoying," said Miss Arden. "Of course I might send a note to Mrs. Hemingway ..." She considered, drumming her fingers on the table.

Both Elizabeth and her father sat quiet, watching her, and trying not to hope that she wouldn't come. Elizabeth looked mournful; Lawrence was anxious.

"No, I can't possibly cut the meeting," Miss Arden said at last. "It's a pity you didn't tell me before."

"It only just occurred to me to-day," Lawrence explained, "or of course I should have."

Miss Arden was hurt; you could see it in her face; hurt and cross.

"Perhaps we could put it off," Elizabeth suggested.

Lawrence thought that was unnecessary of Elizabeth. He shook his head sadly.

"I'm afraid not. I shall be tied to the office all the rest of the week. This is really my one free day." He thought perhaps this sounded too ungracious. "Never mind about the meeting, Anne. I'm sure the Mothers can spare you."

Elizabeth wished that Father were not so anxious that Aunt Anne should accompany them, but she choked the wish down, and said, "Do come, Auntie."

But Miss Arden refused. She went away to the meeting, martyr-like, and Elizabeth felt a dreadful joy at seeing her go.

Home was in a tidy backwater of Kensington, called The Boltons; Lawrence hailed a taxi chunking up the road, and put Elizabeth into it.

"It was a pity your aunt couldn't come," he remarked as he got in beside Elizabeth.

"Yes, wasn't it?" she agreed.

"Though I'm not at all sure she wouldn't have been too tired," he went on.

"One has to be careful that she doesn't overdo it, you know. We probably shan't be back till dinner-time. I shouldn't have liked to feel that we were dragging her about till that hour."

Elizabeth thought that he could not know Aunt Anne very well if he imagined that she would be tired after one afternoon's shopping. A faint suspicion dawned in her mind that Father was talking like this simply to salve his conscience. She banished the suspicion and thought that after all there was some truth in what he said. Aunt Anne was too eager to sacrifice herself to others. She told Lawrence this, and he was pleased with her, and said that she had hit the nail on the head.

It was not until after tea, when three frocks had been chosen, that Elizabeth dared to ask about the silk lingerie. She had become more at ease with Lawrence, and he had liked all the prettiest frocks.

Elizabeth paused tentatively before a shop-window, and blushed.

"Father—I think I ought to have—if you don't mind— just for evening wear—some of—of those things."

Lawrence turned to look at the shop, and then he stared at Elizabeth. She kept her eyes downcast, and thought how awful it was of her to have spoken.

"Well, well!" Lawrence broke into a laugh. "I can't very well go in there with you, can I?"

Elizabeth's lashes fluttered upwards.

"I could go alone—if you'd wait! I've—brought my cheque-book."

The afternoon had been a success; Lawrence felt indulgent.

"Well, in with you," he said. "I wonder what your aunt will say?" Then he thought this was being disloyal, and hastily added, "Of course she won't object, as they're only to wear with the dance-frocks."

"Oh, yes, only with them!" Elizabeth agreed.

She was a long time in the shop, but Lawrence, who had been buying cigars, did not realise this. He patted her arm and hoped that she had got what she wanted.

Elizabeth thought of the piles of silken garments set aside to be sent to her, and stepped out briskly.

"Yes, rather!" she said.

Lawrence said that she was a little puss, and put her into another taxi. On the way home he confided to her that he had long considered buying a car.

Chapter Three

Elizabeth looked so pretty in her new clothes that Miss Arden said nothing about the silken lingerie. She told herself that it was only for the evening, and gradually she was able to believe it.

When Lawrence bought a four-seater coupe she said that she couldn't get over it. Lawrence told her that she wasn't expected to get over it, only into it, and because he was palpably delighted with the joke, Miss Arden and Elizabeth both laughed at it.

Lawrence learned to drive the car, but there was also a chauffeur, which was just as well, as if anything went wrong Lawrence didn't know what to do. He lived in morbid dread of punctures, and whenever the car back-fired, which was often, he got out and felt all the tires. However he was very proud of being able to drive a car, and he looked very important when he sat behind the wheel.

"There's a great deal in driving," he told Mr. Hengist, confidentially. "It's by no means so easy as it looks." He saw a large lorry approaching, and became agonised. Once safely past:—"I suppose any fool can drive a car, but it needs practice and a cool head to be able to drive well."

"Yes, I've no doubt you'll improve in time," said Mr. Hengist cruelly.

Luckily Lawrence was changing gear, a noisy and a perilous process, and he did not hear this remark.

"The fellow who taught me said that it's amazing how dense some people are about learning. Then too, lots of men start driving much too fast. I don't approve of that at all."

"Thank God!" said Mr. Hengist fervently.

"The whole point about a car, to my mind, is enjoyment," Lawrence said, swerving drunkenly to avoid a pothole. "There's nothing enjoyable in scorching." Experimentally and cautiously he removed one hand from the wheel. It was rather daring, he felt, but impressive. "Elizabeth wants me to teach her," he said. "I don't think there'd be any harm in it. Of course I shouldn't let her drive about alone. Either Jenkins or I would go with her in .case of accidents. It was really an excellent idea of mine to buy a car. I can't think why I never did it before. By the way, what do you think of my little girl? I took a hand in choosing her clothes. Poor Anne —she means well, but she can't dress. I don't know whether you've noticed it? I flatter myself Elizabeth looks very well in her new things, very well indeed. What do you think?"

"She's very pretty," Mr. Hengist agreed.

"Not only that, Hengist. Of course you don't know her as I do, because you're not her father, but I assure you her beauty isn't only facial. When I see all these modern young minxes with their cigarettes and their backless gowns, I realise what a complete success Elizabeth's upbringing has been. No offhand manners and horrible slang words, but—well, I often think myself that she's just like a violet. Some poet or other, I've forgotten for the moment who it was, wrote something remarkably apt about a violet. Just fits my little girl. Something about 'modest violet in the dell.' I daresay you know what I mean?"

"No, but it sounds fairly mawkish. I'm willing to admit that Elizabeth has nice manners. She spoils herself by being insincere."

"Ah, that's where you're wrong," said Lawrence. "I don't believe my little girl has ever entertained an unkind thought about anyone. She has such an affectionate disposition."

"When did you discover all this?" Mr. Hengist asked.

Lawrence looked rather hurt.

"It's natural that her father should know what she's really like," he said.

They came into traffic so that out of consideration for his own safety Mr. Hengist forbore to retort. A van-driver asked Lawrence what the ruddy hell he thought he was doing, but otherwise there was no unpleasantness. Lawrence emerged triumphant and remarked that one soon got into the way of guiding a car through traffic.

20

"It would not surprise me if that van-driver was the worse for drink," he said severely. "A most uncalled-for piece of impertinence. What were we saying? Oh yes, about Elizabeth. I'm taking her to Mrs. Carfew's dance on Wednesday, and perhaps to the Opera next week."

"Who are the Carfews?" Mr. Hengist asked.

"Oh, some people Anne called on not so long ago. I know old Carfew in the City, and now that Elizabeth is 'out' I thought it might be as well for Anne to call on Mrs. Carfew. I am making a point of getting to know more people."

"You're certainly doing your duty, even if it is belated," Mr. Hengist admitted grudgingly. "Is your sister going to the dance too?"

Lawrence decided to ignore the first half of this speech; one had to make allowances for Hengist, poor chap. He was becoming quite a crusty old bachelor.

"Well, it's rather difficult," he said. "The invitation is for Elizabeth and 'partner.' I must say, this new custom of expecting a girl to bring her own partner to a dance is a very strange one. I am not at all sure that I approve of it. However, I suppose one must remember *autres temps, autres moeurs*, and as it happened Elizabeth was able to ask the Benson boy to accompany her. There was no invitation either to me or to Anne. Manners are sadly lacking nowadays. Still, I should hardly think that Mrs. Carfew would object to the presence of an extra man, so I shall go too."

"Why?" asked Mr. Hengist. "Elizabeth doesn't need a chaperon at a private dance—or at any other for that matter."

"It is not a question of chaperoning her," Lawrence explained. "It's only natural that I should wish to be present at my little girl's first dance. It's a great pity that Anne cannot come too."

Elizabeth herself was looking forward to the dance with mixed feelings. She wished that she knew the Carfews better, or at any rate, Miss Carfew, who at first sight seemed rather alarming. Smartly dressed athletic girls frightened Elizabeth, who was sure that they despised her, and she could never think of anything to talk about with them. Then, too, she had read in books of girls finding themselves partnerless. How humiliating that would be, but how still more dreadful if she found herself unable to follow a man's style of dancing! She wondered what you said to your partner; whether you made the conversation or whether he did.

She was incredibly nervous on the appointed evening, and sat shivering beside Lawrence in the car, thinking that her hair would come down if she tried to move the pin that was sticking into her head. Her hands were cold, and she felt rather sick, as if she were on her way to the dentist. The light-hearted demeanour of her father and of Denis Benson sitting opposite made her feel much worse; she would have liked to tell them how frightened she was so that they could reassure her, but that was quite impossible.

Some of the nervousness left her when she stood in the ball-room. The orchestra was playing very loudly, and nearly everyone was dancing and did not notice her. Denis took her programme and asked if he might have every third dance.

Elizabeth thought suddenly how nice Denis was to want all those dances. He looked so pleased when she smiled her consent that she felt it was not mere politeness that had made him ask. She had known him for such a long time too that it would not matter so much if she stepped on him or was heavy.

"And this one?" said Denis, "before someone else grabs it?"

No one had been introduced to her yet, so no one was likely to grab it, but it was rather flattering that Denis should think someone might.

"If you like," she said. "You know—I don't dance a bit well. I've only had three lessons."

"Oh, rot!" Denis said, piloting her carefully round one corner. "You dance toppingly. Light as a feather. Jolly tune, what?"

It was the first time Elizabeth had been in a man's arms; she felt bewildered, shy, and unlike herself. Denis held her very close, with one hand over her shoulder-blade; its warmth, through her frock, struck her as being too familiar and just a little horrid. Sometimes his knee touched hers, and that was worse. She thought how she had always hated to be held, even by her father, and wondered whether she would ever grow to like dancing. Occasionally she saw Lawrence, over Denis' shoulder, and whenever she caught his eye he smiled and nodded at her in a way which showed her that he was pleased.

The dance came to an end; Elizabeth slipped out of Denis' arms, panting a little, and flushed. Mrs. Carfew came up, trailing black satin and jet, and murmured names. An alarming kaleidoscope of men scribbled their names on her programme, quite illegibly, and drifted away. Lawrence's voice sounded in her ear.

"Is my little girl enjoying herself?" it asked fondly.

Elizabeth gave him a bright smile, and said yes, it was lovely. Then Denis took her to the room where the refreshments were spread out, and gave her cider-cup which seemed to Elizabeth quite the nicest drink she had ever tasted, and certainly the most daring.

The respite was brief; they heard the orchestra swing into a one-step, and Denis said that they ought to go back to the ball-room. He left her in the doorway, stranded, and went to claim his partner for the dance.

Elizabeth tried to make out the name on her programme, unsuccessfully, and wondered how ever she would recognise its owner. A fair man with a monocle came up to her and bowed.

"I think this is our dance, Miss—Er ...?"

"Oh, is it?" Elizabeth said, wishing that it was not. The fair man looked supercilious and rather bored; she was sure that he danced in a complicated style.

She was rather surprised when he said nothing at all for the first few minutes of the dance, and decided that it was for her to open a conversation. Panic seized her; she could think of nothing to say, and all the time he was staring glassily across the room. His dancing was quite extraordinary, for his whole body seemed to move, his shoulders most of all. She felt stiff and unyielding, and wished that he would not twist and turn so violently. She began to grow hot and miserable, thinking herself a fool to be unable to speak.

But presently the fair man cleared his throat and said something in a weary voice which Elizabeth could not hear.

"I beg your pardon?" she said, knocking her toe against his.

He took a firmer hold on her and repeated his remark.

"I suppose you dance an awful lot?"

"N-no, this is my first dance," Elizabeth answered.

This seemed to discourage him, for he said no more for some time. His next observation was made just as they slid past Mrs. Carfew.

"Not such a bad floor, is it?" he said.

Elizabeth felt herself blushing for him; he could not have seen Mrs. Carfew.

"I think it's awfully good," she replied.

"Pity there's no saxophone," he remarked. "Rotten to have a band without one, don't you think?"

"I don't know—quite—what it is," Elizabeth confessed.

He looked at her blankly, and said, "Oh, really?" He did not speak again until after the dance when he asked if he could get Elizabeth a glass of claret-cup or something. She refused the offer, and then wished that she had accepted it: he looked so disappointed.

"Well, er—better find a place to sit, hadn't we?"

They chose a sofa in a secluded alcove, and the fair man cleared his throat once or twice.

"Ever been to the Hyde Park?" he enquired, after some mental research.

Elizabeth thought he must have a very short memory if he had forgotten already that this was her first dance.

"No. Is it nice? I've always heard that it was lovely."

"Oh . . ." He seemed to deprecate this enthusiasm. "Not so bad." Again he racked his brain. "Have you seen *Buzz*?"

Elizabeth had read a criticism of the *revue* in the *Morning Post*; it was evidently a vulgar performance with a good many bare-backed girls in it.

"No, I haven't," she said primly.

He sighed, and shook his head.

"Wonderful show!" he said fervently.

Her next partner was better; he was younger, and a lucky question brought forth the information that he owned a motor-bicycle. He was quite content to talk about it all the time, and although the description of its engine did not interest Elizabeth, at least she was spared the necessity of thinking out a good opening to a conversation.

Later in the evening Lawrence asked her if she thought him too dull and old to dance. Elizabeth said no, at once, and got up.

"Nothing at all in this modern dancing!" Lawrence puffed, treading heavily on her toes. "All you have to do is to shift from one foot to the other, and occasionally take a sort of sidestep. ... I beg your pardon!" This to the couple with whom he had collided. "Clumsy young bounder!" he whispered in Elizabeth's ear. "I don't see anything in it myself. It's child's play. You know, this room's really rather overcrowded, Elizabeth. You can't move an inch without having someone bang into you. And I can't say that I admire this jazz-music. There isn't any tune about it that I can hear, and the way that fellow keeps blowing the motor-horn is really most ridiculous and out of place."

Elizabeth had no breath to waste in answering. He swung her violently round and, when she stumbled, said reproachfully and with a touch of superiority that she didn't seem to be able to fit her steps to his very well.

Miss Arden was awaiting them at home in a red Pyrenees dressing-gown and with her hair in curl-papers.

Elizabeth hugged her, feeling that she was back in haven after a storm.

"Well, darling, and did you enjoy it?" Miss Arden asked, kissing her.

"Of course she did," Lawrence said, bustling in. "I can tell you, Anne, she was quite a success. Her programme was full up when I saw it."

Aunt Anne was so anxious to hear that Elizabeth had enjoyed herself, you could not possibly tell her how you had hated most of the men you had danced with, or how miserable you had felt when one of those awful pauses fell in the conversation. She would have been distressed, and would think you were blasé or affected.

"Oh, I loved it, Auntie!" Elizabeth said. "I only wish that you could have been there too."

Chapter Four

Sarah Cockburn was the most amazing girl in the world; all the more so because her mother was so quiet and ordinary. Sarah wore flaming jumpers and tweed skirts which showed a large expanse of check stocking. She smoked innumerable cigarettes, elegantly referred to by herself as gaspers, and swept her hair severely back from her forehead. She was a newcomer to the neighbourhood, and Miss Arden took Elizabeth to call on her mother. Elizabeth wore white kid gloves and sat on the edge of the chair, being seen but not heard, and Mrs. Cockburn, in a satin tea-frock, dispensed tea and talked to Aunt Anne about domestic worries, and the difficulty of finding a house.

In the middle of the tea-party Sarah came striding into the room in brogue shoes and the woollen jumper and striped skirt of golf enthusiasts. She did not murmur any apologies for her unpunctuality, but went straight to Aunt Anne and shook hands.

"How d'you do?" she said, and went on to Elizabeth. "B'lieve I saw you in the Brompton Road the other day. I say, you've got nothing to eat!"

Neither Elizabeth nor her aunt knew who Sarah was; Miss Arden looked at her as though she were an escaped lunatic.

"My daughter Sarah," Mrs. Cockburn explained. "Darling, this is Miss Arden, and Miss Elizabeth Arden."

Sarah offered Elizabeth a plate of cakes.

"I don't recommend the pink ones. They usually taste of sawdust," she said frankly, then sat down on a footstool beside the fire and put her cup and saucer on the floor.

"I had no idea you had a daughter." Miss Arden said, and looked inquiringly at Sarah. "I don't think you were at church on Sunday, were you!"

"No, I never go to church," Sarah answered, with a disarming smile. "It bores me horribly, and I come away in a most unholy frame of mind."

26

Elizabeth stared round-eyed. Within less than five minutes this extraordinary girl had committed every breach of social etiquette possible, and now she said that church bored her. She cast a surreptitious glance at Aunt Anne, and saw that her face had assumed the wooden expression it always wore when something had displeased her.

"You've lived here ages, haven't you!" Sarah said, addressing Elizabeth. "What's it like!"

Elizabeth had always been told that the Boltons was the most attractive quarter of London, so central and yet so quiet.

"Oh, it's very nice," she answered. "So convenient, and such a little backwater."

Sarah grimaced.

"Are there any cheery people living here!—or is it frightfully conventional! At first glance it looks rather suburban—the sort of place where people never come to see you unless they're asked."

It was that sort of place, but never before had Elizabeth heard it spoken of in a disparaging way.

"I think—people—are quite good about calling," she said timidly.

Sarah cast her a quick glance, then laughed.

"I believe I'm shocking you. I'm awfully sorry, but I always say the wrong thing. Don't I, Mums!"

"Yes, darling," Mrs. Cockburn agreed placidly. "Miss Arden has been telling me that there's quite a large bridge set here."

"Then you'll be happy," Sarah rejoined. "Mother's a bridge-fiend," she told Elizabeth. "I do hope you don't play?"

"No, I'm too stupid," Elizabeth answered.

"What a heaven-sent excuse! I'm too bad-tempered. If my partner dared to ask me why I'd led a spade in the second round I'm afraid I should chuck something at him. Cigarette?"

"I don't smoke," Elizabeth said, rather regretfully. She thought how lovely it would be to breathe out two long spirals from your nostrils, as Sarah was doing.

She was still dreaming of cigarettes when she walked home with Miss Arden. Miss Arden's voice intruded on the dream.

"On the whole, quite nice people. I thought Mrs. Cockburn a very sweet woman."

"Yes," Elizabeth said.

"The girl is excessively modern, of course, but she's young yet. I daresay she is less affected when one knows her better."

Elizabeth was surprised; she had expected a severe diatribe against Sarah, and could not imagine why Aunt Anne was being so lenient.

"Rather a desirable connaissance," Miss Arden continued. "They seem to be very well connected and to know any amount of interesting people. You must ask Sarah to tea when they have returned my call."

"I'd like to," Elizabeth said, brightening. "I wonder whether she'll come?"

Sarah did come; she told her mother that although Elizabeth was as dull as ditch-water, outside, she rather thought there was something more interesting inside, carefully covered up. She inspected all Elizabeth's books, tried to discuss Galsworthy with her, and ended by asking her to join the private dance-club to which she belonged.

"Awfully cheery show," she assured Elizabeth. "A great pal of mine, Lucy Elmsley, runs it, and as she's a married woman I shouldn't think your aunt 'ud object to your joining."

"I should love to! How kind of you to ask me! The only difficulty is the partner. You see, I don't know many men."

"Well, roll up at the next meeting—it's on Friday— and I'll supply a partner. I think you'd enjoy it."

"I'm sure I should," Elizabeth said. "Only I'll have to ask Aunt Anne. And are you sure it isn't a dreadful nuisance having to find me a partner?"

"Shouldn't have offered to if it were," Sarah said bluntly.

It was Lawrence, and not Miss Arden, who objected to the arrangement. He complained that he did not know Mrs. Elmsley, whoever she might be, and he did not like to let his little girl join what might very well prove to be a fast set. However, Mrs. Cockburn and her husband came in that evening to make up a bridge-four, and Lawrence was so pleased by Mrs. Cockburn's appearance and the excellent game she played that it was only necessary for her to use a very little flattery before he consented graciously to allow Elizabeth to join the club.

So on Friday Elizabeth was driven in fear and trembling to the Knightsbridge Hotel, where the club met. She was purposely late because she had thought how awful it would be to arrive before any of the others, but now, as she entered the ball-room and saw the dense throng of people, she wondered why ever she had been so stupid, and how ever she was to find Sarah in this crowd. Some of the people circling slowly past her no doubt belonged to the club, others were merely habitues of the Knightsbridge, where a public dance club was held. How to distinguish the party to which she belonged, and how to find their table?

Then she saw Sarah in the arms of a very tall man, and Sarah stopped fox-trotting to tell her that their party was sitting in that corner, where those two girls were. She slid back into the throng, and Elizabeth was left to worm her way round the room to where several people were sitting, drinking iced-coffee, and smoking cigarettes.

Elizabeth sat down shyly beside a fair girl who looked rather less terrifying than anyone else, and murmured that Miss Cockburn had told her to come.

The fair girl looked at her and smiled.

"Oh, you must be Elizabeth Arden! So glad you turned up. I'm Lucy Elmsley. How d'you do?"

Elizabeth, who had expected to find Mrs. Elmsley a responsible dowager, gasped.

"That's my husband over there, flirting with May Kimball. Isn't he the limit? George, come and be introduced to Miss Arden!"

George came, and as soon as he smiled Elizabeth thought what a dear he was. He introduced her to several men, and one of them asked if she would like to stagger round the room, now, before the band stopped playing this topping tune. So as Lucy Elmsley had drifted away to where a very fat man was standing, Elizabeth squeezed her way out between two tables, and began to dance with Chubby—this appeared to be her partner's name; he was introduced to her as that.

By the time she and Chubby, who turned out to be a most amusing youth with a vocabulary quite his own, returned to their corner of the room, nearly all the chairs were occupied by the rest of the party.

"I don't think there'd be much wrong with a drink of some sort," Chubby remarked. "Damn, someone's pinched the cigarette I left here. What about some iced-coffee, Miss Arden, or cider-cup?"

Elizabeth thought she would have cider-cup, so Chubby told a waiter to bring it, with two sardines on toast.

"I couldn't possibly eat sardines," Elizabeth protested.

"Good Lord, no!" Chubby said. "Only it's after hours, and the rule of this blasted country is that you can't have intoxicants after hours unless you have supper as well. So you order sardines. Everybody does, an' nobody eats them. Some cove wafts them away when they get too racy, an' they travel on to the next table. You'll see: our sardines'll be looking pretty weary by the time they reach us."

They were certainly dissipated, those sardines, and, they smelt very oily. Someone begged Chubby to bury them in the flower-pot at his elbow. To Elizabeth's horror he promptly rose, and tipped them into the pot, where they probably made excellent manure for the azalea.

Then Sarah came to Elizabeth, with a fair, monocled man at her heels.

"Elizabeth, I want to introduce Mr. Ramsay. The novelist, you know. Stephen, this is Miss Arden."

Stephen Ramsay had grey-blue eyes, and thin cheeks; Elizabeth thought he was interesting, and she admired his teeth, which were very straight and white. She had not read any of his books, which was awkward, but she remembered that she had seen his portrait in the "Bookman."

"Shall I be taking anyone's chair if I sit here?" he asked, placing himself beside Elizabeth.

"Yes, mine," said Chubby, coming away from the flower-pot. "I say, thanks awfully for that dance, Miss Arden. What about it, Sarah?"

"I don't mind," Sarah said graciously. "As long as you're not too energetic."

Stephen Ramsay did not seem to want to dance; he watched Chubby take Sarah on to the floor, and then he looked again at Elizabeth. She wondered whether she ought to say something about his books, but that was so difficult. Instead she asked whether he came often to the club.

"No, I'm a spare man," he answered. His eyes crinkled attractively at the corners. "Cynthia—my sister—got an S. O. S. message from Lucy Elmsley this afternoon to scratch up a male. So here I am. I'm glad I came now."

Because she was very young and nervous Elizabeth said one of those silly things that girls say before they have gained their poise. She asked, why? quite innocently. As soon as the word escaped her she realised that Stephen had paid her a subtle compliment, and she blushed hotly, afraid that he should think she was courting a more direct compliment. To cover her mistake she asked him hurriedly whether he had seen Chubby's way of getting rid of sardines.

"Chubby's quite mad," he said. "He's got unmitigated cheek, and never fails to get away with it."

"I like him," Elizabeth said, not in the least understanding what it was that Chubby got away with.

"Of course. Everyone does. By the way, would you like to dance, or would you rather sit out this one?"

"I'd like to sit it out." She glanced up at him, through her shadowy lashes. "I've never talked to an author before."

His vanity was flattered; he forgave her use of the word "author."

"You looked so scared when Sarah introduced me that I guessed at once you hadn't read my books," he said, laughing.

"No, but I've heard people talking about them," she assured him. "Often. You wrote I Celandine, didn't you?"

"I did. My first, feeble effort. I'm glad you haven't read it."

"I was told that it was good. Why are you glad?"

"Because it wasn't good. The book I've just published never is. The masterpiece is always the next book."

"At that rate there'll never be a masterpiece—in your estimation."

"I hope not. I'd be rather conceited if I ever thought my own book a masterpiece, wouldn't I?"

"I suppose you would. You wouldn't come to dances any more, because you'd think it beneath your dignity."

"Not a bit. I'd come just to show myself, which would be worse. May I introduce you to my sister? She's coming towards us now. Cynny!"

Elizabeth saw that his sister was a fair girl in a wispy black frock with a jazz-sash. She was like her brother, only with blue eyes, rather light and hard.

"Hullo!" she said, and removed her cigarette, in its long black holder, from her mouth.

"Miss Arden—my sister, Mrs. Ruthven."

"How d'you do?" Mrs. Ruthven said. When she spoke she was not like Stephen at all; her words came trenchantly, jerked out. "Don't let Stephen bore you, Miss Arden. He's rather inclined to hold forth."

A glance passed between her and Stephen. Her eyebrows rose infinitesimally; she sat down opposite Elizabeth, on the other side of the little table and waved a casual hand towards her partner.

"My husband. Anthony, ask the Stowe girl to dance. She'll be overcome."

"But I thought—" he began to expostulate.

"Doesn't matter," said Cynthia curtly.

He drifted away; he was amiable and rather fat, with kind eyes. Cynthia stayed and talked to Elizabeth, and Elizabeth discovered that she too wrote, not novels, but poems. She asked all sorts of questions about Elizabeth, but not as though she was really interested. Then, most surprisingly, she asked Elizabeth to come to tea one day, at her flat.

Elizabeth stammered.

"Thank you very much—I should love to," which was not true, because Cynthia repelled her.

"I'll ring you up," Cynthia said. "We'll fix a date." She rose, smiled, and walked away.

"Do go and have tea with her!" Stephen said. "She's rather startling at first, but she's a very good sort at heart."

Elizabeth wondered whether she had been ungracious that he was able to read her thoughts so easily. He was smiling, and she felt more than ever attracted to him.

"And now shall we dance?" he asked.

He danced well, in a way that made her unconscious of her own mistakes, and he was protective and brotherly, as if he had known her all her life. He told her to let herself go a little more, and to take a longer step. Elizabeth became intent on her dancing, and, consequently, danced badly.

"Now I've made you nervous!" he said ruefully. "I'm awfully sorry. Don't pay any attention to me. By the way, have I asked you if you dance here often?"

She laughed, and when she did this her little nose went into fascinating wrinkles, and her eyes danced.

"No, but please don't! How did you know that that was a stock question?"

"A girl told me so once, when I brought it out to her. I admit it's fairly feeble, but you don't know how appallingly difficult it is to think of anything to say to some girls."

This point of view had never before occurred to Elizabeth; ingenuously she told him so.

"No man ought to find any difficulty in talking to you," he said. "If anyone has, then he was without doubt a fool."

She had been looking up at him; now her lashes fell, and a little smile of dawning assurance trembled on her lips. Stephen wanted to kiss her; she was so elusive and fragrant.

No one had ever talked to Elizabeth like this before, or had smiled down at her in quite such a way. He was as different from the man who would like to squeeze her hand and flirt as he was different from the man who was openly bored. Under the warmth of an admiring gaze the petals of shyness unfurled a little way and allowed, he thought, a glimpse of the flower's heart.

"Do you like these shows?" he asked suddenly.

"Yes, I think so. Sometimes it's fun. Do you?"

"Usually they bore me. I find myself thinking that I'd rather be at home. Not to-night."

"Where do you live?" she asked.

"In Kent, not far from Oanbrook. In an old Tudor house with a garden you'd love."

"Should I? Why?"

"Perhaps you wouldn't. If you're a town-bird."

Evidently it was not nice to be a town-bird.

"I don't think I am. I don't know much about the country because I've always lived in London, that's all."

"Well, my garden is made to blend with the house. There are hollyhocks and pansies, and love-in-the-mist, and all the old-fashioned flowers that people have begun to turn their noses up at. And flagged paths, and a big, old cedar, and a stream at the bottom of the field with irises growing beside it."

"It sounds beautiful," she said. "I'm sure there are primroses too, and violets."

"Little wild ones, not the sort one grows in unsightly frames. There's nothing rare in my garden; you might be disappointed. One of my neighbours has a garden full of large labels with Latin names on them much bigger than the poor little plant itself. He wins prizes at the Chelsea flower-show."

The music stopped; Stephen held Elizabeth a moment longer in his arms, then let her go. They went back to their table, and all at once Elizabeth knew that she was enjoying herself.

Stephen went away from the dance with Cynthia and with Cynthia's husband, Anthony, in their two-seater. Anthony drove, and Cynthia was sandwiched tightly between him and Stephen.

"Well, what was the point of it all?" she asked abruptly. "I saw nothing in her."

"Probably you didn't try," Stephen answered.

"Still more probable is it that there's nothing to see."

Stephen was silent; he did not want Cynthia to know how fascinated by Elizabeth he had been; he was fond of Cynthia, she was his pal, but she had a way of being sarcastic when you were not in the mood for sarcasm.

"Moreover," said Cynthia, "she's the last girl in the world I should have expected you to fall for."

"Good lord, Cynny, I'm not in love with her!"

"No, not at present. It'll surprise me if I find there's more to her than a pretty face."

Anthony's voice, puzzled and groping, spoke from the other side of Cynthia.

"What on earth are you two talking about?" he inquired.

"Not a 'what' at all: a 'she.' Didn't you notice, Anthony?"

"No, but then I never do," he said apologetically.

"'Matter of fact I hadn't any time to notice anything this evening except my stud. The confounded laundry has gone and widened the what-you-may-call-it, and the damn thing keeps coming undone, Cynny."

"I'll speak to them about it," she promised, becoming maternal. "What we were talking about was Stephen's latest. Dark girl with eyes."

"Oh, I know," said Anthony. "Pretty kid; I danced with her."

"Well, keep off the grass," Cynthia warned him. "Stephen's got his thumb on her."

Stephen defended himself, laughing.

"It's all rot, Anthony. I don't mind admitting that I was rather attracted. She's refreshing and unmodern. I'm so tired of the slangy, hail-fellow-well-met girls. They haven't got any reserves."

"Um!" said Cynthia profoundly. "Question is, which is the more satisfactory type to live with?"

"There's a lot in that," Anthony agreed, firmly believing that there was, since Cynthia had said it.

"As I haven't got to live with her the question doesn't arise," retorted Stephen.

"And yet," said Cynthia, "you'll come up to town—to see me—on the day I

35

have her to tea."

"I shall, yes," Stephen replied frankly. "I'm interested in her. She's a type."

"Copy for the new book," nodded Anthony. "By the way, how is the new book?"

"Good in parts. I've been hung up over 'Helen.' She puzzles me, and until I met Elizabeth Arden to-night I hadn't been able to find her counterpart."

"Oh, that's what the book's about, is it?" said Cynthia. "The modest violet. You fool, Stephen."

"Cynny, Cynny!" Anthony protested gently. "Don't be cynical, old girl."

"He is a fool, Anthony," she insisted, smiling.

"Yes, of course, but you shouldn't sneer at that girl, darling; she's a nice kid."

"I shan't be allowed to sneer at anybody soon," Cynthia remarked, entirely without rancour.

"'Tisn't necessary, darling, an' I hate it."

"Go on, Anthony," Stephen said encouragingly. "You're the only person I know who can take Cynny down two or three pegs."

"Me?" Anthony leaned forward slightly to look across his wife at Stephen. "Why, Cynny's a lot cleverer'n I am! Queer notions you do get into your head, old man!"

Chapter Five

Lawrence was quite excited when he learned that Elizabeth had met Stephen Ramsay at the dance-club. He seemed to think that it was clever of her, and praiseworthy, for he puffed out his chest slightly and patted her shoulder a great many times, saying, Well, well, well! He wanted to know just what Stephen had said, and Miss Arden, also interested, just how he looked. Elizabeth tried to satisfy both her listeners, but she found it difficult, and floundered badly in her description. She had spent nearly half the evening exclusively with Stephen, but in the cold light of the following morning she could not remember exactly what he looked like. She thought his eyes were grey; certainly he wore an eyeglass, but she felt sure that were she to meet him in the street she would pass him by.

Lawrence was displeased, and remarked in an annoyed tone of voice that Stephen seemed to have made very little impression on Elizabeth.

Elizabeth racked her brains, and managed to recall some stray fragments of their conversation last night, which quite restored Lawrence to good-humour.

"A very bright young man, I should say," he nodded. "I always thought that you might meet some interesting people at the club." He paused, and looked impressively at Elizabeth. "Never neglect an opportunity of getting to know people," he said. "I'm very glad I encouraged you to join the club, very glad indeed."

"Ye-es," Elizabeth agreed doubtfully. "Only I thought that you didn't want me to join it? At first you were so very—"

"Naturally I had to think it over," Lawrence said, frowning. It was tactless and stupid of Elizabeth to remind him of his preliminary mistrust of the club, just as he was forgetting about it. "I should be a pretty sort of father if I gave my consent to all your schemes without sleeping on them first. If I remember rightly you had already suggested staying at home when I finally decided that it would be very nice for you to go."

"Only because you—"

"Don't argue with your father, darling," Miss Arden interposed.

"And," Lawrence went on triumphantly, "I advised you to join the club. If I hadn't done that, in all probability you would have stayed at home. Then you wouldn't have met Ramsay. I must say I am very pleased about that. I read his two books with great interest and I shall like to meet him."

"He lives in the country," said Elizabeth. "I don't think he comes to London much."

"He'll come fast enough if there's an attraction," answered Lawrence playfully. "I have a shrewd notion that my little girl was a great success last night."

Elizabeth tried not to think that her teeth were on edge; she smiled, but shook her head.

"Ah, well, we shall see!" Lawrence said. "Heaven knows I'm not a lion-hunter. Ramsay can stay away or come to call: it's all one to me. And whom else did you meet last night?"

"Oh, lots of people!" Elizabeth said vaguely. "Mr. Ramsay's sister was there with her husband."

"Was she indeed?" Lawrence was becoming more and more complacent. "How did she strike you?"

Elizabeth hesitated, and then compromised.

"I thought she seemed very clever."

"I daresay," Lawrence said wisely. "You liked her?"

"N-no, I don't think I did. She asked me to go to tea with her one day."

"How extremely kind!" he exclaimed. "And pray what is your objection to this lady, Elizabeth?"

"It's—it's hard to explain. She has such an—offhand, curt manner."

"My dear Elizabeth, you shouldn't judge people on their exteriors," Lawrence said severely. "I don't like to hear my little girl flatly condemning someone because she has a queer manner. Then again one has to make allowances for people with brains."

"Why?" Elizabeth asked.

This floored Lawrence completely; he took refuge behind a convenient snub.

"My dear child, if you think a minute you will see how silly that question is. Much—er—much is forgiven a genius."

"Oh, I don't think she's a genius!" Elizabeth said.

"Certainly not. I wasn't suggesting such a thing. Don't fall into that bad habit of catching people up, I beg of you. It's most unbecoming. All I meant was that Mrs.—Mrs.—"

"—Ruthven."

"—Mrs. Ruthven—that's a very distinguished old name—is a clever woman."

"She writes poems."

"There you are, then. Writers very often have small peculiarities. One has to make allowances for them. It would be a dull world if we were all made alike. I strongly advise you to accept Mrs. Ruthven's invitation, if she repeats it. From all I can make out she seems to be a very nice woman. A most desirable connaissance." With that he rose, and went away into his study, taking the Times with him. No one was allowed to look at the paper until he had finished with it, and folded it inside out.

Rather to Elizabeth's surprise, Cynthia Ruthven did repeat her invitation. Some days later a letter came from her to Elizabeth, addressed in a very large and bold handwriting. Lawrence inspected it, and announced that Mrs. Ruthven wrote a good fist, and lived in a very nice part of the world.

"I expect they have to pay a pretty stiff rent for a flat in Hanover Square," he remarked. "They must be quite well off."

Even Aunt Anne thought it an excellent friendship for Elizabeth to make. So Elizabeth wrote to accept the invitation, and wondered secretly whether perhaps Stephen might not be there too. If so it would be really nice, but if not she did not think it would be nice at all.

The Ruthvens' flat was furnished very well, but in a modern style that Elizabeth found rather startling. She was conducted across a hall with a Bakst scheme of decoration to a room which she supposed to be the drawing-room.

Cynthia was lost in the depths of an immense black chair, with her legs crossed and one foot swinging gently in its high-heeled shoe. That, and the blue smoke of her cigarette was all there was to be seen of her. She rose and threw aside the book she had been reading. Elizabeth thought she had never seen anything so marvellous as Cynthia's gown, which was of primrose chiffon, presumably to match the room.

"So glad you've come," Cynthia said, shaking hands. "Where would you like to sit?"

Elizabeth chose the sofa, and at once wished that she had not, for it was so deep and soft that she could not sit upright as she would have liked to have done. She had the uncomfortable feeling that her knees were higher than her chin, and wondered why it was that she could never look graceful or at ease in a lounging position. Other girls did, and they didn't seem to feel at a disadvantage either.

Cynthia curled up again in her original chair, sitting sideways to face

Elizabeth.

"Awfully decent of you to come and see me." she was saying. "It's quite impossible to get to know anyone at a dance."

"I know," said Elizabeth. "And there's never time, somehow, to talk to other girls."

"Quite so. You're looking rather fearfully at my pictures. Do you like them?"

"They're very striking," said Elizabeth politely. "Of course I don't really understand Futurism."

"My dear girl, they're not Futurist pictures!" Cynthia said, amused. "What you're looking at is a Beardsley."

"Oh—is it?" Elizabeth had no idea what a Beardsley was, but she did not like to confess her ignorance. She changed the subject. "I love your yellow curtains, and the black carpet."

"So do I," said Cynthia. "My mother says they make her feel bilious, but then she's addicted to flowered chintzes and pink lampshades."

Elizabeth laughed, but she knew that she too liked pink lampshades.

"Does your mo—Mrs. Ramsay—live in town," she asked.

"Officially. She drifts from Stephen to me, and from me to my uncle, and so on. She's rather a delightful person, not in the least like Stephen or me. One of those incurably vague women, you know, with a gift for saying the opposite to what she means."

"How amusing!" Elizabeth said. She would have liked to make a witty remark, but as usual she could not think of one.

"Most, but trying to live with. She has a habit of getting her affairs into a muddle, and then Stephen or I have to try and unravel them. Anthony's rather more successful than either of us. He's a business man, so he ought to be, I suppose. Here's tea."

Close behind the tea came Stephen, with his monocle screwed firmly into his eye, and his hair waving in a fashion which Elizabeth admired and he thought detestable.

"Hul-lo!" Cynthia drawled.

"Don't sound so pleased!" he answered. "How d'you do, Miss Arden? Been to any more dances since I saw you?"

"Only one," she said, withdrawing her hand from his.

He bent to pick up the plate of hot cakes from the hearth, and offered it to her, smiling irresistibly.

"Do ask me to partner you at the next club-meeting! Or is that cheek?"

Elizabeth's dimples came into play; she looked up at him with a hint of roguishness.

"I thought you didn't like dancing," she said.

"I don't—always," he answered. "Can I be your partner?"

"Squash him," Cynthia advised. "Milk or lemon?"

"Milk, please. I don't know whether I'm going to the next club-dance or not yet."

"When will you know?" demanded Stephen. "I think you're being rather beastly to me. How's the heir, Cynny?"

"Rather pleased with himself," she answered. "He pulled the coffee-pot over at breakfast, and the coffee ran all over Anthony's new trousers. You ought to have heard him swear."

"Oh, have you got a baby?" cried Elizabeth.

"I don't wonder you're surprised," Stephen said. "She doesn't look as though she had, does she? As a matter of fact the kid does her credit. Topping little animal."

Cynthia bit deep into a cake.

"I'm rather surprised myself when I look at him," she said reflectively. "Clever of me to have produced anything so exactly what it ought to be. Nice sentence that."

Elizabeth was rather horrified at Cynthia's attitude towards her baby, and was glad that Aunt Anne was not present to hear her.

"I love babies," she said. "Can I see yours?"

"Certainly, if he won't bore you," Cynthia said, with uplifted eyebrows. "Do you really like babies?"

The idea of not liking babies had never occurred to Elizabeth. Aunt Anne was always sentimental when confronted with one, and Elizabeth had unconsciously adopted the same attitude. The adoration of babies was an instinctive enthusiasm that every girl was supposed to have in her. If you didn't like babies you would either be considered hard and unfeminine, or affected.

"Yes, of course I do," Elizabeth said, opening her eyes wide.

Stephen watched that innocent look and thought it charming.

"I'm awfully glad to hear you say that," he told her. "Most modern girls swear they loathe babies. A form of swank, I think."

"I don't think I'm really a modern girl," Elizabeth said wistfully.

"Most girls honestly dislike babies," said Cynthia trenchantly. "And always have disliked them. The only difference is that nowadays they don't pretend to like them, whereas fifty years ago they did. I hated them before Christopher appeared upon the scene." She nodded towards Elizabeth. "You're an exception to the rule. Stephen, if you've finished tea you might go and collect your nephew."

Stephen departed, and returned presently with Christopher in his arms. He carried the babe in a manner peculiar to his sex, holding him very tightly, with the short frock well rucked up under his arm. Christopher, who was chubby and blue-eyed, grasped a strand of Stephen's hair, and stared solemnly at Elizabeth.

"What a pet!" Elizabeth cried, and rose, advancing towards him.

Christopher promptly dug his head into Stephen's shoulder and gave a protesting kick.

"Chuck it!" advised his uncle. "That happens to be me."

"Is he shy?" Elizabeth asked.

Cynthia rescued Christopher from Stephen's clutch.

"No, it's a new accomplishment, that's all. Sit up, Colombus, and be polite."

However, Christopher refused to have anything to do with Elizabeth, and made manifest his desire to go back to his uncle. Since he showed a tendency to roar when denied this wish he had his way and sat on Stephen's knee making sundry pleased but unintelligible remarks.

"I wonder what he sees in you?" said Cynthia. "Funny thing, Miss Arden, but he finds Stephen most fascinating."

"I can understand his admiration for me," Stephen answered, dodging to avoid a poke in the eye, "but I wish it would find expression in a less strenuous way. Yes, that's my tie, young sir, and you needn't bother to undo it."

"Quite a family man," Cynthia remarked.

Christopher formed the topic of conversation until Elizabeth rose to go. Then Stephen handed him back to his mother, and asked that he might be allowed to drive Elizabeth home in his car.

"Oh, but won't that be taking you out of your way?" she protested.

"No, rather not. Lord, the kid's going to howl!"

"Not at all," said Cynthia, hastily distracting Christopher's attention. "Don't, Cherub, I implore you!

Your papa'll be home soon and you know he's far nicer than Stephen."

Christopher appeared to consider this gravely, and evidently came to the conclusion that there was something in it, for he abandoned his intention of roaring, and instead smiled seraphically.

Elizabeth shook hands with Cynthia, and hoped that she would come to tea with her one day next week. Then Stephen took her out and tucked her into his shining car.

The drive home was all too short; since she had seen Stephen with Christopher Elizabeth thought him nicer than ever, besides it was most thrilling to be on such intimate terms with so famous a novelist.

As luck would have it, Lawrence was just letting himself into the house when Stephen's car pulled up outside. He turned at once, and when he saw Elizabeth, came down the steps again.

"Well, well, so here you are!" he said, and looked inquiringly at Stephen.

"Yes, here I am. This is Mr. Ramsay—my father."

"That's a very well-known name," said Lawrence, shaking Stephen warmly by the hand. "You see in me a humble admirer. Come in for a few minutes, won't you?"

"Thanks, sir. I'd like to if I may. Can you extricate yourself, Miss Arden?"

"Yes, just," Elizabeth answered, emerging from her wrappings. She got out of the car, and they waited for Lawrence to open the front-door.

Aunt Anne was in the drawing-room, and she welcomed Stephen with rather less hostility than was usually apparent in her manner when a man was introduced to her.

Stephen exerted himself to please both her and Lawrence; with both he was successful. Lawrence talked very learnedly about books, and since he was evidently determined to discuss Stephen's latest novel, Stephen gave way after the very shortest of struggles and managed to look as though he were enjoying the discussion.

"A very skilful piece of work," Lawrence said warmly. "Now tell me, had you anyone in mind when you created 'Francis'?"

"Oh, just a type!" Stephen answered evasively.

"Ah, yes, I suppose so. And that bit about 'Patricia' and 'Colonel Longley'—excellent!"

"I'm glad you liked the book, sir," was all Stephen could think of to say. He contrived to change the subject to motor-cars, and immediately Lawrence launched forth into technicalities.

Undoubtedly Stephen was a success.

Chapter Six

Elizabeth's friendship with Stephen grew quickly after that; she feared he must be neglecting his work, so often did his yellow car purr to her door and stop there. He had won the approval of Lawrence; more important still, of Aunt Anne, who described him as a remarkably nice young man. Lawrence said that what he liked about Stephen was his lack of conceit and his modesty when forced to speak of his work. From the day when Stephen brought violets to Miss Arden, Elizabeth heard nothing but praise of him in her home. Miss Arden, fluttered by the gift of flowers—a gift that seemed to recall the days of her youth—saw in it only a delicate attention to herself, and not a wily move in the game Stephen was playing whereby he sought to enlist her sympathies and possible influence on his side.

It was some time before Mr. Hengist met Stephen, but Lawrence saw to it that he had little chance of remaining in ignorance of Stephen's intimacy with the family of Arden. Lawrence formed a habit of dragging Stephen into any conversation, and he introduced his name in a simple and imposing manner. He said, Elizabeth's great friend, Stephen Ramsay, and waited artistically for his audience to interject, Not the novelist? After that it was easy. Mr. Hengist was the only man with whom this delicate opening produced no satisfactory result. Lawrence started neatly with:—

"Well, I'm inclined to agree with what Elizabeth's friend, Stephen Ramsay, says on that subject." He left a pause; Mr. Hengist removed his pipe from his mouth, and inquired:—

"What does he say?"

Lawrence thought this just like Hengist. He had to think very hard to remember what Stephen had said, and even then Mr. Hengist did not ask whether Lawrence was speaking of Stephen Ramsay, the man who wrote "Celandine."

Miss Arden, in a more direct form of attack, managed to arouse Mr. Hengist's interest. Brightly she said:—

"I suppose you've heard that Elizabeth has made a new friend, Mr. Hengist?"

"No," he replied. "Who is it?"

"Someone rather famous," Miss Arden said. "Stephen Ramsay. Of course you've heard of him?"

"Yes, I've read one of his books. What is he like, Elizabeth?"

"I like him very much," she answered.

Mr. Hengist looked at her with slight irony.

"I should like to hear you exchanging views with Ramsay," he remarked.

"I admire his line of thought," Lawrence said profoundly.

Mr. Hengist cocked a humorous eyebrow in his direction.

"Oh, you do, do you?"

"Certainly I do. What's your opinion?"

"Well—" Mr. Hengist started in a leisurely way to refill his pipe— "He's clever, occasionally original, but to my mind he's too inclined to sacrifice sincerity on the altar of wit."

"I don't agree," Lawrence said flatly.

"Furthermore," went on Mr. Hengist, "for one who writes on the psychology of woman he knows very little about woman."

Miss Arden raised severe eyes.

"I'm sure Mr. Ramsay would be quite surprised if he could hear you say that he writes on that subject, Mr. Hengist. I have not yet read his books, but I'm sure—"

"The modern school of novelists," Lawrence interrupted, "is for ever probing into the character of woman. Stephen is young yet. In any case I think his handling of the subject most skilful and delicate."

"There seem to me to be too many books written nowadays on those lines," said Miss Arden. "I consider it most unnecessary."

When Mr. Hengist at last met Stephen he seemed to like him. He discussed the Novel with Stephen, who grew quite excited, and ran his long fingers through his hair until it became riotous, and curled more than ever. He talked of Petronius Arbiter, and Lawrence coughed, with a warning glance towards Elizabeth. As Elizabeth had never heard of Petronius this precaution was useless. Mr. Hengist then said, take Le Sage, for instance, and once more they were plunged into a discussion. Lawrence informed everybody that he could see nothing in these Satirists, and that he thought that the adventures of Gil Bias de Santillone had better have been left untold.

"Ah, then you are probably no admirer of Smollett either?" Stephen said.

"No, I can't say that I am," Lawrence answered with perfect truth, having but the haziest notion of Smollett's identity.

"Smollett?" grunted Mr. Hengist. "A copyist, Ramsay. No Le Sage, no Smollett."

"Not entirely, sir," Stephen maintained.

Elizabeth sat silent, withdrawn into herself, thinking how clever Stephen was, and how delightful it was to know him. She was reading "Celandine" in her spare time and trying to see Stephen in it. That was difficult, even rather perturbing because "Celandine" was a queer book, she thought, and sometimes, if she read it aright, rather broad. Much of it she did not understand; passages of obscure meaning caused her to wrinkle her brow and wonder whether she was dense, or just innocent. Yet it was surely impossible that the Stephen she knew, the man she thought to be the real Stephen, would write of things of which he would not speak to his girl-friends. Or if he wrote them, then he had for the moment assumed a pose, and was no longer himself but perhaps one of his own characters.

Stephen knew that she was reading his book, and although he wanted her to read it and to like it, he was also anxious and strangely diffident.

"You're wasting your time," he said once. "It's mere froth. Don't bother."

"You behave as though you don't want me to read it," she teased him.

"I don't. Yes, I do. Oh, lord, I don't know whether I do or don't! I'll write something better, more worthy of your notice. The style of that's bad—in parts. And it's muddle-headed too, I think."

"No, no!" she said. "You mustn't say that! It's good, I know it is!"

At that he laughed, but he was pleased, secretly.

"All right, go on with it. Only when you've come to the end, be candid with me!"

"Very well." She looked up at him. "Sometimes it puzzles me because I can't imagine that you really wrote it. Is it really you?"

He thought for a moment.

"I believe so—most of it. It's difficult to probe beneath one's self-deceit, but—yes, I think it's me. So if you don't like it after all, it'll mean you don't like me."

She shook her head.

"No, for I shall know that the parts I don't like aren't really you."

"They're probably more me than the parts you do like," he said seriously, but again she shook her head.

For him her fascination grew, till it was sweet to see her quietly sitting by the fire with the red light from the coals casting her profile into relief against the dark wall. It was sweeter still to dance with her and to feel her slim body in his arms, young and fragrant, and to look down into her face so near to his. He loved the dark hair bound closely to her head, and her lashes curling upward, or lying still against the cream of her skin, shading her eyes. He was awed in her presence, loving her innocence and the little ingenuous things that she said. Her silences seemed fraught with deep reflection; he wondered what were her thoughts, and what lay behind the softness of her eyes. That they were gentle, like herself, he knew, very young perhaps, and perhaps a little shy.

She was aloof with him, retreating within herself. Sentimental he thought, how virginal! She could never be intimate with him as other girls would be. She would bring everything there was in her, all her thoughts and her fancies, all the places in her soul kept secret, unspoiled to her husband. Then, as he saw her, in imagination, a bride, his hands clenched and his breath came faster, and he thought of the treasures that were hers to unfold, the frailty, and the exquisite purity. Young and immature she was, too young and too sweet to hold strong alien opinions, young enough to be yet plastic, with intelligence to comprehend and to absorb a man's teaching.

It would be joy to lay a guiding, artist's hand on her mind still unformed, joy, greater still, to be sure, as he was sure, that no other man's lips had touched hers, to know that she was wholly his, with no old, forgotten flirtations lying behind her.

That would gall him, he felt; he would never take to wife the girl who was careless of her kisses and flirted with every man who came. He knew many such, liked them, had flirted with them, and knew that there was no harm in them beyond a certain volatility. It was not through Puritan spectacles that he regarded them; he knew them to be products merely of the new age, who had thrown away restraints in the same light-hearted way that they had thrown away their corsets. No doubt this recklessness, this brazen flaunting of charms that were more alluring veiled, was of no more than surface depth, yet he felt, singularly egotistic, that he would not choose a wife from this short-skirted, sleeveless sisterhood, but would rather, Oriental-wise, take a girl like Elizabeth, whom no other man should know.

If Elizabeth were old-fashioned, then how well she would blend with the flowers of his garden. She belonged to the age of Sweet-Williams and London Pride; he pictured her, a maid of long ago, demurely gowned, with a tiny posy of flowers in her hands. Cynthia said that she harked from Mid-Victorian times, but Cynthia was wrong. The Elizabeth round whom he built his whimsical fancies belonged to no age, but was symbolic of the eternal dream woman. Least of all could she be typical of an age that was ugly, and saw indecencies everywhere, even in piano legs.

Cynthia could not shatter his rosy dream, hard though she might try. Cynthia said, For God's sake, come out of the mists! and wondered what had happened to him. She told him that he was cheating himself, that the Elizabeth he was in love with was an Elizabeth of his imagination and not the true one. He thought her jealous, even feline, and his beliefs remained unshaken. He coaxed his mother to call on Miss Arden and eagerly awaited her verdict.

"Such an alarming woman!" she said, smiling sweetly up at him. "Of course I said all the wrong things, Stephen. Wasn't it dreadful of me?" His mother might be vague and aimless, incapable of any reasonable thought, but she was his mother and he adored her. Now he laughed, and kissed her hand.

"You always do, mater, so what's the odds? You wouldn't be you if you didn't."

"No, I suppose I shouldn't," she agreed. "Do you like me as I am, darling?"

"Yes. Who was the alarming woman?"

"Oh, not Elizabeth, Stephen! Miss Arden. Her skirt dipped at the back and she said you were a charming young man."

"Well, that ought to have pleased you," he pointed out.

"No, darling, not at all. No one but myself ought to know that you're charming. Where was I?"

"You said Miss Arden alarmed you."

Mrs. Ramsay put down her tea-cup.

"Did I? No, she didn't exactly alarm me, except that she was so correct. I don't really know the word I want."

"Never mind about Miss Arden. Did you see Elizabeth?"

"Yes, she poured out the tea, and she didn't forget that I don't like mine strong. Quite a dear girl. She reminds me of someone, only I can't remember who. Someone who lived at some place beginning with a B, I think. You must know, Stephen. No, I've got it. Marion Tapley; she died before you were born, poor thing. Yes, and she lived at Weybridge, and I remember thinking at the time that she just suited the place. She had an impediment in her speech."

"Hang it all, mater, Elizabeth hasn't got an impediment—"

"What a horrible idea, darling! I shouldn't have liked her at all if she had. As a matter of fact she has a very pretty voice. Such an asset! Do you remember Kate Dalkeith? Poor dear, she was almost ugly, but what a beautiful voice!"

"Yes, mater, but we're not talking about Kate Dalkeith."

She smiled happily across at him.

"Nor we are. I've lost myself again. Oh, yes, about Elizabeth! Very young, Stephen."

"Nearly twenty, mater."

"Well, darling, that is very young. I don't know how old you are—at least, of course, I do, but I've forgotten for the moment."

"Twenty-seven."

"Dear me, Stephen, what a dreadful thought! Why, Cynthia must be twenty-five."

"She is. You gave her that diamond brooch on her birthday."

"So I did." Mrs. Ramsay nodded pensively. "With an emerald in the middle."

Stephen brought his cup to her to be replenished. Her small white hands fluttered over the tea-tray, from milk-jug to sugar bowl.

"You don't really like Elizabeth, mater?"

"Yes, I do, Stephen. Why not?"

"You don't give me the impression—"

"My dear, do I ever give people a right impression? Elizabeth seemed to me a very sweet child. But isn't she rather a throw-back? Or do I mean a missing-link?"

"Good lord, I hope not! You mean that she's old-fashioned?"

"So prim," she explained.

There fell a tiny pause.

"That's rather a beastly word, mater."

Mrs. Ramsay put down the slice of bread and butter she had so carefully folded in half.

"I'm sure it isn't. What have I said that was awful?"

"Prim."

"Oh, that! It's not awful at all, Stephen. I thought I'd said something I shouldn't from your expression."

"So you did. Elizabeth could never be prim."

"Couldn't she, darling? I expect you know her a lot better than I do."

This was unsatisfactory. Stephen glowered into the fire.

"You've allowed Cynthia to influence your judgment, mater."

"Dear Cynny! So domineering. No, I don't mean domineering. Downright. That's better."

"What did she say about Elizabeth?"

"I can't remember that she said anything. Oh yes, she did! She said Elizabeth hadn't got a mind of her own! That's rather true, Stephen."

"It's not. She's shy and reserved."

"I expect it's the aunt," Mrs. Ramsay said placably. "She won't let Elizabeth have a mind of her own; she wants her to have her mind. Stephen, that's rather clever. Now I know where you get your brains from."

He laughed, but reluctantly and like a sulky boy.

"Because Elizabeth doesn't smoke and doesn't always say exactly what she thinks, whether it's rude or not, Cynthia condemns her. That's just like Cynthia. Beastly intolerance."

"Yes, but we Ramsays are always dreadfully outspoken, dear."

"What's that got to do with it?"

"Lots. You see, Stephen, you've always been used to terribly frank people, and you're the same yourself."

He rose and went to the fire, one hand on the mantelpiece and the other deep in his trouser-pocket. He spoke, looking down into the fire, and not at his mother.

"What are you driving at, mater?"

"Only that you've never been interested in a girl as you're interested in Elizabeth, dear hoy."

"No." He began to play with one of the china ornaments near his hand.

"And you sent me to see what I thought of her. Didn't you?"

"I suppose— Yes. You know, this is rather—"

"Dreadfully. Well, I like Elizabeth, but I don't know why I'd like her if I had to."

He raised his head, and Mrs. Ramsay saw that his eyes were crinkling at the corners. That hinted smile was reflected on her lips at once.

"Wouldn't you feel the same about any girl, mater?"

"Yes, I expect I should. Of course, darling, you'll do as you please, and I shall be nice about it— Don't you think I should be a charming mother-in-law?—only don't rush into anything with your eyes shut. That would hurt me terribly."

"I'm not a bit likely to do that, mater."

"Yes, you are, Stephen. You're so like your father."

The smile grew.

"Well, if he rushed into marriage with you with his eyes shut I can't do better than to follow his example and shut my eyes."

"My dear, what a beautiful compliment! But Elizabeth isn't like me, you know."

He looked wistfully down at her.

"I thought you'd get on with her so well, mater. She is like you in some ways—at least, I think so."

Mrs. Ramsay went to him and put her hand up to stroke his cheek.

"Poor boy! I expect I shall get on with her splendidly when I see her away from her aunt. Anyway, don't let's worry! Only I do so wish it had been Nina Trelawney."

He moved one shoulder impatiently, and the vase he had played with, fell into the hearth and was smashed.

"Damn. There was never any chance of that, mater. Sorry about the vase. Was it valuable?"

"No, not a bit, I hated it. Break its twin."

He obeyed, absent-mindedly. Mrs. Ramsay watched the work of destruction with great interest. Then Stephen began to laugh.

"Mater, how mad!"

"Yes, but doesn't china make a fascinating sound when it smashes? Can't we break anything else?"

"No, not to-day. Come down to Queen's Halt next week and we'll break those awful china dogs Cousin Freda sent us."

"What a splendid idea, Stephen! We might break the Crown Derby plates too."

"No, we can't do that," he objected. "Not Crown Derby. I don't think I could."

"Think how blatant they are, Stephen. I'm sure I could."

"I know. Still . . . They're too good to break."

"That makes it all the more exciting. We'd feel so wicked," she said, dimpling. The dimples disappeared. "Elizabeth wouldn't understand about smashing china, darling, would she?"

Chapter Seven

It was inconceivable that you could like a man and not his nearest relations. Excuses had to be found for Mrs. Ramsay and were quickly forthcoming. She was eccentric; it was deplorable, but an excuse; she was absent-minded: a fault, but one that made her the more attractive. Lawrence located her in Debrett; she came of ancient stock, and not only had she married into the County, but she was herself County. Lawrence realized to the full the significance of this magic word; it was better in these days to be County than Titled. Mrs. Ramsay's eccentricity pointed to no lack of breeding, but rather to her nobility. Miss Arden said that it was refreshing to meet anyone so delightfully unconventional.

In an introspective mood Elizabeth knew herself to be drifting towards an alien pool. There was no mistaking Stephen's ardour; it was obvious to all, so obvious that sly jokes were cut by Lawrence and Aunt Anne at her expense. About Stephen there could be nothing alien, but in the world where he dwelt was Cynthia, incomprehensible in her speech and manners, and Mrs. Ramsay, incomprehensible too, and from Elizabeth, poles apart.

Elizabeth felt it dimly, then thought herself morbid in her imaginings. She was bred in an atmosphere of class-distinction; she knew that in Miss Arden's eyes she stood upon the brink of a successful marriage. She had thought about it many times, seeing herself the wife of a famous novelist, hearing herself referred to as County. It was snobbery, she knew, and scolded herself for indulging the vice, but the secret thrill remained, dominating her judgment.

In Miss Arden's attitude towards her was a new tenderness; did she forget some trifling behest or errand, Miss Arden would smile mysteriously and say, We're very forgetful nowadays, aren't we? with no annoyance, hut an evident satisfaction.

"I am in love," Elizabeth thought. "I must be in love."

But how difficult it was to distinguish between love and like! If love meant pleasure felt in Stephen's company, and pride in his appearance, she loved. If it meant that she would be sorry never again to see Stephen, then surely she loved. Other girls spoke of heartaches, of longing and despair, but how often had she proved that other girls were different? Violent emotions bordered on indecency; the nearest approach to violence that she had achieved was an inward shudder of pure delight when Stephen was masterfully gentle, possessive.

She saw herself fragile and precious in his eyes, and was glad. His tall proportions and his strength pleased her, and she loved to be asked:—

"Who is that awfully good-looking man you danced with the other night?"

She seemed to herself to grow in stature when she answered that it was a great friend, Stephen Ramsay, the novelist. How immeasurably proud she would be if ever she could say: It is my husband.

"Are you in love with Stephen?" Sarah asked her.

It was the first direct allusion; Lawrence and Aunt Anne dealt in innuendoes. Elizabeth blushed deeply and was embarrassed.

"Sarah!"

"Anyway it's as plain as a pike-staff that he's head over ears in love with you. Any amount of girls have run after him, but I've never seen him so absolutely struck before."

This was immensely satisfying; Elizabeth's eyelids drooped, and she smiled.

"You're damn' lucky," said Sarah candidly. "There aren't many Stephens in this world."

Elizabeth thought of the scores of men whom she had met, and with whom she had danced.

"No, there aren't," she agreed, wondering how it was that she had never thought of this before.

Sarah looked at her curiously.

"Are you in love with him? You needn't mind telling me."

"Sarah—you do—ask awful questions!" Elizabeth said. "I—don't think I know. I like him ever so much—as a friend."

"Personally," said Sarah, lighting a fresh cigarette from the stump of her old one, "I should imagine he'd make rather a jolly husband. Bit temperamental perhaps, and fairly selfish, but—can't think of the word I want—understanding and—considerate."

"If he's selfish—but I'm sure he isn't, Sarah—how can he be considerate?"

"Selfish in the small everyday things of life, like insisting on going to Scotland when you'd set your heart on France, and considerate in the—the bigger things. Have you got what I'm driving at?"

Elizabeth knew from the constrained note in Sarah's voice that she was talking of something in marriage that was dark and mysterious. Suddenly she longed for the courage to confess ignorance and beg enlightenment. But years of training stood in her way, and the implanted belief that knowledge was wrong.

"Oh, yes!" she said vaguely.

"Taking it all in all," Sarah went on reflectively, "he might be a lot worse. He wouldn't do for me, and I shouldn't have said that he'd do for you either. Still . . . S'pose I'll be congratulating you ere long?"

"Oh, do be quiet!" begged Elizabeth, rosy-cheeked.

Sarah rose to go.

"Well, I think you're jolly lucky," she remarked.

Everybody seemed to think that, although no one was so outspoken as Sarah. Lawrence cast up his eyes comically when Stephen's impetuous knock sounded on the front-door, and murmured,

"Oh, Elizabeth, Elizabeth! I suppose I shall be *de trop* now?"

And Miss Arden smiled as at a hidden thought, and gave Elizabeth's hand a little squeeze.

She was a heroine of romance all at once, and all things were forgiven her on the score that she was in love. She had never before felt so important, nor taken so prominent and conspicuous a place in the opinions of her relatives. It was embarrassing sometimes, but always delightful.

And how much more important she would be if she married Stephen and became mistress of a house of her own. Aunt Anne would have to admit then that she was really and truly grown-up, and no one would be able to say, Elizabeth, go and tidy your room, as though she were still only a little girl. More than that: once she was married she could do anything she liked without reproach, all the little things that a girl could not do. She would always have a partner at hand, and she would be able to give parties of her own without having first to ask permission.

She saw herself ordering her own groceries, and superintending her own maids. That would be fun. She would pour Stephen's coffee out at breakfast, and say all the proper wifely things to him. And he would talk to her about his new book; perhaps, even, he would read passages to her and ask her advice.

Then the tiny fear sprang up again, How shall I hold my own with his mother and .his sister? I am not of his world. The fear was hateful, and grew larger as she dwelt upon it. She brushed it aside then, thinking, I am not marrying them; it will not matter. She gave herself up to romantic imaginings, and presently saw herself, married to Stephen, a transformed being, no longer shy, no longer tongue-tied or ignorant, but the woman she longed to be and would never be.

She began to count the days that had passed since she had met Stephen. It was three months, only that, a very little time in which to learn to know a man. She wondered whether she did know Stephen, and whether any girl knew her man before she was irrevocably tied to him. By devious paths she approached Miss Arden with this question, saying nervously at last.

"I suppose—Auntie—marriage is always—rather a— plunge in the dark?"

"Nonsense, child!" Miss Arden said briskly. "What on earth do you mean?"

"Only that—it's difficult to know—can one possibly know—what a man is really like—before one marries him? I mean—one doesn't know anyone—properly—till one has lived in the same house with them. And—and wouldn't it be—rather dreadful—if after all—it turned out that one had made a mistake?"

"My dear Elizabeth, you're getting morbid," Miss Arden said flatly. "You've been mooning about indoors too much, and reading silly books."

Elizabeth's fingers gripped together till the knuckles shone white.

"Aunt Anne—I don't believe I know—quite what—it will mean."

Miss Arden knitted faster than ever, and did not look at Elizabeth.

"The best thing you can do, my dear, is to go for a brisk walk in the Park," she said repressively. "You don't know what you're talking about."

Elizabeth got up, and stood for a moment looking down at Miss Arden.

"Oughtn't I to know?" she said quietly.

"My dear Elizabeth, you can take it from me that if you love your husband all these silly fancies of yours are groundless. Now run along and put your hat on."

Instead of the Thorn

Elizabeth went slowly out of the room. For the first time in her life a great regret took possession of her, and a great want.

"I wish my mother hadn't died."

She had never felt this want before, but now it entered deep into her soul and told her that she was lonely and helpless, lacking a guiding hand. Aunt Anne became suddenly useless and apart from her, Lawrence a stranger. She felt that she stood alone and that there was no one to help or to advise her. Dimly, subconsciously she knew that Aunt Anne was no more to her than Lawrence, a creature who loved her but did not know her, whom she did not know.

It was in this mood that Stephen found her, alone in the drawing-room.

He came unannounced into the room, quickly as always, and shut the door behind him with a little, decided click.

Elizabeth was sitting in a big chair beside the fire, with an open book on her knees. She was not reading, but looking wistfully down into the fire; her mouth drooped, her eyes were laden with shadows. She did not turn because she thought it was only the parlour-maid who had come to set out the table for tea, and for a moment Stephen stood quite still with his hand still on the door-knob, watching her.

Then, wondering, she raised her head, and he saw a tinge of colour creep into her cheeks.

"Stephen! I didn't know it was you." She had sat for so long in the half-light, all alone; she was so glad to see him. It was as though he had known of her loneliness and her unhappiness, and had come because she needed him. She rose and went towards him with little, hurried steps, holding out her hands. "I'm so *glad* you've come!" she said, like a child, and with a tiny catch in her voice.

His hands came out to meet hers, and clasped them warmly together, and kept them so.

"Elizabeth! Why, you poor little thing, what's the matter?"

He sounded so sympathetic and anxious, and so tenderly possessive that a rush of hot tears sprang to Elizabeth's eyes and glittered on the end of her lashes. She tried to smile and to draw her hands away.

"N-nothing. I—I don't know. I was lonely."

It seemed an infamous thing that she should be lonely, or that anyone should, however indirectly, have caused those wonderful eyes to brim with tears. Stephen bent his head over the hands in his, and kissed them.

"Dear little Elizabeth!" he said. "What a damned shame!"

She was startled; he felt her pulses leap under his fingers, and looked up again, smiling.

"Don't be so scared, dear! Come and tell me all about it." He knew now that his mind was made up; he would not leave this room until he had told her how greatly he loved her; her tears and her helplessness had brought matters between them to a head.

Elizabeth knew also, blamed herself yet was glad. She let him put her back into her chair, and quivering watched him sit down on a low stool at her feet.

"There—there isn't anything to tell. It was only being alone—and silly. I'm awfully sorry I was such an idiot."

"You weren't. You couldn't be," he said quietly.

"Oh, but I was! I was just being—morbid. It sounds frightfully stupid, because I never knew her, but I—I wanted my mother."

His eyes darkened, and again he held her hands.

"Stupid? Did you think that I shouldn't understand, Elizabeth?"

She was drawing back into her shell; she thought it could not have been herself who had made that confidence.

"I don't see how you can. I don't understand it myself. Please—please, will you let me go?"

"No. I want you to let me keep you and take care of you all your life, Elizabeth. I love you. Oh, my darling, you're trembling! You're not afraid of me—you couldn't be!" He was on his feet now, and had pulled her up to stand before him. "Elizabeth, little wild bird! I love you so *much!*"

She started to struggle; it was the impossibility of breaking away from him against his will that made her shrink suddenly towards him; that, and the marvellous feeling of security his strength gave her. Without knowing why, she began to cry, very softly, with her face buried in his coat. His arms were tight about her, she felt his lips on her hair, and presently his fingers came under her chin and forced her head up that he might look into her eyes. She bore his look for a moment, and then her lashes fell and she felt his lips hard-pressed against her mouth.

He was gentle with her after that, knowing her fright, and dried her tears with his own large handkerchief, laughing at her a little, but very tenderly.

"Little babe! Oh, my darling, I'll be so good to you! You shall never be lonely again, never! Elizabeth, dearest one, say that you love me! Say it quickly!"

Her senses were whirling; she was no longer Elizabeth, but some strange, mad girl who had been kissed by a man who was not her father. She was being swept off her feet by a swift tide of unreality and things unknown.

Stephen gave her a quick hug; she gasped and put her hands up against his chest.

"Say it, you little witch! If you don't I'll—"

She flung her head back to avoid the threatened kiss, and pulled away from him as far as his arms would let her.

"I love you," she stammered. "Let me go! Please, Stephen, please!"

His arms slackened from about her shoulders, but he took her face between his hands and very gently kissed her.

Nothing he could have done would have made so great an appeal to her as his present forbearance. She felt his iron self-control and loved him for it. His passion had frightened her, even though it carried all before it, but his consideration now drove out her fear. Shyly she returned his kiss, then drooped her head and laid nervous fingers on his coat-sleeve.

He wanted to pick her up, but something warned him that he must not. It was in keeping with his ideal of her that she should be timid; he must be careful, and not forget her frailty. So he drew her down to sit beside him on the sofa and began to play with her little hand.

"When will your father be home, sweetheart? I just can't wait."

"I don't know—the usual time— Oh, Stephen, are you *sure?*"

"My darling! Am I sure! Elizabeth, you won't make me wait too long?"

"Would you—if I wanted to?" she asked, peeping up at him. "Would you, Stephen?"

His fingers crushed hers against his lips.

"I—yes, if you wished. But don't, Elizabeth, don't!"

It was marvellous to think that anyone so big and masterful would give way to her so humbly. She pulled her hand from his and showed him her whitened fingers.

"Look! How cruel, Stephen!"

He was all contrition at once; she saw herself precious in his eyes, and tilted her head, a faint smile of new-born confidence on her lips.

Then, after what seemed a very little while, Lawrence's key grated in the front door lock, and Stephen sprang up.

"I never knew that I could be in such a fever of anxiety!" he said. "Wait here, my darling, won't you?"

"Yes," she answered, and raised her hand to brush a piece of fluff from his coat.

His eyes laughed, and again he caught her in his arms.

"Oh, you darling!" he said, and went striding out to meet Lawrence.

Chapter Eight

It was not very long before Miss Arden came in. She found Elizabeth wrapped in dreams, slowly regaining her balance.

"Well, well, nothing to do?" she exclaimed. "Haven't you any sewing, my dear?"

Her voice interrupted the pleasant reverie and irritated Elizabeth. She looked up, and that tiny, triumphant smile again curved her lips.

"Stephen is here," she said.

Miss Arden glanced round the room as though he were hidden somewhere in it.

"Where?" she asked. "His car is not outside."

"I suppose he took a taxi," Elizabeth answered. "He's with Father."

Miss Arden jumped and stared very hard at Elizabeth.

"My dear?"

"We're—we're going to be married," Elizabeth said simply.

Miss Arden dropped her furs and her bag and almost fell upon her niece.

"Oh, my darling! my dearest child!" she cried. "What —What can I say?" She kissed Elizabeth, and fondled her hair. Her eyes were wet. "I don't know how I shall bear it, or what I shall do without you! But I'm very, very glad, for your sake. If I have to give you up to any man I'd sooner it was to Stephen. Oh, darling, are you very happy?"

"I think I am," Elizabeth said conscientiously.

"I Think! Elizabeth, surely, surely—"

"No, of course I'm happy. It's only that it was so sudden—I don't quite know where I am or what's happening."

"My dear, I understand! I'm not a bit surprised, of course, at your news. Onlookers see most of the game, don't they, love? Oh dear, and you're so young! I had hoped— What are we going to do without you? Stephen Ramsay too, of all people! I don't fancy that your father will make any objection. He's such a charming young man, as I told his mother, and so well-connected. Darling, really I don't know whether I'm on my head or my heels! If only your poor dear mother were alive, how proud she would be! She'd understand what I'm feeling, too. It seems only yesterday that you were playing with your doll."

Then Lawrence came bustling in with Stephen behind him, and, pouncing upon his daughter, kissed her, twice.

"Well, well, well! So my little girl wants to be married, does she? And a very obstinate, pushing husband you'll have, my dear! I have been forced—yes, forced at the sword's point so to speak—to give my consent to an early marriage. Many, many congratulations, Elizabeth, but more to Stephen. You little know what a treasure you are going to possess, young man."

"I do know, sir, none better," Stephen said promptly.

Lawrence heaved a great sigh.

"Not as I, her father, know. It's going to be a great gap in our lives, eh,

Anne?"

"I can't bear to think of it," she answered. "But I do congratulate you, both. And I do hope you aren't going to force Elizabeth into too early a marriage, Stephen."

"I couldn't force her into anything, Miss Arden," he replied, smiling. "But I'm impatient. Can you wonder?"

"No, oh no, but there's so much to be thought of, and so much to be done."

"Long engagements," said Lawrence unexpectedly, "are a mistake. We'll discuss all that at some future date. Meanwhile, Stephen tells me he has promised to be at his mother's flat by half-past six."

"A dinner-party," Stephen explained, grimacing. "If it wasn't the mater's party—"

"Oh, but of course you must go!" Elizabeth said quickly. She was anxious to put an end to this trying scene, and stepped forward to his side. "I'll come and see you off."

Outside, in the hall, he put his arms about her and kissed her eyelids.

"If you only knew how often I've longed to do that!" he murmured. "Your father was a brick, Elizabeth. Don't let them persuade you into putting off the wedding! Let it be soon, sweetheart, I can't wait!"

"Not too soon!" she begged. "You don't understand, Stephen, I must have time. I—I've got to get used to the feel of being engaged first."

"Poor little precious, you shan't be rushed and badgered! Elizabeth, until I can get you a real, proper ring, will you wear this?" He drew the signet ring from his little finger.

"I'd like to," she said, and gave him her hand.

*

Cynthia was with his mother, and Anthony. As Stephen came impetuously into the drawing-room, Anthony, pen in hand, was saying,

"But, look here, mater, you must remember where that missing twenty pounds went to!"

"I don't, a bit," Mrs. Ramsay said placidly, then caught sight of her son.

"Stephen, Anthony's bullying me."

Stephen bent to kiss the top of her head.

"What a shame! And what have yon been doing?"

"He says I must account for a horrible twenty pounds. Put it down as incidental expenses, Anthony."

"Can't. Everything is incidental expenses! And *really*, mater, this isn't the way to keep an account-book."

"Isn't it, darling? You show me, then."

Anthony grinned, and shut the book.

"Showed you last week, my dear. Not a bit of good."

"Don't worry her," Stephen said. "She likes to be in a muddle. I'll go through with her later. She probably bought a Chippendale chair with that twenty pounds."

Mrs. Ramsay sat up.

"No, not a chair, a mirror. Stephen, you're perfectly wonderful! I should never have remembered! How did you do it?"

"Long association with you helped, mater. I've news for you."

"How nice! Good news?"

Stephen went to the fireplace and stood with his back to it. Mrs. Ramsay saw that his chin was tilted a little as though for battle.

"Very good news. I am engaged to be married to Elizabeth Arden."

Heavily weighted, his words fell into a strained silence. Then Cynthia moved, jerking her head.

"Oh, damnation!" she said forcibly.

"Thanks," said Stephen. "Anything else?"

"Go to the devil your own silly way!"

Stephen's hands went into his pockets, tight clenched. There was blazing light at the back of his eyes, and the corners of his mouth twitched slightly.

"Yes? What exactly do you mean by that?"

"What I say!"

Anthony heaved himself out of his chair.

"No, she doesn't. Gently, Cynthia, now! Congratulations, old man, an' all that sort of thing. Nice little girl, Elizabeth."

Mrs. Ramsay came to Stephen, and put her hands up to hold the lapels of his coat.

"Please don't frown at me, Stephen dear! If you're very happy, I am too. Didn't I say I should be? Somebody bring me a footstool, I can't reach him, and I want to kiss him."

"You're a dear, mater," Stephen said, and hugged her. "You won't be able to help loving Elizabeth when you know her better."

"Of course I shan't. Can I congratulate her, or does that look as though I'm too proud of you?"

Cynthia rose and walked out of the room.

"Don't be huffy, old man!" Anthony begged. "You know what she is. She doesn't mean anything."

"I do indeed know what she is," said Stephen grimly. "Of all the shrewish—"

Anthony put his pipe down on the mantelpiece.

"That'll do, Stephen," he drawled.

"I daresay it suits you to shut your eyes to her abominable behaviour!" Stephen sneered.

"If you've got anything more to say, you can come outside and say it," Anthony warned him softly. "I'm willing to admit that Cynthia shouldn't have said what she did, but if you think I'm going to let you—"

"I'll say what I like about Cynthia! You seem to forget that I've got the rotten bad luck to be her brother!"

"And you—" Anthony planted himself firmly before Stephen, "seem to forget that I have the extraordinary good luck to be her husband."

"Very extraordinary!" Stephen snapped.

"I think it's time I began to cry," Mrs. Ramsay said plaintively. "Don't quarrel, you dear silly creatures. Anthony, don't pay any attention to Stephen. Goodness me, you ought to know the Ramsay temper by now!"

Anthony picked up his pipe.

"Pity it isn't kept under control," he remarked, very levelly.

"Damn it all," Stephen said fiercely, "anyone would think I started the row!"

"Never mind who started it!" begged Mrs. Ramsay. "And be nice to Cynthia, Stephen, just to please me. You can be so awfully nice if you try."

"Be nice to her! What am I expected to do? Apologise for marrying a girl whom she doesn't happen to like?"

Mrs. Ramsay stroked his coat sleeve.

"It's only because she's so proud of you, dearest, and because she'd set her heart on your marrying Nina. She's sorry by now that she was so tactless."

Stephen was slightly mollified, but still he scowled.

"Jolly way to- have the news of one's engagement received," he said.

"Horrid, darling, but I'm glad that you're going to be happy, and so is Anthony."

The door opened; Cynthia came back into the room with her hat and gloves on. Stephen went forward.

"Going to congratulate me, Cynny?"

"I don't suppose it matters to you what I say," she answered bitterly.

"Cynthia, do behave properly!" sighed her mother. "I won't have you all quarrelling round me. And Stephen's going to kill Anthony—or Anthony's going to kill Stephen, I'm not sure which—and it'll be most unpleasant. All over you too, and it isn't anything to do with you really."

"You needn't bother to fight over me," Cynthia said. She hesitated, and then held out her hand. "Sorry, Stephen. I'll write to Elizabeth to-night."

"Thanks, old girl."

"Very handsome," commented Anthony. "I'd better take her home before she spoils it. Cheerio, mater; good luck, Stephen. Come on, my lady."

Cynthia released Stephen's hand.

"Perhaps I'd better," she admitted. "Time you and Stephen dressed for your party, mater."

So Stephen and his mother were left alone, and for a long time stood with linked arms before the fire. At last Mrs. Ramsay spoke.

"Soon, Stephen?"

"I hope so, mater."

Mrs. Ramsay stifled a tiny sigh, and looked up, smiling.

"I'll give Elizabeth the pearls as a wedding-present, shall I?"

He pressed her elbow slightly.

"No, dear. You won't."

"I'd like to, Stephen. Truly."

"Elizabeth wouldn't like you to. Nor should I. But you're a very nice little mater to think of it."

"Aren't I?" she nodded, pleased.

Chapter Nine

Following close upon a letter from Mrs. Ramsay, Stephen came to the Boltons' next morning and caught Elizabeth up into his arms.

"Oh . . . don't!" she cried, in agitation.

He laughed at her, and held her for yet another moment; then he set her gently on her feet, and put a little leather case into her hand.

"Darling, there's your first fetter," he said gaily. "Tell me if you like it! I've had at least twelve jewellers' shops upside down this morning, looking for a ring that would express you."

Elizabeth opened the case, and of habit, said, How lovely! She had dreamed of sapphires, deep twinkling gems, and Stephen brought her a cluster of pearls set in a diamond circle.

"It looked so exactly like you, Elizabeth. But if you don't care about it I'll change it. I ought to have asked you your favourite stone, oughtn't I?"

"Of course I like it. Thank you very much, Stephen. It's perfectly beautiful. Only it means tears. Had you forgotten?"

He drew his signet-ring from her finger and slipped his gift on in its place.

"'Fraid it's too big. Sweetheart, you don't really care about that silly old superstition, do you?"

She shook her head, smiling.

"No. I said it to tease you. It is too big, Stephen— just a bit."

"Sickening. What can I measure your dear little finger with?" She hunted in Miss Arden's work-bag for tape and carefully he tied a knot about her finger.

"Stephen, Mrs. Ram—your mother—has written an awfully nice letter to me. I'm going to tea with her this afternoon."

"Oh, splendid!" he said. "I told her last night. You'll love her, Elizabeth."

"I'm feeling—dreadfully shy—about going to see her," she confessed. She laid a hand upon his coat-sleeve, and glanced up at him in the bewitching, childlike way she had.

His arm went round her.

"My darling, you couldn't be shy of the mater! She's far more likely to be shy of you, little babe."

"Is she?" Elizabeth looked surprised. "But why? Won't she like me as a—as a daughter-in-law?"

"Elizabeth! How dare you? She'll love you—just as I do. No, not as I do at all. Darling, I adore your hair, it smells of all the flowers in the world, but I'd like to see your face."

She turned it upwards in blushing obedience. She saw his eyes grow dark and grave.

"Elizabeth—" He stopped and quite gently kissed her.

"There's so much I want to say, and I can't say it without sounding like a third-rate novel. I'd like to say all the things that I thought I never should say. I want to tell you that your eyes are like pansies, all velvety and soft, but I know quite well from the solemn look on your face that you'll think I'm just phrase-making."

She had not thought it; his whimsicality and the quick predominance of his humour puzzled her; she had not imagined that her lover would be like this, and laugh even when he said that she was beautiful. The tiny catch in his voice told her that although he joked, his feeling for her was serious, more serious perhaps than he dared to show? her. And yet his joking was a jarring note to her. Love-making was something that was holy and solemn, like going to church; he should not have laughed. After yesterday everything seemed a little flat. She had expected to feel a heroine's exultation when Stephen slipped the ring on to her finger, but the ring was too big, and she had wanted sapphires.

He left her when Miss Arden came in, and she spent the morning wondering what Mrs. Ramsay would say to her, and what she would say to Mrs. Ramsay.

But Mrs. Ramsay made everything easy. When Elizabeth entered her drawing-room she came forward quickly and held out both her hands.

"Elizabeth, can I congratulate you, or does that sound as though I were too proud of my son?"

Then Elizabeth laughed, and kissed her, and some of the tension was gone.

"It was so nice of you to ask me to come to-day," Elizabeth stammered.

"My dear, of course I wanted to see you at once. We hardly know one another, do we? Still, I always believe what Stephen tells me because he's usually right, and he says that I shall love you. Oh, do sit down!"

"Stephen says that I shall love you too," Elizabeth smiled.

"Please do! I'm a horribly spoiled person, and I can't bear it if people don't like me. By the way, I must introduce you to Thomas. Such a darling. Thomas, where are you?"

Thomas, who was a bull terrier, came stiffly from behind the sofa, and snuffed enquiringly at Elizabeth's ankles. She patted him and fondled his ears, and he put his forepaws on her knee.

"What a blessing!" sighed Mrs. Ramsay. "It's most awkward when Thomas won't be polite to my friends. I'm glad he likes you. Have you got a dog?"

"No, but I've always wanted one," Elizabeth answered. "My aunt doesn't care for them. What a beautiful head Thomas has."

"Hasn't he? You know, he rules my life, which is sometimes most tiresome. That's the worst of a dog—yes, and the best too—if you're really and truly fond of them you can't stir without them, and then where are you?" She began to pour out the tea. "I was at Seaford. At least, that's where Thomas landed me. Such an awful place; you can't wear a hat there without being conspicuous."

"But why did Thomas land you at Seaford?" Elizabeth asked, considerably mystified.

"Oh, didn't I explain?" Mrs. Ramsay handed her a plate and made a vague gesture of invitation towards the cake-stand. "The only hotel that would receive Thomas was one at Seaford. No, I believe there was one at Eastbourne, but I couldn't possibly go there, could I? You can't go *without* a hat there, without being conspicuous. No medium. So I went to Seaford, and Thomas loved it. Do have some toast."

Elizabeth took the toast, and as there didn't seem to be anything to say she was silent. Mrs. Ramsay gave Thomas a lump of sugar, remarking that it was exceedingly bad for him, and leaned back in her chair, smiling at Elizabeth.

"Poor child, you little know what a mad family you're marrying into. Someone ought to have warned you. Did Stephen?"

"No," said Elizabeth, laughing a little.

"What a shame. Still, you've met most of us, haven't you? Even Anthony, and he isn't mad at all. Quite the reverse, poor old thing. Then there's the Outer Circle: aunts, you know, and one uncle. Quite a darling, and never will go to bed before three in the morning. I believe there are some cousins, only I've forgotten for the moment which they are. Relations are rather trying, aren't they? especially cousins. So elusive. You meet them once in a blue moon and feel you ought to love them whereas really you hope to goodness you'll never see them again. Are you cursed with them?"

"No, I've no relations except my father and my aunt. My mother was an only child, you see. Oh—as a matter of fact I think I have got some cousins somewhere. Second ones, or once-removed. I don't quite know, but I've never seen them."

"There you are!" Mrs. Ramsay nodded. "One day they'll turn up, and you'll think, What awful people! Backwoodsmen. They always are."

"Back what?" Elizabeth asked, much amused.

"Backwoodsmen. Isn't that right? Country-bumpkins, who come on a visit to town and buy clothes at Selfridge's."

"Oh, I see! Yes, I believe mine are like that. They live in the Isle of Wight."

"I didn't know anybody did," Mrs. Ramsay said innocently. "I always thought the Isle of Wight was just a place everyone went to in the summer. That's why I never did. Try some of that cake. I bought it myself because it looked like the Albert Memorial."

"Oh, that eyesore!" Elizabeth cried.

"My dear, it's wonderful. I go and stare at it periodically and gasp."

"But don't you think it's ugly?" Elizabeth asked.

"Marvellously. It's just as though an ancient Greek did all the stone work at the base and Joseph Lyons came and put the chocolate wedding-cake on top. I wonder whether he did? I must ask Stephen. Yes, and that's brought us back to Stephen. The Albert Memorial and Stephen. How dreadful! When is he going to take you down to Queen's Halt?"

"He hasn't said anything about it—yet. You see—it was only yesterday that he—that we—"

"So it was! Such an attractive house, Elizabeth—in the summer. Ingle nooks and beamed ceilings. Yes, and a warming-pan. Rather draughty in winter—not the warming-pan, but the house. Stephen's grandfather pushed I don't know how much Louis Quinze furniture into it, and it simply shrieked. However, we've got rid of it all now, so you needn't be alarmed." Her hands began to wander over the tea-tray again, and she looked worried. "I'm sure I haven't said all the things I ought to say. I've had no experience, you see, and it's difficult. Anthony simply said, Please can I marry Cynthia? and I answered, Yes, if you take care of her. I can't very well tell you to take care of Stephen, can I?"

"I—I will, though," Elizabeth said.

"Yes, I think perhaps you will. The best thing I can say is, Be as happy as you can and—and never give him kippers for breakfast. He hates them."

Elizabeth took this quite seriously, and made a mental note of it.

"Before we—before we're married, will you please tell me all those sort of things that I ought to know?" she asked diffidently.

"My dear, I don't know them myself," Mrs. Ramsay said. "I only remember about the kippers because Stephen once threw one out of the window. By the tail. It looked so pathetic, and the garden was infested by cats for days afterwards."

"Threw it out of the window?" Elizabeth gasped. "*Stephen?*"

"Dear me, yes. Quite a dreadful exhibition, wasn't it? I remember old Mrs. Taunton was staying with us at the time and she was quite surprised. Rather shocked too, and really one can't wonder at it. Still, it did look funny."

"But what an extraordinary thing to do," Elizabeth said slowly.

"Most. So inconsiderate too, because I couldn't bear to think of a kipper lying in the garden, and we all had to go out and look for it after breakfast. Thomas found it, didn't you, my pet?"

It was funny, as recounted by Mrs. Ramsay, and Elizabeth laughed, but privately she wondered what she would think if ever Stephen did such a thing in her presence. Something of this was reflected in her face, for, after a pause, Mrs. Ramsay said,

"You mustn't think that throwing kippers out of the window is one of Stephen's vices, my dear. In fact, I've never known him do it before or since. On that particular occasion something had gone wrong with his novel, and he vented his wrath on the kipper. Careless of me to have offered him one."

"I shall take good care never to have kippers," Elizabeth remarked. "But seriously, Mrs. Ramsay, will you tell me all his likes and dislikes, and—and—that sort of thing?"

"I would if I could," Mrs. Ramsay assured her, with a disarming smile. "Only I can't, because I don't remember. If I think of anything I'll write it down on a piece of paper and lose it. And I can't tell you anything about housekeeping, because I'm a very bad housekeeper. I never know what day the washing comes home, or whether I've paid the books or not. You won't have to worry about that unless you want to, because Nana housekeeps at Queen's Halt. Nana is Stephen's old nurse; such a treasure. She knows everything."

"I expect she'll teach me then," Elizabeth said slowly. "Is she—very formidable?"

"No, I don't think so. She's rather fussy about not bringing mud into the house, and I don't think she approves of Stephen's books, but she's really quite harmless. She'll like you, I expect. By the way, when are you going to get married, or don't you know?"

"Oh, I—we—haven't thought about that yet!" Elizabeth said, shrinking. "There's—there's heaps of time."

"I shouldn't hurry it too much," Mrs. Ramsay said. "Stephen will want to carry you off at once, but—oh, I'd wait a little while!"

Elizabeth looked at her, and again the thought came to her that Mrs. Ramsay did not want Stephen to marry her. She began to fumble with the bead-bag she carried.

"Why, Mrs. Ramsay?" she asked hesitantly.

"Because you don't know one another very well yet, my dear. Do I sound as though I were being nasty? I'm not a bit really. Only Stephen's the queerest creature on God's earth, and it would be better for you if you knew what sort of moods he was likely to have, before you married him."

"Moods ..." Elizabeth repeated. "Is he—moody?"

"My child, he calls it 'artistic temperament.' So much nicer. Awfully interesting, but sometimes rather trying. His father had it too." Then Mrs. Ramsay realised that she was saying things to separate Stephen from Elizabeth, and she managed to stop herself, and to smile. "But he's always charming, and—if you go about it the right way— easy to manage. How dreadful of us to talk about him like this! He wanted to come to tea to-day, and I wouldn't let him. I preferred to have my future daughter to myself."

"I'm glad you did," Elizabeth said. "It's easier in a way—to get to know one another. I was—awfully pleased to be able to come."

"Rather an ordeal," Mrs. Ramsay commented.

"Oh, no!" Elizabeth assured her. "Not a bit!"

Mrs. Ramsay felt glad that Cynthia was not there. Cynthia would have been triumphant; perhaps she would even have sneered.

"I want you to come and see me just whenever you feel like it," Mrs. Ramsay said. "I Don't bother to ring up; come."

"Thank you—it's very kind of you," Elizabeth stammered.

"It isn't a bit. I want to get to know you, and I want you to know me. So much more satisfactory for both of us. So drop in on me, won't you? I can't bear ceremony."

"I should love to," Elizabeth said; but Mrs. Ramsay knew that she would wait to be invited.

Chapter Ten

Elizabeth wanted to "show off" her engagement to Mr. Hengist. It was the way Mr. Hengist spoke and looked, the little ironical things he said that made her want to do this. Mr. Hengist thought her stupid; he laughed at her, and said, For God's sake be natural! Now surely he would recognise that she was not stupid: how could she be when Stephen Ramsay had chosen her for his wife? She had been proud to introduce Stephen to Mr. Hengist as a friend; she was immeasurably proud to speak of him as "my fiance." The mantle of his brilliancy seemed in some mysterious way to have fallen about her shoulders; she held her head higher; in imagination she was Mrs. Stephen Ramsay "whom you *must* know, my dear!"

Yet, in the end, it was disappointing, and Mr. Hengist was unresponding and unimpressed. It was queer how Elizabeth cared for his opinion, and liked him even when he annoyed her most.

He came one evening to smoke a pipe with Lawrence, and because Lawrence was out, he went into the drawing-room, where Elizabeth sat with Miss Arden.

"Aha!" Miss Arden cried archly, "you've come to congratulate our little Elizabeth!"

Mr. Hengist shook hands with them both in his quiet way, and said, after the tiniest pause,

"Yes. I suppose so. I hope you'll be very happy, Elizabeth."

"Well, I must say that's not very enthusiastic!" Miss Arden said, still arch, but with a touch of acidity in her voice.

"Isn't it? I hardly know Ramsay. If you and Lawrence are pleased—"

"Pleased! We're delighted—for Elizabeth's sake."

"Then it seems to be most satisfactory," he said calmly.

Elizabeth thought how grudgingly he had spoken, how detached was his manner. Pique made her cheeks rosy and her eyes bright, and when Miss Arden went to fetch her knitting, she looked challengingly at Mr. Hengist, and said,

"Why did you congratulate me in such a funny way, Mr. Hengist? Aren't you glad?"

"Very, if you are."

"Of course I am! I shouldn't be engaged if I—if I didn't love Stephen."

"Wouldn't you?" Mr. Hengist looked at her in that quizzical way he had, just as though he didn't believe her.

Elizabeth was tired with a long day's shopping, and pettish.

"I wish you'd say what you really think!" she said rather snappishly, like Miss Arden.

Mr. Hengist started to knock his pipe out against the fender; the measured, staccato sound irritated her, and she jerked her head crossly.

"My dear Elizabeth," Mr. Hengist said slowly, "don't you realize that that is the last thing in the world you want?"

She was startled, and her eyelids flew wide.

"I don't know what you mean!"

"You ask me to say what I really think. That would be the truth, Elizabeth—the thing you've run away from all your life."

"I haven't!" she said hotly. "It's only what *you* think! I—I do want you to tell me your real opinion!"

"Very well," he answered. He shifted his shoulders into the chair, as though he were digging himself in. "I think that you're making a mistake—and I'm sorry."

Elizabeth gripped the arms of her chair, staring at him.

"How—how can you say such a horrible thing? I— making a mistake? I think it's most unkind of you! And how can you know?"

"I didn't think you'd care for my honest opinion, did I?" he replied, unruffled. "But you asked for it, and I'm going to give it. No one has ever made you look into yourself. Ever done it? Of course you haven't. You cheat,

Elizabeth."

"I don't! Oh, I don't!"

"You cheat yourself, which is far worse than cheating other people. It isn't all your fault, but it's time you stopped. I know you think you're in love with Ramsay— perhaps you are. I don't think so. Yes, that's a pretty beastly thing to say, isn't it? It's necessary though. You believe in the thing you either want to believe in, or that your—other people—expect you to believe in. You've read sickly trash, and you're susceptible to glamour. There's glamour about Ramsay; it's caught you. Ask yourself, child, whether you would still be in love with him if he were on the Stock Exchange."

"Yes!"

"Then you 're in love, and I withdraw all I have said."

"You don't believe me?"

"No, I don't. You haven't learned the meaning of love yet, but your mind has become a kind of sentimental sponge which makes it receptive to a fancied emotion. Do you see what I mean?"

"I'd rather not see," Elizabeth said frigidly.

"I know that. It's your attitude towards everything that's unpleasant. But I warn you, Elizabeth—and I speak as one who's very fond of you—that sooner or later you'll have to face unpleasantness. Your rosy, gossamer little world'll be torn up, and it'll be a shock. I don't want to see you hurt in that way. Facts have a way of forcing themselves upon you; you'd better face 'em now, and start being honest. And, Elizabeth, I hate to see you cheating yourself. It's rotten, and it's cowardly."

Her underlip trembled; he wondered whether she were about to cry.

"I don't see what—all this—has got to do with—my engagement!"

"Everything. With all his faults, Ramsay's honest— as honest as a man can be. A bit blind, perhaps, but sincere. Doesn't it rather stand to reason that you'll be in danger of clashing?"

"Stephen knows me better than you do!"

He smiled in boundless wisdom.

"He will, child, certainly. He's in love with you now, and being an idealist—almost a romantic, I think—he doesn't see any faults in you. When a man's deeply in love, he doesn't."

"I think you're being—unkind and—and cruel, Mr. Hengist."

"I expect you do, and I'm sorry. If I didn't love you I shouldn't bother to upset you. I want you to consider well before you plunge into marriage with Ramsay. If you're really in love with him incompatibility of temperament and ideals won't matter. If you're not—well, your chance of happiness is slender."

Elizabeth tried to capture dignity, but her voice quivered.

"It—seems to me, Mr. Hengist, that you think—Stephen has made a mistake."

"I do," he said. "He's not your sort. You're poles apart. I believe in affinities, you know. If you marry him you'll very soon see the need for adaptation, and as he's a man it's you who'll have to adapt yourself. Even then—oh, Elizabeth, you're only a kid, and I'm afraid you're going to make a mess of things!"

"I think—it's a matter for me to decide."

"Certainly it is."

"What is more, my father entirely approves."

Mr. Hengist started to say, Your father be damned, and recovered himself in time.

"Auntie too," Elizabeth said gently.

"Oh, lord!" groaned Mr. Hengist.

To Lawrence he said more, forcibly, but Lawrence put his finger-tips together and was blandly complacent. You could make no impression on him; he wanted to have Stephen, Ramsay as a son : in-law.

And all the time Stephen was kicking against the barriers that were attendant upon engagement. Hotly he desired Elizabeth, and chafed against restraint. She was his, but not his. He could take her out in his car, to dances, to the theatre; he could sit alone with her at her home but all the time he was conscious of the convenances hedging them round and witholding Elizabeth.

He would not take her to see Queen's Halt. Tentatively she suggested it, and he laughed, and the blood stole up to the roots of his hair as he confessed his whimsical fancy.

"I don't want to take you there until you're my wife, sweetheart. I can't explain why not, and I suppose it sounds ridiculous, but I—well, I won't. I'm getting incurably sentimental. All your fault, you adorable little angel. Soon I shall be seized with a longing to lift you over the threshold. Wouldn't it be awful?"

"I think it would be rather attractive," she said, reflecting.

"All right, I'll do it, and brave the sniggers of the cook and the housemaid. It's a bet."

"Would they snigger? It wouldn't be very nice, then."

"Sure to. Probably think me mad. Oh, no, they'd say, Ah, well, he's a writer, with an indulgent smile. You can do anything if you're a writer, darling. Awfully useful. People rather expect you to be eccentric. Provided you wrote or painted they'd say, How delightfully Bohemian, if you turned up at a dinner-party in a tweed coat."

"Or threw kippers out of the window," Elizabeth added, remembering.

His eyes narrowed in a puzzled way peculiar to him.

"What's the joke?"

"Mrs. Ramsay—I mean, mater—said you did that once."

"Did I? Oh, yes, I know! How base of mater! If I promise never to do it again can our engagement stand?"

"Stephen, you silly!"

"Elizabeth, you pet! When will you marry me?"

It always came back to that. He argued until her excuses seemed foolish; her defences were weakening; she thought how masterful he was.

"My things aren't nearly ready yet."

"Damn your things, darling."

"I must get my trousseau together, Stephen. You know I must. You don't want a dowdy wife, do you?"

"Don't care a bit as long as I get her. You don't suppose I'm marrying your clothes, do you?"

"Yes, but I can't, Stephen. Not yet. Please wait just a little while. We've been engaged such a short time."

That was how it ended, always. Then at last one day he pleaded so adroitly and with such winning fervour that she named her date, promising to marry him in June, if her father consented. It would make their engagement of three months' duration; he must admit that it was short.

He began to plan their honeymoon; she listened breathlessly while he spoke of Paris and Brittany, or perhaps Florence, and Rome and Sicily. She was dazzled and eager. Life was beautiful.

Lawrence put forward no objections; it was Miss Arden who begged Elizabeth to wait. Lawrence said that he should like to see his little girl married among the roses, and was she to be married from a hotel or from home?

That diverted Miss Arden's thoughts a little; the battle raged over Elizabeth, and in the end Lawrence won. She was to be married from a hotel, with a champagne breakfast. It was all very exciting and queer, and there was so much to be done that Elizabeth's thoughts rarely travelled further than to the wedding itself. "Afterwards" was in the misty future; now there was her dress to be made, and her going-away frock to be chosen.

And as the time drew nearer she began to wish that it were over, and looked forward to the actual date as a day when all the wearisome preparations should be over and she might pause to draw breath.

Stephen grumbled at her constant preoccupation, but he submitted because he knew that soon, very soon, it would all be over, and he would be able to carry her off, away from a fussy aunt and trite father, and away from excited and admiring girl-friends.

It seemed to him that Elizabeth had no time to give him now; she was busy trying on clothes or acknowledging presents. She was looking tired, too, and there was no sense of repose in her home. Miss Arden saw to it that everyone, including herself, was in a continual state of bustle. She enjoyed it, and spent the day running up and downstairs, forgetting first this and then that, and growing steadily wearier and, therefore, more irritable.

When Stephen came he bore Elizabeth off in his car, motoring her out to lunch at some quiet, lovely spot, waiting on her with tender, solicitous care, treating her, she thought, as though she were made of porcelain. It was so pleasant that she found herself counting the days to her wedding, almost longing to get away from home and her strenuous aunt.

Her bridesmaids worried her too, with their chatter and their giggling enthusiasm. Sarah was the only one of them she liked to have with her for any length of time; the others were all "nice" girls, approved of by Miss Arden.

She saw Cynthia Ruthven many times, and Cynthia was always civil. She knew that Cynthia did not like her. Anthony was different; you could not be afraid of him, any more than you could be afraid of Mrs. Ramsay, or of Stephen's aunt who lost all her luggage on the way to town and could still smile. She did not care much for Stephen's best man, John Caryll, who spoke in a drawl and quoted unknown verses, but she knew that he was clever, and supposed, sighing, that one must make allowances for him.

Lawrence, full of plans and importance, was in his element, and Miss Arden's way. He criticised all Elizabeth's clothes, to Miss Arden's annoyance. Elizabeth knew that his taste was good, and listened to all that he had to say. Since she was soon to leave him his interference and his mannerisms hardly irritated her at all, but she wished he would not embrace her so often or so lingeringly.

But if Lawrence was outwardly concerned only with the trivialities attached to a wedding, inwardly a greater problem was worrying him. Parental duty, before so light a burden, became suddenly heavy and brought a frown to his brows. He felt himself responsible and so carried his responsibility to Miss Arden.

She knew that he had something on his mind by the way he fidgetted and allowed his pipe to go out. Twice he cleared his throat and seemed about to speak, yet did not. Only when Miss Arden folded up her work before going to bed did be manage to broach the question that bothered him.

"Er—Anne!" he said casually, scraping out the bowl of his pipe.

"Yes? What is it, Lawrence?"

He thought, and rightly, that it was going to be difficult. Very badly he wanted to abandon his attempt, but for once sense of duty triumphed.

"Um— Well. Er—there's something I rather wanted to say to you. Ask you about, you know."

"Yes?" she said again.

"It's—well, of course I'm only Elizabeth's father, and —well, you know what I mean. Naturally I can't speak to her, but—er—well, I've been wondering whether we— er—oughtn't to—er—ask someone—a—a married woman, I mean—to—to—well, have a talk with Elizabeth. Don't you—er—think so?"

Miss Arden sat very straight. He did not look at her, but began to fold the evening paper, fiercely. Miss Arden's voice was dangerous.

"I don't think I quite understand you, Lawrence," she said. He knew that she did understand, and was angry.

"Well, er—I don't know—how much—er, I mean, what Elizabeth knows, but she—um—I can't help feeling that perhaps if Mrs. Cockburn talked to her a bit—before she's married ..."

"May I ask why Mrs. Cockburn is to be put in my place?" said Miss Arden icily.

"Well, but—hang it all, Anne, you're not a married woman, and—and it's not a job for a—a spinster."

"I can assure you, Lawrence, that I am perfectly capable of telling Elizabeth all that she ought to know. I fail to see that this is your department."

"No, er—quite. Only Elizabeth hasn't got a mother, and—well, she's very—er—innocent. Besides it's not— not a pleasant task for you, and—"

"I am not at all likely to shirk my responsibilities."

"Now, Anne—now, really, Anne, did I suggest such a thing? All I meant was—"

"You would be most ill-advised to ask Mrs. Cockburn to interfere or anyone else for that matter. A great deal of nonsense is talked nowadays on this subject. Provided the man is nice it is most undesirable that girls should know too much. You may take it from me, Lawrence, that it simply puts silly ideas into their heads."

Lawrence wanted to tell Anne that as she had never been married she knew nothing about it, but he dared not.

"Yes, yes, I daresay. But at the same time I don't think it's—well, fair."

"Really, Lawrence! I should never have thought that you would have fallen for this modern craze of telling girls everything."

"It's not exactly— What I mean is, it isn't fair to—"

"If you haven't enough faith in Stephen—"

"Not fair to him," Lawrence said surprisingly.

Miss Arden stared at him with uplifted brows.

"I don't understand you."

"Not fair to either of them—beastly for Stephen."

"I think you're making mountains out of molehills."

Lawrence was silent, wondering whether this were indeed so. If it were, his course was easy to see: he could relapse into inanition. After all, he supposed that Anne must know Elizabeth better than he did, and could be trusted to do and say what was right.

"Well, anyhow, Anne, you must find out just what Elizabeth—"

"My dear Lawrence, you can safely leave it to me," Miss Arden interrupted. She spoke with finality.

"As long as you tell her what she ought to know—"

"I shall do all that is necessary."

Lawrence sighed with fast returning comfort of mind. "I expect you know best, Anne. I leave it to you." He went to bed with the pleasant conviction of having performed a disagreeable duty. Incidentally, he had sloughed his responsibility. It rested on Anne's shoulders now, and on her conscience.

Chapter Eleven

Elizabeth awoke on her wedding-morning with an odd feeling of mingled excitement and foreboding. As she lay in bed she could see her new trunks, one open, with her evening-frocks, carefully folded in tissue-paper, bulging up out of the tray; the other locked and strapped, and with the initials E. R. shining on the side, in big, black letters. E. R.—Elizabeth Ramsay. How funny it sounded, and how unreal. She repeated it to herself, half-dreaming, and then fell to wondering how Stephen felt this morning; whether he too were excited, and whether he knew, or guessed, that underneath his bride-to-be's excitement, vague melancholy lurked, and a certain shrinking.

Her mind wandered back to last night. She and Aunt Anne had laid the last things in those trunks, and had marked the last batch of handkerchiefs. And while she had packed that taffeta dance-frock that peeped above the side of the box Aunt Anne had talked, very quickly and mysteriously, of things that Elizabeth only partially comprehended.

Thinking it over now, Elizabeth subconsciously compared her aunt's words to the pills she had been made to swallow in her childhood, smothered in raspberry jam. You had never tasted the pills: there was too much jam, but you had felt that they were there, and that they were nasty. Just so had Aunt Anne talked last night, telling you nothing, but hinting that you were about to enter on quite a new life, filled with new experiences, some of them not pleasant.

She had wanted to know more, and yet she had been thankful when Aunt Anne stopped. She had been shy, and red in the face, and she made Elizabeth shy, more withdrawn into herself.

How dismal her room looked, dismantled, and with one wardrobe door yawning to show dark emptiness within. How queer to think that this was the last time she would lie in bed in her room, waiting to be called. She had never before realised how much she loved her room, everything there was in it, and its exquisite privacy. That brought her to another disturbing thought. She tried to picture Stephen here, and thought how impossible it was; how impossible, and how embarrassing. Probably she would not feel that in a new, strange room. And yet . . . Hurriedly she switched her mind away from that picture, and turned on her side to look at the bridal dress, laid over the back of a chair. How pretty it was, with its soft, dull folds, and its long train. It would be nice to wear her mother's veil, too, and to carry the sheaf of lilies that would arrive this morning. The going-away frock was packed in that suit-case; she would change from her wedding-dress to that in the hotel. It was queer to think that even your brushes and combs were new, a wedding present from Aunt Anne. It was as though you became a different person all at once when you had a fitted dressing-case of your own, and threw away all your old clothes.

The housemaid came with a can of hot water, and congratulated Elizabeth as she pulled up the blinds. Everyone seemed to think that this was the happiest day of your life; no one realised how mixed were your feelings.

She got up, and slowly dressed, putting on an old skirt and a knitted jumper. Stephen's present to her lay in the flat velvet case on the dressing-table. He had brought it yesterday, but she thought she would not wear it until she changed into her wedding-dress. But she opened the case, so that while she brushed her hair she could look at the long string of pearls, and occasionally touch them.

She was to he married at twelve, so there would not be much time to attend to all the countless little jobs that were left. Perhaps that was as well. If you had nothing to do you might brood, and grow unhappy at the thought of leaving your home.

Lawrence looked unfamiliar at the breakfast-table, already dressed, save for the flower in his button-hole. When Elizabeth entered, he said, Here she is! as though he had been anxiously awaiting her. Miss Arden rose and kissed her with tears in her eyes, and said, My darling. Elizabeth clung to her for a moment, and then turned to open her letters.

The morning passed in a dream. More presents came and had to be acknowledged. She had to ring up the shop that was supplying her shoes, and tell them to send at once. Then Sarah appeared, ready, as she said, for the fray. Sarah was going to help her to dress, with Miss Arden; Sarah was cheerful, and full of jokes; she made Elizabeth laugh.

The orange-blossom was exotic in scent, and heavy. They fixed her wreath over her veil and coaxed her hair into curls about her ears.

"How pale you are, my darling!" Miss Arden sighed.

"Rot!" said Sarah briskly. "Now for the pearls! Elizabeth, you lucky little beast!"

The pearls lay milk-white against her neck, and rose slightly with the heave and fall of her breast. The lilies lay upon the table, tied with white satin ribbon, and beside them her long kid gloves reposed chastely between folds of tissue paper.

They told her to look at herself in the glass. She saw a stranger, white and with apprehensive eyes.

"It hangs well," she said, in a gasp. "I think—if you'd put a pin just there ..."

Then Sarah said she must fly; someone came to take the trunks to the station cloakroom; Miss Arden hurried away to put the finishing touches to her own toilette.

Elizabeth wandered about her room, to see that nothing had been forgotten. How funny it would be to see Stephen in a cut-away coat and top-hat! Yesterday when he came he had said that his boot-maker hadn't sent yet. She wondered whether he had had to ring up too, and whether it was an unlucky sign. Stephen had said that he was getting the wind up, but that he looked to John to pull him through. Perhaps John would pull her through too; he looked as though he would be able to do anything.

Lawrence called up the stairs to tell them that Aunt Anne's car was waiting, with Mrs. Cockburn, who was to accompany her, inside. Aunt Anne answered that she was just coming, and returned to Elizabeth's room, pulling on her gloves.

"Ready, darling? Come down and show your father how lovely you are." She picked up Elizabeth's coat of white fur, and then put it down again, and held out her arms. Elizabeth went to her, in a rush. The tears were trembling on the end of her lashes.

"Oh, Auntie—oh, Auntie!"

Lawrence called again, impatiently. They went down to him, and when he saw Elizabeth he said, Well, well, well! a sure sign that he was impressed. Aunt Anne was fussy, and said, Take care you don't crush her dress. She said you must not forget your gloves, and then she was gone in a whirl of mauve silk, into the waiting car.

Elizabeth sat down on a straight hard chair in the drawing-room. It was as though she were in a dentist's waiting-room. Something inside her was thumping, thumping. The drawing-room was unreal, Lawrence too, and herself. Ten to twelve ... on any other day she would just be coming into the house after a morning's shopping. To-day she sat attendant upon an unknown fate, in the drawing-room, clasping in her hands a great sheaf of pale lilies.

And now that the moment was so close when she would step out of the old life into the new, an intangible dread took possession of her, numbing her faculties towards every feeling but the one fear that she was walking blindfold on the brink of a precipice, and that one careless step might send her over the edge, to smash upon the rocks she knew to lurk in the abyss.

"Couldn't have had a better day," Lawrence said, standing, watch in hand, at the window.

"No. Isn't it perfect?" she answered.

"Car ought to be here any minute now. What about putting your coat on?" He held it ready, and managed to gather up her veil in one hand.

She felt more than ever that she was in the dentist's waiting-room, and that soon, very soon, the door would open and a sepulchral voice say, Miss Arden, please!

"Here it is!" Lawrence exclaimed. "Is my button-hole all right, Elizabeth?"

"Yes, quite," she said. "Ought—ought we to start?"

"Yes, we're a bit late. Doesn't matter, of course, but if you're ready—?"

"Quite," she said, gathering up her train.

The bridesmaids were in the church porch, laughing and talking. One of them cried, Here she is! and suddenly Elizabeth realised that she was the chief figure to-day, and that they were all waiting for her. Somewhere within the church people were turning to see whether she were coming; she would have to walk up the aisle, between the rows of smiling faces, until she reached the place where Stephen stood, with the capable John.

She laid her little cold hand on her father's arm; someone spread out her train behind her; Lawrence whispered fondly in her ear. They went out of the golden sunshine into the cool grey church.

She saw nothing, could distinguish no one in the blurred mass of people, until she felt her hand taken in a strong clasp and knew that Stephen was there. He said something; she did not know what it was, but she smiled and fixed her eyes on the black and white thing before her that was the clergyman.

Dearly beloved, we are gathered together . . .

What a lot he was saying in that queer, droning voice . . . what was it all about? Marriage, and something to do with children. How strong the lilies smelt!

Wilt thou love her, comfort her, honour . . .

He was speaking now to Stephen. It was beautiful.

In sickness and in health.

A lump rose in her throat. How straight Stephen stood; how deep and grave and unfaltering sounded his voice. Now it was her turn; she heard her own voice speak, quite clearly. She was not so nervous after all.

I, Stephen, take thee, Elizabeth . . .

She loved Stephen's voice; it was manly and stern and protective. She took his hand, and began to speak after the clergyman, looking at him, and wondering what made his cheeks so plump and red.

Someone moved beyond Stephen; it was Caryll, of course, with the ring, ready to the instant. She put up her hand and saw the gold circlet slip over her knuckle. She was married; the rest of the ceremony was nothing.

In the vestry there was noise and many kisses. Elizabeth saw Mrs. Ramsay, all in grey with floating draperies and soft plumes; Cynthia, severely swathed in blue; Aunt Anne, dabbing at her eyes; Anthony, hot and beaming, and Lawrence, shaking hands with the clergyman.

She signed her name, conscious of Stephen beside her; then turned to speak to Mrs. Ramsay.

"Has anyone told you that you look an angel?" Mrs. Ramsay said. "Because you do. Stephen had to go and fetch his boots, poor darling. Wasn't it trying? Stephen, I congratulate you. I believe I've said the right thing. I must tell Anthony." She drifted away, presumably to do so, and Elizabeth discovered that she was shaking hands with Cynthia.

"Congratulations," Cynthia said. "I knew you'd make a lovely bride."

Stephen was kissing Aunt Anne. How nice of him to think of that!

"Well, Mrs. Ramsay?" said Lawrence jocularly.

She smiled up at him; Stephen spoke at her elbow.

"That sounds wonderful, sir. Almost too good to be true."

They went back again into the church; the wedding-march sounded in her ears, triumphant; she thought that she heard bells, pealing. Her head went up, her cheeks were burning, and her hand lay on Stephen's arm.

In the car they sat side by side, not speaking at first, for Stephen's head was bent over her fingers. Then at last he looked up, and spoke huskily, almost as though he were awed.

"Little white bride," he said, and again she smiled, wistfully, thinking, This is not myself, it is a dream.

In the reception-room at the hotel they stood side by side, shaking hands with their guests, laughing, talking, and being congratulated. Everyone said what a pretty wedding it was, and did they see the man with the camera outside the church?

"Famous Novelist Weds," Sarah said teasingly.

"Anthony wouldn't let me bring Thomas," Mrs. Ramsay complained. "Such a shame. Elizabeth, who is that dear man who kissed you in the vestry?"

"This needs looking into," Stephen remarked solemnly. "Divulge his name, Elizabeth."

"Only Mr. Hengist," she answered, laughing.

"Introduce him," commanded Mrs. Ramsay. "Oh, I suppose you're too busy! Will nobody introduce me to Mr. Hengist?"

Mr. Hengist himself came forward, and presently they heard Mrs. Ramsay tell him that Thomas had eaten the bow someone tied about his neck.

The breakfast was a great success; champagne revived Elizabeth from the weariness that was stealing over her, but Stephen had to help her to cut the cake.

Healths were drunk; Stephen made a speech, and John Cary murmured to Elizabeth, Quite a witty effort, what? He then caused salmon mayonnaise to be put before her, and she ate some of it, rather to her own surprise.

Lawrence and Mrs. Ramsay, at the far end of the table appeared to be engaged in close and earnest conversation, about food; Miss Arden was inclined to be lachrymose. Beside her Anthony sought to cheer and amuse.

The vigilant best man was looking at his wrist-watch; he touched Elizabeth's arm and told her that it was time she went away to change. She caught Miss Arden's eye, and they rose.

Mrs. Ramsay whispered to Mr. Hengist,

"Poor darling, Miss Arden will cry! Not poor darling Miss Arden. Poor darling Elizabeth. Do you think I can go with them, and help? Then the aunt won't cry."

"Yes, do!" Mr. Hengist said. "She might easily upset Elizabeth."

So Mrs. Ramsay came floating towards Elizabeth, and asked with a winning smile if she might come too. John Caryll marched Stephen away, and a maid-servant conducted Elizabeth to her room where her travelling garments were laid out in readiness for her.

Miss Arden had no chance to weep because Mrs. Ramsay talked so hard and so madly. She made Elizabeth laugh, and it seemed that she had left her sunshade in the church and didn't know what had become of her handkerchief.

Lawrence came presently to say goodbye to Elizabeth. He was genuinely affected, and kissed her twice.

She went out into the passage, dove-grey now, with a saucy little hat on her head. Mr. Hengist was there, to wish her the best, the very best, of luck. He went with them out of the hall, and Elizabeth felt that she never liked him so much.

Stephen was waiting, hat in hand, John at his elbow. John had the railway tickets, and was coming to Victoria to put them into their train. He looked so conscientious and so dogged that Elizabeth wondered whether he would consent to leave them at the station, or whether he would insist on accompanying them on their honeymoon.

Stephen stepped forward, his eyes on Elizabeth's face. Lawrence met him, and took his hand.

"I give her to you," he said. "Take care of her."

"I will," Stephen said, just as he had said it in the church.

"Oh, my darling, I hope you'll be happy!" Miss Arden said, on a half-sob.

"I can't cry, because I've lost my hanky," sighed Mrs. Ramsay. "I'm not at all sure that I ought to either. Does the bridegroom's mother cry, or not? I forgot to ask Anthony."

"'Bout time we pushed off, what?" John drawled. "Look out for the confetti."

Hurried kisses followed. Elizabeth took Stephen's hand and ran. As they emerged into the sunshine confetti showered above them. They got into the car, waved, called messages, and were gone.

Stephen began to brush the confetti from Elizabeth's coat.

"That scoundrel Anthony's tied a boot on the back of the car," he said.

"Ah, I was afraid it had been forgotten!" John remarked, showing his relief. "Not at all a bad show, was it?"

"Don't speak about it as though it were a musical comedy," protested Stephen.

"I think it was rather like one," Elizabeth reflected.

The drive through the streets to Victoria was soon over. At the station Stephen and Elizabeth found that, John having shouldered all responsibility, there was nothing to be done but to walk on to the platform and into the carriage which, by some unknown means, John had managed to reserve for them. There were five minutes to spare; they sat opposite each other, and John stood leaning in at the window, saying,

"Might let me have a line from Paris to say you arrived safely. Luggage is in the rear. Better put the tickets in your pocket-book, Stephen. Wish I'd brought the odd slipper. Might have hung it on the door."

"Oh, thank goodness you didn't bring it!" Elizabeth cried.

A paper-boy passed; John bought the *Morning Post*, the *Sketch*, the *Bystander*, the *Sportsman*, and *Eve*, and handed them to Elizabeth.

"In case you get bored with Stephen, Mrs. Ramsay."

"Thank you very much, but I don't think I shall," she smiled.

"You never know," he said. "Well, you're off. Best of luck, an' all that, what? Don't forget to send me a post card."

The train began to move. Stephen leaned out of the window.

"Righto. Thanks again, old chap, for all you've done. Couldn't have got through without you!"

The train slid out of the station; Stephen drew his head in, and stood for a moment looking down at Elizabeth. Then he sat down beside her, and caught her against his heart.

"At last!" he said, and kissed her, not gently at all, but hard and fiercely, on her mouth. "Mine! *Mine!*"

Chapter Twelve

Afterwards, when she was able to look back upon her honeymoon as from a great distance, calmly, Elizabeth realised that it was the fact of living for the first time in a foreign country, in an inevitably bizarre atmosphere, which to some extent mitigated the shock that marriage gave her. In England, amongst English people and accustomed surroundings she could not have borne it, but in Paris nothing was real, not even herself. The fairy-like beauty of the place helped her; in England beauty would not have struck her, because she knew English scenery so well that it had become cheap in her eyes. In Paris everything was strange, even the noises which she heard in the streets. That, and the foreign tongue, the different race and the swiftly moving kaleidoscope of events ever since her wedding, all helped to strengthen the fancy that the honeymoon was a dream, sometimes pleasant, sometimes evil. It was a new word, a new Stephen, and—yes, a new Elizabeth. She knew that Stephen's patience and his understanding were qualities not many men possessed: instinct told her that. She was immensely grateful to him for his consideration and his forbearance, but the depths of her nature were unstirred by his passion. She felt only distaste, which must, she knew, be hidden.

She would not permit herself to think of Miss Arden, because her thoughts would have been laden with bitterness. It was inconceivable that she could criticise or condemn her aunt's actions. She had a feeling that Aunt Anne had betrayed her—no not quite that:—let her down. She must not think, then, of Aunt Anne, who had allowed her to take this irrevocable step with her eyes blindfolded.

Yet there was much in the new life that was more delightful than anything she had ever known. There was always someone at hand whose only task in life seemed to be to care for her and give her everything she might want. Her smallest wish was gratified at once; her frown made Stephen anxious, her smile made him happy. The sense of power this gave her was wonderful; it was wonderful too to be everything in one man's eyes.

The ornate decoration of their bedroom in the hotel at Paris, its gilt and brocade furniture and general opulence, and its total dissimilarity from any other bedroom she had known, made it easier for her to see, without embarrassment, Stephen's shirt flung over a chair, and his pajamas on the bed.

He was untidy; that distressed her. His clothing—she was astonished to see how much there was of it—overflowed from the adjoining dressing-room into her bedroom. She wondered whether any ordinary bride would have liked to see it there, cheek by jowl with her own *chiffons*. She hated it. She hated his unshaven face in the morning, and his ruffled hair; his presence in the room filled her with an emotion near to repulsion; she hid it behind a valiant smile, but he knew that it was there, and it worried him. Then he told himself that this intensely shy attitude was in keeping with his ideal of her; she would grow out of it; he tried to think that he would not have liked it had it been otherwise. But it hurt him when he kissed her awake one morning, and felt her wince. He was careful never to do that again. He came into her room when she was dressing to go to the Opera; the instinctive clutching of her kimono about her gave him pain. He laughed at her, and took her in his arms; she sighed, like a child that is overwrought, and let him kiss her. Her helplessness made him more gentle still; she was so fragile, so easily frightened.

She did not know Stephen. She realised that now, and thought that the love that survived seeing a man unwashed and unshaven before breakfast must be great indeed. It was queer that she had never, before her marriage, speculated on her possible feelings towards these little, ugly intimacies of their life together. How foolishly innocent she had been! How unfair it was that girls should be tossed into marriage unprepared, and with the rose-veil of innocence still wrapped about them. It meant a rude awakening, a shock, a tearing asunder of that romantic veil. You were jerked into a new life of which you knew nothing, and you were expected to fit into it at once, as though it were not wholly alien to your nature. She was glad that the honeymoon was to be a long one. She would have time to adapt herself, outwardly at least, before she was faced with the ordeal of meeting her people again, and her friends. She dreaded lest they should perceive her true feelings; dreaded her aunt's tentative questions, or Sarah's, not tentative at all, but grossly frank.

They went from Paris to Florence. Again she was exhilarated by the change of surroundings, of beauty, and of quaintness. Stephen talked of the Renaissance; she was awed by the knowledge he displayed: she liked to go out with him and hear him talk. He said that she was an inveterate sight-seer because she roamed daily through first this picture gallery and then that. She answered breathlessly, I've so longed to see all this!

"You're happy?" he asked her. The anxiety throbbed in his voice.

"Oh, Stephen!"

"Yes, but that doesn't tell me anything," he pointed out.

"Of *course* I'm happy!"

"Cheers! Let's go on to Rome!"

"We shall have to buy another small trunk, then," she answered practically. "All those things we bought ...!"

Her sense of duty was strong, and made him laugh. If there were a hole in his sock it must be mended at once; she would do nothing else until that was finished.

"Never mind that!" he said impatiently. "I want to drive you out to Fiesole."

"I must do this first," she answered. "And there's a button off your pajamas."

"Damn my pajamas. I didn't marry you for that."

"But, Stephen—"

"Do it some other time and come out now."

"I *can't*, Stephen. There are heaps of odd jobs I must see to. Why must we go to Fiesole to-day? Won't tomorrow do as well?"

He sulked; that was another side of him she had never suspected to be there. It astonished her and made her unhappy. She could not understand why it was so imperative to go to Fiesole to-day. There seemed to be no reason; to-morrow would have done as well, or better, and yet Stephen sulked. She wondered when he would make it up; in the end it was she who coaxed him round. Then he was repentant, and would have done anything she wished to show that he was sorry.

She liked to plan ahead; he preferred to act on the impulse of the moment. "Looking forward" was the nicest part of an event to Elizabeth; to him it was the most irksome. She, of long training, was always punctual to meals; he, unless she urged him, never. If it were a matter of catching a train she would be ready half an hour too soon, and would wear a worried frown and a restless air until they were safely in the train, and their luggage too. He, ten minutes before it was time to drive to the station, would stroll out and buy a pair of gloves. It drove her to distraction; it meant that they would be late and would have to run to catch the train. If Stephen left his walking-stick behind, Elizabeth fussed to retrieve it. Stephen only laughed, and said, I'll buy another.

He saw things from a different standpoint; he said things she would not have dreamed of saying.

"Don't wear that hat, Elizabeth; I simply loathe it!"

She thought that she could not have heard aright. She had been taught from earliest childhood that personal remarks of a disparaging nature, even between the nearest of relations, were not only rude, but unkind as well.

"You—loathe it?" she repeated blankly.

"Mm. Doesn't suit you, darling. Do take it off!"

She did so, slowly. The hurt she felt showed in her face, so that he came to her and put his hands on her shoulders.

"Why, Elizabeth, you're not offended, are you? I didn't mean to hurt you, sweetest! It's only that that particular shade of blue takes all the colour out of your dear little face."

"I—see. Which hat would you like me to wear?"

"The little brown one. Let's burn the blue atrocity."

"Stephen! We couldn't possibly! It's new!"

"Well, never mind if it is. I'm not going to let you wear it, so why hang on to it?"

"I couldn't bum it. It would be such waste."

"Give it to the housemaid, then."

"Yes, I might do that," she agreed. "It seems rather dreadful, though."

At Rome he spoke to her of his income, and found her woefully ignorant of all money-matters. In the Arden household it was considered a breach of manners if you spoke of money as Stephen spoke of it. You did not enquire into another person's means, nor did that person offer to expound them to you. She had no idea what was her father's income; to speak of it would have been almost as grave a solecism as was the discussion of a prospective will. Such subjects were considered to be extremely delicate, and as such were kept hidden. She imagined that Stephen must feel as uncomfortable when he laid his affairs before her as did she. She supposed he had made some sort of declaration to her father. She knew from novels that this was usual, but she would have died sooner than have asked Lawrence what had been divulged. He did not volunteer to enlighten her; such a course was counter to his creed.

Stephen spoke of bequests and investments, and book-rights. She sat silent, with eyes downcast at first, then laid a gentle hand on his arm.

"Stephen dear, I—I don't want to know all this."

"Does it bore you, precious? I'm awfully sorry, but we'd better have it out. Then you'll know how we stand." His eyes twinkled. "If I grow stingy you'll know whether it's from poverty or miserliness!"

"You needn't tell me," she said earnestly. "Truly, you needn't!"

He looked at her, and the truth dawned on him.

"You quaint little morsel! Why should you be embarrassed?"

Mentally she squirmed under the teasing note in his voice. She hated him to make fun of her.

"Oh—embarrassed! It's just that I don't think money a particularly interesting topic. Do you?"

"Not as compared to some others. Isn't it interesting to know where your money comes from?"

"I—do you think it is?"

"I want to know what you think."

"Well, no. At least—I've never thought about it."

"What a haphazard training!" he smiled. "Didn't your father talk to you about his business and how he makes his money?"

"Oh, no!" she said, shocked.

"Good Lord! You know, 'Lisbeth, that attitude's awfully Victorian. Artificial and insincere. You're not a Victorian."

"Isn't it nice to be one?"

"No. Of course it isn't. Not in that way."

"I suppose Aunt Anne's Victorian, though?"

"Out and out."

She was up in arms at once.

"You speak as though you don't like my aunt."

"Rot! I like her very much—parts of her. I don't like some things about her, naturally."

"Naturally?"

"Hang it all, darling, you probably don't like some things about my mother!"

"I like your mother very much. And anyway I shouldn't say I didn't to you."

"Wouldn't you? Why not?"

She thought him extraordinary; she had never imagined that he would be so difficult to understand.

"It wouldn't be polite—or considerate to your feelings."

"But, Elizabeth my dear, there's no such thing as that kind of politeness between husband and wife! If there is you're building up a barrier between us."

"How can you say such a thing? Of course I'm not!"

"Of course you are. Tell me now, do you like Cynthia?"

"I—I hardly know her."

He pulled her on to his knees, where she sat stiffly, ill-at-ease.

"Say right out that you don't, you little humbug!"

She winced at that, and her eyes filled with tears. It was as though Mr. Hengist had spoken.

"If you think—that—of me—!"

He was remorseful at once, and petted her back to happiness. When she smiled again he reverted to the discussion of his affairs, telling her what he proposed to settle on her for her private use. She did not like that; it seemed wrong, and she tried to protest.

"But, Stephen, I've—I've got quite a lot of money of my own. You know I have—from my mother."

"I want you to use my money, beloved."

"It—it isn't necessary! I'd rather—" She stopped, seeing the look of hurt steal into his face. "Are you sure you can afford it?" she ended lamely.

That delighted him; he roared with laughter, and thought her adorable.

The days flew past; Elizabeth felt as though she had been married a very long time and yet was not acclimatised to the new conditions of life. Physical contact with Stephen grew less revolting, but no less unpleasant. She went through a phase of feeling herself degraded, and although she put the fancy from her, knowing that it was absurd, it preyed upon her nerves so that they became jangled and on edge. She began to jump at sudden noises, and grew restless, sometimes even morbid. Deep in her soul lingered a tiny fear that Mr. Hengist had been right when he said that she did not really love Stephen. The fear was so terrible, so shocking, that she stifled it and would not admit of its presence. The complications that must inevitably arise, did she acknowledge the fear, effectually prevented her from doing so. She assured herself that nothing was wrong, that she would grow accustomed to her new life, and would, in after days, look back upon this phase as the morbid imaginings of a nervous bride.

Just as she had first been thankful that her honeymoon should be spent abroad, so now, was she desirous of returning to England. Hotel life was becoming tedious; much as she enjoyed sight-seeing, the constant round of amusement began to pall on her. She thought that it would be easier to settle down if she were installed in her own house, with work to do, and time to rest. Stephen too would have work to do, and something besides his love for her to occupy his thoughts. They would have a chance to learn to live together, not at fever heat, but in the "take it for granted way" that she had dreamed of. She wanted placidity not passion, because she was very young and undeveloped, and did not understand that placidity comes in middle-life, not in the first years of marriage..

In more senses than one the honeymoon was strenuous. She began to wish for more society; perhaps, if she had really loved Stephen, she would not wish that. As it was she was anxious to see Sarah again, and her other friends, but she did not like to suggest to Stephen that they should go home.

In the end it was he who broached the question. Typewritten letters came to him, and he became sometimes rather *distrait*. At last he spoke to Elizabeth, tentatively suggesting that they should leave Italy.

"Jackson—my agent, darling, you remember—writes that Edwards and Tollemache are agitating about my next book. Would you mind very much if we thought about returning soon? I ought to get to work on 'Caraway Seeds' as soon as possible."

"Of course not," she replied instantly. "We'll go as soon as you like."

"You're sure you don't mind?"

"Not a bit. I've loved being in Italy, but I'd like to go home now and see everybody again, and—oh, and hear English spoken!"

He was relieved. He had been afraid that she would not like to have her honeymoon curtailed. They had arranged to be away three months; they had stayed only two.

"I say, I am glad! I was afraid you'd be disappointed. I'll write off at once to Nana and tell her we're coming. By the way, what date shall I fix?"

"I don't mind, Stephen. Just when you like."

"Nice, adaptable person! I had a sort of an idea that we might put in a week in town before we go down to Queen's Halt, and see all our respective relations?"

"Oh, how lovely. Can you really spare the time?"

"Yes, rather. I'll go and write to Nana and a hotel in town at once."

"I must write to Aunt Anne," she said. "If you're going to write your letters here I'll go down to the lounge. I know what it is when you start."

"All right, my lady," he retorted, seating himself at the table. "You needn't think I don't know why you're going into the lounge."

She paused, her hand on the door-knob.

"Oh, why?"

"To flirt with the Italian Count," he said solemnly.

Chapter Thirteen

Elizabeth stood at the window of her room at Queen's Hotel, and looked with contented eyes down into the dusky street. The sounds, the dull, lovely greyness, even the smells, were London, and therefore, home. She stood for a long time, resting her cheek against the window, watching the traffic and the scurrying pedestrians. She was tired, for she and Stephen had arrived in London that same day in the early afternoon, but she had been resting on her bed, thinking how important she would feel this evening when she entertained her father and her aunt to dinner. It was sweet of Stephen to postpone the invitation to his mother until to-morrow; little things like that, which he did, warmed her heart towards him and made her think that, after all, she was lucky in her choice of husbands. She had protested at the time, saying that of course they must ask Mrs. Ramsay, but Stephen had stood firm.

"Your turn to-day," he had said. "Mine to-morrow."

"Stephen, it's dear of you, but *really* I'd rather you rang up Mater and—"

"Naughty little fibber! You wouldn't."

"But I'd simply hate to offend your mother—or hurt her—"

"She won't be offended or hurt, darling. She isn't that sort. I shall go along to see her this afternoon. She'll understand."

"Then I shall come too," Elizabeth said.

"No, you won't. You're going to rest. You're dog-tired already. You shall give me all the messages you like for Mater, and I'll do my best to deliver them."

She gave way to him, hoping that it was not wrong to do so. It was nearly time to dress for dinner now, but Stephen had not yet returned. She was watching the street for him, wrapped in a blissfulness she had not felt during all her honeymoon. In England things would be easier. Curiously enough, now that the honeymoon was over and she was to meet her aunt and father as a wife of two months I standing she felt a great pride in Stephen, and in herself for possessing him for a husband.

The bitterness she felt towards Miss Arden was still there, but so hidden and smothered that she was hardly conscious of it. At the moment she felt only excitement at the prospect of seeing her again: excitement and importance. Now at last she was grown-up, and a creature of account.

She turned from the window to survey her room again, letting her eyes dwell lovingly on each solid and massive piece of furniture, emblems of respectability so sadly lacking abroad. It was warm, a golden September evening, but she had had a fire lit in the grate just so that she might look at it and feel that she was really in England. Central-heating was all very well, but it was not companionable.

Lunch on the dining-car of the train up from Dover had been delightful, because it was so dull and English. There was boiled cod—on dining-cars there always was—and roast beef, and fruit tart, things she had never imagined she would yearn for. And here, in this solid and respectable bedroom she had had tea—real Tea with a capital letter—triangular morsels of bread and butter, and deadly plum cake, cut in strips. It was horrible, but no other country in the world could—or would—manufacture it. She ate it all.

The chamber-maid came in, heralded by a discreet knock. She was prim and middle-aged, heavy-footed, and clumsy. Elizabeth loved her.

"What a beautiful evening, isn't it?" she said, just to hear an English answer.

"Yes, madam. Will you have the blinds drawn now?"

"Please," Elizabeth said, coming away from the window.

The blinds were jerked down, curtain rings rattled along a brass rod.

"Is there anything else you'd like, madam?"

"No, thank you."

The maid went out, and Elizabeth opened the door of her wardrobe to select a frock.

She had almost finished dressing before she heard Stephen in the adjoining room. He called through the communicating door.

"Can I come in, 'Lisbeth?"

"Yes, do. You're awfully late. I'm nearly ready."

He entered.

"Am I? Doesn't matter. You'll want to see your people alone. I shan't be long. London looks good, doesn't she?"

"So quiet and restful," she nodded. "Was Mater in?"

"Rather, the darling! Sent her love to you. She's coming round to see you to-morrow morning. That all right? I said I'd ring her up if it wasn't."

"Oh, quite all right! Only it's I who ought to go to her. Are you sure she didn't mind?"

"Not a bit. She quite understands that you want to see your own people first. Did you sleep at all this afternoon, dear?"

"I dozed. I was too happy to sleep. Tea was so glorious—with plum cake."

"O, Lord! Don't, don't start rhapsodising over that cod again, darling! I can't bear it, and I know you're going to!"

She laughed.

"You don't understand. It was because it was so typically English."

"God-forsaken."

"You can't have a God-forsaken cod," she said.

"How topping! Of course you can. God-forsaken cod. What a brilliant inspiration! Wish I'd thought of it."

"You did. And it really hasn't any sense at all."

"None of the really funny things have. Lord, look at the time! Have you got my studs?"

"They're in the little silver box on your dressing-table. You'll find your dress-shirts in the second long drawer. Hurry up, won't you?"

"'Lisbeth, you *haven't* unpacked my things?"

"Yes, I have. Naturally."

"Darling, I wish you hadn't. You're really most disobedient. Didn't I expressly command you to rest?"

"Stephen, *do* hurry up! I did rest—and anyway what cheek to talk about your express commands!"

"Love, honour and obey," he quoted severely.

"Oh, go along!" she begged.

Someone knocked on the door.

"Come in!" Elizabeth called, opening her jewel-case.

The door was opened slightly and a page-boy announced that Mr. and Miss Arden were in the lounge.

Elizabeth slipped a ring on her finger, and jumped up, snapping a bracelet round her arm.

"All right, I'll come. Stephen, go and get dressed quickly! I'd no idea it was quite so late. That clock must be slow. I'm simply *dying* to see Auntie—and Father! Do I look all right?"

"Perfect," he said. "Give me *one* kiss before you go, and I'll be quick. Otherwise I won't."

"You're idiotic," she said, but she kissed him, hurriedly.

The Ardens were watching the lift eagerly; Elizabeth stepped out of it and almost ran towards them.

"Auntie! Father!"

There was laughter and kisses, Miss Arden's arm about her waist, countless questions, none answered, and then more kisses.

"Let me look at you, my darling!" Miss Arden said at last, and stood back to survey her niece. She sighed, and took Elizabeth's hand. "Oh, my dear child!"

"You're looking well," Lawrence remarked, with satisfaction. "Never seen you look better."

"Oh, she looks *tired*!" Miss Arden cried. "I do *hope* you haven't been overdoing it, dear?"

"Not a bit, Auntie. I'm not really tired, either. It's just the effect of the journey. How are you? and you, father?"

"Oh, *I'm* all right," Miss Arden said.

"We miss our little girl," Lawrence added, in a melancholy voice. "And where is my son-in-law?"

Elizabeth gave an excited little laugh. She was seated between them on the sofa, one hand held by Miss Arden, the other by Lawrence.

"Isn't he dreadful to be so late? He went to see Mater and only got back a few minutes ago. However, he promised to hurry. I want you to myself for a bit." She squeezed their hands. "It's so lovely to be back and to see you both again!"

"How did you enjoy Florence?" Lawrence asked.

"Yes, tell us all about it!" begged Miss Arden.

"Oh, it was beautiful! I can't tell you how beautiful! Rome too, in a different way. And Paris! I took heaps of snapshots. I'll show them to you after dinner. Stephen was awfully rude about my photography. He says I shall develop into an album-fiend. Isn't it horrid of him? Auntie, I've liked cod to-day for the first time! They had it on the train, and it thrilled me. Only I daren't say so to Stephen because he hates it." So she chattered, switching from one triviality to another, conscious of being unnatural. She felt that she was talking somewhat as Stephen talked, and wondered why. It was curious that she should do it to the Ardens and not to him.

Then Stephen came downstairs, two at a time, and Elizabeth thought how tall and good-looking he was, and how well-tailored.

"Here you are!" she said. "I've been telling them about my snapshots."

Stephen kissed Miss Arden and shook hands with Lawrence, warmly.

"How jolly to see you again! Don't encourage 'Lisbeth, I implore you! She produces snapshot after snapshot, points to a misshapen splosh in the background, and says, 'And *that's* Stephen!' Do you like Martini, Miss Arden, or would you prefer a vermouth?"

"Nothing for me, thank you, Stephen," she answered.

"'Lisbeth?" He asked her out of courtesy; she never drank cocktails.

"Vermouth, please, Stephen," she said, as though she had been in the habit of imbibing it for years.

Dinner was a merry function that evening; they all talked, and together. It seemed to Elizabeth that she had seldom been so bright in conversation. Perhaps it was the cocktail, and the wicked sparkle of champagne in her glass. After dinner Stephen took Lawrence into the billiard-room, and Elizabeth and her aunt went upstairs for a quiet talk.

They sat before the fire in Elizabeth's room, and constraint fell upon them. Elizabeth was reduced to producing her snapshots.

"Our little girl has quite blossomed forth," Lawrence said on the way home. Then, as Miss Arden was silent, he added in a hurt tone, "Don't you think so?"

"She has changed," Miss Arden said.

"Oh, nonsense!" Lawrence replied uneasily. It was really rather mean of Anne to try and spoil his evening.

"She isn't herself. She's thinner too."

"All your imagination!" Lawrence said loudly. "*I* saw no change in her—except that she has, as I say, blossomed forth."

"I daresay you didn't. You're only a man."

Lawrence was accustomed to hear his sex referred to in a disparaging way,

104

but to-night it annoyed him.

"That's as may be. I am at least Elizabeth's father."

"It's not to be expected that you would notice things as I do."

"I repeat, you're imagining it. Next you'll say that her marriage is not a success!"

"I hope not," she said seriously.

"Good gracious, Anne! Well, really! It's a good thing we don't all see things in this morbid way! It struck me that Elizabeth was in great spirits. In fact, a thoroughly happy bride."

"I daresay," Miss Arden said crushingly. "All I know is that she's changed, and doesn't look well."

This was very disturbing. Lawrence cleared his throat and sought for an answer.

"A honeymoon is often rather a trying period," he said airily. Then, as Miss Arden opened her mouth to retaliate, he added hastily, "Time will show."

"Yes," said Miss Arden, and left it at that.

*

Mrs. Ramsay appeared next morning soon after breakfast, one end of her fur trailing behind her.

"My dear, I nearly lost my note-case in the street, only such a dear boy picked it up and ran after me with it. How are you, darling? and did you have a jolly time? What an adequate way of putting it!"

"I'm very well, thank you. It's so nice of you to come to see me. I ought to have called on you with Stephen yesterday, but he made me rest instead. I do hope you'll forgive me!"

Mrs. Ramsay sat down in a large chair; the rest of her fur slid to the floor and remained there until a solicitous page-boy came to pick it up.

"What nonsense, dear! I didn't want to see you a bit yesterday, any more than you wanted to see me. I only wanted Stephen. Isn't that delightfully rude, and don't I put things badly? Did you get that frock in Paris? It's charming."

"Rue de la Paix," Elizabeth said. "I'm—afraid I was awfully extravagant."

"One always is. Paris makes me reckless. Such a nice, wicked feeling. I wish I'd brought Thomas. He's dying to see his new relation."

"Oh, dear Thomas! He wouldn't have been allowed here, so it's just as well you didn't bring him, perhaps."

"What a shame! Don't you think I could have got round that burly porter? Never mind, though. Did you feel gory and mediaeval in Florence?"

"N-no, not exactly. What a wonderful place it is!"

"Isn't it? Funnily enough, Stephen's father took me there on my honeymoon. I don't remember where we stayed, but I know that George lost his stud one night and had all the staff into our room to help him find it. So trying for me; I was dressing, you see, and at that time I hadn't grown accustomed to George's ways."

Elizabeth laughed, and there fell a silence. Mrs. Ramsay started off again.

"As usual I began at the wrong end of the stick. I didn't come to talk about George's stud—no one ever found it, by the way. I don't think George ever really got over it— Where was I? Oh, yes! What I wanted to say was, how lovely it is to see you both home again! Stephen's very happy, my dear. I'd like to thank you for making him so, but I know that's quite out of place. Cynny's coming to call soon, but she said she wasn't going to inflict herself on you at once. I expect you're pretty tired, aren't you?"

"Oh—not really," Elizabeth replied.

Mrs. Ramsay cast her a fleeting glance.

"Well, you look it, darling. I shall speak severely to Stephen. He mustn't let you overdo it. He's a strenuous boy, you know. Always was. Never would lie still in his perambulator. Dear me, it's awfully hard to realize that he's married!"

"Yes, I expect it must be. I—I find it hard to realise that I'm married sometimes!"

Then Stephen came in, and Elizabeth was able to sit quiet while he talked. It was strange that she could not be bright and conversational with Mrs. Ramsay when she had been so talkative to her own relations. You couldn't get rid of the feeling that, in spite of her inconsequence, Mrs. Ramsay was clever, far cleverer than you were yourself. That tied your tongue; you were afraid to advance an opinion because your opinions were always so different from those of the Ramsays. You felt too that the Ramsays thought privately that you were very ordinary. Not Stephen, of course.

Mrs. Ramsay went to have tea with Cynthia that afternoon, and Cynthia curled her lip, and said, Well?

"Oh, Cynny, I don't know!" Mrs. Ramsay sighed. "She's—a dear little thing, but I can't get any further with her! I've tried and tried, but she makes me nervous, and I can't say what I want to. I talk the most arrant nonsense, and she smiles, and says, Yes, I know. So very uninspiring. I wish I could get beneath her—her perfect manners."

"Probably you wouldn't find anything," Cynthia said.

"Darling, that's horribly ill-natured. I won't believe that it's true. Poor child! I can't help feeling sorry for her."

"Good lord, why?"

"Well, my dear, Stephen's very like his father, and— and not a bit like Elizabeth."

"Funny point of view. If I'm sorry for anyone I'm sorry for Stephen—tied to a pretty face."

Mrs. Ramsay rescued her gloves from Thomas.

"So nice to sit opposite Elizabeth's face every morning at breakfast," she murmured.

"Are you being sarcastic, mater?"

"No, not at all. I mean it. The thing that bothers me is—Cynny, this is between you and me alone—I don't—I can't be sure that Elizabeth cares for Stephen —*really* cares for him."

"Oh!" said Cynthia, and set her cup down with a click. "That's it, is it? God help them both, then, for they won't help themselves."

"Cynny, I'm not sure—it's only just a—a sort of feeling that I have, and I may be quite wrong!"

"Yes, I understand. What attracted her? Money, or fame?"

"Don't, my dear! It—it sounds so crude and hateful. I've probably been misled by her manner. And then, of course, she's shy. That aunt, too. I wish I could get near Elizabeth. I'd be such a lot of use to her. Only I can't. She holds me off, she's so—so proper. What a horrible word!"

Cynthia selected a cake with some deliberation.

"What about Stephen?"

Mrs. Ramsay did not answer for a moment. Then she looked across at Cynthia and spoke quite slowly, and with none of her usual sparkle.

"I believe what he wants me to believe. Everything is all right."

"I see," said Cynthia.

Chapter Fourteen

Queen's Halt lay in a hollow beyond Cranbrook, with a giant elm for gate-keeper, and slim poplars as sentinels around.

Legend, or history, ascribed its name to the passing of Queen Bess, who was supposed to have rested there a night in the course of one of her pilgrimages. It was more probable that if the Queen had journeyed this way she would have chosen the Manor as her halt, a mile on, up the hill, but the Ribblemeres, who had lived there since the beginning of things, laid no claim to this distinction and showed no desire to wrest its title from the old white house below.

Queen's Halt, gabled and beamed, with friendly windows, and squat chimneys, and swallows nesting under the eaves, stretched itself in the middle of its garden, which had grown and spread about it on many levels.

Before it the flower gardens lay, and the new tennis-court; on either side the orchards and the old pleasance, and behind, an uneven yard with moss padding between the flagstones and an aged pump keeping watch beside the rain-tub.

The yard merged into a meadow, studded over with chestnut-trees and oaks, through which a little stream, crystal-clear, bubbled and sang its way over the rounded pebbles on its bed. Violets grew there in the spring, and irises, pale primroses and blue forget-me-nots, and all the year round hens, speckled, and buff, and white, were dotted here and there on the grass, walking at will about the coops, languidly searching for grubs. Sweet-faced ducks waddied in solemn procession from the yard to the stream and stayed there, half in, half out of the water. Beyond the stream the wood began, straggling at first, then dense —with Kentish undergrowth, and alive with scuttling, bobtailed rabbits.

The orchard, born at a distance from the house, to the east, had wandered through many years nearer and nearer to the house, and spread stray apple-trees and plum all amongst the flowers in the garden. So that in the spring white blossoms and palest pink fluttered down like snow upon the daffodils and lay, flecks of foam, upon the close-cut turf.

In September, when Elizabeth first saw it, the garden was rich and warm beneath the changing tints, and the house basked golden in the autumn sun. Very slowly were the leaves turning, so that here and there, peeping from out the softer green, splashes of red and orange showed, heralds of the year's decline. The late roses were wide-spread, trembling before their approaching end, and all about them the Canterbury bells nodded to each other, and the lavender waved, thick and fragrant on either side the flagged walks. Beyond were masses of phlox, purple and white, and palest pink. Blue bordering flowers stretched at their feet, and a few tall lilies stood about them, pure white with golden hearts. Asters flaunted every colour on a neighbouring bed, and beside the old wall of mellow red, the sweet-peas rambled, casting their scent about them.

A hedge of yew with an arch clipped in the centre shut the sunk rock-garden from view. You walked down the flagged path, over the tiny flowers that pushed their way up between the cracks, and stood beneath the arch, at the top of the moss-grown steps that wound their rustic way down through the terraced rockery to the pond below. There gold-fish dwelt, and frogs, beneath a fountain playing rainbow-coloured in the sun, and there a mournful willow bowed its head until its whispering leaves dipped listless to the water's edge.

Elizabeth cried out when first she saw Queen's Halt, thinking it the most beautiful home on earth. Everything in it, all its quaint, old furniture, every plant in the garden she thought delightful, only Nana, tall and prim, made her shy and ill-at-ease. She had expected the old nurse of fiction, buxom and smiling, domineering perhaps, but kind. She found a thin woman with an impassive countenance, w T ho treated her with quiet respect, and with ceremony handed over the keys.

Just as Mrs. Ramsay found it impossible to pierce beneath Elizabeth's outward veil, so did Elizabeth, in her turn, find it impossible to become intimate with Nana. She thought perhaps Nana was jealous, and disapproving; no trace of those feelings was apparent in her bearing. Her manners were unimpeachable; if she disagreed with Elizabeth she put forward her own suggestion with deference, and showed no desire to domineer. She baffled Elizabeth with her calmness, and her tight smile. Elizabeth hated her.

Stephen was afraid that Elizabeth might be dull at first, buried as she was in the depths of the country. She assured him that there was no fear of it. While the country was there to explore, while the fowls required attention, and while rabbits scuttled in the woods boredom, for her, would be impossible. There were Stephen's dogs too to be exercised and groomed, three of them, all different. Of Hector, the Irish wolfhound, she was at first nervous. She had never seen so large a dog before, but she was careful to hide her alarm of him in case Stephen should laugh, or not understand. The silky cocker, Flo, was her favourite, because Flo was gentle, and had liquid, mournful eyes. But Flo would never willingly leave Stephen.

She was older than the others and preferred to be under Stephen's desk when Elizabeth went with Hector, and Jerry, the Airedale, for a tramp through the woods.

"Keeping house," the duty to which Elizabeth had so eagerly looked forward, proved to be less pleasant than she had expected, and not a duty at all, but a hobby. For years Nana had held the reins of this office; Elizabeth acknowledged that it would be unfair to wrest them from her. Nana assumed that Elizabeth would find the task onerous; Stephen would not hear of her attempting it. Sadly she thought, how little they understood her! She assumed joint responsibility with Nana; Stephen laughed, thinking it a child's hobby.

Almost at once after their return he plunged into the work that awaited him. Elizabeth looked with awe upon the sheets of scrawled manuscript, marvelled that he could write so fast and in so great a muddle. His study, he said, was inviolate. She asked, Against me? He told her not to say silly things. It was inviolate against all spring-cleaning or tidying invasion. She pointed to the dust upon his desk.

"I like it," he said simply.

"But how extraordinary!" she exclaimed.

"Have you ever looked at dust with the sun on it?" he asked.

She never had; she considered the question absurd.

"It's perfectly beautiful," he said.

She ventured to arrange a bowl of roses on his desk, the petals fell; he ordered that the bowl should be removed. She was hurt, but she said nothing.

In imagination she had seen herself seated quietly in the room while he wrote, sewing, or perhaps with a book. When first she made this dream reality, and tiptoed into the room, he spoke impatiently, and without raising his head.

"Yes, what is it!"

"It's all right," she said in a low, soothing voice that she would have assumed when speaking to a sick person. "It's only me."

He looked up then, and his frown disappeared.

"Oh, you, darling! What do you want?"

"Nothing," she said. "I've just brought my work in here. Don't stop writing. I shan't talk to you."

He watched her sit down on the sofa. There was a doubtful look in his eyes, but she did not see it. After a few moments he bent again over his paper, and went on writing.

She was morbidly anxious to make no sound, therefore she sneezed, stifling it to a tiny noise in her throat. Again Stephen looked up, amused.

"Darling, what a funny little noise! What was it?"

"A sneeze," she said. "I'm so sorry! I didn't mean to disturb you."

"How awfully conscientious! 'Lisbeth, if that's one of my socks, give it to Nana! I don't want you to slave over my things."

"I'm not. Stephen, if you talk to me I shall feel I'm hindering you."

He went on with his work, but he wrote more slowly now, and spasmodically. In the pauses between the hurried scratching of his pen he stared out of the window, chin in hand. Elizabeth watched him covertly.

"The lawn wants mowing," Stephen said, absent-mindedly.

"I'm afraid you're not getting on very fast," she replied, in some concern. "Does my being here worry you?"

"Not in the least. The only thing that worries me is Geoffrey. I'm not at all sure that I shan't give him another name."

"Is Geoffrey your hero?" she said.

He made a grimace.

"You little horror! It sounds .like a Victorian melodrama."

"What does?" she said, bewildered. "Hero?"

"Of course. One pictures a golden-haired and blue-eyed young colossus, with the strength of a lion and the face and bearing of an archangel. Don't ask me what my 'villain' is like!"

"But if you don't call him your 'hero,' what are you to call him?"

"Geoffrey. No, Norman. God, what an inspiration! Norman! It's perfect. It changes the whole disposition of the man. Elizabeth dear, go and pick flowers, or feed the fowls, or bathe in the stream. I'm going to tear all this up and start afresh."

She gathered up her work.

"I'm worrying you? You'd rather I went?"

He had pulled fresh paper towards him, and was scribbling fast.

"No, dearest, but I shan't be pleasant company until I've started Norman in life, so you'd better go. I don't want to bore you."

"Oh, I'd rather stay! I shan't speak," she said.

At half-past four she crept out. Her stealthy departure irritated him. He wanted to tell her to walk like a reasonable being, but he checked the impulse, for fear of hurting her feelings. She re-appeared presently, bringing him some tea.

"Thanks," he said curtly, and allowed it to grow cold. Not until after six did he awake from his abstraction; then he found that Elizabeth was still in the room.

"Darling, you haven't been here all the time?"

"Yes, I have. I liked it."

"I wish you wouldn't, babe. I don't want you to stuff indoors just because the spirit moves me. It worries me."

"I've been quite happy," she repeated.

Soon their neighbours began to call. The first of them was Nina Trelawney, who came quickly up the drive one afternoon on an informal visit. She found Elizabeth under the cedar-tree on the lawn, and went to her.

"I'm sure you're Elizabeth!" she said, as soon as she was near enough for her voice to be heard. "You answer so exactly to Stephen's description. I'm Nina Trelawney. If he hasn't told you of me, it's extremely objectionable of him. How do you do?"

Elizabeth shook hands nervously.

"Yes, of course my husband has spoken of you," she said conventionally. "How kind of you to come and see me! Won't you sit down?"

Nina chose a deck chair, and sank into it.

"This isn't a really, truly call," she explained, with a friendly smile. "I'm coming with my mother to leave cards in the approved manner very soon. I felt I couldn't wait until then, though, so I came to-day, just to say how awfully glad I am that you and Stephen have arrived. Oh, and to extend a welcome! Isn't that a lovely expression? I found it in a book. How is Stephen?"

"Very well, thank you. Very busy too. You'll stay to tea with me, won't you?"

"Thanks, I hoped you'd ask me to. I was awfully sorry I couldn't come to your wedding. I had the accursed plague, you know. 'Flu. Mother told me that it was a charming affair, which made it much worse for me, not being there. Is Stephen working now? Can I shout to him in a loud voice?"

"Oh, *no!*" Elizabeth said earnestly. "He hates to be disturbed!"

Nina looked at her, then at the end of her sunshade, with which she was prodding the ground.

"Yes, I know, but don't you think it's good for him?"

"I wouldn't interrupt his work for worlds," Elizabeth said. "I—I suppose you've known him for a long time?"

"Our acquaintance started in the perambulator," Nina nodded. "We tried to poke each other's eyes out. Metaphorically, we still try. That's the worst of being brought up as brother and sister. One never troubles to be polite, and horrible fights ensue. How do you like the Halt?"

Elizabeth had not known that Stephen's friendship with Nina was of so long a date. It was rather unpleasant to think that he had known Nina years and years before he had met his wife. Only, of course, it was silly to feel like that about it.

"I think Halt is lovely," she said. "The garden fascinates me especially. It's so unexpected and rambling."

"And so delightfully disorderly," Nina added. "I love a garden without rhyme or reason. Our own is perfectly soul-killing. My father's an expert gardener and botanist, and he loves symmetrical beds and colour schemes. The result is like a mathematician's idea of heaven. This is the sort of garden you can love. You wouldn't feel a criminal either if you picked flowers from it."

"Can't you in yours?" Elizabeth asked, smiling.

"Oh, dear me, no! Everything's too rare and precious. Besides you can't pick a flower with a five-syllabled Latin name, can you? Aren't we talking rot? Do tell me, has anyone called yet?"

"You're the first," Elizabeth answered.

"Am I really? How nice! By the way, I didn't see you in church on Sunday, ma'am!"

"N-no!" Elizabeth frowned slightly. "Stephen wouldn't go, and I was too shy to go alone."

"How base of Stephen! He's got a down on churchgoing, hasn't he? I remember he once came to see Mummy and inveighed against convention and—and—oh, yes, pusillanimity!"

"I don't quite see that," Elizabeth confessed.

"Nor did we till he explained. With truly great magnanimity he informed us that he had no objection to people going to church if they really wanted to, but what he *did* object to—most rampantly—was people going to church for fear of what their neighbours would say if they didn't. That was the pusillanimity. He loathes and abhors the Tomlinsons—you'll meet them soon—because they daren't play tennis on Sunday for fear the Drurys, next door, should hear the balls. Personally, I sympathise with the Tomlinsons. I always wilt when a disapproving eye is bent upon me."

"But does Stephen never go to church?" Elizabeth asked.

"I believe he wanders down occasionally to obscure services. I never see him at the fashionable time. Of course, if he were a newcomer and displayed this shocking laxity no one would call. As it is, 'Ramsays' are an institution, and known to be queer. 'Just a little eccentric, my dear, but such a brilliant young man.' You know the style. Oh, here comes Nana!" She jumped up, and walked to meet her. "How do you do, Nana? I introduced myself to Elizabeth—by the way, can I call you that, Elizabeth?"

"Please do," Elizabeth said, feeling that she, as the married woman, should have had the initiative here.

"Well, Miss Nina!" Nana said. "And does Mr. Stephen know you're here?"

"No, and Elizabeth won't let me shriek to him," Nina said gaily. "I believe she spoils him, Nana."

Nana gave her tight-lipped smile, and looked at Elizabeth.

"Will you have tea here, madam, or indoors?"

"Which would you like?" Elizabeth asked her guest.

"Here, please; it's more exciting. Earwigs never drop into one's tea indoors. Oh, there is Stephen!"

Steph came sauntering out of the library window, which was flung open to let the warm, rose-scented air into his room. He was looking very untidy, Elizabeth thought, in old grey flannels and a tweed coat. When he saw Nina he shouted, Hullo and hurried towards her.

"I say, old girl, this is topping of you! Have you been here long? Why did no one tell me? How are you, kid?"

Elizabeth was considerably taken aback to see him implant a brotherly kiss on Nina's cheek, and give her shoulders a quick hug.

"Jolly quiet, weren't you?" he remarked. He smiled down at Elizabeth. "She generally heralds her arrival with loud cries."

"I was afraid you wouldn't want to be disturbed," Elizabeth explained.

Nina sat down again and opened her sunshade.

"I was severely checked. I think you're very lucky to have such a nice wife, Stephen."

"I am," he said. "You're not in the sun, Nina, so why the outspread umbrella?"

"'Tisn't an umbrella," she protested. "If you weren't so abominably dense, you'd grasp the fact that it's a new sunshade, and I'm ostentatiously displaying its glories." She tilted a laughing face towards Elizabeth. "Don't you think it's rather lovely?" she inquired. "The strange flower just under the butterfly excited Daddy's interest. He had an idea that it's a *Tetrapetalous Argemene Mexicana*, but he isn't sure. Anyway, I tell people that it is, because it sounds so impressive."

"What is it in its week-day clothes?" asked Stephen, poking daisies into the buckle of Elizabeth's shoe. He was seated on the grass, between their chairs.

"My dear, I haven't a notion! I hope no one ever tells me, because it's sure to be something quite ordinary and unromantic."

Tea was brought on a folding table, which Nina prophesied would collapse, and immediately the midges and caterpillars made themselves felt. As Elizabeth poured out she took covert stock of Nina, and admitted, reluctantly, that she was pretty, in a vivacious way, and very appealing. Perhaps that was because she was so small and thin, and because her face was so mobile. She had strange eyes, always changing; they were attractive too, both in mischief and in gravity.

Nina fished a fly out of her cup.

"Victim number one. Luckily I'm not a vegetarian. How's Geoffrey, Stephen?"

"He isn't," Stephen answered, selecting a sandwich from the dish. "How very timid cucumber can be. You bite one end, and it evacuates the sandwich hurriedly at the other end."

"But why is Geoffrey not?" Nina demanded.

"He became Norman half-way through the book," Stephen explained.

"And it was all torn up," added Elizabeth.

"How drastic! Still, what a lot of things he can do now he's Norman. Norman could fail to catch the train; Geoffrey would have to be there ten minutes before it started."

"Exactly," Stephen said. "As Norman he was able to jilt Caroline with perfect grace. As Geoffrey he became a cad from that moment."

"I don't see it a bit," Elizabeth declared. "He'd be a cad anyway."

"No, not at all. If you capture everyone's sympathy you're not a cad. Norman does, you see. Naturally."

"Just because of his name? Stephen, how silly you are!" She said it all laughingly, but she felt that he really was silly.

"What a horrid insult!" Nina said. "Never mind, Stephen, I appreciate the true inwardness of Norman. What does Cynny think? Or doesn't she know?"

"Of course she does. I notified the whole family in a series of telephone calls. Cynny said, Marvellous! he can murder Caroline. I hadn't thought of that. Mater was inclined to be upset. She said, Poor dear Geoffrey! I once had a canary called Geoffrey. That revelation sealed his doom."

Nina gave a little spurt of laughter.

"Oh, how sweet of Aunt Charmian! Something invariably reminds her of something else, delightfully irrelevant."

Elizabeth picked up the milk-jug.

"The only sane member of the family was Anthony. He sent a telegram:—'It leaves me cold.' That amused me."

Instead of the Thorn

"Neither you nor Anthony," Stephen said, "has a soul. Nina, d'you remember the day mater had a tea-fight under this very tree and Bertie Tyrell withdrew to the bank and wrote a poem about introspection?"

"Oh, lord yes! And read it to Lady Ribblemere." She turned to Elizabeth. "Nobody understood the poem; it was all dots. When Bertie got to the last line, which was 'God! I am glad,' Lady Ribblemere said 'Dear me!' in a most surprised voice."

"Yes," nodded Stephen, "and then she billowed over to Bertie's wife, and said, 'Can you tell me who is that extraordinary person?'"

"How awful!" Elizabeth interjected, feeling that she ought to say something.

"Well, I don't know," pondered Stephen. "If you're Futuristic at a tea-fight you must expect the worst. By the way, we must ask the Tyrells down, 'Lisbeth. They'll amuse you."

"You'd better not," said Nina. "Bertie's got a marmoset, and he won't go anywhere without it. He brought it down to us for the week-end, and it made havoc amongst the *Saxifraga TJmbrosa.*"

"The animal showed a considerable amount of discrimination then," said Stephen.

Nina gathered up her belongings, and rose.

"No, it was purely vindictive. It removed the cockatoo's crest. Mother nearly committed suicide. Thank you very much for my nice tea, Elizabeth. The next time you see me I shall have white kid gloves on. You'll know what that means. We'll bring Daddy to call on you too, and he'll walk round the garden, saying, 'Charming, charming! What induced you to plant the peonies in so unsuitable a spot?' Only he won't call them peonies, so you'll be none the wiser. Goodbye, both of you! I've enjoyed myself awfully."

"We'll walk with you to the gate," Elizabeth said.

"I shan't," Stephen murmured. "I'm busy."

"Stephen!" Elizabeth exclaimed, just a little shocked.

Chapter Fifteen

Lady Ribblemere from the Manor was the next to call. She filled the drawing-room, or so it seemed to Elizabeth, and talked heavily, but kindly, about hardy perennials and young ducklings. Then she said,

"So you went to Florence on your honeymoon. That must have been very delightful! The Uffizzi and—and that sort of thing. I always think it so good for one to travel. One is inclined to become insular, don't you think? But of course when you get to my age you prefer home-comforts. And how is Stephen?"

"Very well, thank you." Elizabeth wondered how often she would have to answer this question. "Hard at work."

"Ah, then I will not disturb him!" Lady Ribblemere said, rising ponderously. "I will just look in at him and say how do you do?"

Feeling entirely helpless, Elizabeth followed her into the library. Stephen looked up, and rose, putting down his pen.

"No, don't get up," said Lady Ribblemere. "I shall feel I am interrupting you if you do. I only popped in to see how you were, and to tell you how pleased we all are to see you back again, with your wife."

Stephen shook hands, saying that Lady Ribblemere was very kind.

"And how is your dear mother?" she went on. "It is quite an age since I saw her."

"She's flourishing, thank you," Stephen answered. "Won't you sit down?"

"No, I really mustn't stay a moment," she said, choosing the sofa. "I was on my way out when I decided to look in on you. And how is Cynthia?"

"She's suffering from a slight cold at the moment, but it's nothing much," Stephen answered.

"Ah, I am sorry to hear that. It is to be hoped the dear baby won't catch it. How is the baby?"

Elizabeth, seated beside her, replied to this question.

"So bonny," she said. "Cynthia writes that he is learning to walk. Isn't he forward?"

Lady Ribblemere looked rather concerned, and shook her head so that the plumes in her enormous hat nodded like a row of mandarins.

"I do not think that Cynthia should allow him to walk yet," she said. "I don't believe in forcing children. None of mine walked at his age. Dear me, I have not asked after Mr. Ruthven! I hope he is well?"

"Yes, quite, thank you. I believe they are both going to Scotland next month."

"That will be very nice, I am sure. I used to go to Scotland myself in my husband's shooting days. Dear me, is that your spaniel I see under the table? So you still have her! Come along, little doggy! Come along!"

Flo retired further under the table.

"How is Sir George?" asked Stephen, catching Elizabeth's eye as he said it.

"Thank you, he is as well as can be expected. I always say that when you pass the age of fifty it is not to be supposed that you will feel the same as you did at thirty."

"Er—no," said Stephen.

Lady Ribblemere's glance wandered round the room.

"Is that your new book I see on the table?"

"The beginning of it," Stephen smiled.

"How very interesting! Dear me, I am sure no one would have said when you were a little boy that you would grow into a writer! I think I must really try and read one of your novels. I remember my husband was very pleased with them, but, as you know, I seldom read fiction nowadays. At my age one feels that it is rather waste of time." She turned to Elizabeth. "It must be very interesting to have a writer for a husband. I expect you read his books together?"

N-no, said Elizabeth. "I am hoping to be allowed to see this one soon."

"You should read it to her, Stephen. She would be able to help you. And now I must really be going. Tell me, Stephen, is that a new photograph of little Christopher I see on the mantelpiece?"

Stephen handed it to her.

"Cynthia sent it to me a few days ago. He's growing quite large, isn't he?"

Lady Ribblemere began to fumble in her lap for her lorgnettes. Through them she stared at the photograph.

"Dear me, yes! He's very like Mr. Ruthven, don't you think? Not at all like

Georgette Heyer

Cynthia, the dear little man. Yes, that is very interesting. If I remember rightly, you are his godfather?"

"I am. It's an onerous position."

"Ah, I daresay," Lady Ribblemere said vaguely. "It seems incredible that Cynthia should have a child of her own. Time flies indeed. Which reminds me that I must be going." She heaved herself out of the sofa. "No, do not trouble to escort me to the gate, Stephen. I shall feel that I am interrupting you in your work. You and your wife must come up to dine with us one evening. Perhaps the Vicar and Mrs. Edmondston would come too. I must arrange it. Goodbye, Mrs. Ramsay, or may I call you Elizabeth? We have had a delightful little talk. I wish you would not come with me, Stephen; I am sure you are very busy." Her voice died away in the passage; Elizabeth drew a deep breath, and started to giggle. When Stephen came back he was scowling; Elizabeth became grave at once.

"Damn the woman!" snapped Stephen. "What on earth did you bring her in here for?"

Elizabeth shrank slightly from the roughness of his voice.

"I didn't. She—just came. I couldn't help it."

"Good lord, I should think you might have raked up some excuse! Infernal old wind-bag. Of course that's the end of my work for to-day."

"Really, Stephen, I don't see why you need be so angry about it!" Elizabeth said, hurt. "After all, she didn't stay long, and she was very kind and nice."

Stephen groaned.

"Good God, can't you understand that a thing like that's enough to put me off for a week?"

"No, I can't," Elizabeth said, angry in her turn. "And anyway I'm not going to be talked to like that! Anyone would think it was my fault!"

"Well, I do think you might have said that I was out, or ill," he grumbled.

"If people take the trouble to call on us, the least you can do is to receive them pleasantly," said Elizabeth, quoting largely from Miss Arden.

"I have yet to learn that it is the man's duty to receive calls," Stephen replied sarcastically. "And as for Lady Ribblemere—I can't bear the woman.

She's positively rude. Fancy saying that she considered novel-reading waste of time! Beastly bad form."

"Well, I like her. I think it was very kind of her to come and call."

"Elizabeth, don't talk such damned rot! I'm willing to admit that she's kind, but you can't possibly *like* her! There's nothing to like."

"I don't agree at all. I think you're very fault-finding and quarrelsome."

He softened.

"Sorry, darling. I didn't mean to quarrel with you. Pretend that you like Lady Ribblemere, if you want to. It doesn't really matter."

She reddened.

"I am not pretending. Why do you always say that?"

He put his arm round her waist.

"Because you do, 'Lisbeth. You know you do."

She did not know it, but he had discovered it long ago, and it irritated him. For as long as she continued to shrink from crude facts, and honesty, there could be no real intimacy between them. That he did not quite realise, but he could not help feeling that her extreme delicacy bordered on prudery. A dozen times a day he made her blush. He was at first amused, then slightly impatient.

"Elizabeth, you really can't be shy with me!"

"I don't think one need talk about such things," she said repressively.

That always baffled him; he wished he understood her better, or had the power to break through her reserve. Because she wanted it, he gave her some of his manuscript to read. When she had finished he asked her opinion. After a tiny pause she said,

"It's very good."

That drove the artist in him to a frenzy.

"Good? Yes, but what else? How does it strike you?"

"Oh—I like it—quite!"

"You mean you don't like it. Well, why not?"

"Oh, no, Stephen! Of course I don't mean that!"

"My dear girl," he said sharply, "say what you think, for God's sake, and don't bother about being polite."

"But, Stephen, I— It's only perhaps that I don't quite understand some of it. And—and sometimes—I expect I'm old-fashioned—isn't it rather—broad?"

"It's perfectly straight-forward, if that's what you mean. What of the style? Do you like it, or not? I shouldn't ask for your criticism if I didn't want it, Elizabeth."

"Oh, the *style!*" she said, wondering what was the proper thing to say about it. "Yes, that's very good, I think."

He seemed to shrug his shoulders, then turned away. She knew that she had failed him, and was wretched.

Nina and her parents came to call. Elizabeth liked Mrs. Trelawney, who was quiet and full of common-sense. Mr. Trelawney did just what his daughter had said he would do. He walked with Stephen round the garden, and said, Charming! in an absent-minded way many times. He offered to send them some cuttings from a rare plant; Elizabeth thanked him, and said that she would love to have them. When the Trelawneys had departed Stephen asked her what on earth she had said that for?

"Well, what else could I say?" she demanded, wide-eyed.

"Why, that you didn't really understand horticulture, and it would be waste to give his rarities to you."

She was aghast.

"Stephen! But how rude!"

"No, not a bit. You could have said it so that he would have understood perfectly."

"I wouldn't have hurt his feelings for worlds!"

"They wouldn't have been hurt. He's far more likely to feel hurt when he sees those cuttings withering in an alien soil. For you *don't* know anything about 'em, 'Lisbeth, and they're sure to die. Besides which, sooner or later he'll discover that you aren't a gardener, however much you pretend. Then he'll be annoyed."

"I had to try to take an interest in his hobby," she protested. It was strange how often she seemed to do the wrong thing; strange and sad.

He laughed, kissing her hair.

"Yes, but you carried it to excess, darling. I was convulsed with inward amusement when you nodded wisely at his botanical terms."

Other people called, some nice, some negligible, others definitely nasty. Then began the wearisome ordeal of returning calls. To Elizabeth, who had never visited without her aunt, it was a terrifying ceremonial. She was overcome with nervousness, and could never think of anything to say. And«after the calls came invitations, some to tea, others to dinner. She preferred the dinner invitations, for Stephen was present then, to support her. He refused to accompany her out to tea; he said that his work was sufficient excuse. She could not agree; she had always imagined that a novelist had plenty of spare-time on his hands. Stephen seemed to have none. Even when he did cease work she knew that he was thinking of his book; thinking and planning. It was extraordinary that he could be so absorbed so soon after their marriage. She feared he was working too hard; when he sat up until three and four in the morning she worried, and often went downstairs to make him come to bed.

She would find him in the library, his head bent over the paper, his hand travelling fast, across and across. He would be dishevelled, totally abstracted, sometimes not noticing her entrance.

"Stephen dear, do come up to bed!" she would say softly. "I'm sure it isn't good for you to work so late."

"All right, darling. In a minute."

Sighing she would seat herself on the arm of a chair, watching and waiting. The patience she displayed irritated him more than any petulance would have done. The feeling that she was there preyed upon his nerves; the flow of words came less easily, then stopped. In exasperation he would fling down his pen.

"Oh, darling, *please* don't sit and wait for me! It worries me to distraction."

"It worries me to know that you're sitting up so late," she would answer gravely.

"Very well, dear; I'll come."

Georgette Heyer

It ended in him sleeping for the time in his dressing-room so that he should not disturb her. That showed her how great a hold his work had over him. While the mood for writing was on him he had no thought for anything else, no other passion, no other love.

But when, reluctantly, he suggested the change, her heart leaped within her. Once again she could be private, and alone. Only when she slept by herself did she realise to the full how she hated to have Stephen with her. She had borne it because she had not the courage, morally, to protest; she felt now that she could never resume the old relations.

And yet, dual to this feeling, came the wave of jealousy whenever Nina visited them. That was often; it seemed that Nina was more intimate with this house, and with Stephen, than she could ever be. Nina wanted to be friends; she wanted Elizabeth to come and see her as often as she came to Queen's Halt. It was not in Elizabeth's nature to do so. She could not be friends with Nina; they were not akin, and Nina knew so much. She could not even take part in a general conversation when Nina was there. She did not understand Nina's conversation, she could not follow her allusions. She tried; she even pretended that she recognised some obscure quotation, but she knew, miserably, that Nina was not deceived.

Nina seemed to be necessary to Stephen, too. He had always some question to put to her, some point on which he wanted her advice. He read passages to Elizabeth, and asked which she preferred. She did not know. When Nina came Stephen put them before her, and the result was very different.

"Nina, I want your opinion. This—or this?"

Then Nina would read, and as soon as she had read she knew which variant was best.

"My dear old Stephen, are you going in for Euphuism?" she would say mockingly, flipping one sheet towards him.

It was extraordinary how his face could light up.

"You think that? Yes, you're right. Good lord, why didn't I see it?"

Nina was always ready with her criticism; evidently Stephen respected it. Nina would look up from the manuscript, point to a word and say,

125

"I almost think I'd prefer the Norman word here, old man. You've scratched it out, but it's a nicer rhythm."

Sometimes he disagreed, and they would argue; sometimes they would discuss situations in the book which Elizabeth thought too frank to be mentioned. And always Nina embraced her in the discussion.

"Elizabeth, can *you* convince Stephen that no girl would behave as Caroline does with Carlyle?"

That aspect of it had never struck Elizabeth; she only knew that Caroline's behaviour shocked her.

"I don't care for that part of the book, I must say," she answered.

"No, because it's false. Norman's misdemeanours aren't great enough to make her go off with Carlyle, Stephen. Do you think so, Elizabeth?"

"No," Elizabeth said. "Because Caroline didn't seem to be that sort of girl. I thought at first that she was quite nice."

"Elizabeth loves a book full of thoroughly nice people— or black-dyed villains," Stephen said teasingly.

"So do I, upon occasion. I think you're in danger of becoming a decadent, Stephen. Bilious Byronism. Oh, Elizabeth, what a brilliant thought! *Isn't* Stephen Byronic?"

"I don't know," Elizabeth said. "I don't read Byron."

"Oh, but you should! He's not at all without merit."

"I don't think I should care for his poems," Elizabeth said primly.

Soon after that she suggested to Stephen that she should invite Lawrence and Miss Arden down for the week-end.

"And perhaps Auntie would stay on longer."

It was the last thing in the world that Stephen desired just then, and he tried, selfishly, to postpone the invitation.

"Wouldn't it be better if we waited until I'm through with my book?" he asked, thinking what death to inspiration Lawrence would be.

"But it would only be for a week-end, Stephen! And if Auntie stayed on longer she wouldn't interfere with you."

"Just as you like, darling."

"Of course, if you don't *want* them—"

"Rot, 'Lisbeth! If you'd like to have them to stay now, I'm perfectly agreeable."

"I'll write at once," she said.

The invitation was accepted; the visit passed quite pleasantly. Stephen laid aside his work from Friday till Monday, and gave himself up to Lawrence. Miss Arden sat with Elizabeth in secluded corners, and talked little nothings.

When they had gone, other people, Stephen's friends, began to invite themselves. The Tyrells drifted in quite unexpectedly one afternoon; Elizabeth was completely flustered, and somewhat annoyed. Stephen, on the other hand, was delighted. It did not matter to him that the visitors' beds were not aired, or sufficient food provided for them. It did not seem to matter much to the Tyrells either, who were the maddest, most happy-go-lucky pair Elizabeth had ever met, but it drove the poor hostess to a frenzy. They dropped cigarette-ash on the carpet, they sat up late talking drama, poetry, and art till Elizabeth nearly dropped asleep from sheer boredom. Luckily the marmoset had met with an accident and died, so she was spared that intrusion into her neat home. She wondered what Aunt Anne would think could she but see Bertie Tyrell cross-legged on the floor, dangerously waving a coffee-cup in mid-air the better to point his arguments. She could hardly believe that it was really herself who entertained these oddities from another world. How much rather would she have held a quiet, sedate tea-party, where no guest would talk of Azurism, or Exposition of the Nude, or Gothic style of writing. What it was all about she had no idea. When she begged enlightenment of Stephen, he laughed, and assured her that no one knew, least of all the Tyrells.

"Are they talking nonsense, then?" she asked, puzzled.

"Not exactly. They're striving after something, but they don't yet know what it is. It's interesting, I think. I like to hear them propound their views."

"I find them rather boring," she sighed.

"Poor little sweetheart! You must just learn to laugh at them, as I do. Then they become funny."

After the Tyrells came Mrs. Ramsay, with Thomas. Elizabeth dreaded a dog-fight, but she was assured that Thomas was well acquainted with Hector, and Jerry, and Flo. Mrs. Ramsay sprang from her cart into her son's arms, and hugged him.

"My darlings, I'm so pleased to see you again! How beautifully the trees have turned! Elizabeth, does the Halt hold an awful fascination for you? It does for me— especially when I'm away from it. Dear Nana, I think I've lost my hat-box. Do you suppose it can have jumped out of the car?"

"No, madam. You've left it behind," Nana said with conviction.

"Perhaps I have. How tiresome! Stephen, have you grown, or is it because I haven't seen you for over a month?"

They took her into the house; she noticed little changes, and remarked on them, approvingly. But when Elizabeth went with her upstairs she walked straight to Elizabeth's room, and then checked, laughing.

"How silly of me! Please, where am I to go?"

"It must seem very funny—for you to come to your own home—with me here," Elizabeth said. "I prepared the Blue room for you. I thought that would be nicest." She opened the door for Mrs. Ramsay to pass through.

"My dear, this is positively thrilling!" Mrs. Ramsay said. "I've never slept here before. Thank you for putting those flowers on the table. Oh, here's Nana! Nana, must I unpack, or will you?"

"It would be a nice thing if I let you do it, madam! If you go along down to tea I'll see to your things. Have you lost your keys, or shall I find them in your handbag?"

"I don't know at all," Mrs. Ramsay said brightly. Then she took Elizabeth's arm, and went out with her.

After tea she explored the house. When she saw the made bed in Stephen's dressing-room she paused for a moment in her flow of conversation, but picked up the thread almost immediately. In Elizabeth's room she pottered about, looking at photographs, and fiddling with the ornaments upon the mantelpiece. Suddenly she looked up at Elizabeth, and spoke lightly, yet with anxiety in her voice.

"Darling, don't you sleep together?"

Elizabeth blushed hotly.

"It's—Stephen thought—while he's writing—I mean, he sits up so late. He was afraid it—it disturbed me. It's only—for a time."

"Yes, of course. I see. You are happy, aren't you, Elizabeth?"

"Yes, I'm very happy," Elizabeth said. "Did Stephen tell you that Father and Auntie came to stay with us?"

"No, but how jolly! By the way, has everybody called? Oh, and did Lady Ribblemere ask after all the family in turn?"

Elizabeth smiled.

"Yes. I wanted to laugh rather, but she was really very kind."

"She's quite a dear, only so dreadfully tedious. I must go and see her, I think. I heard that the Tyrells came on a surprise-visit! What a shock for you. I always go to bed early when they stay with me."

"I didn't like to do that," said Elizabeth. "I—Mr. Tyrell has some very—queer ideas."

"Most immoral, my dear. I hope you told him so. Nothing pleases him more. Next time you see him you'll find that he has dropped Free Love and taken up Christian Science. So volatile. No, I don't mean that. What do I mean? Let's go and ask Stephen."

"I expect he's writing," Elizabeth warned her.

"Then he'll have to stop." Away went Mrs. Ramsay, downstairs to the library, with Elizabeth at her heels. "Stephen, stop writing and help me!"

"What's the matter?" he asked.

"I want to know what the word is I want instead of volatile."

He laughed.

"Context, please."

"My dear, I've forgotten what it was. Elizabeth, do come to the rescue!"

Elizabeth explained, much to Mrs. Ramsay's admiration.

"You probably meant versatile," said Stephen. "Not that it fits at all."

"Doesn't it, Stephen? Never mind, let's pretend that it does. I'm afraid I'm disturbing you, as Lady Ribblemere would say. I'd like to see the fowls, please, Elizabeth."

When she had thoroughly inspected everything, Mrs. Ramsay came to the conclusion that Elizabeth was an excellent housekeeper, and said so.

"I try to be," Elizabeth said, warming under the praise. "But it's difficult sometimes. People drop in without any warning—and things like that."

"Don't let it worry you," Mrs. Ramsay advised. "It's a mistake. I did, when I was first married, but I grew out of it. One has to do a lot of adapting."

"Yes," Elizabeth said slowly. "Yes—one has."

"If ever you want advice—or help," Mrs. Ramsay went on, "come to me. Will you?"

"It's—it's very kind of you—" Elizabeth stammered.

"No, not a bit. Generally I'm hopelessly unpractical, but I do know a great many things about the Ramsays. Of course, if you had a mother of your own, you wouldn't need me. But as it is—when—I mean, if—you get in a fix—or you want to talk to someone—come to me. I'm quite safe."

"Thank you very much indeed," Elizabeth said. "I will."

Mrs. Ramsay stayed at Queen's Halt for a week, and before she left she went for a long walk with Stephen, through the woods. Little by little she coaxed him to talk to her of Elizabeth, and of himself.

"I don't know, mater. I just—don't—know," he said in answer to her question, Were they happy? "I—love Elizabeth, you see. I—I don't think I could live without her. Only, sometimes—I wonder— She's such a babe still. It's something I can't talk about, mater. It's between us two alone."

"Yes, darling. I don't want you to try to talk about it. Only, Stephen, don't be too absorbed in your book. That's only a thing. Elizabeth's more than that."

"Oh, come now, mater, I can't be expected to chuck work just because I'm married! Other men have to be away all day at an office."

"I know, dear. But they come away from their work, and don't have to sit up until the small hours at it."

He was silent for a moment.

"I do my best work at night, mater. You know that. And there are weeks when I don't touch a pen from one day's end to another."

"My dear, if you're selfish in refusing to—to adapt yourself to Elizabeth, it's unfair to her. I think you've got a long way to go—both of you."

Chapter Sixteen

Towards the end of October Stephen's pen began to run dry; he grew restless, short-tempered, and finally decided that he would give up attempting to write for a few weeks. So the manuscript was locked in a drawer, and Stephen emerged from his absorption. He suggested that they should go to London for a time; Elizabeth was only too delighted. She had contrived to amuse herself successfully, with the house and the garden, and the car, which she had learned to drive, but these were, after all, only Things. She longed to see her family again, and London; she longed too to be free from Queen's Halt and its traditions just for a short breathing space, and to escape from Nina, with her abstruse witticisms, and flood of reminiscence. Those reminiscences galled Elizabeth, but she had not the courage to say so. Sooner or later, when Stephen and Nina were together, would crop up those deadly words, Do you remember? To the third person who did not remember, who did not know, or want to know, the people mentioned, who saw no humour in the old jokes and catchwords, the reminiscences were not only boring, but unbelievably annoying. They implied a close intimacy between Stephen and Nina, an age-long friendship, and a perfect understanding.

So Elizabeth was glad to leave Queen's Halt, even though it meant hotel life for a spell. That did not seem to matter, somehow, especially since they were to have a private sitting-room. The sitting-room was Stephen's suggestion: he thought she would not care to entertain her friends in the public lounge. In little things like that which had to do with her comfort and well-being, he was consideration itself. She realised that she had still only to mention a wish. If it were in his power to do so, he would grant it at once.

The Ardens welcomed Elizabeth to town with open arms; she was often at the Boltons, trying to feel that the old life was not closed to her. But it was closed, and she knew it. It was left far behind, just as far behind as the new

Instead of the Thorn

life was far ahead.

She was pleased to see Sarah again. Sarah was going to Switzerland for winter-sports; it was fun to help choose the clothes she would need. She and Sarah shopped together, and went to picture-galleries while Stephen held long business interviews with his agent, and other people. Elizabeth was not interested in business; she did not want to know that Stephen had sold his Rubber shares and was doing a little flutter in Oil; she was not really interested to hear that he had changed his publisher. She did not appreciate the significance of publishers.

Cynthia and Anthony had returned from Scotland, and Cynthia was making a determined effort to become intimate with Elizabeth. Elizabeth wished that she would not; Mrs. Ramsay she had come to love; Cynthia she felt she could never love.

"What's Stephen's book like?" Cynthia asked. "The institution of Norman was a splash of genius."

"He's only done half," Elizabeth answered. "It's clever, I think."

"Yes, cleverness is his besetting sin," Cynthia said. "That, and facility."

Elizabeth did not quite understand.

"Facility? But—"

"You don't agree? I think he writes too easily. Nicely balanced sentences trickle off his pen, and he doesn't have to prune or re-write."

"I should have thought that that was an advantage."

"From the viewpoint of celerity, undoubtedly," Cynthia said curtly.

That was how Cynthia puzzled you. She said things that you felt to be clever, or apt, yet that you could not understand. Elizabeth, instead of meeting bluntness with bluntness, would nod wisely, and never say in frankness, I don't understand; please explain. She hoped all the time that no one would perceive her ignorance, or think her dull and stupid.

She was rather surprised to find that with her own family she could talk, quite brightly, rather like Stephen, or Nina. Lawrence said again that she had blossomed forth. With him she felt that she had; with her husband, and his family, the old reticence and nervousness returned.

132

At a subscription dance to which she and Stephen, and the Ruthvens went, she met Wendell.

Wendell was tall, and dark, with very soft brown eyes, and a smiling face. Stephen, when he was dancing with Elizabeth, saw him, and exclaimed.

"Hullo! There's old Wendell!"

"Who is he?" Elizabeth asked.

"Chap who was in my battalion out in Flanders. Very cheery." He piloted Elizabeth across the room, and managed to attract Wendell's attention. After the dance Wendell came to the Ramsay table, and Stephen introduced him to Elizabeth. He looked at her in admiration; Stephen said that he must come to dinner with them one night.

"I'd love to!" Wendell said eagerly. "Topping to meet you again!"

Elizabeth was at her best in moments like these. She smiled, and endorsed Stephen's invitation, and said that she would write and suggest a day. Wendell thanked her and said that it was awfully good of her. Then he had to hurry back to his own party, and they did not speak to him again that evening.

He came to dine with them later in the week, alone, and Elizabeth liked him. He was gay, and he made jokes that she could follow. She wondered rather what Stephen found attractive in him, for he was certainly not particularly clever, and quite ignorant of matters literary. He and Stephen "talked War," and Elizabeth listened with interest. That type of reminiscence was not galling, but amusing. Then, too, Wendell evidently thought her charming. She read the admiration in his eyes, and expanded to it. She was at her best, and she knew that she was being a good hostess for once.

"I say, Mrs. Ramsay, isn't it a bit strenuous being married to a gilded novelist? D'you have to make learned remarks about his books? Jolly fatiguing, what?"

"Oh, no!" she answered, laughing. "I don't know enough about novel-writing to criticise. All I do is to drag him away from his work to come and talk to me."

"Shouldn't think he needs much dragging," Wendell said.

Elizabeth dimpled.

"Oh yes, he does! While he's writing he hasn't any use for me. I think he's in love with his heroine—I mean, the girl in his book."

"What an unblushing lie!" Stephen remarked.

"P'raps his heroine is you," suggested Wendell.

"Me? Good gracious, no! She's a dreadful creature!"

Then they all laughed, Elizabeth too, when she realized what she had said.

They went into the billiard-room after dinner, and as no one else was there, Elizabeth let Stephen and Wendell teach her how to play. She enjoyed that, even when she miscued three times in succession. Stephen said, Rotten!

Wendell told him to shut up. He assured Elizabeth that she was learning fast, and would make a fine player. They played three-handed billiards, and Wendell had Elizabeth as his partner.

"As a handicap?" she asked, smiling.

"Not much! Come on, Mrs. Ramsay, we'll have to pull our socks up with a vengeance. Stephen's played the game before."

He was a delightful partner; he coached her zealously, in spite of a running fire of commentary from Stephen.

"Now then, Mrs. Ramsay, we've got him on toast. If you can cannon off the white on to that cushion, with just a leetle left-hand side on, you'll—"

"If you tell her to put side on she won't hit it at all," Stephen interrupted.

"Don't be so rude!" Elizabeth protested. "Go on, Mr. Wendell, I'm listening."

"Well, you want to hit the white very nearly half-ball, then you'll cannon off this cushion on to the red."

"Not she," said Stephen. "Look here, darling! aim to hit the red half-ball—don't bother about any side—and the chances are you'll go into the middle pocket."

"Shut up, Stephen; you're muddling me. Will you mind if I miss this, Mr. Wendell?"

"No, rather not. Yes, that's right. Let your cue follow."

Of course she did miss the shot, and Stephen said, I told you so. Wendell was more complimentary.

"Jolly good attempt. Just hadn't got legs enough. Hullo, look at old Stephen! Billiards by One Who Knows. Well, let's see what we can do with it."

They played until two men who were staying in the hotel came in. Then Elizabeth put up her cue, and sat down to watch.

Decidedly the evening was a success.

After that they saw Wendell often. He asked them to dine with him, and go to a theatre. The piece was a revue, but Elizabeth enjoyed every moment of it. They went to supper afterwards at the Savoy, a thing Elizabeth had never done before.

"You like Wendell?" Stephen asked her, later.

"Oh, yes! Don't you?" she replied.

"Quite a good chap. We must get him to come down to the Halt some time or other. Did I hear you say you were going with him to Twickenham?"

"He did ask me," she admitted. "I've never seen a Rugger-match. Do you mind if I go, Stephen?"

"Mind? Good lord, no, darling! Why should I?"

She went with Wendell, several times. He made one of the party Stephen got up to go to Sandown Park; he formed a habit of ringing up many times in the week to see whether the Ramsays couldn't come along with him to a show that night, or a motor-drive that afternoon. Easily, almost unconsciously, he and Elizabeth drifted into close friendship. Christian names came naturally; it was as though she had known Wendell all her life. In conversation with him no mental effort was required; sometimes, even, she felt herself to be intellectually his superior. That was rather a refreshing change. It was she who suggested that he should visit them at the Halt. He jumped at the invitation.

"I say, how topping! Yes, I'd love to. Please don't forget, Betty, or I shall be compelled to remind you!"

"No, I won't forget," she promised. "Only I'm afraid it will be rather dull for you. We haven't got a hard court, but there are some golf-links quite near to us."

"You'll take me round while Stephen mugs over his book," he said.

"Oh, I can hardly play at all! I'm awfully stupid at games, Charles."

"Rot! I bet you can play well enough really. You're so frightfully modest, that's all."

Aunt Anne met Wendell one afternoon when she came unexpectedly to see her niece. Wendell was with Elizabeth, having tea; Stephen had gone out to interview his typist.

Miss Arden was rather surprised to find a strange man with Elizabeth, surprised and rather disapproving.

"Oh, Auntie dear, how lovely to see you! This is Mr. Wendell. Charles, this is my aunt, Miss Arden."

Wendell did not stay very long, and as soon as he had gone, Miss Arden asked,

"My dear, who is that young man?"

"A friend of Stephen, Auntie. I like him very much; he's so energetic and cheery."

"Does Stephen know that you entertain him in his absence?"

Elizabeth stiffened, inwardly furious at her aunt's interference.

"Of course Stephen knows. I'm—I'm not a child, Auntie."

"Oh, if Stephen knows—!" Miss Arden said, trying to feel relieved. But she mentioned the occurrence to Lawrence that night, and said that she hoped that it was all right.

Lawrence pooh-poohed her misgivings. It was only natural that his little girl should have men-friends. Why, her marriage itself enabled her to do so!

"Yes, but—I've wondered—sometimes—whether everything is—quite as it should be—between Stephen and Elizabeth."

"Nonsense, my dear Anne, nonsense! I never saw a more devoted couple! All your imagination! And if it weren't, I for one know Elizabeth too well to suspect her of carrying on an intrigue with another man!"

"Lawrence! How can yon? I never dreamed of such a thing! Only—sometimes—a friendship like that—isn't very wise."

Georgette Heyer

"No one nowadays thinks anything of a platonic friendship," Lawrence said loftily. "It's perfectly usual and natural."

Miss Arden rose to leave the room. But before she went she delivered a Parthian shot.

"I don't believe there's any such thing as platonic friendship," she said flatly.

She was not alone in her belief, or her disapproval. Cynthia had seen Wendell. On many occasions she had been included in the parties of which he was a member, and she realised that Elizabeth liked him more than she knew. Having come to the conclusion that Elizabeth neither loved nor understood Stephen, Cynthia thought her friendship with a man of Wendell's calibre dangerous. Inwardly she raged, for she felt herself to be impotent. Elizabeth did not like her; therefore she would not be advised by her. It was equally impossible to drop a word of warning in Stephen's ear. That, she knew, would be disastrous, almost criminal. Philosophically she thought, If Stephen chooses to be a blind fool, he must take the consequences. To Anthony, however, she spoke her mind, characteristically.

"I do not like the Tertium Quid," she drawled, over Christopher's curly head.

Anthony looked up.

"What?"

"Kipling," said Cynthia.

"Yes, I know. Who?"

"The treacle-eyed Wendell."

Anthony was interested, and put down his book.

"Really? But why Tertium Quid?"

Cynthia addressed her son.

"My cherub, will you be stupid, like your father, when you grow up? I love stupid men."

Christopher grinned cheerfully, and said Dad-dad-dad.

"I don't see it, Cynny," Anthony said.

"I know you don't, but it's none the less obvious. The treacle-eyed one has

137

found the soft spot in Elizabeth's heart."

"D'you honestly think that, Cynny? He doesn't shine much beside Stephen."

"No matter. He admires, he adulates. What more does Elizabeth want?"

"That's unfair, Cynthia. Beastly unfair."

"My dear, I shall begin to be jealous of Elizabeth soon."

He smiled.

"I like her, Cyn. Probably because I'm stupid. I think she's a thoroughly nice little thing. You know, Stephen's at all joy, if you have to live with him."

"No. He wanted a very different wife."

"I'm not so sure. I know you and Mater had set your hearts on Nina, but I always thought you were wrong."

"Nina, or someone like her. Someone who had the same interests as Stephen. Someone brainy."

Anthony began to knock his pipe out.

"Funny how you clever women go off the rails," he remarked. "Take a simple example. Ourselves. I don't know a darn thing about verse; I can't grasp mysticism, and I loathe William Morris. What about it?"

Cynthia threw up her hand.

"Yes. *Touché.* Perhaps we're exceptional."

"Not likely. If Stephen had married Nina they'd have quarrelled from morn till night. Each one striving to go one better than the other."

Cynthia rested her cheek against Christopher's little round head.

"You may be right. You often are. But I can't believe that Stephen's marriage is a success."

"I don't see why it shouldn't be—eventually," said Anthony.

Chapter Seventeen

The visit to town lasted until the New Year. Stephen had wished to go back to Queen's Halt at the end of November, but when he saw how much Elizabeth was enjoying this time in London, of his own free will he suggested that they should lengthen their stay. They spent Christmas with the Ardens, and Stephen bore it well, on the whole. When it was over he said that another time he thought that they would either go abroad, or invite friends to the Halt. That was what he felt about Christmas with the Ardens.

Stephen began to grow tired of Wendell.

"That chap's always hanging round us," he said one day.

Elizabeth looked up quickly.

"Don't you like him, Stephen?"

"Fairly. I get a bit bored with him. Don't you? Rather vapid, but quite a cheery sort of blighter."

"I'm rather sorry for him," Elizabeth said. "He doesn't seem to have any people, or anywhere much to go to."

"Seems to have this place," he remarked humorously. "I'm always falling over him."

"Well, shall we not ask him to come so often?" she said. "If he bores you—"

"Oh no, darling! It's not as bad as that. If he amuses you, and you like him, why should we choke him off?"

"He does amuse me," she said. "I think he's good fun."

"All right, then. Long live Charles Wendell. I suppose we ought to ask him to join our theatre party next week. We owe him an invitation. Don't we?"

"Do we? Oh yes! The party he got up at Claridges. That was awfully jolly, wasn't it?"

"Yes. I didn't care much for the stray girl who came with the Parchetts, but otherwise it was a good show. Ring him up and ask him for next week. Or I will, if you like."

"I'd rather you did," she said.

The theatre-party dined first at the Berkeley. The Ruthvens were present, and Sarah, and Cynthia was rather short with Wendell. Anthony, however, was as pleasant as ever. He sat on one side of Elizabeth, Wendell on the other. Elizabeth thought that Anthony was a darling. She could not understand why he had married Cynthia. Elizabeth and the two men talked airily of nothing; Stephen and Sarah and Cynthia discussed Galsworthy and Conrad. Occasionally conversation became general, but the party split most naturally into two.

At the theatre Wendell sat next to Elizabeth, and whispered to her, "Stephen's sister—jolly clever an' all that, but a bit alarming, what?"

She agreed whole-heartedly, but disloyalty was not one of her failings.

"She wants knowing," was all she said.

"Oh, quite, quite!" he answered hurriedly.

After the theatre they went back to the Ramsays' hotel for supper, and Wendell asked Cynthia if she did not think the play jolly good. Cynthia said, Spasmodically.

"Rather outspoken, of course," he said. "Personally I like to hear a spade called a spade, though."

"Undoubtedly," Cynthia replied, "but it is not always necessary to call it a 'bloody shovel.'"

That was awful of Cynthia; even Stephen looked annoyed. Elizabeth began to talk quickly about the electric-light signs in Piccadilly Circus.

"Cyn, you are the limit," Stephen told her, aside.

"Sorry. Treacle-eyes arouse the worst in me."

Stephen's shoulders began to shake.

"Apt little devil! I never noticed them till you mentioned it."

"You're often rather blind," said Cynthia calmly.

A few days later, Mr. Hengist, who had been abroad on business, returned, and lunched with Stephen at his club. He went on afterwards to see Elizabeth, and found her sewing in her private room.

"Well, child?" he said.

Elizabeth jumped up.

"Mr. Hengist! How nice of you to come! Did Stephen bring you?"

He kissed her, clumsily.

"No; he went on to the City. How are you, my dear?"

"Very well indeed, thanks," she answered. "And you?"

"Not so young as I was. Are you reading this?" He picked up a book from the table.

"No; Stephen is. I can't get on with Yeats."

"A pity," he said. "Still reading Victoria Cross and Charles Garvice?"

"Oh, I never did!" she protested. "How unfair! Anyway, I shouldn't dare to with Stephen in the offing. The cigarettes are in that box at your elbow. Do have one!"

"I'd rather have a pipe, if you don't mind the smell of it."

She laughed at him.

"You know I don't mind! You're very polite to me all at once."

His eyes twinkled.

"It's a nice change, isn't it? It'll wear off, Elizabeth. I'm shy just at the moment. How do you like Stephen now you're married to him?"

"Very much, thank you," she smiled. "How do you like him?"

"I always did. I think he's a man in a thousand."

She opened her eyes at that.

"Do you? Why?"

"To have put up with you all this time," he parried. "Tell me about your home. I don't trust your father's description."

"It's perfectly lovely," she answered. "Tudor, you know, with an enchanting garden. Will you come down to stay with us in the spring?"

"Certainly, if you ask me. And don't invite me to come when your father and aunt are with you. I see them any day of the week."

It was just what she had intended to do; already she had begun to plan.

"Not? But— Anyone would think you didn't like them!"

"Your aunt and I don't hit it off very well, as you know. I'd rather come alone to see you."

She did not quite know what to say. She had known that Miss Arden did not always approve of Mr. Hengist, but it had never occurred to her that Mr. Hengist did not like her aunt. She decided to change the subject.

"I saw my first Rugger-match just lately," she said. "A friend of Stephen's took me. It was so exciting."

Mr. Hengist's eyes gleamed suddenly, and he took his pipe out of his mouth.

"Still at it, Elizabeth," he said drily.

She did not understand at all. She was glad that the page-boy came in at that moment. Mr. Hengist was so queer.

The page told her that Wendell had called to see her. She said, "Ask him to come up, please," and turned once more to Mr. Hengist.

"Funnily enough it was Mr. Wendell who took me to Twickenham. He was with Stephen at the Front."

"Oh, really?" said Mr. Hengist, politely but not with any great show of interest.

Wendell came in; mentally Mr. Hengist said, Dresses too well; don't like his eyes.

"Hullo, Charles!" Elizabeth said vivaciously. "How nice of you to come and see me! Mr. Hengist, may I introduce Mr. Wendell?"

Both men murmured something inaudible.

"Look here, Betty, what I really came round for was to ask you if you'd care to run out with me in the car and have tea somewhere. Topping day, an' all that. If you wrap up well don't you know ...?"

"It's very kind of you, Charles, but I'm afraid I can't. Stay and have tea here instead. Stephen will be in very soon."

Mr. Hengist rose.

"Don't refuse on my account," he said. "I must be going. I only just dropped in to see you."

"Oh, don't go!" she cried. "I should so like you to stop to tea! I can go motoring with Charles any day of the week!"

Mr. Hengist thought, Can you indeed? but aloud he repeated that he must go.

On the way home he did some hard thinking. He had never seen Elizabeth so sprightly, or so coquettish. And all for a man who dressed too well.

"Gaiety male chorus," said Mr. Hengist to a lamp-post.

But in the first week of January Stephen took Elizabeth home, and left Wendell with no more than a casual invitation to come and visit them some time or other.

At Queen's Halt Stephen, whose fingers had itched for a pen during the past weeks, drew forth his manuscript and set to work on it once more. Elizabeth tried to read William Morris, curled up beside the fire. Outside everything was damp and cold, the garden bare, the trees gaunt and shimmering against a grey sky.

The wonder of it was that Stephen could see beauty even in this dripping landscape. Elizabeth could not; she could only see that it was dreary and cold. The beds, stripped of their flowers, depressed her; the sky above was uniformly drab, lowering and chill.

Lady Ribblemere invited her to Afternoon Bridge. Elizabeth refused the invitation, saying that she did not really play. Lady Ribblemere said, Never mind, we are none of us good. In a misguided moment Elizabeth went. She had always absented herself from her aunt's bridge-parties; she did not know the evil spell which Bridge casts over people; she had no idea that Bridge could transform a kindly, good-natured woman into a shrewish harpy. She was appalled to see how polish and good manners fell from Lady Ribblemere and her guests.

They cut for partners; everyone smiled and was polite. Elizabeth said nervously that she must warn them that she was a beginner. They were so encouraging that she took heart. Her partner was Mrs. Edmondston, the Vicar's wife.

As soon as the hands were dealt round an air of gloom, of despair, and of suspicious secrecy descended on the three other women. Lady Ribblemere said, in an Oh-if-I-must-declare voice, One spade.

Then Elizabeth said, No, in quite the wrong tone of voice. She discovered soon that if you said No, you must say it wearily, and as though you were bored and wanted to stop playing and go home.

Mrs. Ffolliot, who had seemed at first a gay little woman with laughing eyes, also said No, very crossly. Elizabeth's partner shrugged and proclaimed, One No Trump. Everyone said No to that, which made Mrs. Edmondston look more annoyed than ever. The game was played; that was easy. The worst came afterwards, when Mrs. Edmondston told Elizabeth that she had absolutely given the game away with that idiotic lead in the second round.

"I should have thought you must have *known* from my lead that I had the ace, queen, knave!" she snapped.

Elizabeth could only falter, I'm sorry. The worst thing of all, though, was when, at the end of the three rubbers, she found herself a winner. Mrs. Edmondston was pleased; their opponents were not.

"Never seen such cards!" Mrs. Ffolliot exclaimed peevishly. "Why, in that last hand I'd hardly one court card! Even then if you hadn't thrown away your king, Lady Ribblemere, we might have had a chance."

"You over called my hand in the previous round," Lady Ribblemere retorted with dignity. "But our opponents had all the luck. I always think it so strange how the luck favours one side. Really, a very poor game to-day. So unequal. Dear me, all those honours, Mrs. Edmondston? I do not recollect— Oh, no doubt you are right! Yes, a very poor game."

Yet all Elizabeth said to Stephen was, I didn't enjoy it very much.

That was the end of her career as a Bridge Player; thereafter she steadfastly refused all invitations; it was too alarming, and too unpleasant.

Stephen still occupied the bed in his dressing-room; a slight attack of influenza furnished Elizabeth with an excuse to keep him there. She began to dread the finish of his book; nothing would serve her as an excuse then. She did not know what she would do; she dared not think of that.

Nina was more often than ever at Queen's Halt, for she too was writing a book. Elizabeth felt that it was purely competitive, or perhaps just a reason to come and talk to Stephen. Nina stood on no ceremony; she never rang the front-door bell, but walked straight into the hall and shouted to Elizabeth, or to Stephen. After all, she thought, it was her house, not Nina's, and she had not asked her to treat it as her own.

Nina insisted on reading chapters to Stephen. Elizabeth listened in growing bewilderment, to the haze of words. To her they were meaningless, sometimes even Stephen could not understand them.

"Look here, what is this supposed to be?" he demanded once. "Burlesque, tragedy, or satire?"

"What do you think?" Nina asked.

"Good lord, I don't know! Cut out the talk and get down to facts. If only you wouldn't try and be so damned clever in every second sentence!"

"You don't like it?" Nina became defensive, ready to fight.

"Oh yes, parts of it! I can't stand that maundering Edwin-person, though. Mixture of Voltaire and Destoievsky."

"I believe I have been influenced by the Russian school."

"Judging by the morbidity I should say you have. Come off the roof, Nina, and leave the Russians alone, God help them!"

Then they would argue, banteringly, intimately, till Elizabeth could have screamed. Sometimes Nina grew heated over the argument, furious with Stephen for his imperturbable teasing. Then he would shake her, or pinch her nose, and call her a silly little ass, and tell her to shut up.

"What do you think of the blasted book?" he asked Elizabeth, when Nina had departed.

"I do wish you wouldn't use such language, Stephen. I daresay the book is all right, but I get very tired of hearing nothing but books, books, books all day long."

He was hurt by the acidity in her voice, and drew back.

"Sorry if I've bored you," he said.

"Oh, I don't object to hearing 'book' from you!" she said.

"Thanks very much," Stephen answered drily.

Her nerves were on edge; every little thing jarred upon her; she began to think herself neglected, miserable, and to long for congenial companionship. Stephen never was in time for meals; he ignored both gongs; she had always to go and fetch him.

"Stephen dear, I wish you'd try and be more punctual!" she would sigh. "Or say when you'd like to have dinner. It's not fair to the servants if you're always late. It upsets everything."

No one had ever expected him to be punctual; no one had worried him, or cared at what hour he dined.

"My dear girl, the servants are used to my ways. It never has upset them and I don't see why it should now."

"It keeps everything back," she complained. "It makes it very difficult for me, too."

"Well, I'm sorry, 'Lisbeth," he said. There was finality in his voice. Elizabeth remembered that Mrs. Ramsay had said it was she who would have to do the adapting.

"Yes, that's all very well," she said, "but I do think you might consider me sometimes."

He looked at her, then came and sat down beside her.

"What is it, darling? Why so cross?"

"I'm not cross."

He tried to draw her on to his knee, but she shrank from him, and slipped away. He rose quickly.

"Elizabeth!"

She was trembling; she did not want him to touch her, yet she could not face the difficulties and the terrible trouble that would come if she told him so.

"I—I've got a headache. Pm tired."

"But why did you flinch?"

"I didn't! I didn't!"

"You did. It's not the first time either. For God's sake, *tell* me, Elizabeth. What is it?"

No, she could not bear it. It was all so hard and so awful. The easiest thing was to smother your feelings, and to keep up the wretched pretence. She went to him.

"Oh, Stephen, how silly you are! I just feel out of sorts and otherwise-minded."

The anxious look in his eyes, the little worried frown, aroused her pity, and the mother in her. She tiptoed, to kiss him, and stroked his cheek.

"Don't be angry with me, Stephen dear."

His arms went round her.

"Oh, my darling! Angry with you!"

Cynthia came down for the week-end, with Christopher; she was polite and friendly towards Elizabeth, but there was antipathy between them. Christopher was adorable, and Elizabeth loved him. He was so fat and seraphic, and so determined. When you did something to amuse him he chuckled, and said, Again! He went on saying, Again, louder and louder, until you obeyed him. Cynthia sat in a big armchair, and Elizabeth played with Christopher at her feet.

"You ought to have one of your own," Cynthia said, quite gently.

Elizabeth pretended not to hear. How blunt Cynthia was!

But Stephen wanted it; Elizabeth knew that, and it frightened her. Once he spoke of it; she said, Not yet; I couldn't. She was too young, she was not in very good health: so she evaded him.

Neither was happy, neither could speak of their unhappiness to anyone. Stephen knew now that Elizabeth was fighting to keep him away from her; that hurt almost unbearably. There seemed to be pitfalls all about him; one wrong step, he felt, would land him in one of them. He clung to the hope that Elizabeth was suffering from the depressing after-effects of influenza. She would get over it in time, if he were inconsiderate now, and forced her to yield to him, something terrible might happen to their marriage. He was not a fool; he could feel that disaster was hovering about them. If he were gentle and kind, they might come safely through this stormy period. Elizabeth was so young and so fragile, so easily scared; he could only wait, he thought. She should not be forced into submission; she made it impossible for him to talk to her, reasonably, as he would have liked to have done.

As for Wendell, it was easy to see that he was attracted to Elizabeth. That Elizabeth had, or could ever have, a more tender feeling towards him than friendship was impossible. That conviction was deeply rooted. Stephen could see no danger in allowing Wendell to visit them, if Elizabeth wanted it. Of all men, he, with his too-soft eyes, and too-full lips, was the least likely to exercise fascination over Elizabeth. When she awoke to a full realisation of love it would be for her husband, never for Wendell. You could not think of Elizabeth and Wendell together: it was loathsome, yes, ludicrous too. It was not as though Elizabeth's code of morals was elastic; it was rigid and strict.

Wendell, Stephen felt, could never be a danger.

So when, in March, he invited himself to Queen's Halt for a long week-end, Stephen said,

"What do you feel about it, darling?"

"Oh—I don't really care!" she said. "Just as you like, Stephen."

"No, just as you like. If you think it'll be a nuisance we'll put him off."

"I don't think we ought to do that—I'd rather like to see him again. He's fun."

"Righto, 'Lisbeth," he said.

Chapter Eighteen

Wendell arrived on Friday, in a new car. He said that he had had her all out last week and she touched seventy. Not bad for a little bus like that, was it? He brought Elizabeth an enormous box of chocolates, and some hothouse roses. She took them as graceful gifts to the hostess, and thanked him very much. Then he said, By Jove, topping place this, what? and admired the what-you-may-call it in the hall.

"Oh, the warming-pan!" Elizabeth said.

"Yes. Jolly picturesque and quaint, an' all that. Hullo! Nice little spaniel, that. Envy you this place, Ramsay, 'pon my word I do. 'Spose you're a great gardener, Betty, what?"

"No, I'm very stupid about it," Elizabeth said. "The gardener says I pick the wrong flowers. Are you fond of the country?"

"Oh, rather! Country in winter—jolly nice, you know. Hunting, an' all that. Had a very good day a month ago with the Quorn. Pal o' mine belongs. D'you hunt?"

"I don't ride at all. Stephen does, only he doesn't care for hunting."

Wendell stared at Stephen.

"What, not really?"

"I'm a conscientious objector," Stephen said.

"Oh—fox gets a damn fine run for its money," Wendell said vaguely. "Even chances, don't you know?"

"I wasn't really thinking about the fox, but about the mere human."

Wendell was nonplussed. Queer chap, Ramsay.

"Human? Don't quite get you."

"I like to discourage the primeval instinct," Stephen said.

"Oh—er—quite, quite!" Wendell answered, totally at sea. "You writing chaps always have funny notions. I say, Betty, I brought my golf clubs. You promised to take me round, remember?"

"I think you'd better go with Stephen," she smiled. "My golf is very little better than my billiards."

"Then it's jolly good," he said stoutly. "Stephen's got to write his book."

Next morning she did take him round the golf-course, to prepare him, he said, for his round with Stephen in the afternoon. They did not play very seriously, but they talked a lot.

Wendell, striding along beside Elizabeth, said,

"Not looking awfully fit, are you, Bets? Tired, I mean, and a bit thin."

She thought how kind it was of him, and how sympathetic, to ask her.

"I had 'flu in January, and I haven't really got over it yet."

"Should think it's pretty dull for you, buried down here, with Stephen writing all day," he remarked.

"Sometimes it is," she sighed. "I was brought up in town you see. It's rather a change."

"Yes, rather. Rotten for you. Any decent people living here?"

"Oh—well, one or two. They're quite nice, but not very great friends of mine."

Wendell nodded, just as though he quite understood. He didn't ask her to be more explicit; that was so refreshing.

"You ought to get Stephen to take a flat in town," he said. "Be near your friends, and all that."

"I don't think he would," she said lightly. "He's so fond of the Halt. He was brought up here, just as I was brought up in town."

"Very bad luck," he nodded. "What d'you do with yourself all day?"

That was just it. She didn't do anything—at least, nothing specific. If only there was something that she could do it would be different. Easier, not so dull and boring.

"Oh, I—exercise the dogs, and do the shopping—some of it—and people call—and that sort of thing."

"Sounds pretty deadly," he remarked. "What I mean is, no variety. Any cheery people about?"

"Not very. There's the Church-set—they go to Mothers' Meetings and Infant Welfare Societies. It's not very exciting. Then there's the Bridge-set—they're rather mixed up together, those two. I can't play bridge. And there's the literary set. We're that," she added, rather bitterly.

"Can't stand literary shop. I say, that's a bad brick, but you know what I mean! I'm not clever enough, what? Don't know what to say when people start talking 'bout 'technique,' an' form, an' 'influence of the Russian school.' You know the sort of stuff."

"Yes, I know." She did know. You could not live a day Stephen and Cynthia and Nina and the Tyrells without knowing.

"Daresay it's awfully interesting if you're in the trade yourself. It's all Greek to me. I know when I like a book, but I can't tell you what the style's like, or what the publisher's name is. Don't see that it matters, personally. Can't say that I often remember the blinking author's name."

"I don't see that it matters either," Elizabeth sighed. "But the first thing Ste—any writer asks about a book is, Who published it?"

"Awful strain of the what-you-may-call-it. Intellect. Good word, that. Expect you'll start writing yourself soon. Force of example, what?"

"Goodness, no! I can't even write a decent letter, and my taste in literature is bad."

"Lord! Is it? Daren't speak about mine to Stephen. I like a good yarn—exciting, an' not too long. Can't stand these—what d'you call it?—psy—psychological novels, whatever that may be. Lot of rot, I call it."

"Introspection," said Elizabeth. "I know. I like Dickens and Mrs. Humphry Ward, and—books like theirs. Not too deep. I tried to read Meredith a little while ago."

"Never heard of him."

"He's dreadful," Elizabeth said. "I couldn't make head or tail of him. And Hardy—well, I don't approve of the sort of book he writes."

"Ah, quite!" Wendell answered profoundly.

"And Bernard Shaw, and Chesterton and Galsworthy —I just can't get on with them."

"Shouldn't try."

"Oh, I've given it up! I'm too old to be re-educated. I don't really appreciate Stephen's books. Not in the proper way."

"I tackled one of 'em the other day. Bit beyond me. Awfully clever, of course, an' that sort of thing."

"Yes, he's very clever," Elizabeth agreed.

"Always feel a bit of a fool when Stephen's about," he confided. "Jolly nice chap, though."

"I think I do too," she said, half to herself.

"Oh, I say, what priceless rot. I bet you've got a lot tucked away under that topping hair of yours, Betty."

She blushed. She was flattered, but she felt vaguely that she ought not to allow Wendell to say these things.

Married women ought not to flirt with their husband's friends.

"No good pretending you're a fool," Wendell continued. "Frightfully wise look in your eye, don't you know? Mysterious, an' all that sort of thing."

That was interesting, and a surprise to her. She looked up at him.

"Mysterious? Whatever do you mean?"

By Jove, she was a pretty kid! Fascinating. That innocent little face. Inviting mouth too, and pretty teeth. Lovely dimples when she smiled. Too jolly attractive by far.

"Oh, what I once heard a poet-johnny call 'unfathomable.' Lot behind."

She walked on faster; the dimples peeped out.

"How silly! You're not to say such things. You'll make me vain."

"You vain? Rot, Betty, rot! Imposs. Ab-solutely. Lucky chap, Stephen."

"Why do you insist on calling me Betty?" she asked. "No one's ever done such a thing before."

"That's why. Suits you, too. I like nicknames, you know. Cosier. More pally. See what I mean?"

"No, I don't think I do," she said primly.

Stephen went out with Wendell all the afternoon, and in the evening Nina came to dine. Elizabeth was worried about the trifle. There wasn't enough wine in it, and she was afraid it would not go round. That distracted her attention; she was not at ease until dinner was over, and then she began to worry about the coffee, hoping that it would not be muddy as it was last night.

"Nina," Stephen said, when they were gathered about the drawing-room fire. "What's this I hear about young Hemingway?"

"Shut up!" said Nina. "Nothing at all."

"Keep your hair on!" he advised her. "No need to give yourself away."

She laughed, and flushed. Elizabeth suggested that they should "do something."

After some discussion they played vingt-et-un and poker, because Wendell suggested it. Elizabeth lost, but she enjoyed the game because no one took it very seriously. It didn't matter if you could not remember poker-rules, especially as Stephen and Wendell argued about it, and seemed to have quite different rules. It was a complicated game, Elizabeth thought, but it didn't matter much if everyone had a different conception of its laws.

Wendell said it was a pity there wasn't a gramophone. Nina answered quickly that she wouldn't have come if there had been, and Elizabeth agreed with Wendell that they could have got up an impromptu dance if they had had a gramophone.

"'Lisbeth, would you really like one?" Stephen asked eagerly.

"Not if you hate them."

"That's just my pose. Snobbery, I think. We'll go up to town next week and get one. Why didn't you demand one before?"

"Mechanical music," said Nina, laughing. "I shall go on being snobbish. I once listened to a pianola. I did really, Stephen."

"I had one in my rooms at college," Wendell said. "You can get a lot of fun out of a pianola. Just as good as a piano, and not half the fag."

"Oh, no, they're dreadful!" Elizabeth said suddenly. "So horribly churned out."

"Hurray!" Nina cried. "Down with pianolas and barrel-organs. Elizabeth, have you ever heard Musetta's song on a barrel-organ? It fascinated me. Like a dog against its will. I stood on the curb-stone and shivered all down my spine. Yes, and gave the man sixpence to play it again. Nobody understood my feelings except Aunt Charmian, and she said, Like looking at snakes."

"Just what mater would say," Stephen remarked. "Do you know my mother, Wendell?"

"No, haven't had the pleasure of meeting her yet."

"When you do," Stephen said, "she'll probably say, 'Ah, I once had a chauffeur whose name was Charles.' So don't say I didn't warn you."

"A chauffeur?" Wendell repeated, in mystification.

"Or a parrot, or a pet duck. Anything that's thoroughly uncomplimentary," Nina explained. "She always does it. When I was born she begged mother not to call me Nina as she'd once had a cat of that name and it died."

"Oh, I see!" Wendell said, and laughed, trying to sound as though he really did see and was amused.

He didn't like Nina; Elizabeth could see that. When Nina had gone, he said,

"Pretty girl, what? Always get the wind up with those clever women. Never know what they're driving at. More in Stephen's line than mine, so I let him do all the talking."

That touched Elizabeth on the raw. Nina was "in Stephen's line"—how well she knew that! Nina and Stephen understood one another; they had the same interests, and they thought the same things funny. They talked nonsense to each other, and neither thought that it was nonsense. Or if they did, they considered that it was amusing to be silly and inconsequent. Elizabeth didn't think it amusing at all. It got on her nerves; it was a strain to have to follow their line of thought. Not only that. It was usually impossible.

Stephen's book was finished at last, and had gone to his typist. The publishers were impatient to see it; there was no doubt that they would accept it. Already they had begun to advertise.

"That's off my chest!" Stephen said. "They wanted to publish in the spring; I insist on June or later. Just before the summer holidays. Next there'll be my typist's idiocy to correct, and then—oh, ghastly job—proofs! And, Elizabeth—" he caught her in his arms. "I want my wife!"

She hoped he would not notice the hard beating of her heart. Why was he so insistent? Couldn't he understand that she wanted to be left alone?

He was coaxing, petting her.

"Darling, it's had a dull brute of a husband for months, but I'm free now. And I won't sit up till four o'clock in the morning any more. Oh, and I'll try to be punctual to meals! So can we go and have another honeymoon, please?"

"I'd—rather—stay here," she faltered. "Or—London—I don't mind—but—one can only have—one honeymoon."

"Nonsense, babe! We can have as many as we like!" he said gaily. "One every year."

"I—I'd *prefer* to stay here," she said urgently. "I've —never seen—the Halt in the spring. And there are those eggs hatching out. Ducklings and chickens. I couldn't miss them. The garden, too. Primroses. If—if you want a holiday—I don't want to be a wet-blanket. *You* go away—if you want to."

His arms fell away from her.

"Good God, Elizabeth, you can't think I want a holiday from you? We haven't been married a year yet!"

"I didn't mean that! I only thought— Husbands *do* go away by themselves. I know they do. It's—it's good for them. I could have Auntie to stay with me, too. Oh, and Sarah!"

She could see the frown gathering in his eyes; she dreaded an outbreak of his temper.

"Your Aunt! Sarah! Where do I come in, I'd like to know? It seems to me that I don't come in at all!"

"Oh, you can't think that I—I didn't mean that a bit!"

With an effort he choked back his rising anger, and spoke levelly, holding Elizabeth's hands.

"I wish you'd tell me just what you do mean," he said. "I can't keep up with these half-sentences and—innuendoes. In my family we speak out. Can't you do the same, Elizabeth? Am I to understand that you want me to go away?"

It was what she had meant, but now that he put the wish into words she was frightened of it, and shrank away.

"Oh, *no!* How could you think that?"

He sighed faintly, looking at her.

"My dear, I don't know what to think. You hold me off with a pitch-fork."

"I—I don't! It's—it's your imagination!"

"It's not. Else why am I still excluded from your room? I don't like my dressing-room, Elizabeth."

She was silent. There was nothing she could say.

"You're not being fair to me," he said quietly. "I happen to be human, you see. You expect too much—or should I say too little?"

"It's you who expect too much of me!" she cried, goaded to it.

He stood very still. For a moment there was silence; Elizabeth dared not look up.

"Do I?" Stephen said slowly. "Oh!"

"You—you expect me to like living here—in the country, and you expect me to like your friends—and everything! And I don't! oh, I don't!" A sob rose in her throat.

"You don't? A minute ago you said you wanted to stay here. Who don't you like? Is it Nina?"

She was embarrassed, and sought to dissemble.

"I ought not to have said that. I didn't really mean it. Things—get on my nerves. Please don't pay any attention to it!"

Then his temper surged up, exasperated and hurt, and white-hot. He crushed her hands together; she saw the flame in his eyes and knew fear.

"God, can't you be honest with me?" The words bit. "Say what you think, and damn my feelings! How can I help to straighten things out if you lie, and lie all the time? Say that you loathe Nina! Say you loathe the Halt, and Me, and let's have it out! You may like groping about in a fog. I don't! I was taught to be straight forward, not to cheat and lie!"

"How dare you?" she gasped. "Oh, how dare you? I hate you! How *could* you say such a thing to me? How could you? Oh, I *hate* you!"

The grip on her wrists was torture.

"Yes, we've got it out now," he said grimly. "You hate me. Don't try and say you didn't mean it! I'd rather have it straight from the shoulder like that, than be fooled and cheated, and held at arm's length!"

She was sobered for an instant, appalled at the storm she had roused.

"Ah, I didn't mean that! I—I don't hate you, Stephen! You—oh, you know I don't!"

"I don't know it. I'm beginning to feel that I know nothing about you. You're wrapped round in a net-work of hypocritical evasions! You may think it's fair to me; I don't! D'you think I'm a fool to be deceived by your talk of 'influenza' and 'to-morrow'? You don't mean to live with me as my wife. You're hoping the desire'll die in me. You—little—fool, don't you *understand?*"

"Let go my hands! You think me a fool! Oh yes, I've known that for a long time!"

"If you can cheat yourself into imagining that I'll be content to live with you as we're living now you certainly are a fool. Good God, Elizabeth, I love you!"

"You don't! You'd never—treat me like this—!"

He laughed; it was an ugly sound, savage and mirthless.

"I've treated you as though you were made of porcelain. You know that. I've been a damned fool! And you thought I'd keep it up for ever! Heavens, don't you know what a man's like yet? What do you suppose I married you for? To look at? That's what I've been doing for the past months. Do you realise *that?* Do you think it's a natural state of affairs? Do you think it's fair to me, this—this platonic arrangement of yours? What do you take me for, Elizabeth? An iceberg, like yourself? I'm not. Got that? And I've had enough of this life we're leading! I thought if I were patient—hell, *patient!* —you'd come to me of your own free will." Again he laughed. "Instead of that you take advantage of my patience, and draw farther away from me! Oh yes, you can look outraged, and if you like you can think yourself an insulted saint! But you're not! You made a bargain with me when you married me, and now you refuse to fulfill your part of it. Yes, and I'm a brute to expect it of you, aren't I? I ought to be satisfied with your presence in my home, thankful that you let me kiss you! When you find that I want more than that from my Wife, you think me unreasonable! You sit on your pinnacle of false righteousness and never see that you're cheating me of what is my right!"

She had stopped struggling; she tried to cling to dignity, to stand straight and to face the flame of Stephen's eyes.

But she was trembling from head to foot, from stark terror, and a sense of violated decency.

"I—never—dreamed you would—s-say such things—to me!" How her teeth chattered! She tried to smother the Fear, but it was too great. Were all men such primitive monsters as this? "Let me go! You Ye—you Ye hurting me! How dare you—say such things to—me? I think you Ye horrible—horrible!"

"I daresay you do. You've heard the truth for once, and it shocks you. And you've shown me that it's folly— crass folly—to let a woman have her own way! The strong yielding to the weak!" Again she shrank from that ugly laugh. "I tell you, Elizabeth, it's women like you who make men into beasts! That's what you think me, isn't it? Isn't it?"

"Yes!" she cried. Dry sobs shook her. "Yes, yes, yes! You're hateful, cruel, unjust!"

"My God!" he said. "Yes, you think that. You can't see that it's you who are cruel and you who are unjust! So long as I'll submit like a weak nincompoop to your unnatural ruling I'm decent and nice. But when I refuse to give way to you any longer, then I'm cruel and unjust! Well, you can go on thinking that for as long as you're fool enough. But I'll be master. Do you understand that? We've tried your way, and it's no good. Now we'll try mine, my lady."

"You—can't mean—you can't, can't mean—you'd f-force me—?"

Instead of the Thorn

"Can't I?" There was savagery in his voice, and unleashed passion. "You shall yield or you shall be made to yield. I mean that!"

Then, before she could cry out, or struggle, he dragged her roughly into his arms, and kissed her as he had never kissed her before, fiercely and hard, in anger, full on her agonised mouth.

She was helpless; his arms were like steel, and as merciless; she felt that she was suffocating and that the remnants of her sanity were slipping from her. She tried to scream, and could not; fought madly, but could not break away one inch. Then she was released, suddenly, so that she staggered backwards, panting and in wildest alarm, catching at a chair-back for support.

Through a haze she saw Stephen stride to the door and go out. She sank quivering into the chair and crouched there, listening. She heard the front-door slam, and the excited barking of the dogs. The sound of hasty, nervous footsteps died away on the gravel path; the barking grew fainter, and stopped.

She did not know how long she cowered in the chair after Stephen had gone, or how long it was before the chaotic, racing thoughts grew calmer and more reasonable. The Fear was less now Stephen had gone, but when he came back it would return, more awful this time, impossible to control. She had seen the real Stephen, the primitive Stephen, and the sight appalled her. There was no longer safety under his roof. He was merciless and powerful. He could force his will on her.

She lifted her shaking hands and looked with dilated eyes at her bruised wrists. That was Stephen. Brutal, ruthless. She had not known. All this time she had never so much as guessed at the presence of a Monster in Stephen. Were all men like that? Not gentle and admiring and kind as they showed themselves at first, but coarse and hard, like brutes. You could not fight; you were weak and helpless. A man could do what he liked with you; yes, with one hand tied behind him. Life was a nightmare, no longer a romance, a nightmare from which there was no escape.

Escape. . . . That checked her thoughts. Escape. She started up, looking at the clock. Her knees were trembling. Suppose he returned suddenly? Before

158

she had had time to go. To go. Right away. Alone. Leaving all this horror behind. Only she must be quick. What was it Stephen had said?—"You shall yield or you shall be made to yield. I mean that." If she had found it hard to bear him before when he was gentle, how much harder would it be now that he was angry and a stranger?

She straightened her hair. It would not do to let the servants see her panic. She must be calm. Not let them suspect.

Jenkins was polishing the brass-work on the car. How surprised he looked! but respectful, sympathetic. He was sorry madam had had bad news. Yes, if madam could be ready at once he thought he could drive her to Tonbridge in time to catch the four-ten to London. Only he'd have to put the car along a bit.

That didn't matter. If there were an accident and she were killed, so much the better. She went indoors, up to her room.

Rose was there dusting. Rose was sympathetic too, and helped her to pack a suit-case. Nana came; how she hated Nana!

"I did not hear the telephone bell ring, madam."

Nana suspected. Let her, then. She would be done with them all soon. Let them think what they liked.

It was strange that she could think so coolly when every nerve was stretched to breaking-point. Money. She'd drawn a cheque on Wednesday. That was all right. Her cheque-book. She'd have to have her account transferred to London. That didn't matter now. And the rest of her clothes. Something would have to be done. No good worrying about that now. Nana's impassive face. What was Nana to tell the master? Nothing. She would write a note. He'd understand.

She wrote in the library, at Stephen's desk, with the car waiting for her outside. How did one begin a letter like this? "Dear Stephen"—how silly that would be! Better to start straight away.

"I've gone. I couldn't stop. I've told the servants I'd had a telephone call from home. You needn't worry about me, I've got plenty of money. I'm sorry if it's been my fault. Elizabeth."

She put it in an envelope and sealed it. An apology for a letter. Stephen would have done it better, probably. Only she wasn't a novelist. It would have to stand as it was. There was no time to re-write it.

She went out to the car, and got in.

"I do 'ope it's nothing serious, ma'am!" Rose said.

Nothing serious! If only they knew! Well, they would know soon.

"No, I hope not. Ready, Jenkins."

"We shall be seeing you again in a few days, madam?" That was Nana. Never. Never again.

"Oh, yes, I expect so!" Lying. That was lying, real lying. Stephen could accuse her with justice now. Liar and cheat. Stephen, Mr. Hengist. Liar and cheat, liar and cheat.

Chapter Nineteen

There was a hotel off Baker Street, quite a small one. Someone had told her about it, and the name stuck in her mind. She told the taxi-driver to take her there. All the way up to town she had wondered where to go, or what to do. The first thought had been home. She had no home. She had left the Boltons for Queen's Halt. Now she had left that, and there was no home. She could not go back to the Boltons. She thought of her aunt's horror and distress, Lawrence's anger. They would not understand. They would try to make her go back to Stephen. They might even say that she had disgraced them. Well . . . She supposed she had, only how much were they to blame? She didn't want to see them. If she had been an innocent, pretending fool, it was their fault. They had taught her to pretend to be ignorant. They had reared her in a rose-mist, and given her, like that, into a man's power. Aunt Anne would never see that it was all her fault. She would talk meaningless platitudes. She could not see Aunt Anne yet. Not until she had become calm after this awful storm.

There was Mrs. Ramsay. She had said, If ever you want help, come to me. Yes, but you couldn't run away from a man to his mother. Mrs. Ramsay's sympathies would be with Stephen. You could not possibly go to her; soon she would hate you because you did not love her son.

That was a fact, and she faced it. She didn't love Stephen. She had never loved him. Therein had she cheated; that at least was true. She wasn't cheating now whatever she had done in the past. All those things Stephen had said. . . . True? perhaps they were. She had made an end of it though. She hadn't been able to pretend any longer. He had made that impossible. In a way, she supposed she had been forced into this, first honest action. She would have gone on pretending if Stephen had not torn down her barricades. It was Stephen who had brought matters to a climax, by his anger and his rebellious passion. She could not look back on that without a shudder. Pretence was over. She had done something dreadful in running away; had she been calmer or more sane she would never have done it: she would not, she thought, have had the courage. But since, in a moment of frightened madness, she had done it, she would never go back. Well, that was being honest. Only how maddening it all was! Stephen had said that honesty was a virtue. Mr. Hengist, too. Running away from your husband wasn't a virtue, though. It was wicked, and she, Elizabeth Arden, had done it.

She would try to go on being honest; that, in part, was why she wrote to Stephen on the day after her arrival in town.

He came to the hotel; she had expected that, and she had braced herself to meet him. She was afraid; she dreaded seeing him, dreaded the inevitable argument. Even now, had her fear of him been less, she would have given in and returned to Queen's Halt, because it was so awful to quarrel, and so much more natural to her to obey than to stand by her own resolves. Yet there was in her a curious streak of obstinacy. It showed itself sometimes in the details of life, and now it reared up its head to face this great disaster. In madness had she taken the biggest, most momentous step of her life; it would be easier to go on than to turn back; easier after the first struggle.

She was in her bedroom when Stephen came. The hall-porter fetched her, and immediately her pulses started to race again.

Stephen was very pale. She found him in the deserted lounge, standing with his back to the fire, tight-lipped, and with hard anxious eyes. There was no trace of the demon in his face, but Elizabeth felt, It is there, covered up. It is always there. I can never go back to him.

Neither spoke for a long minute. She was trembling; when Stephen stepped forward she shrank.

"I've come to take you home, Elizabeth."

She shook her head.

"I—c-can't."

There fell another silence. The ticking of the marble clock on the mantelpiece dinned in Elizabeth's ears.

"Where can we talk without being disturbed?" Stephen asked abruptly.

Her voice was unsteady; she tried to calm it, and herself.

"N-no one is likely to c-come in," she said. "The—the people who live here—go out to work—all day. There— there isn't anything—to say—really, Stephen! Please don't—please don't argue!"

"There's everything to say, Elizabeth. You know that."

"No, no. Please—oh, please leave me alone! I—I can't come back to you! I can't! I—you said I ch-cheated you, and—and I think—it's true." She took a deep breath. "I—never really—loved you. I—I'm sorry, Stephen." It was out. She had said it; she had been frank, but what an effort it had cost her!

"You did love me once. It was my abominable temper the other day that frightened you. I've come to apologise for that. If you will—come back to me—it shall be on your—own—terms."

"Oh, I can't, I can't! Please don't! Please don't!"

"You must come back. In time—you'll learn—to care, perhaps."

"No, no! You—you don't understand! I can't! I'd r-rather die!"

He winced.

"Elizabeth, we're not living in a neurotic novel! You can't leave me like this! It's unthinkable!"

"I—I have left you! I— can't live with you! I didn't know—I couldn't— I—I won't cheat you—any more— so I've—I've run away."

He tried to take her hand; she evaded him.

"I'd no right to say what I did, Elizabeth. I'll try to make you happy if only you'll trust me again! I'll—I'll try to be content with your companionship. Can't you forgive me?"

"No—please, no! Please let me go! It's not f-fair— you—you couldn't be con-content and—I—you couldn't make me happy. I—I'm not a companion to you. I— don't understand you. Nina does. She can—be your companion. I can't! I can't!"

"Nina! Good God, what is Nina compared with you?"

"I—I don't know. I didn't mean— Don't be angry! I can't bear it. It's—it's been a mistake. I can't go on— I can't go on!"

"You mean that the sight of me is hateful to you?"

It was. She could not forget his face when they had quarrelled. Cruelty and desire. Horrible. Horrible.

"Oh, I—no, no! It's only— Oh, I'm so tired of it all! I want to be left alone! I want to be—to be able to *think!* It was a mistake. Everything!"

"I'll never believe that. I've made you think so with my damned temper. Together we—could make it a success. Ah, Elizabeth, we could! Forget what I said, and let's start afresh! Elizabeth, you must! I can't possibly let you go like this! You don't understand!"

"Oh, don't, don't! Don't make me! Please don't make me!"

Words, arguments rained about her. She listened, quivering, to Stephen's pleading, his reasoning, even his anger. At last, looking drearily up at him, she said,

"If—if you make me come back now—I think I shall die. Leave me—just for a *little* while!"

That was cheating. Gaining time—putting him off with false hopes. She would never go back, only she could not tell him so. He would find out in time.

Her words gave him pause. In silence he paced the room, thinking, thinking. He could see that Elizabeth was beside herself; he could see too that for the moment at least she was in deadly fear of him, fear and repulsion. All his thoughts were concentrated on the determination to save this marriage of theirs from the rocks. The look of weakening despair on Elizabeth's face cut him to the quick, but he realised that she was in earnest. He could not believe that she would always be so. He would not believe that. The other day he had driven her to desperate, incontinent flight by anger, and by precipitate action. He must be careful now; he would do nothing to drive her further from him. In anger he had uttered threats which he would never have carried out. It was not in his nature to coerce the thing he loved most. He would never have done so, only she did not know that and he could not convince her. In her present mood she was capable of any madness; he would not drive her to it. He clung to the hope that time would soften her, and make her wiser. Just now it would be cruel to force her against her will. Cruel and perhaps disastrous. She would come back to him if he insisted; he knew that. But the spiritual part of her would go farther and farther away. That might never come back. How easily could he ruin everything now!

She was frightened, watching him with great, apprehensive eyes. Pity for her helplessness and her fear took possession of him. After all, she was hardly more than a child. She must be comforted, re-assured.

He went to her, and sat down beside her, taking her hand. The hardness had gone from his face, and when he spoke his voice was quiet, free from that disturbing passion.

"All right, Elizabeth. Don't look so scared. Listen to me, dear."

Her hand lay passive in his; her eyes did not waver from his face.

"If you are set on it you shall stay away from me for a time, as you suggest. I'm not going to force you into anything. I might do it, and we might settle down—quite comfortably. But we shouldn't ever be happy. Not as I want to be happy. So I'll let you go. Oh, not for ever, Elizabeth! I couldn't do that, and you mustn't ask me to. You don't hate me; I'm sure of that. It's only that you— haven't learned the meaning of Love. You won't learn it if I make you come back to me against your will. I see that. But I want you to remember, Elizabeth, that if I chose I could make you. Instead of that, I suggest that we—agree to separate for a time. I won't try to see you or worry you in any way during that time, but if you feel—that you don't mean, after all, what you've said today, I want you to send for me. I want you to promise that you will. If at the end of the time—you still feel the same—I suppose—we shall have to—make some sort of an—arrangement. Will you agree to that? If you won't, then I shall take you home with me to-day."

"Yes, oh yes!" she breathed thankfully. Then she realised the sacrifice Stephen was willing to make for her sake, and the hope he cherished. Some unknown impulse made her say quickly, "Stephen—I shan't change! It's— it's not fair to you—this arrangement. Let—let me go now—altogether!"

"I can't. You wouldn't be able to understand if I explained. Just believe that I can't."

She was holding fast to her courage. Again she managed to speak frankly.

"I—don't want to—lead you on—under false pretences! I've—I've done enough of that! You'll—hope—all the time—and it'll be—no good!"

"I'm willing to risk that. I'm going into this with my eyes open. Only, Elizabeth, I want you to think it over all the time, sanely. Don't let—other people—influence you. If you're happy without me—I'll—I'll set you free. But if you're not, if you're lonely, or miserable, then send for me. Promise me that!"

She had tried to make him see how she felt; she had tried to be honest. She could do no more.

"Yes, Stephen. I—I promise."

His hand tightened on hers.

"You see, 'Lisbeth, we—we can't end like this. I— That's not possible. But this is the only way—that I can see—to give our happiness a chance. And we must do that, Elizabeth. We _must_. I can't believe that this is the end of our life together. I know it isn't. It's—an interlude. We'll look back on it some day, and smile, and wonder what was the matter with us. I suppose most married people go through a period of—dissension, only with us it's more acute, more dangerous. So whatever we do, Elizabeth, don't let us plunge in the dark. You don't know your own mind yet. A year from now it'll be different. You'll know—at least, I think so—one way or the other."

She looked curiously up at him.

"You're—willing to wait—all that time?"

"Yes, if eventually—we come together again. It won't take so long as that. I—I *hope* it won't. I don't know— I may be talking nonsense, but I feel that we've got—just a chance."

"You—you may change," she reminded him nervously. "You may find that—that you don't love me—after all."

He smiled, crookedly.

"No, I shan't do that. I do love you. That can't change."

"I'm—I'm not a companion to you. A thousand things that I do—or don't do—irritate you."

"But still I love you. It makes all the difference, 'Lisbeth. If you really love, those little irritations don't matter—except momentarily. You get above them. They do matter to you—because—you don't—love me. And because I know that you don't—love anyone else—I feel there's hope. There's no other man. You just haven't learned to love. That's all."

"I don't think—I shall ever learn," she said wistfully. "I—I wasn't meant to be married."

"You were, 'Lisbeth. Only you haven't grown up yet. I'm beginning to see that. A year will make a difference in you. And, 'Lisbeth, promise me this!—If ever you need me, or want my help, you won't let pride stand in the way? Send for me. I shan't come if you don't, you see."

She hesitated.

"It's not much to ask, 'Lisbeth," he said, rather sadly.

"No, oh no! I—I will promise. Th-thank you. I— suppose I've—treated you—very badly. I'm—sorry. It —it hasn't been all my fault, Stephen."

"I know that. A lot of it's been my fault, and a lot— your upbringing. You haven't had a fair start. Well, you shall have it now, 'Lisbeth. By yourself. And—I think—we'd better discuss things from the business point of view now." He paused, fighting the longing to take her in his arms. "Do you propose to stay here, or will you take a little flat somewhere?"

"I think—I shall stay here. I—I like it. I couldn't afford a flat."

"You can afford what you like, Elizabeth. You don't imagine I am going to let you provide for yourself? Your allowance will be paid into whatever branch you name."

"Oh, please no! I—I couldn't, Stephen!"

"You must," he said. "You're still my wife."

"I shan't touch it!" she said vehemently. "I couldn't! You can't make me do that!"

He shrugged, but she saw his mouth set obstinately.

"It will be paid in. Give me credit for some pride too, Elizabeth."

Again she gave way.

"Very well. But—I shan't touch it."

"But it'll be there. Surely I'm not as hateful to you as that?"

"No—but—I couldn't!"

There was a pause.

"Shall your things be sent to you here?" Stephen asked.

"Yes, p-please. I—I think I shall go away—for a time. To the sea, perhaps. By myself."

His eyelids flickered.

"Take Sarah," he said. "You're such a—babe."

"I—I'd rather go alone. I shan't come to any harm. I—I don't want to see anyone—for a bit."

He was frowning. He looked down at her.

"May I give you the address of some rooms? I know the landlady. I'd feel happier about you, 'Lisbeth."

"Oh—if you like! Thank you."

He drew out his pocket-book and wrote an address.

"At Torquay," he said, giving the slip of paper into her hand. "I think you'll like it." He rose, and she saw that his face was almost haggard. "I think—that's all. Except—Goodbye."

She rose also.

"And—and thank you. I do—appreciate—what you're doing for me. I'm—I'm sorry for—everything. I suppose—my people—know?"

"No. I rang up to ask if you were there—but I was careful not to—let them suspect. ... You see, I thought then that—well, never mind."

"I shall have to tell them," she said. Then she put out her hand. "Goodbye, Stephen."

He took her hand and kissed it for a long moment.

"No, 'Lisbeth. Only— *au revoir*."

Chapter Twenty

Elizabeth left London almost immediately for Torquay. Mentally she was bruised. All these months of strain had preyed on her nerves, so that now her whole system cried out for peace and rest. She left most of her baggage at Baker Street, and with one small trunk journeyed west.

Before she left she wrote to her aunt and to her father, a joint letter. She was amazed at her own curtness when she read the letter over; it seemed as though all the softness and affection had gone out of her. Baldly, reticently she told her family what had happened. She would say nothing that was disloyal to Stephen; it was just "a mistake," and they had agreed to part "at any rate for a time." She begged that neither Lawrence nor Miss Arden would follow her to Torquay; she wanted to be alone, but when she returned to London she would come to see them.

She thought, How strange that I should write like this to my people! Only a year ago I could not have done it. I thought that I adored them. Was I pretending then, or have I changed?

Their answers reached her at Torquay. A wail ran through Miss Arden's six-paged letter, a wail against the brutality and selfishness of men, a wail for her niece's unhappiness. Without hearing the facts she ranged herself on Elizabeth's side. Men were beasts; men cared only for themselves; men were everything that was loathsome. Elizabeth must come home, and "forget all about it." Elizabeth must surely want her aunt at such a time. She at least understood and sympathised.

Elizabeth read it through slowly, dispassionately. Yes, Aunt was being kind, but it was too late. She was left far behind; she belonged to the past, that other world. She didn't understand. The letter went on to the fire, not in anger or impatience, but in sadness.

Lawrence began, My dear little girl. That jarred. Lawrence took her parting from Stephen as a personal insult to himself. He was astonished, grieved; he was sure he did not know what his little girl was thinking about. He had approved Stephen as a husband for her; she must return to Stephen at once. Really, he thought she had taken leave of her senses.

That letter followed Miss Arden's into the fire. They couldn't understand; they didn't even see how much they were to blame.

Torquay soothed her. She, who had never been by herself before, now gloried in her freedom. Stephen wrote briefly that he was going abroad for a time, but that letters addressed to his agent would find him. Elizabeth felt that she could breathe more freely now that there was no fear of meeting her husband.

Her landlady was sometimes rather trying. She would come up to Elizabeth's sitting-room on some pretext or other, and would stand there by the door, her hands under her apron, indulging in reminiscence. Mostly it was, Fancy now! To think of Mr. Stephen—I should say Ramsay—being grown up and married, as you might say.

Elizabeth smiled always, and answered,

"It must seem strange."

"Well, it do, ma'am, an' that's a fact. Why, it seems only yesterday they was 'ere—'im and 'is ma, an' Miss Cynthia. Lor', an' she's married too! Well, reely, I find it 'ard to believe, ma'am."

"She has a son—a dear little chap," Elizabeth said.

"Has she reely, ma'am? Well, I do declare! An' how's Mrs. Ramsay, if I may ask?"

"Very well, I believe. I—I haven't seen her for some little time."

"Ah, well, she were what I call a real lady. Not one of your C3 ladies. I remember she were always losing something, an' the nurse an' Master Stephen—I should say Mr. Ramsay—was always runnin' round after her. Well, I must say she did make me laugh." Then Mrs Benson would draw a deep breath and start off again.

"And now Mr. Stephen—I should say Mr. Ramsay—has got a wife of his own! I read 'is book what came out a year ago. If I may pass the remark I should say that it was a very pretty tale, I'm shore. When I think of 'im sitting in this very room with 'is ma—well, he couldn't 'ave bin moreen twelve—lookin' after 'er, quite the man, as I says to Mrs. Ramsay—well, reely, it does make you think, don't it?"

Elizabeth agreed that it did.

"I took quite a fancy to 'im, I must say. Well, 'e 'ad such a way with him an' all. I'm the man o' the fam'ly, 'e says to me. I got to look after me mother and Cynthia. Well, I thought, if that isn't touching! An' so 'es married. Will 'e be coming down 'ere at all, ma'am, if I may make so bold as to ask?"

"Er—no," Elizabeth said. "I—I've come—by myself, on a—rest-cure."

That always aroused Mrs. Benson's sympathy and interest. She told Elizabeth all about her own ailments, and how her pore 'usband used to suffer somethink cruel, 'e did, from 'is inside. A floating kidney, 'e 'ad, and she could assure Elizabeth it weren't no joke, because you couldn't ever tell where it 'ud get to next, as one might say.

Elizabeth usually terminated these gruesome recollections by going out for a walk. Nothing else would stop Mrs. Benson, once she had got into the swing of her narration.

She remained at Torquay for a month, leading a life of indolence and much thought. Then loneliness came to her, and she longed for companionship. *Whose* companionship she did not know. Not Miss Arden's, certainly, or her father's.

She went back to London, to the little south room that had been kept for her. You could hear the roar of the traffic in Baker Street from it, not aggressively, but as from a great distance. That in itself was company. If you craned out of the window and looked along the street you could see the gay red omnibuses pass the end of the road. But it was lonely in the hotel. Save for one old lady, who objected to all newcomers, she was by herself there all day. The other people snatched hasty breakfasts early in the morning, and did not appear again until dinner-time.

Miss Arden was upset that Elizabeth would not come back to live at home.

In that resolve Elizabeth was unshakeable. She could give no reasons, because they would have hurt Miss Arden; she could only repeat that she wanted to live alone.

Lawrence fumed and was aggrieved. It was impossible that his little girl should do such a thing. If she refused to return to her husband—really, he would never have believed that Elizabeth could be so selfish and unreasonable— she must live under the shelter of her father's roof. That was his last word.

It wasn't his last word by any means, but his arguments made no impression on Elizabeth. She listened wearily, and when he had finished, said,

"I'm sorry, father. I prefer to stay where I am."

"And pray what am I to say to Stephen?" Lawrence inquired. "Do you suppose he will approve of this—this independence? I never heard of such a thing. I'm most disappointed in you, Elizabeth. I can't get over your behaviour."

"I'm sorry. Stephen knows what I am doing. He quite approves."

"I don't know what the world's coming to!" Lawrence said. "I should have thought the least Stephen could do would have been to come and see me. Instead of that he writes me a letter, stating the facts in what I can only call a very curt way. The whole affair is most disgraceful and uncalled for. If you want my opinion, there it is."

She didn't want it. He was futile and tiresome. If only he would leave her alone! If only Miss Arden would not say, Oh, my dear, I'm not surprised! I *felt* it coming! Miss Arden wanted to hear the full story; she worried Elizabeth to tell her everything. In desperation Elizabeth said,

"It's between Stephen and me. I can't tell anyone. Please leave me alone!"

Then Miss Arden would look hurt, and shake her head.

"How you've *changed*, Elizabeth!" she would sigh.

Elizabeth's visits home grew less and less frequent. Often when Miss Arden came to her hotel she told the porter to say that she had gone out. Aunt Anne meant to be kind, but she made matters worse.

Then, one afternoon when she was darning stockings in her bedroom, Mr. Hengist's card was brought up to her. That drove the colour from her cheeks; she felt she could not face him, and yet that she must. She went down to the lounge and stood against the door, looking at him in unhappy defiance, at bay.

"Hullo, Elizabeth," he said, coming forward. "You're not looking very fit, my dear. I didn't come to see you before as I thought you'd want to be alone."

The defiance went out of her; gratefully she took his hand.

"It's so—nice of you to come," was all she could say. "Sit down—there's only one horrid old lady in at the moment, and she lives in the drawing-room. You'll stay to tea, won't you?"

"No, I want you to come out to tea with me," he said.

She sat down opposite him, on the other side of the fireplace.

"Thank you very much. I'm—I'm afraid I'm in disgrace, though." She smiled, rather pitifully.

"My dear child, your father's a nice old stick, but he's a fool."

She gasped.

"Good gracious, Mr. Hengist!"

"You know that as well as I do," he said. "Your aunt too. Well-meaning, which makes it worse. Where's Stephen?"

"I think—in Spain."

He nodded.

"Seen any of his relations?"

"Oh, no!" she shuddered. "I daren't! I couldn't!"

"Um! Well, you've made a fairly good mess of things, Elizabeth."

"Don't say, I told you so!" she begged. There was a catch in her voice.

"It's the last thing in the world I should say. What I want to know is, Are you any happier now that you've chucked Stephen and started out on your own?"

She looked down at her wedding-ring, and twisted it in silence for a moment.

"I think—I shall be."

"But you're not at present?"

"Oh ...! I'm glad to be free. If Father and Aunt Anne—wouldn't—wouldn't make things so hard—I should be very happy, I think."

He started to fill the inevitable pipe, but she saw the twinkle in his eye.

"All right. We'll see. Question is, what are you going to do?"

"Do?" She looked startled.

"Yes, do. Going to live an aimless life in a hotel?"

"Oh, no, of course not! I—I'm afraid I haven't thought about it much just yet."

"Well, I suggest that you do think about it. You'll soon get bored if you've no occupation."

He was unexpected and cheerful; she felt that he was her best friend. He was very outspoken, of course, but how kind!

"What can I do?" she asked. "I don't think I have any special qualifications."

"Not one," he agreed candidly.

"I can drive a car," she pointed out, rather piqued.

"I shouldn't, recommend a job as chauffeuse. Too tiring."

"I can tell you what I would rather like to do," she said suddenly, "I'd like to help in a creche. Children, you know."

"Not a bad idea," he said. "Two days a week stunt. Not at all bad."

"Of course, one doesn't get paid for that sort of work," she said.

He blew a cloud of smoke.

"Oh! Want money?"

"Well, yes. I—I shall want some."

"Haven't you an allowance?"

She flushed.

"I won't touch a penny of it!"

"Quite right," said Mr. Hengist. "Don't."

She looked up eagerly.

"Oh, you do see that I can't?"

"Certainly. If you let a man down you can't live on his money."

There was a long silence.

"Do you—think—that, Mr. Hengist?"

"What, that you've let Stephen down? Yes. What do you think?"

"I—you don't quite—understand."

"My dear child, don't start that parrot-cry. It means nothing. You married Stephen, you found marriage wasn't quite as jolly as you thought it was going to be, so you chucked it up. However, I didn't come to talk about that. It's nothing to do with me. You can settle your own differences."

"Mr. Hengist—I want you to realize that—whether I've behaved badly—or not—I'm not going back—to Stephen."

"All right, don't. I think you'll be throwing away an exceedingly nice husband, but that's your lookout. *Revenons à nos moutons.* What do you propose to do?"

Mr. Hengist was not taking her seriously; he talked as though she were still a child, not as though she were a woman who had taken a great step in life.

"I don't know," she said peevishly. "I shall have to think about it." Then an idea occurred to her, and she leaned forward. "Oh, Mr. Hengist, how much ought I to give the waitress here? And the chambermaid, and the porter?"

He was puzzled.

"Give them? Give them what?"

"Tips. I've—I've never done it, and it is so difficult to know. I—I think one does it regularly, only how much ought I to give?"

"I've no idea," he said brazenly. "That's one of the drawbacks of being on your own, isn't it?"

"I don't regret it," she said quickly. "Only—I'm thinking of going into rooms."

"Won't you be rather lonely?"

"Oh, no! I've—I've my friends, and anyway I hardly ever speak to the other people here. I should be much more comfortable in rooms. In fact, I've been looking at one or two, and I've almost decided to move into some further down the street. They're very clean and nice, and I liked the landlady. I should be awfully happy in a little place by myself."

"Would you?" Again Mr. Hengist's eyes twinkled. "Then I should move into them by all means. You might take in typewriting."

She was dubious.

"What sort of typewriting? I haven't got a machine, and they're awfully expensive to buy. Besides, I don't know how to type."

"Easily learn," he said. "As a matter of fact I've got a machine I don't want. I'll bring it along."

She looked rather suspicious.

"You've got a machine?"

"Yes," he lied cheerfully. "I bought it not long ago, and I've hardly used it. A Remington. You can have it."

"It's awfully kind of you," she said. "You'll—you'll let me pay for it—won't you?"

"No, I will not!" said Mr. Hengist loudly. "Upon my word, Elizabeth, things have come to a pretty pass if I can't give you a typewriter if I wish!"

She laughed.

"I didn't mean to hurt your feelings!" she said. "I don't believe you've got a typewriter at all. Have you?"

"Never you mind," he growled. "Any more nonsense about paying from you, and I wash my hands of you!"

"Oh, please!" she begged. "I won't mention the word again! Thank you very, very much!"

Mr. Hengist struck another match.

"You learn to typewrite decently—mind you use your brain, Elizabeth!—and then we I'll see about getting work. I know several people who might be willing to give you a trial. There's old Chilton, who writes articles for the *Cornhill*. If you can type literary stuff with intelligence hell recommend you fast enough. He knows a lot of literary people. It would be interesting work, too."

"Yes, I think I should like it," she said. "If I'm not too stupid to learn."

"No one's too stupid to learn," said Mr. Hengist. "Go and put your things on, child, and come along out to tea."

Chapter Twenty-One

The removal from the hotel to her new rooms was nervous work. First there was the ordeal of giving notice; then the worse ordeal of tipping the staff, and wondering whether she had given the page-boy enough. The taxi-driver was surly and would not carry her trunks up to her rooms. He and the landlady "had words" and a small crowd gathered round to share in the fun. Only Elizabeth did not think that it was fun; she longed for someone— Mr. Hengist, perhaps—to come and take charge of the situation. When you had a man with you these disturbances did not happen, or if they did you had nothing to do with them. There was no one to come to the rescue; Elizabeth had to bribe a loafer to carry her trunks upstairs. The landlady dogged his footsteps, warning him to wipe them muddy boots and not to knock the paint off the door, or else he'd hear about it.

Then when the transport had been effected and the improvised porter lavishly tipped, the landlady came up to Elizabeth's bedroom and asked brightly what she had ordered for her dinner, as nothing had come yet.

Elizabeth had forgotten to order anything. She said blankly,

"Oh—er—I am dining out to-night!"

"What about breakfast, ma'am?" inquired Mrs. Cotton.

"I—well, to tell the truth, I forgot about breakfast. I—I'll bring in some eggs."

"Well, as long as I *know*," Mrs. Cotton said. "Thompson, the greengrocer up the road, 'as very nice eggs. Very nice indeed they are. P'raps you'll be dealing with 'im, ma'am?"

"Yes, if—if he's reliable. I don't know the shops in this district. Can you advise me?"

"I'm sure I shall be very pleased to do anything I can to 'elp," Mrs. Cotton said obligingly. "There's Dimson, the butcher. I always 'ave said and I always shall say that barring accidents you couldn't do no better than to go to 'im. As to grocers, well, there you are! You've got Sainsbury's just around the corner, or the 'Ome Colonial, though I must say their new man what comes down this way is not at all what I'd call a gentleman. 'Owever, that's neither 'ere nor there, and I 'ope I knows 'ow to keep a man in 'is place. No, realy, I should say you couldn't do better than to try the 'Ome Colonial. And Mr. Williams, I'm sure 'e'd be only too glad to supply you with bread, an' flour an' that. 'E's a very obliging man, ma'am."

"All right," Elizabeth said. "Perhaps you'd ask him to call for orders?"

"Certainly," said Mrs. Cotton.

Elizabeth unpacked, and tried to make her sitting-room look more like home. The thought that she must dine out depressed her, but if there was no food in the house there was nothing else to be done. As she was getting ready to go, Mrs. Cotton appeared again, with a latch-key.

"The gentleman as used to 'ave these rooms was very pertickler about 'aving a key," she remarked, standing half in and half out of the doorway. "I just popped up to ask if you'd like to 'ave it now 'e's gorn. It saves me 'aving to come up them basement stairs every time you come in, and reely what with my 'eart and my rheumatics, well, there! You know what it is, ma'am!"

"Thank you; I should like to have a key," Elizabeth said, taking it. "Thanks very much."

"It's a great convenience," said Mrs. Cotton.

Elizabeth partook of a frugal meal at a tea-shop in the near vicinity. She bought an evening paper to read; she had never before known what a number of divorces there were. She read one case till her face grew hot as she pictured herself in the witness-box. After that she studied the racing news and the report of the debate in the Commons.

She spent the evening alternately staring into the fire and reading what seemed to be a very dull book.

"It will be better later," she thought. "When I'm more used to being by myself—and when I've got something to do."

Miss Arden came to see her next morning. She found Elizabeth composing a list of groceries.

"Oh, my darling!" she said, for no particular reason.

"Hullo, Auntie! Sit down," Elizabeth said. She had been feeling miserable and helpless, but she would not let Miss Arden see this. "I'm making a list. Such an awful job! I've no idea what quantities of everything I'll want!"

"If only you would come home!" Miss Arden sighed. "I can't bear to think of you all by yourself. It's not fitting. You're so young and inexperienced. When I think of that man—"

"Please don't let's talk about Stephen!" Elizabeth said. "I'm enjoying myself no end. How many pounds of sugar shall I order?"

"Two of each sort. Oh, my dear child, I don't know how you can be so cheerful! It's such a dreadful thing to happen! In our family, too! If your poor mother could but see—"

"Do you think I'll need any rice? I never eat it, but is it used for anything but puddings?"

"No. And if you had to live by yourself—but I cannot see why you want to—you might at least have come to South Kensington. Being here is nearly as bad as being out of town. 'Bus 30 is always full, and it means I have to take the Underground and then change. Really, Elizabeth, I don't understand you. I should have thought that you'd have wanted to be with us at such a time."

Elizabeth was silent.

"You've changed, Elizabeth. I said so to your father as soon as I saw you after your honeymoon. Only of course he couldn't see it. Men are so blind. So selfishly blind. They only care for themselves. Poor child, you've found that out."

"No," Elizabeth said. "No. Stephen—hasn't been— selfish. He—he was—anything but that."

"It's sweet of you to stand up for him, my dear, but I know what husbands are."

"That's rather clever of you, Aunt, considering that you've never had one," Elizabeth said smoothly. She was surprised at herself; it was the sort of thing Stephen might have said.

"It is not necessary to be married to know these things," Miss Arden said, with heightened colour. "And if Stephen was not selfish, I should like to know why you have left him."

"We won't discuss it," Elizabeth said. "Did I tell you that Mr. Hengist has found an amusement for me?"

The bait was successful; Miss Arden followed it into fresh waters.

"Oh, that man! I really don't know how I have been able to put up with him all these years. I daresay he means well, but his manners leave much to be desired and he is far too fond of interfering in what doesn't concern him."

"At all events," Elizabeth interrupted, "he's solved my difficulty."

"What difficulty? If you wanted advice or help, darling, I think you might have come to me. I know it is the fashion nowadays to go to anyone sooner than one's nearest and dearest, but I am not quite a fool, Elizabeth."

"I didn't want help. At least, I didn't know that I wanted it until Mr. Hengist came to see me."

"Oh, so he has been to see you? He said so little when I told him what had happened that I could hardly make out whether he was interested or bored."

"I expect he was bored," said Elizabeth audaciously. "Anyway, he suggested that as I must have occupation of some kind I should learn to type."

"If that isn't just like a man!" Miss Arden exclaimed; "Learn to type, indeed! Oh, yes, I know very well what that means! Stuffing indoors all day over a noisy typewriter! I hope to goodness you won't do anything so foolish."

It was so long since Elizabeth had been in the habit of obeying her aunt's orders and listening to her disapproving criticism, that she was irritated now and impatient. It was not thus that she had been criticised during the past year.

"I'm certainly going to learn. Then I'm going to take in work—literary work. It'll be great fun and I shall enjoy it." She expected strenuous opposition; she was surprised and interested to see Miss Arden collapse.

"Well, I think it's great nonsense, and most injudicious of Mr. Hengist to suggest it. I shall tell him so when next I see him. And pray, have you considered how you are to afford a typewriter?"

"Mr. Hengist is giving me one."

"Oh, indeed! He takes a great deal on himself, I must say. It's not even as though he were related to us. I should have thought you might have consulted your father or me."

"I don't think either of you would be much good," Elizabeth said. "You don't know people who'd want typing done, do you?"

"That's entirely beside the point, Elizabeth."

Elizabeth said nothing.

"Aren't you going out this morning?" Miss Arden asked. "A beautiful day like this! You mustn't mope about indoors. It's not good for you."

How dreadful it was to feel that you would like to wring your aunt's neck! You must be getting more depraved than you knew.

"Yes, I'm going out to do my shopping. If you'll wait while I put my hat on we might walk along together."

"I'll come and see your bedroom," Miss Arden said. "Oh, it leads out of this? That's convenient, at any rate."

While Elizabeth searched in her wardrobe for a hat, Miss Arden inspected the dressing-table.

"Dear me, Elizabeth, where did you get this lovely powder-bowl?"

There was a pause.

"Stephen gave it to me," Elizabeth said shortly.

"Oh!" Miss Arden put it down as though it were red-hot. "Is that a photograph of Mrs. Ramsay? I wonder that you have that on your mantelpiece."

"I'm very fond of her."

"Are you, my dear? You know, I never really cared for her. We always thought she was rather extraordinary. If only one could look ahead! That terrible sister too! What is she doing now?"

"I've no idea. I've not met Cynthia for some time. I see she brought out another book of poems the other day."

Miss Arden said, "Oh!" very coldly, and inspected a pile of books.

"Those are going in the other room," Elizabeth said. "I'm having some shelves put up."

"Ah, the old favourites!" Miss Arden said, opening a copy of "Little Dorrit."

"I see you have some new ones. Who is Rose Macauley, my dear? I don't think I have read any of her books."

"She's clever. Beyond me."

"And what is this? Shelley! I'm afraid his poems would not appeal to me."

"I love them," Elizabeth said. "Just the sound of them. Cynthia sent me that on my birthday. I'd never read Shelley before. Are you ready, Aunt?"

They went out, and on the stairs met Mrs. Cotton who was on her way up to ask Elizabeth whether she wanted the spinach cooked for lunch or dinner. Also, could "the gal" get into Elizabeth's sitting-room to sweep yet?

"I don't know how you can stand that woman," Miss Arden said as soon as the front-door closed behind them. "I don't think you'll like living by yourself for long, Elizabeth. It's a miserable sort of existence."

"We shall see," Elizabeth answered lightly.

Mr. Hengist came round with the Remington that evening, and stayed for an hour, helping Elizabeth to move some of the .furniture. He showed her how to work the typewriter, and, very thoughtfully, brought a sheaf of paper with him, which he left with her. After he had departed, Elizabeth sat down to master her new toy until nearly eleven o'clock. A decided bang on the floor above made her remember the time, and she put the machine away, hoping that she had not kept the top-floor lodger awake for very long.

She soon learned to type creditably, and to show Mr. Hengist how she had progressed she typed him a letter.

Another week, she thought, would see a marked improvement both in speed and correctness.

Mrs. Cotton came up to her room every morning after breakfast to hear Elizabeth's menu for the day. Elizabeth discovered that her culinary powers were limited. Mrs. Cotton had two stock dishes which she suggested to Elizabeth every day. One was, "a nice dish of tripe with onions to suit," and the other a treacle tart. Elizabeth did not think that the two synchronised.

On one of these visitations Mrs. Cotton ventured to inquire into Elizabeth's history.

"Mrs. Pearson, what lives in the 'ouse next door, she says to me yesterday,

'Well, Mrs. Cotton,' she says, 'so I see you've got a new visitor.' 'Yes, Mrs. Pearson,' I says, 'I 'ave. A Mrs. Ramsay,' I says. 'Well,' she says, 'she do look young to be married an' all. And is 'er 'usband alive?' she says. Well, I answers her pretty sharp, ma'am. 'I'm not one to be prying into what don't concern me,' I says. She looked very silly at that, ma'am."

"Oh?" said Elizabeth. "I think perhaps I'll order cutlets for to-night."

"Cutlets?" Mrs. Cotton said dubiously. "Of course, it's just as you like, ma'am, but if you'd asked me I'd 'ave suggested a nice piece of steak with mash. You see, you don't 'appen to care for tripe an' onions, do you?"

"No, thank you," Elizabeth said hurriedly. "I think I'll stick to cutlets."

"Well, if that's what you *fancy*, ma'am . . . And what would you like to follow? I was thinking a treacle tart 'ud go well after the steak."

"Cutlets," Elizabeth corrected. "With tomatoes."

"Yes, ma'am. An' some mash."

"Can you do Scotch woodcock?" Elizabeth asked. "I think I'll have a savoury instead of pudding."

Mrs. Cotton looked vacant.

"Oh, yes, I can *do* it," she said. "Only the kitchener's difficult when it comes to them little knick-knacks."

"I see," Elizabeth said. "What about Welsh Rare-bit?"

Mrs. Cotton brightened.

"Yes, that 'ud be just the thing, ma'am. It was on the tip of my tongue to suggest it, as you might say. Cutlets and a nice bit of Welsh Rarebit to follow." She lingered in the doorway, and Elizabeth wondered what she wanted. "My 'usband 'e used to be very partial to Welsh Rarebit, 'e did. But then there's no knowing what fancies a man'll take to, is there, ma'am?"

"No," said Elizabeth.

"You'll pardon the liberty, ma'am, but you looking so young an' all, an' Mrs. Pearson passing the remark like she did, I do 'ope as 'ow you 'aven't lorst your 'usband. Not seeing 'im an' you not mentioning 'is name— Well, there it is. I'm not one for poking an' prying into what don't concern me, but I've 'ad a bit of trouble myself, what with my pore 'usband 'aving a stroke in the Strand, and 'im being carried straight away to the 'rspital—well, what I mean is, I know what it is to 'ave trouble one way and another." She paused for breath. Elizabeth dipped her pen in the ink.

"My husband is quite well, thank you. He is in Spain —on business."

Mrs. Cotton seemed to be much relieved at this piece of intelligence. She prepared to depart.

"Ah, well, I daresay as 'ow we shall be seeing 'im before very long then," she said optimistically.

Elizabeth wanted to throw something at her, something very hard and sharp.

"How criminal I'm getting!" she thought. "First I want to kill Aunt Anne, and now Mrs. Cotton. Either I've changed—or I was always like it, only more controlled. I wanted to kill Father the other day, too. I think I'd better go for a walk." Then she thought how like Aunt Anne that was, and smiled. "Funny. It's only just lately that I've begun to notice those—idiosyncrasies in her. I'm getting critical. Critical and bad-tempered." She paused, staring out of the window. "Over-critical. About my people. They're nice. Really nice. It's just the little, outside things that make me want to kill them. Not seeing things as I see them. Annoying. Awfully annoying. Well ... if I criticise them like that—Aunt Anne especially, because I love her—did I—was I over-critical of Stephen's friends and—and him? Did I let the outward things get on my nerves? . . . But it wasn't only that. It was the other thing. Fear. Repulsion. Because I didn't love him. Only as a friend. Other girls can't feel as I felt about that physical side. There wouldn't be any marriages if they did. So if I'd loved him it would have been all right. I didn't love him. I didn't know what love was. I still don't know. Perhaps I was too young. I was too young. I didn't know anything about men, or about marriage. I didn't even know what my own feelings were. I was—oh, I was just a child! How could I know? And no one could see it. Aunt Anne, Father—Stephen himself. Yes, Mr. Hengist knew. Mr. Hengist knew everything. He tried to warn me that day when I was so angry. He was the only one. Nobody else thought, or cared, or prepared me in the least. Couldn't Aunt Anne see that I wasn't fit to be married? Couldn't she have told me what it meant?

... No. Of course she couldn't. She didn't know. You can't know if you've no experience. But you might guess a little. Enough to see that it isn't fair to let a girl as innocent as I was be married. It's worse than unfair; it's cruel and wicked. Girls ought to be told. Just as soon as possible. So that you can get used to it—the idea of it—and know what you've got to face. It isn't surprising that things went wrong. My honeymoon ... I don't know how I bore that. I must have been dazed. Numb. Then when I came home the numbness wore off. It was as if I'd had an awful blow and the bruise took some time before it showed itself. It was my nerves, I think. In pieces. All the little silly things that made me cross. The Tyrells. Stephen being late for meals. Idiotic things. That was nerves. Then the row. That finished it. It was just as well that happened. It made me realise. If I'd gone on much longer something worse might have happened. It was awful, but it put an end to it. Put an end to everything. Spoiled Stephen's life. Mine was spoiled before that. Spoiled before I'd begun to live. I've nothing now. Only a typewriter. And I might have had—oh, I might have had so much!" Her gaze fell from the roof-tops opposite. Tears came, and rolled unheeded down her cheeks.

Chapter Twenty-Two

The weeks dragged by, it seemed to Elizabeth, inch by inch. By June with the aid of Mr. Hengist she had obtained a small clientele for whom she typed. That was interesting sometimes, sometimes instructive, and occasionally dull. One man sent her magazine stories, very illegibly written. Elizabeth was amused by the series that came from his pen. They were called "The Adventures of Colin Cardew," and there seemed to be no reason why they should ever come to an end. Elizabeth followed Colin into Chinatown, where he escaped death by two inches, or into a gang of gentlemen-crooks where he escaped death by one inch, and watched with a cynical eye his efforts to win the heart of a perverse lady who rejoiced in the name of Griselda Gordon. Colin became a part of Elizabeth's life. She told her family or Mr. Hengist that Colin has got himself into another mess. I really don't see how he can escape this time. But of course he will." Miss Arden thought it all very silly, and said so. Mr. Hengist said, "Thank God she's learning to be silly!" which Miss Arden thought sillier than ever.

Another man sent Elizabeth articles on abstruse subjects. He wrote very neatly, which was just as well, for he filled his pages with archaeological names. Elizabeth was appalled at first, but she grew accustomed to it.

Stephen's book was published in June. Elizabeth bought a copy, and went every week to a Free Library to look for reviews. Although she did not love Stephen she could still be interested in his work.

It was in July that she met Wendell. She was walking on Regent Street when his car came up behind her, and stopped.

"Betty! I say, old girl! Betty!"

She turned swiftly, flushed, and stood still.

"Oh—hullo, Charles," she said nervously.

Wendell opened the door of the car for her to enter.

"By Jove, what a splash of luck, what? Get in, Bets; I haven't seen you for ages. Where are you living now?"

So he knew? She wondered how, and whether everyone knew.

"I—I haven't time, Charles. I—I've got some shopping to do."

"Rot!" he said. "No, come on, Betty, you must!"

She got into the car. It slid forward, up the street.

"My dear old thing, I'm simply delighted to see you!" Wendell said. "Awfully sorry to hear that you and Stephen have separated, an' all that sort of thing. Where are you living?"

"Just off Baker Street. How did you hear about— about Stephen and me?"

"Well, really, I don't know," he said. "How does one hear these things? Rumour, what? Soon gets about, you know."

She did not know. She thought it horrible.

"I see," she said. "What have you been doing since I last saw you?"

"Oh, the usual sort of things. Just got back from a month's fishing. Topping good sport. Look here, Betty, I'm damned glad to see you again! What about a dinner to-night and a show?"

"Oh, I couldn't possibly—thank you very much!"

"Why not? Going out already?"

"No, but—"

"Well, that's settled then. Mustn't go into retirement, Betty. Not at all good for you."

"I'm not," she said. "Only I don't really feel much like—"

"Oh, I say, Betty, do come! Be a sport! Why won't you?"

"It's awfully nice of you, Charles, but—"

"Do!" he coaxed, laying one hand on hers. "I haven't seen you for such ages!"

She wanted to go. She liked Wendell, and, after all, what harm was there in it?

"Very well, I will. Thanks very much."

"I'll call for you at seven then," he said promptly. "What's the address?"

She told him. How nice it was to think she was going to dinner and a theatre again!

She enjoyed the evening; Wendell made her laugh, and the dinner was exceedingly good. He took her home in a taxi afterwards, and parted from her on her doorstep, saying that he'd be round to see her to-morrow. He wasn't going to lose sight of her again.

He came in time for tea, and found her typewriting. Mrs. Cotton conducted him to Elizabeth's sitting-room, because it was "the gal's" afternoon out.

"Oh, Lord, what are you doing?" he exclaimed, throwing his hat on to a chair. "Betty, fancy you grinding over a blasted typewriter! What's the joke?"

"No joke at all," she said, giving him her hand. "I love it. Sit down, won't you? I must just finish this off. Can we have tea soon, please, Mrs. Cotton?"

"Certainly, ma'am," Mrs. Cotton said graciously. "The kettle's just on the bile, as one might say."

"Priceless old bean," Wendell remarked as soon as Mrs. Cotton had departed. "Hope you weren't awfully tired after last night, Betty?"

"No, not a bit. I loved every moment of it."

"Oh, splendid! Well do it again, what? Am I going to have tea with you?"

"Not if you talk to me while I'm busy," she smiled, typing harder than ever.

"Can't help it," he said. "However d'you manage to do that so fast? I love to see your sweet little fingers dodging about the keyboard like that."

She looked up gravely, reproof in her eyes. He was not abashed.

"Well, I do, Bets," he said.

Elizabeth typed on until grampus-breathing without heralded the approach of Mrs. Cotton. She came in with the tea-tray and proceeded to lay the table:

"I cut some extry bread an' butter," she informed Elizabeth. "If you want anything else just ring the bell an' I'll pop up."

"Thanks," Elizabeth said. "I don't think we shall want anything."

"Well, you never know," Mrs. Cotton said philosophically, and went out.

"You couldn't be dull with her about the place," Wendell said.

"One can have too much of a good thing," Elizabeth answered. "She's told me about every illness she's ever had, and all her relations' illnesses."

"Jolly gruesome. Is Stephen down at Queen's Halt, or is it true that he's buzzed off abroad?"

"He's in Spain. At least, I think so."

"Romantic, what? When did you leave him? Long ago?"

"March." Elizabeth wished that he would not talk about it. "Sugar?"

"Three lumps, please. Well, I'd never have thought it of you, Betty. Very fine effort, what?"

She was silent; it had not struck her in that light.

"Tell you what we must do," Wendell said. "Run down to Roehampton and see some polo. Ever seen any?"

"Yes, several times. At Hurlingham. I'd like that, Charles. Only you mustn't spoil me."

"Couldn't." Then he started to tell her about his newest car, and how he had taken the little 'bus down to Brooklands last week to see what she could do. He did not go until past six, and it did not seem as though he would have gone then if Elizabeth had not promised to go for a motor-drive with him on Sunday.

Sarah and her old friends she had shunned. They looked at her with curious eyes, and were inquisitive. Wendell was different. You couldn't possibly be offended by him. And after these long weeks of loneliness, what bliss it was to meet someone again who liked you, and didn't disapprove of your conduct. There was another thing: it was pleasant to enjoy a man's company again. There were things men did for you, like helping you into your coat, and holding doors for you to pass through, that your own sex did not do. When you were with a man, too, he looked after everything; it was his job. All you had to do was to sit still and let him wait on you.

So she allowed Wendell to come to see her, and she allowed herself to go out with him. Stephen had introduced him to her; he was Stephen's friend, and hers. His high spirits refreshed her. Sometimes they impelled him to say things that he should not have said, but she told herself that was merely his natural effervescence. He took her snubs well; she thought him easy to manage.

She found herself leaning on him for support and advice. She was not made to stand alone. Little disturbances worried her out of all proportions; it was misery to be by herself, bliss to know that there was a cheerful friend at hand to turn to. There was Mr. Hengist, but his business occupied most of his time. Elizabeth wanted a man who was always free, and always ready to help.

Wendell put up her bookshelves and hung her pictures; he went out to buy cake when she found there was none for tea; he was like an elder brother, full of fun, only more admiring. She liked his admiration, she was pleased when he brought her chocolates or flowers. She thought the friendship purely platonic, as it had always been. Her marriage protected her. When you were married you could entertain men; she believed that firmly. Moreover she had been told so many times that she was a prude. She would not be prudish now.

They motored out to Burford Bridge, and Elizabeth cried how lovely the trees were against the blue of the sky. Wendell said, "Yes, rather. See that new Crossley over there? By Jove, she was a fine car!" Elizabeth was impatient; she felt that nice as he was Wendell had no appreciation of beauty. He laughed at her, and tried to admire as she admired. Sometimes he said things to her which she did not quite understand; then he would laugh again, and change the subject. Or he would make some remark that had the effect of making her draw back. He would say, I love those stockings of yours, Betty. There was nothing in it, she thought. Only the way he said it made her shy. Occasionally he was not delicate in the choice of a subject for conversation; he said things that made her blush. Nothing, really. Only you felt that there was a meaning behind, something you did not want to understand. That was his modernity, she thought. Men were free in their talk to women nowadays.

Once he told her an anecdote, and at the end waited for her to laugh. She did not see the point; she shook her head and that made him laugh, in rather a silly way.

"Haven't you seen it, Betty? Good Lord, and you're a married woman!"

"No, I haven't seen it. What is it?" she asked, gravely dignified.

"Oh, my dear girl, I can't explain a joke of that kind!"

"I see. Then please don't try."

"You runny little prude!" he exclaimed. "Are you really Innocent Isobel from the country, or are you Pitting it on?"

She was deeply affronted.

"Don't talk to me like that, Charles. I don't know why you should find my 'innocence' so hard to understand."

"Don't you? By Jove, I should have thought the reason was pretty obvious."

She got up, pale, and with furious eyes.

"Really? Perhaps you'll tell me, then?"

"Well, hang it all, when a girl leaves her husband—"

"I think you'd better go, Charles."

He jumped up, and put his arm round her shoulders.

"Oh, don't be snorty, Bets! I was only pulling your leg. Sorry if you're cross about it. Kiss and be friends."

She freed herself from his embrace.

"I am cross. I'm—hurt that you could think I'd understand a nasty joke."

"I say, Betty, live and let live! I didn't mean anything, you know. Anyway, I'm awfully sorry. Please, teacher, I won't do it no more! Didn't know you were so innocent, that was all."

She forgave him, but she knew that he did not really believe in her innocence. He thought she was pretending. That side of him was the one she did not like.

When next they went to a theatre together he was more familiar with her than before, but careful to say nothing which might shock her. He brought her home in a taxi, and took her right up into her sitting-room.

That worried her; she felt that she ought not to allow it, but how difficult it was to know what to do! She was convinced of his good intentions; his attitude was one of sympathetic friendship. She thought, How kind it is of him to try to cheer me up like this! She had come to believe that she was dull and stupid; even she undervalued her beauty, and the fascination of her smile. That made Wendell's attentions more kind, more altruistic. To say, You may not come up to my room at this time in the evening, was to insult him. She could not do that. She had no reason to impute evil motives to him; it seemed impossible to part from him on the doorstep without wounding his feelings. He handed her out of the taxi, and said, Give me your latch-key, Betty. She gave it, and he opened the front-door for her to enter. They stood in the hall under a faded oleograph, and Wendell said lightly,

"I'll see you up the stairs. Who knows? There might be a bogy round the corner." He took her arm and led her upstairs. Within her sitting-room, she stood irresolute, hoping that he would say goodnight and go. Instead, he said coaxingly, "Can I stay for a few minutes and talk over the play? It's not late. Oh, I say, tea?"

She always made tea for herself before going to bed. The kettle was on the grate, the tray ready upon the table. She could not tell Wendell to go; it would be so rude and so ungracious.

"Just a few minutes then," she said. "Do smoke!"

He sat down and offered his cigarette-case to Elizabeth.

"Don't you ever?" he asked.

"No. Never."

"Why not? Don't you like it?"

"I've never tried," she confessed.

"Good Lord! You'd better start, old thing."

"I don't think I dare. Supposing I felt ill?"

"What rot! Do take one, Betty! It's so dull to smoke alone!"

She laughed, and feeling very daring, selected a gold-tipped cigarette. Wendell lit it for her, she tried not to feel distaste at smoking a cigarette his lips had touched, and puffed away valiantly. It was not very nice, she thought, and the smoke would get into her eyes, hut she persevered. Wendell laughed at her, and said that she looked too pricelessly funny for words. He stayed until close upon midnight, entertaining her with anecdotes and the more amusing of his war experiences. Time sped by unheeded, until the aggressive clock on the mantelpiece struck the quarter. Then Wendell jumped up, and said, By George, he'd no idea it was so late. Elizabeth followed him downstairs to bolt the front door. He lingered for a moment on the doorstep; she wondered why, and suddenly felt nervous. Then Wendell said, Well, cherio, old thing; and hurried away. Elizabeth thought, What a fool I am to be nervous of Charles.

When she entered her sitting-room again she found that Wendell had left his cigarette-case on the table. She determined to smoke again to-morrow.

Lawrence and Miss Arden came to tea next day, and when Lawrence kissed Elizabeth, he sighed, and shook his head. Miss Arden sat beside Elizabeth on the sofa, and held her hand. When she visited Elizabeth alone, she complained of Elizabeth's behaviour; when Lawrence was there she was staunch in her championship of Elizabeth's cause.

"My darling, you're looking so tired!" she said. "Quite pale and worn-out. I do wish you would come away with me next week."

Mrs. Cotton shaking the tea cloth on to the table, and solicitously patting down the corners, joined in the conversation. She could never resist it; on the days when Elizabeth entertained, the "gal" was not permitted to lay the tea.

"That's what I says, ma'am, begging your pardon. Well, reely, Mrs. Ramsay's such a worker, you'd hardly believe it. I'm shore it fair goes to my 'ea,rt sometimes to see 'er banging away at that typewriter! 'Well,' I says, 'ma'am, I do wish as how you'd go and lay down for a bit on your bed. There's nothing like a good lay down every afternoon, is there, ma'am?'"

"No," Miss Arden said frigidly. "What are you making, Elizabeth? Another jumper?"

"Rather a pretty colour, isn't it?" Elizabeth answered. "I like knitting. It's so restful."

Mrs. Cotton waited for a moment, fidgeting with the tray-cloth. Feeling, however, that there was no excuse for remaining any longer, she went out, shutting the door very slowly and softly behind her.

"A most objectionable woman!" Lawrence said. "Pushing herself into the conversation like that. And why will that class say 'lay' instead of 'lie'? Nothing irritates me more."

"It is rather awful, isn't it?" Elizabeth agreed. "Stephen would say, 'She must think you're oviparous.'"

The mention of Stephen was met with uncomfortable silence. Elizabeth flushed, and spoke again.

"I hope you'll have good weather for your fishing, father. Is it next week that you go?"

"Wednesday," Lawrence said. Gloom descended upon him. "Whether I shall enjoy it is another matter. I am almost sorry I allowed myself to be persuaded, into accepting the invitation. When I think of my little girl living apart from her husband, and alone in London."

"Oh, father, don't! It sounds like a third-rate novel! 'Alone in London' or the 'Trials of Truda.'"

"I am glad you can see something funny in the situation," Lawrence said huffily. "Personally I fail to appreciate the humour you appear to find in it."

"Now, Lawrence!" Miss Arden said warningly. "Elizabeth, won't you reconsider your decision and come with me to Cousin Flora's? She'd love to have you. You know she said so."

"Yes, I know. It's quite impossible though, and I've already written to refuse. It would mean giving up my work, and I don't want to do that."

"Oh, that work!" Miss Arden exclaimed. "You're ruining your health over it. How I wish that you would listen to older and wiser advice!"

"That is the last thing in the world the modern generation thinks of doing," Lawrence said sarcastically.

Elizabeth smiled, not pleasantly at all, but in a set, furious way.

"As far as I remember, father, Mr. Hengist is considerable older than you are. He advised me to take up some sort of work."

"Hengist, indeed!" Lawrence snorted.

A week later they had both left London; in an unholy frame of mind Elizabeth said, Thank goodness!

Chapter Twenty-Three

Wendell said,

"Can't shake hands, Betty, 'cos they're all over petrol. Can I wash?"

That was rather difficult, because there was no washbasin in the bathroom. Elizabeth explained.

"Well, but I must get the petrol off. Can't I do it in your room?"

She flushed. Then she thought, I suppose it's a reasonable request; anyway, why not? She opened the door into her bedroom, and Wendell went in.

"Lovely view," he remarked, nodding towards the window. "All mews and chimney-pots. Are you going to pour some water out for me with your own fair hands?"

She did so, and he picked up her soap.

"Topping scent. Now I know what makes you smell so heavenly. Betty, I love your sponge!"

She began to feel uncomfortable.

"Do you? Here's a towel."

"And your funny little toothbrush. Oh, thanks!" Drying his hands, he wandered to the window, and her dressing-table. "Lots of pots and things.

Just like you, Betty. All little and pretty. Have you got one of those priceless powder-puffs? You know—the beaver ones. Girl I know produced one at a dance the other night. Can I look?" He awaited no permission, but lifted the lid of her powder-bowl. She stood in the doorway, fidgeting.

"Do hurry up, Charles!"

He came to her, and put his arm round her waist, giving her a quick squeeze.

"Straight-laced little Puritan. One of these days I really will shock you. Didn't it like me to admire its powder-puff, then?"

"Don't be so idiotic!" she said, but tempered it with a laugh.

They went back into the sitting-room; Elizabeth was excited; it was so delightfully wicked to let Wendell flirt with her.

"Have you seen the show at the Vaudeville, Betty?" he asked. "There's an absolutely wonderful woman playing in the revue; knocks Delysia into a cocked hat. By Jove, she is hot stuff! Beautiful too. Shows just about as much of herself as she can, without overstepping the limit."

"How horrible!" Elizabeth said.

He was not at all abashed, but roared with laughter, and would have pinched her arm if she had not quickly withdrawn it.

"No good my asking you to come and see it then, I suppose?"

"No," she said.

He ought not to say these things to her. She could not imagine why he did it.

On their way out of London on Sunday they drove through Hyde Park. Elizabeth, to her surprise, saw Nina and Mrs. Trelawney. They saw her, she knew, but they looked away quickly and became interested in a nearby tree. Elizabeth blushed hotly, and was silent for a long while. For the first time in her life someone had cut her.

Sarah, who met Elizabeth and Wendell at Roehampton, was downright to the point of rudeness in her disapproval. She went to tea with Elizabeth, and asked,

"Who was that man you were with at Ranelagh yesterday?"

Elizabeth did not appreciate that tone from Sarah. Coldly she answered, "You've met him. Charles Wendell."

"Oh, that weed!" Sarah said scornfully. "What on earth do you see in him?"

Elizabeth's eyes began to flash.

"I like him. He is a friend of mine."

"Yes, so it seems. You ought to be jolly careful whom you go about with, placed as you are."

Criticism of her actions from an unmarried girl was something Elizabeth could not brook.

"Thank you, Sarah, I am quite capable of looking after myself."

"Looks like it," Sarah said. "Personally, I never had a weakness for brown-eyed fops. Furthermore, I don't like his round and vacant face."

"Indeed?" Elizabeth said sweetly. "But did I ask for your opinion?"

Sarah glanced at her critically.

"Um, yes. You're waking up a bit. A year ago you'd have been too soft to snub me. Seriously, however, be careful, Elizabeth."

"Have some more cake," Elizabeth said. "I know Charles rather better than you do."

That ended it. Sarah wanted to say much more, but she dared not in face of Elizabeth's changed attitude. All she said was,

"Funny what a queer streak of obstinacy you've got."

Elizabeth was kinder than ever to Wendell after that, just to show "people" how little she cared what they thought. Mrs. Trelawney's snub had enraged her, made her feel brazen and devil-may-care.

Wendell was delighted with this mood, and became more audacious. He dropped a kiss on her bare shoulder one evening, and was surprised that Elizabeth recoiled.

"Charles!"

"Fascinating little devil!" he retorted, fumbling in his case for a cigarette.

"You mustn't do that," she said. "I—I don't like it."

"Oh, sorry—sorry! Have a Turk?"

"No, thank you. I mean it, Charles."

He laughed; he didn't believe her; she saw that. She knew then that she ought to keep him at a greater distance, but the gay life they were leading, coming as it did after a long stretch of dull, eventless days, had excited her. There was risk, too, in playing with Charles, and that she could not resist. After all, he knew that she was married, and there wasn't really anything serious in their flirtations. Only she would have to be careful.

She had never been on terms such as these with a man. Before she met Stephen her flirtations were hardly worthy of the name; she had been too shy. The primeval instinct within her urged her along this dangerous path. It was fun, and there was no harm in it; she believed fondly that it would be quite easy, always, to keep Charles at arm's length.

In Bond Street, standing outside a hat-shop and wishing that she could still afford to buy hats here, Elizabeth met Mrs. Ramsay.

A hand was laid on her arm; a voice said,

"Elizabeth, are you going to cut me? Please don't! I hate people to cut me."

Elizabeth turned, blushing, and could not meet Mrs. Ramsay's eyes. She could hear the constraint in Mrs. Ramsay's voice, and the forced lightness. She shook hands, stammering, and saw that Cynthia's car, with Cynthia at the wheel, was standing a few yards away from them.

"My dear, why haven't you been to see me all this time?" Mrs. Ramsay asked. "Don't you remember the bargain we made, when we were watching those adorable ducks?"

Elizabeth hesitated; she thought, You never asked me to come. Mrs. Ramsay seemed to read the thought.

"Oh, I know! I didn't write or come to see you. Horrid of me. I think I'm sorry. Will you come? Not if you don't want to, of course. I promised Stephen I wouldn't bother you."

"Th-thank you," Elizabeth said. "It's—very, very kind of you. I—I know that—and I think it's sweet of you—"

"But you won't come. Well, don't forget that I've asked you. If you do want help at any time or—or advice —don't forget that I'm there, waiting. Dear me, that sounds as though I should sit at home all day, listening for the bell to ring. What a dreadful occupation! Don't forget, Elizabeth. I'm—I'm not really—so terribly biassed. At least, I try not to be, and anyway we were friends, weren't we? What crowds of people! I can't possibly talk here. Goodbye, my dear."

She was gone in a moment, leaving Elizabeth softened, and unhappy. Mater was so awfully nice. Not many mothers would speak to their erring daughters-in-law as she had spoken. Of course she hated you; how could she help it? You couldn't blame her for that; Stephen was her son.

Cynthia let in the clutch with a jerk.

"Good Lord!" she said. Her tone was eloquent.

"Yes. Well, I know, darling, but what could I do?"

"I should have thought you'd have run a mile sooner than meet her."

"Oh, no, Cynny, not at my age and certainly not in this skirt. And if I—what's the word I want?—indulge (how clever of me!) indulge my private feelings I shan't make matters any better between them. And I want to do that, Cynny."

"He's well rid of her," Cynthia said.

"That's just what he isn't, darling. Or if he is, he'll never realise it, so what's the good of talking like that? He's miserable—and she's miserable too."

"Oh?" Cynthia looked at her for a fleeting moment.

"Yes, darling. And so pale and thin."

"I'm glad to hear it. She's spoiled Stephen's life."

"I won't believe it. She'll go back to him. She must go back to him."

"Like a romance. Not she. Far more likely to hop off with the Tertium Quid."

"Oh, no! Elizabeth would never do that. She isn't that sort a bit. Besides Thomas liked her."

"Quite conclusive," Cynthia said.

"Moreover, darling—what a gorgeous word!—Anthony thinks it'll come right in the end."

"Anthony's a fool, then."

"Not a bit, Cynny. Anyway, that doesn't matter a bit. The only thing that matters is that Stephen loves her."

"And she doesn't love Stephen. A hopeless situation."

Mrs. Ramsay sighed.

"I know. Dear me, how tiresome and awful it all is! I'm sorry for Elizabeth. I can't help being sorry for her. She was too young. She couldn't possibly know her own mind."

"Hasn't got one to know. No grit either. Having married Stephen she ought to have stuck it out."

"Yes, darling, but it wouldn't have improved matters. Not in the long run. She couldn't have made Stephen happy that way."

"Nor this."

"You don't know, Cynny. We none of us know yet. Since I've seen her I feel ever so much more hopeful. Because she is so palpably wretched."

"You think she's fallen in love with Stephen when he wasn't there to be fallen in love with?"

"How quaint! Of course I don't. Absence makes the heart grow fonder. Only more often than not it doesn't. I think she misses Stephen."

Cynthia lifted one gauntleted hand and struck the steering wheel with it, smartly.

"Well she may! I can't think of her without boiling over! That she couldn't see how dear Stephen is, and how absolutely white! He 'got on her nerves'! I could have cried when he told us that. Stephen! Got on her nerves! My God, she doesn't deserve to have him back again! Why couldn't the silly, silly fool fall in love with Nina? Why must he eat his heart on a selfish, empty-headed little nonentity like Elizabeth?"

"Darling, I wish you wouldn't. You'll run into something in a minute, and we shall be killed. So unpleasant. Nina and Stephen were never attracted to one another that way, though I must say I did think so at one time. Stephen marries a nonentity, and Nina becomes perfectly maudlin about a fond, foolish youth whose name I never can remember. Which reminds me that I do wish she'd get married and have done with it. She's positively wearisome in this love-lorn condition. Another thing, Cynny:—If Elizabeth returns to

Stephen, it'll be a very good thing that Nina'll have gone with her horrible soldier to India. Nina was partly the cause of the trouble. I'm perfectly sure of it."

"Probably," Cynthia said. "Elizabeth's silly enough for anything."

"For goodness' sake, mind this 'bus!" implored Mrs. Ramsay. "I can't possibly be killed to-day; I've got Colonel Farncombe coming to dinner."

Chapter Twenty-Four

At Ripley on Sunday, Elizabeth met John Cary. She was lunching with Wendell in a room crowded with holiday-makers when Caryll and two other men appeared in the doorway. She exclaimed when she saw him, and was carried back, mentally, to her wedding-day, on which occasion he had been such an efficient best-man.

He came now to her table, and shook hands.

"Er—how do you do? Very delightful to meet again like this. You're—er—staying in town, aren't you?"

"Yes. Oh, Mr. Wendell—Mr. Caryll!"

Caryll looked hard at Wendell, then bowed, and said, "How do you do?" in a voice that was quite expressionless. He turned again to Elizabeth.

"Beautiful place this, isn't it, Mrs. Ramsay? I suppose you motored down?"

"Mr. Wendell brought me," she nodded. "I mustn't keep you from your friends. Perhaps we shall meet again some time."

"I hope so," he said. Then he bowed again to Wendell, and walked away to where his friends were sitting. Elizabeth began to crumble her bread, eyes downcast. Wendell's voice made her look up.

"Cheery sort of bloke, what? Got a face like an unripe apple. Who is he?"

"One of Stephen's friends," she said unwillingly. The gaiety had gone out of her; Caryll had spoiled this day's enjoyment. She felt that he thought her contemptible, and was sorry when she met him again, outside the hotel when Wendell had gone to fetch his car.

Cary spoke of the lake, and asked Elizabeth whether she had seen it in spring, when the rhododendrons cast their reflection deep into the water.

Then abruptly, and not looking at her, he said,

"I met Stephen in Paris, Mrs. Ramsay."

"Yes?" she said, not very steadily.

He was silent for a moment, but turned to face her presently, and held out his hand.

"I'm infernally sorry that things have gone wrong between you. I hope they'll right themselves—eventually."

"Thank you," she said. She put her hand in his, and was surprised at the warmth of his clasp.

"I'm very fond of Stephen, you know. You mustn't be offended at my—shall we call it officiousness? Gave me a bit of a shock when I met him in Paris without you."

"Wasn't he well?" she asked, tugging at her gloves.

"He looked very ill. Bodily he was all right, I suppose."

Elizabeth said nothing.

"I can't help feeling responsible," Caryll went on, with a smile. "I steered you through the actual ceremony, you see. And, as I say, Stephen's a great friend of mine. You're not offended with me?"

"No," she said. "Of—course not."

He saw Wendell's car, coming towards them.

"The worst of this place is that it's so public," he said. "Trippers always spoil beauty when they come in hoards, don't they? I've seen half-a-dozen people I know already."

He was drawling slightly; Elizabeth wondered what lay behind his words. She would have liked to ask him, but she could not summon up sufficient courage. And Wendell was coming towards them.

He did not like Wendell; that was obvious. It was as though he disapproved of him, probably because Wendell was with her. Yet there was nothing wrong in going out with Wendell, she argued. It was all perfectly above board, besides which nowadays everyone had men friends and no one thought anything of it. . . . Above board . . . Well, was it? She hadn't tried to conceal anything; she didn't go with Wendell secretly, but she had not told her aunt or her father of her close friendship with him. She hadn't told Mr. Hengist either; she hadn't mentioned Wendell's name to him. Why, she did not know, for again and again she told herself, as now, that she was doing no wrong.

She wondered what Stephen would think, if he knew. But Stephen had introduced Wendell to her. He was broad-minded, too, and—after all, since her life with Stephen was at an end it didn't matter what he would think.

Only she wished that Wendell's car, with her in it, had not drawn up beside Cynthia's in a hold-up in Piccadilly that day last week. At the time she had felt ashamed to be with Wendell; Cynthia's cold bow had made her feel hot and wretched. Again she had argued herself out of that state of mind. What right had Cynthia to criticise her actions? Cynthia of course was prejudiced. Elizabeth was very glad Mrs. Ramsay had not been there also. You could not help being fond of her; it would be dreadful if she bowed as Cynthia had bowed, as to a chance acquaintance—no, not even as cordially as that.

Towards the end of August, when Miss Arden was still out of town, Elizabeth again fell a victim to influenza. She fought her illness for days, but at last succumbed, aching from head to foot, wanting only to sleep, never to wake again.

Mrs. Cotton thought she should write to Miss Arden. Lonely and unhappy though she was, Elizabeth would not do this. She did not want her aunt; she thought she wanted no one.

Wendell was away, Sarah, and Mr. Hengist. Only the doctor came to see Elizabeth, and Mrs. Cotton. She thought, Last time I had 'flu how good Stephen was to me. People sent me flowers too, and they rang up to enquire. It seems as though no one cares now. Mater sent great Madonna lilies . . . like my wedding bouquet . . . How heavy their scent was ... in the church.

It was funny how desperately ill influenza could make you feel. You only wanted to die; you could get no rest, and the hot August nights seemed interminable. Silly to have stayed in town all August. She had never done that before. Those holidays of her childhood! Cromer and St. Margaret's Bay, and Swanage where you met everyone you least wanted to meet. All that was long ago, ever so far away, lost in the past.

Mrs. Cotton was kind, but how she talked! She stayed for what seemed hours, at the foot of the bed, telling Elizabeth how she had once had a nephew what died of "'flu turned to double pneumonia." It was not very cheering, and it was horrible to be called "pore dear" by your landlady. Still more horrible was it to lie in bed all day long and all night, alone, too ill to read, and too ill to sleep. She longed for someone to come to see her, someone who would be kind and sympathetic, and bring her flowers to put on the table by the bed. Yet still she would not let Mrs. Cotton send for Miss Arden. Her aunt would say, I told you so, and she would insist on taking her away to the sea. Elizabeth did not want that, and pride refused to allow her to tell anyone that she was ill.

Convalescence came, and with it still deeper depression. Elizabeth crawled about the house, and later, round the streets. She thought then that being ill was perhaps better than convalescence. You were miserable, yes, but not so miserable as when you were up, and dressed, and trying to pursue your life's ordinary course.

She had to think of meals again; that was dreadful when the contemplation of food made you feel sick. And Mrs. Cotton suggested every morning that she should cook Elizabeth a nice dish of tripe and onions. In desperation Elizabeth would say, I'll have fish. Turbot. Boiled. When it was put before her she recoiled from it, and lunched off bread and butter, and, occasionally, an egg. Mrs. Cotton said, It do seem crool to waste all that beautiful turbot. In a peevish mood Elizabeth answered, It isn't beautiful; it's ugly. Mrs. Cotton shook her head and murmured, Ah, pore dear! If only you could get out more an' take the air!

It was just what Elizabeth could not do. She thought her legs were made of cotton-wool; they would not bear her many yards. Vaguely she felt that she ought to hire a carriage to drive her round the Park, but she had never done this, and she didn't know how one did it, or what it would cost, or what one tipped the coachman. It was all too difficult and too worrying. She let the matter slide, entirely apathetic. Instead of driving out she sat in an armchair by her window, and for the second time read Stephen's new book.

Even that wearied her. The book would lie open on her knee while she looked dreamily out of the window, listening to the muffled roar of traffic in the distance.

When she had made up her mind to live alone, five months ago, she had had no conception of the difficulties that would rise up to grin at her inexperience. She had imagined that it would be easy to regulate her life. Big obstacles there might be, she had thought; she knew now that there were none. It was the tiny details that harassed her so: small household matters which sounded so trivial when one mentioned them. When you were ignorant and nervous these obstacles became almost insurmountable. How could you know what groceries you would need when you had never done any housekeeping without assistance? How could you know about tips when someone else had always done the tipping, without consulting you?

Tips worried her more than anything. Everyone who did something for you seemed to require a tip. The "gal" required many; if they were not forthcoming she became slow in answering the bell, and lazy in sweeping Elizabeth's rooms.

The worst of it was, you couldn't ask advice about these things. They were too silly. People would laugh, and think you a fool, or they would say wisely, Ah, *now* you see how unfitted you are to live alone. Aunt Anne would say that; that was why Elizabeth was so anxious never to let Aunt Anne know how lost she felt, and how lonely.

When Wendell came again she was overjoyed. He seemed to be the only real friend she had, excepting Mr. Hengist, who was so old.

Wendell exclaimed at her wan looks and thin frame. He behaved as though it were his fault that she had been ill; he blamed himself for having been away all this time.

"You couldn't have done anything, Charles," she said, smiling.

"Oh, I don't know! Might have sent some flowers to cheer you on. Might have hotted up your landlady a bit, too. I say, Betty, you do look rotten! Tell you what! You must let me tool you round in the car. Do you good, what?"

She yearned to be out of town, if only for a few hours.

"Oh, I'd love to! How good you are to me, Charles!"

"I could be a lot better if you'd let me," he said.

"I'm sure you couldn't," she answered, in innocence.

He took her to the river, and punted her up it one hot afternoon. She lay blissfully upon many cushions, watching Wendell's brown, muscular arms at work with the long pole. He looked nice in flannels, she thought. It was wonderful that the creases in his trousers remained so straight and new. He wore a silk shirt, open at the neck, and where the tan left off, his skin gleamed very white.

He was tidy, always. In his place Stephen's hair would be ruffled and wild. Wendell's remained sleek and shining, brushed severely back from his forehead. His shoe-laces never came untied, either, and as he never thrust his hands into them, his coat-pockets retained their slim shape.

Wendell looked down at Elizabeth, drawing the pole clear of the water.

"Comfy?"

"Awfully," she murmured lazily.

"That's good. You're just the right figure for lying in a punt. Most women either look all leg, or—or like bolsters. You look top hole. So jolly graceful an' all that sort of thing."

She laughed, but secretly she was delighted at the compliment. The punt glided forward; Wendell spoke again, looking across the water to the farther bank.

"Heard from Ramsay lately, Betty?"

She was started out of drowsiness.

"No. Why?"

"What I mean is—is your separation permanent, or— or only temporary?"

"Permanent," she said.

"Yes—well, you'll be getting a divorce I s'pose?"

She had not thought of it; the word had an ugly sound.

"I really don't know. How lovely those swans are over there!"

He took the hint and said no more. But he had disturbed Elizabeth.

They were slipping almost imperceptibly into a greater intimacy. It seemed natural to Elizabeth that Wendell should visit her as often as he did; she hardly realised how much of his time was spent with her, and certainly had no suspicions that he was taking advantage of her loneliness and depressed spirits to insinuate himself further into her confidence.

Mr. Hengist, meeting Wendell in Elizabeth's room, afterwards said, Be careful, Elizabeth. I do not like that young man. Elizabeth was indignant on Wendell's behalf. Wendell was kind, and jolly; he was after all quite young.

For how much had his youth to account! Little things that he did or said Elizabeth excused on this score. But she could not excuse his behaviour when he called to take her out to dinner and found her still dressing in her bedroom. He knocked on the door and asked, Can I come in? Elizabeth answered, No; I am just coming.

"Oh, rot!" Wendell said, and opened the door.

Elizabeth was fully dressed, but the clothes she had shed were scattered about in disorder. She stood before the mirror, gazing in open-eyed astonishment at Wendell.

"Charles!"

"Betty, you are a little prude!" he said, laughing. His glance wandered round the room; he strolled forward. "Do buck up, you adorable little idiot! Where's your cloak?"

She was deeply affronted. Speechless she watched him finger the pots on her dressing-table.

"Betty, what topping scent you use! Hullo, is this rouge? Oh, sold again!"

"Please wait for me in the other room," she said stiffly.

He turned to look at her.

"Why— Good Lord, Betty, I should think we'd got far enough for me to come into your room without you turning up your nose about it!"

"What do you mean? Far enough? I don't understand you!"

He hesitated, then shrugged, and went to the door.

"Funny kid. All right, I'll go. Don't be haughty, Betty. After all . . ." Then he went out.

He was changing, she thought. Something in him made her nervous, and yet she liked him. She knew that, because when he came to see her she was conscious of elation and a certain breathlessness. She wondered, Is it possible that I can love this man? The suspicion frightened her; she put it from her at once. She thought, I must not see so much of him; perhaps it is wrong.

Only how difficult it was to put a check on their intimacy. It seemed to have grown out of hand; she had allowed it to go too far.

People were talking: Mr. Hengist, for instance. He put a wrong construction on her friendship with Wendell; it was horrible of him, but did others think as he thought? Elizabeth felt herself to be impotent, a straw in a whirlpool, swirled away against her will.

She tried, tactfully, to warn Wendell that they must be more discreet. He took her by the shoulders and said, "Damn the scandal-mongers! Are you giving me the chuck, Betty?"

All his kindnesses leaped to her mind.

"Oh, no!" she said, in distress. "How could you think that? Only ..."

"There aren't any 'onlys.' I'm—I'm—dashed fond of you, old thing."

She wanted to say, You are too fond of me, but she could not.

"We must be more careful," she murmured.

She was not looking at him, or she would have seen the light that sprang to his eyes and realised the interpretation he put on her words.

"I wish you'd make up your mind to get a divorce," he said under his breath. "Sometimes I don't understand you, Betty."

She did not understand herself; she smiled, wanly, and turned away.

Mrs. Cotton's manner was changing, too. She said aggrievedly,

"Of course, ma'am, I have to be careful. Well, what I mean is in my position, you've got to be. I must say, a nicer spoken gentlemen than Mr. Wendell I never met, but what with 'im cornin' 'ere so late an' all—well, what I say is, I've got my good name to think of, haven't I?"

Elizabeth was humiliated. Her cheeks burned when she realised to the full Mrs. Cotton's insinuation. That anyone should think her that kind of woman was a sickening shock. In agitation she told Wendell, haltingly, and begged him not to visit her so often.

He listened, frowning.

"You'll say I'm compromising you next!" he said, sneering.

"Oh, you don't mean to! I—I know that— Only people think such—awful things!"

"I like that! I compromise you! I don't see what right you've got to be injured at this stage, I must say."

She shrank from him.

"Why—what do you mean?"

He was angry, but he managed to laugh.

"Oh, I don't mean anything. Matter of fact—I didn't mean to let it go—as far as this. But you damn' well go to my head—and— Oh, Betty, you know I love you! I'm —I'm mad about you. Get a divorce—Ramsay'ud give it to you, wouldn't he? Or if he won't, come away with me! Betty, I— Oh, my God, I can't stand this sort of thing much longer! You don't know what it means to me to wait like this."

"Stop!" she whispered. "For heaven's sake, stop! You don't know what you're saying— You—I don't— I never thought—you felt like that!"

His cheeks were dark; she was frightened all at once, and clung to a chair-back, staring up at him.

"You must have known! Good Lord, you're not as innocent as all that, Betty! You never thought I was just being a 'friend'! A man wants more than friendship from a girl like you! You know it! What are you backing out of it for now? Because I asked you to come away with me? You surely didn't think— Betty, I'm asking you to marry me! I don't care a hang what people say! If you 'll get a divorce I'll wait. Only—if Ramsay refuses—"

"Charles, you must stop! You must stop! I couldn't possibly! I—I'm awfully fond of you—but I don't love you! I—I'm sorry if you ever thought I did, but—"

"If I ever thought it! Look here, Betty, it's no good pretending like this! Why did you encourage me to come here if you never meant anything more than friendship?"

She could not speak; her knees were trembling; it seemed as though he were stripping decencies away and imputing evil to her.

He took a quick step towards her.

"You were just playing with me, were you? Never meant anything? And then when I—couldn't hold myself in any longer you behave like a plaster-saint. That's rich, by God! That's really rich!"

"Don't, oh don't! You—you can't mean what you're saying! I—I thought you were just—being kind to me— because I was unhappy! I never dreamed—"

"Never dreamed I was in love with you! And you expect me to believe that?"

Her eyes sank. She had suspected; she had thought the suspicion ugly, fearful, and she had turned her back on it. She had pretended that Wendell's attentions were those of a friend only; she had wanted to believe that, so she had believed it.

He laughed shortly.

"It won't wash. You knew all right. Well, what's the matter now? Why have you suddenly turned cool? What have I done? Strikes me I've been pretty patient! You showed me clearly enough what you wanted."

"Oh, I didn't, I didn't!" she cried passionately. "How dare you say such a thing? How dare you?"

"You led me on! You know jolly well that you did! I don't know what your game was—I don't want to know! Pretty low-down, it seems. I suppose you just wanted an exciting flirtation? Well, you chose the wrong man to play that game with, I can tell you."

She was gripping the chair-back with all her might; there was not a vestige of colour in her face, but her eyes were flaming.

"You're—insulting me! You wouldn't—dare—if my husband was here!"

"Your husband! I like that! You'd better leave him out of the discussion. You chucked him, you encouraged me to dance attendance on you, and then you talk about insults! Yes, and you're the injured saint! You know well enough that this is your own fault. I'd never have 'insulted' you if you hadn't shown me that you wanted me to. Your talk of 'being more careful'! What did that mean, my lady?"

"You're horrible, horrible!" she panted. "That you should think *that* of me!"

"And what did you suppose I'd think? When a woman leaves her husband and allows another man to take her about and visit her every day, what is a man to think?"

"I asked you not to!" she flashed. "You know I did!"

"Yes, in a way that meant you'd be jolly disappointed if I obeyed you!"

So that was how he read her anxiety not to wound his feelings? She felt sick, disgusted.

"If I'd known what you were really like, I'd never have let you *speak* to me!" she said.

"All I can say is, if you imagined that I'd be content with a thus-far-and-no-further arrangement, you were a fool. You're one of those women who play with fire and then blame the fire when it burns them! You got what you asked for, and this outraged virtue air you're putting on is a bit out of place! Good Lord, what do you suppose people are thinking?"

She started.

"Thinking?" she echoed numbly.

"Yes, thinking. You've been everywhere with me for months. What did that damned Ruthven woman think when she saw you with me? What did Caryll think when he met us at Ripley? And old Johnson, at Ranelagh? They thought what I thought—what anyone'ud think! And you pretend to be perfectly innocent and blameless!"

Her body seemed on fire; she saw Wendell through a mist.

"What—do they—think?" she whispered.

"They think I'm your lover," he said brutally. "Everyone thinks so. What else are they to think? You can bet your life Ramsay thinks so too. If you're not jolly careful he'll divorce you. That'll upset your damned virtue a bit!"

"And you—" she tried to steady her voice— "And you—knowing this—deliberately—compromised me! Please—go!"

His eyes fell; colour crept into his face, and he laughed uneasily.

"I wanted you," he said. "I was mad for you. How was I to know you were so guileless? You're not a schoolgirl. You're a married woman—who's left her husband."

"Is that an excuse for you to insult me like this?"

"A woman in your position," he retorted, "who behaves as you've behaved—"

"Go away!" she cried, between quivering lips. "You've no right to speak to me like that! Stephen would kill you if he could hear! You only do it because you know I'm alone! You coward, you coward!"

"Stephen's far more likely to set detectives on to you," he said mockingly.

Up went her head.

"Do you suppose that my husband would believe these —vile tales?" she asked proudly.

"Oh no, of course not!" he sneered. "And you'd be able to deny that you'd been everywhere with me for months, wouldn't you? You'd be able to deny that I've been up in your room until past midnight too! You'd try and cheat him as you've cheated me. I hope you succeed, that's all."

"Don't say any more!" she gasped. "Go at once! If you don't, I'll ring till Mrs. Cotton comes! Go away, and never, never let me see you again!"

"Yes, that's it! You've had all the fun you want out of me, and now I'm to go. Well, I'm not going yet. Not until I wish to." With a sudden movement he twisted the chair from between them and then, before she could escape, caught her roughly in his arms and pressed his hot lips against her panting mouth.

His arms clamped hers to her sides; she could not struggle or cry out; she felt that she was suffocating, deadly nausea took possession of her, and her taut muscles relaxed until she lay limp in Wendell's violent embrace, almost fainting.

Footsteps sounded; someone knocked on the door.

"Are you there, ma'am?" called the "gal." "There's a letter for you, just come."

Chapter Twenty-Five

Wendell had gone. Elizabeth crouched in one corner of the sofa, sobbing drily, and twisting her crumpled handkerchief between her fingers. The thought dominant in her mind was that of all things she most needed a protector. She saw now, too late, to what risks she had exposed herself; badly she wanted Stephen, who was the only man in the world who was capable of understanding, and helping her. If Lawrence had been different, she thought, she could have turned to him, but Lawrence had never been really a father to her, and would now condemn her indiscretion in triumph. There was Mr. Hengist, but he was after all only a friend, and one of a previous generation. She knew no one but Stephen who would be of use now.

In wonderment she remembered how she had thought Stephen coarse and brutal. It seemed ludicrous, now that she had seen into Wendell's soul. Wendell had said, I thought what any man would have thought. But Wendell did not know Stephen. In his place Stephen would have had the insight to realise the limit of her affections; Stephen would surely not have misconstrued her words as Wendell had done.

She passed her handkerchief across her lips, still trembling. Her mouth was bruised from Wendell's kisses; there were marks on her shoulder where his fingers had dug into her flesh. That was Horror. Her eyes dilated as she dwelt upon that violent embrace; it was Horror such as she had never known; fear of Stephen's passion was as nothing beside it. She had felt sick with loathing; she was still sick, at heart.

Self-hatred and shame swept over her. She was not as bad as Wendell thought, but how bad only she knew. It was the old fault, borne in upon her this time with a force that wounded mortally. She had deceived herself as always. She had faced only that which was pleasant and easy. The ugly truth she had shunned, cheating herself into a belief that her friendship with Wendell was orthodox and blameless. He had rudely torn away her illusions, battered through pretence, cruelly and coarsely.

Mr. Hengist had warned her that one day her cheating would lead her into serious difficulties. He could not have foreseen anything so serious as this.

Instead of the Thorn

Lack of moral courage, inability to look truth in the face when it was unpleasant, had brought her to an unbelievable climax. People were talking about her, scandalously; they believed the worst thing possible of her who had always prided herself on her delicate purity.

She thought now, I am not good at all. I knew that Charles was in love with me. I pretended that I didn't know.

She had been wrong from the beginning, when she permitted Charles to visit her. She ought never to have done that. She had known that it was wrong even then, for she had been careful never to let her relations guess that Wendell was in town. She remembered her blushing discomfort when Mr. Hengist had discovered them together. If it had been right to entertain Wendell in her room she would have felt no discomfort.

He had said, You must have known. That was the truth. He had wanted to know what her game was. She had let him imagine that she wanted his love. Thinking it over carefully she realised that she had wanted it, or, at least, his admiration. She had liked to feel that he admired her so ardently, but she had wanted to keep him at arm's length, worshipping. That was unfair, cheating again.

Another man would not have denounced her as Wendell had done, but Wendell was right in much that he said. Only she hadn't realised what she was doing until he spread the facts before her eyes, and made her see.

In her overwrought condition she saw herself in her worst colours, and exaggerated her faults until it seemed to her that she had no virtue left, no honour or decency. In shame she thought, I almost believed that I loved Charles. If his love-making had been more gentle, if hot temper had not overmastered him, who knew but that she might have given way to his pleading, cheating herself into thinking that she loved him because she was lonely and helpless? In her innermost self she had speculated on her chance of happiness with such a man as Wendell. She must have been mad. If she had not been able to bear Stephen's love, how could she have borne the passion of a man sensual where Stephen was controlled, brutal and crude where Stephen was gentle? The instant Wendell's lips had touched hers she

212

knew that she hated him, and was afraid. She had known before, when he had said things calculated to offend her. She had known it when he invaded her bedroom, and laughed at her intimate possessions. Only she had not chosen to acknowledge the instinctive dislike.

All those jokes Wendell had made. . . . She hadn't understood them, but she had known that they were vulgar. He had thought her coarse enough to enjoy them from his lips because she had left her husband. Probably he put a false construction on that too.

That brought her back to Stephen. She saw now, in face of Wendell's turbulent ardour, that Stephen had been exceptional in his treatment of her. It seemed funny to think that she had been afraid of him on that awful day of their quarrel and parting. She had thought him a monster; compared with Wendell he had been a lamb.

And now people were coupling her name with that of Wendell: sniggering probably, exaggerating surely. They were saying, My dear, have you heard? Stephen Ramsay's wife has gone off with another man! Gloating over it . . . glad of an excuse to be scandalous. That was what Stephen would have to bear when he came home. Nudges, and whispering, and side-long glances cast in his direction. It wasn't only on herself she had brought shame, but on him too. And he'd been generous in letting her go. This was how she had repaid him.

Wendell had said, He's far more likely to set detectives on to you. Would he do that? She felt very cold. No, he was too chivalrous, too generous. He'd hear her explanation first. He'd believe her, too. She thought that he would believe her.

She became conscious of cigarette smoke lying heavy on the air. Wendell's Turkish cigarettes. She dragged herself up and went to the window, throwing it open to let out this reminder of his presence. Her head was aching, her cheeks still hot. She stood at the open window, letting the cool air sweep into the room.

The next day brought a long letter from Wendell, abjectly apologising for his "unpardonable behaviour," imploring her to forgive him and let things be as they were. He had not meant a word he had said; he was kicking himself for his caddishness; it was Betty's beauty and his love for her that had made him lose his head.

She wrote carefully in answer. Their friendship was at an end; it would be impossible to pick up the threads again. She realised that she had been at fault; she was sorry, but it would be better for them not to meet again.

He called, bringing flowers; Elizabeth sent them back. Again he wrote; she did not answer his letter. A last letter came telling her that she had broken his heart and that he was going to Scotland for the shooting.

Lawrence and Miss Arden were back in town, Lawrence with tanned cheeks and a country manner. Miss Arden wrung her hands over Elizabeth's poor health, and said again and again, Why *didn't* you send for me?

Miss Arden tried to discover Elizabeth's plans for the future; Elizabeth, whose mind was in a chaotic state, hardly knew herself.

"Darling," Miss Arden said, "you must see that this sort of an existence is impossible. I'm not suggesting for an instant that you return to that man, but you're far too young to live alone."

"I expect I shall go into a tiny flat," Elizabeth said vaguely. "I could quite well afford it now that I've got on so with my typing."

"My dear child," Miss Arden said flatly, "it's not to be thought of. Really, when you've got a home waiting for you, I can't understand this attitude of yours. Anyone would think you disliked your old home. I'm sure I don't know what has happened to you. You never used to be like this."

"I'm sorry," Elizabeth sighed. "I'm not going to live at home again. I can't."

"Can't? Nonsense! You don't want to!"

The old Elizabeth started to say, Oh, Auntie, it's pot that at all! The new Elizabeth intervened and with an effort said,

"No, I don't. Not now. Things have changed."

"Well, really, Elizabeth! They certainly have changed if those are your feelings. I'm sure I don't know what your poor father and I have done to deserve this coldness from you."

Elizabeth was silent; she was too tired to explain or to reassure.

"Am I to understand," Miss Arden continued, "that you propose to spend the rest of your life in this indefinite fashion?"

The rest of her life. ... It had a sinister ring. Elizabeth shivered.

"No. I've got till March to—to make up my mind."

Miss Arden raised her brows.

"Indeed? March? What do you mean?"

"Stephen said—I might have a year."

Miss Arden achieved a shudder at the mention of Stephen's name.

"It's the first I've heard of it! Do you mean to say that you are thinking of *returning* to that man?"

"Don't you want me to?" Elizabeth asked curiously.

"I? My darling, of course not! You've never seen fit to confide in me, but I know that he must have treated you abominably."

Somehow that jarred. Did Aunt Anne tell all her friends that Stephen had treated his wife abominably?

"I never said that, Aunt."

"Oh, my dear, give me credit for some intuition! I could see it in your face!"

"Then my face lied—like the rest of me!" Elizabeth said bitterly.

Miss Arden stared at her.

"Dear child, what is the matter with you?" she inquired anxiously.

"Stephen didn't treat me badly. If—if anyone is to blame it's myself. I can't go into all that now. If I don't—if I feel I can't—go back to him—I suppose we shall have to get a divorce."

Miss Arden had never dreamed of anything so dreadful.

"Elizabeth, what on earth are you thinking about? Divorce! Pray have a little consideration for your father's feelings and mine! You may not know it, but divorce is a very disgraceful thing."

"Oh, I know it," Elizabeth answered. "I've read case after case. What else can I do?"

"There is such a thing as agreeing to remain apart," Miss Arden said sarcastically, and with the air of having solved the problem. "It is not necessary to fly to spectacular extremes."

"It wouldn't be fair," Elizabeth said. "Stephen might want to—to marry again!" It was difficult to say that, horrible to think of it. But it was something that had to be faced.

"H'm! I should like to meet the girl who would marry a *divorce* Miss Arden remarked."

That aspect had never struck Elizabeth; she sat very still, thinking.

When Miss Arden had gone she went to her desk, and from the bottom of the drawer in it, pulled out a photograph of Stephen. She stood it on the table and looked at it for a long time. It had lain in the drawer all these months, because she had never dared to look at it. That was rather queer, since she had been able to look upon Wendell's face, in the flesh. Subconsciously she compared them, and again thought, I must have been mad ever to have preferred Charles to Stephen. His mouth should have warned me. His eyes, too.

She sank her chin into her hand, and still watching the picture, mused on her married life.

She hadn't appreciated the good in Stephen, the forbearance and the tenderness; she hadn't tried to understand him. He was clever; in his work she had failed him. She was his wife, and yet she hadn't allowed him to be intimate with her; she had held herself apart and thought him coarse when he spoke of things which Elizabeth had been taught to consider unmentionable. Things about which she had permitted Wendell to make jokes; Wendell, who was nothing to her. Yet it was Wendell who had taught her to listen to sex-matters without a blush; he had spoken in innuendoes, Stephen would have spoken bluntly. Stephen's way, of the two, was best.

She hadn't liked his friends. They were all so different to anyone she had met before. In time, perhaps, she could have learned to tolerate them, only she hadn't given herself time.

Bridge at Lady Ribblemere's house. How awful that had been! Yet she hadn't told Stephen. He had been annoyed at her reticence. He had said, Surely you can say what you really think to me? That was the trouble. She couldn't. Dimly she felt, If I had told Stephen all about it, it would have been better. All the little things that happened like the Vicar's wife saying that she feared I was not a conscientious Churchwoman. Stephen would have said, The cheek of the woman! and we'd have laughed, and it wouldn't have mattered any longer how the Vicar's wife annoyed me.

If she could have her married life over again, how different would she be! Now that she had known the wretchedness of living alone, in town, she could appreciate Queen's Halt, and Stephen. It seemed that she could not exist without a husband, even though she did not love him, even though she had been unhappy with him. She supposed that if you had once been married you could not go back to an unmarried state without feeling a void, and a great want.

But if she went back to Stephen it must be as his wife. That was the obstacle that stood in the way. It would need more courage than she possessed. If she could return on platonic terms, she would do so to-morrow. She couldn't. She thought that if Stephen still loved her and wanted her he would accept those terms, but they would be unfair to him, and the day of unfairness was over. It must be all or nothing; she had put shams and pretence aside. How hard that was only she knew, but she had learned a bitter lesson, and she made up her mind that she would profit by it. If she went back to Stephen she would be frank with him. He should know that she did not love him, so that if he did not want her like that, he might reject her.

He might not want her; he might have ceased to love her. It would be hard to send for him, hard for her pride. And if he did not come, how humiliated would she be! Then she thought, I can't be more humiliated than I am now.

Wendell had knocked the pedestal from beneath her feet. She had played with Wendell, knowing in her heart of hearts that he was unsafe, knowing too that it was wrong. And Wendell had shown her to herself as she was. Her spirit still writhed under his accusations, for exaggerated though they were, each one contained a grain of truth.

Mr. Hengist came to see her, and pointed a stern finger.

"Knocked yourself up, I hear. You're losing your looks, child."

She smiled, but wearily, for she knew that this was so. The glass showed her pallor and her thinness; the glass showed tiny lines upon her forehead. She had aged.

"Have you come to scold me?" she asked. "Please don't!"

"Not at all. I never scold. I merely offer good advice which you seldom take."

"Oh!" she protested.

"Quite true. My advice now is, Go away."

"Where?" she asked listlessly.

"Where would you like to go?"

She shook her head.

"I don't know."

"The sea?"

"Oh, no! That means crowds of holiday-makers and a horrible band."

"Um! You never really liked the seaside, did you?"

"No," she said. "Never."

"Congratulations," said Mr. Hengist.

She was puzzled; then she understood.

"Yes, I'm learning," she said. "It's a slow business. A year ago I should have said that I loved the sea."

"I know you would. You're getting on, Elizabeth. What about a farm-house in the country?"

Her face lit up.

"Oh—I think I should like that! Only—it's rather difficult. You see I wouldn't go away with Aunt Anne when she asked me."

"Certainly not. She's the last person in the world you want. Go by yourself. Will you?"

"Do you know of a farm-house that would take me in?"

"Yes, and I'll make all the arrangements." He rose and laid a clumsy hand on her shoulder. "Go and fight out your battles alone, Elizabeth. I've hope of you yet."

Georgette Heyer

Chapter Twenty-Six

Miss Arden's indignation when it was made known to her that Elizabeth contemplated a change of air, alone, knew no bounds. Elizabeth felt herself to be unkind and ungracious, but she could not bear the thought of taking Miss Arden with her. In this she was supported by Lawrence, who said very aggrievedly that of course it didn't matter what became of him, but if Elizabeth was going to drag her aunt away he would be made exceedingly uncomfortable, and would probably have to live at his club. However, he said, he was accustomed to having his convenience disregarded, and heaven knew that he was not so selfish that he would expect Anne to deny herself anything for his sake. He begged her not to consider him in the slightest; no doubt Elizabeth's need of her was greater than his, although Elizabeth had not consulted either of them when she made this new, and really rather unnecessary plan.

He wore a martyr-like expression for some days, awaiting Miss Arden's decision, and frequently implored her to please herself. Then another idea occurred to him, and he remarked that it was most unreasonable of Elizabeth to want her aunt to accompany her to such an out-of-the-way hole as Wood End. He told Miss Arden that there was no need for her to sacrifice her comforts and enjoyment for Elizabeth. She would not like to be buried in the heart of the country at this time of the year; it was sure to be damp, and everyone knew that the autumn was a dangerous season. In fact, speaking perfectly dispassionately, he strongly advised Anne to remain at home. A nice thing it would be if she caught cold in an old-fashioned and draughty farm-house.

So Elizabeth went to Wood End alone and stayed there for a month, until October's red and gold gave place to November's sullen grey.

The open-air life, and the great quiet of the country did her good. The livestock on the farm interested her; after some hesitation she learned to milk the cows, under the friendly and amused eye of the farmer, a bluff and direct person with an enormous beard and bright red cheeks.

She was somewhat taken aback by him at first, and a little shocked. As soon as she arrived at the farm a large sheep-dog, bob-tailed and shaggy, bounded up to her and was effusive. She hugged it, a lump in her throat; till now she had hardly realised how much she had missed the dogs at the Halt.

"Oh, you darling!" she cried. "What a beautiful dog!" She looked up at the farmer. "Isn't he a dear?"

Mr. Gabriel smiled widely down upon her.

"Not a dog, madam. She's a bitch. Get down, Nellie, get down!"

If your dog was a female you called her a lady-dog. The word bitch fell on amazed ears. Elizabeth hurried away after Mrs. Gabriel to her bedroom.

Mrs. Gabriel was fat and motherly. She took Elizabeth to a long, low-ceilinged room upstairs, with an uneven floor and small casement windows. Chintz curtains framed them, with cottage frills. The bed was a four-poster, all the furniture old and worm-eaten, Jacobean, Elizabeth saw at once.

Outside, the fields stretched away in patchwork to the far woods, and below the window, in the paved yard, some Cochin-China hens searched for grubs in the cracks. There was a partially demolished hay-rick beyond the yard; the scent of it came up to Elizabeth's room, fragrant and sweet.

"Oh, what a beautiful place!" she exclaimed. "How quaint and fascinating! Don't you love it?"

"Yes, madam," Mrs. Gabriel said simply. "Most people do. Mr. Hengist comes here often."

"He never told me about it till now. I wish I'd known of it before."

"Never mind, you'll come again—often."

"I shall," Elizabeth said. "If you'll have me."

"We're always glad to have Mr. Hengist's friends, madam. I hope you'll be comfortable. It's not the right time of year to come to a farm, properly speaking, but there's always plenty to interest you, if you're fond of animals."

"I am, oh I am! I wonder, will Mr. Gabriel take me round?"

"Why, surely!" his wife said, smiling.

Under Mr. .Gabriel's wing Elizabeth inspected everything, and learned that if a pig drank water it was a sign of illness, and that, of all climates under the sun, England's was the worst.

Gabriel had tales to tell of nearly all his animals. Elizabeth heard with interest that the Jersey cow, Emily, had had bad trouble in her last calving, and that he and Mrs. Gabriel had almost despaired of saving the calf's life. She saw the calf, a sturdy young heifer, and soon knew every cow and pig apart. She thought how lovely it would be to have a farm, especially in the spring, when the lambs came. Then she remembered that there was a farm quite near to Queen's Halt. She had never taken very much interest in it, probably because she had been too much occupied in dwelling upon her grievances. What a fool she had been!

"I wish this were spring-time!" she said impulsively. "Lambs are so sweet!"

"You'd best come again, next year," Gabriel answered. "There 'll be lambs and sucking-pigs and chickens. Spring the best time for a lady to come on a farm. If you'd been here earlier in the year you could have helped my wife rear the lamb we had to take from its mother. She had to feed it from a bottle."

"I wish I had been here! I'd like to have seen Nellie's puppies, too."

"Beautiful litter," he agreed.

"Perhaps you'd like to have a pup out of her next one?" Mrs. Gabriel suggested.

"Oh, yes, I would! How lovely!" Elizabeth cried.

"Well, it'll give you something to do, won't it, my dear?"

Elizabeth looked at her.

"How did you know I—wanted that?"

"I sort of guessed, dearie. If you've no babies, have a dog. It's nice to have something to love and do for."

"No—I haven't any—children," Elizabeth said.

"I knew that. It's not in your face. They'll come, maybe."

Elizabeth thought it unlikely—not impossible, but improbable. During her visit to Wood End she fought her battle, as Mr. Hengist had thought she would fight it. The problem of her future was turned over and over; she argued this way and that, striving desperately to be honest with herself, excusing herself never, but rather exaggerating the blame that was due to her.

Mrs. Gabriel was a help; she was ready to talk or to be silent, whichever you wished, and when she talked stray scraps of her life's philosophy came out. In a manner free from impertinence she asked where Elizabeth's husband was. She spoke as a woman more than double Elizabeth's age, and Elizabeth told her that Stephen was abroad. They had parted.

Mrs. Gabriel nodded, banging the rolling-pin down upon the pastry. Her shapely arms were bare to the elbow; Elizabeth marvelled at the fine texture of the skin, and the plump firmness of the flesh beneath. There was kindness in the grey eyes that regarded Elizabeth; it impelled her to speak, almost against her will.

"It was all too—difficult," she said haltingly. "I—I made a mess of it."

"I daresay," Mrs. Gabriel answered. "There's a deal of give and take in marriage, and girls don't realise it." She rested her rolling-pin up on end, and smiled across at Elizabeth. "The man takes and the woman gives. Leastways, I've always found it so."

Elizabeth, seated on a small table against the wall, munching apples, said wistfully,

"Have you, Mrs. Gabriel?"

"It comes more natural to us, you see, and a man's a great weak creature when all's said and done, without much more understanding than a baby. You're to humour a man. Lord, that's what we're here for! It's a poor woman who's got no man to manage."

"If he can be managed."

The rolling-pin went vigorously to and fro. Mrs. Gabriel chuckled; it was a comfortable sound, full of wisdom.

"You can take it from me, my dear, the man that can't be managed don't exist. I never met one that couldn't be twisted round the finger of some woman, if she had the mind to do it." She looked up, and her smile embraced Elizabeth. "Bless you, I've been through it, too. We most of us have, only there's some as takes it harder than others. You start off thinking everything's like a feather-bed, and you find that it isn't."

"No. More like a bed of—of thorns."

"Oh, not always, dearie. When you're courting, of course, you've got it all your own way, and your man's on his best behaviour. He brings you flowers and what-not, and pets you and cossets you as though you was made of china. You're the weak one, then, and you think it'll always be the same. But when you're married, it changes. Men can't keep up their best behaviour for long. It seems kind of exhausting. The best thing you can do is to remember that he's a baby in most things, and start feeling motherly as soon as may be."

"Motherly?" Elizabeth offered the core of her apple to Nellie, who politely accepted it and placed it under the table. "Can one?"

"The best wives do, dearie. It's a great help to you if you can keep it in mind. My gracious, don't I know what a worriting creature a man can be? But, Lord, they don't mean anything! It's the way they're made, and to make allowances for them is the way we're made."

"It—it isn't the way I'm made," Elizabeth said sadly. "I didn't seem able to—make allowances."

"Girls don't. They grow into it, though. You see, dearie, a man's selfish. He can't help it; he don't have to bear what we bear. At the best he's stupid when it comes to understanding how we women feel. We don't really like him any the less for that."

"Are men selfish?" Elizabeth asked. "All of them?"

"More or less, mostly more. Because they don't understand. So the woman's got to be unselfish. Stands to reason she must be, or how would she fit in? A man doesn't fit, ever. He doesn't know how to. You go out and look at our cock. He makes a deal of noise when he finds a fat grub to eat, but when the hens come fluttering round to see what it is, he gobbles it up himself."

"Y-es. It seems rather hard—and unfair."

"My dear, don't you get thinking this is a fair world for women, because it isn't. I'm not saying that if we could start all over again we wouldn't have things different, but seeing as how they are as they are, we've made the best of 'em, and we've learned to fit in as quickly as possible. You've got to put up with a lot, the Lord knows! but it's worth it in the long run."

Elizabeth chose another apple from the basket on her knees.

"I wonder—did Mr. Hengist—send me to you—on purpose?"

"That's telling," smiled Mrs. Gabriel. "Maybe he did. He told me you hadn't got a mother, my dear, and p'raps he thought it would be a good thing if you could have a talk with someone that was a mother. He knows my life hasn't been all honeysuckle. It's no good talking to someone as hasn't been through any of your sort of trouble."

"No. I—please, go on. No one's ever—spoken to me like this before. Not—sensible—and—and helpfully."

"People don't. I remember when I quarrelled with Gabriel there was a lady living down at the White Cottage who came and talked a heap of nonsense about duty and love and I don't know what beside. She'd come and sit here and talk by the hour, until my mother told me not to listen to her rubbish, but to get on with my cooking. I remember too, one thing my mother said to me."

"What was it?" said Elizabeth.

"She said, 'Don't get thinking Gabriel's a brute because he doesn't always understand the way you feel.' That's sound advice, my dear. Men want a lot, and the best way is to let 'em have it, as much as you can. It's easier then to get your own way when you want it." She paused, and her smile grew. "And don't forget to let him think it's his way. It doesn't matter to us whether we seem to be ruling or not, as long as we are, but it does matter to a man. He's a pernickety, difficult creature, and it doesn't do to let him see who's cock of the walk. Let him think he is, and the bigger he talks, the smaller he acts. Let him talk. He likes it, and it makes him feel good. You see, a man's got to feel good and masterful, or he's only half a man."

Elizabeth folded her hands over the basket. Gravely she looked at Mrs. Gabriel.

"You know an awful lot," she said.

"I ought to. I've reared a husband and three boys, and that's enough for any woman. They've all leaned on me till it's a wonder I'm not worn to a skeleton!"

Elizabeth laughed.

"No, I'm still fat, thank goodness. People used to talk to me about woman leaning on man. My goodness, you soon find out who does the leaning! A man needs propping up more times than you can count, the great, helpless zany! When things go wrong a man turns to his wife, and it's her job to bolster him up a bit, and keep cheerful. He don't bear troubles in silence: he tells 'em to his wife, like when his little finger aches. Leastways, he does if his wife's a good one. We keep most of our troubles to ourselves, because a man wouldn't understand, though he'd try hard, bless him! And that's another thing, my dear! All through your life you've got to listen to your man's upsets, but don't you worrit him with yours. He'll soon get tired of it, and you'll most likely lose him."

"That's one-sided, too," Elizabeth said.

"In a way, my dear. Still, most women want to hear their man's troubles. They coax 'em out of him; he likes it better that way. It's the motherly feeling I told you about. You want to be always running behind to pick him up when he falls down, and start him off again."

"That's what I didn't do," Elizabeth said slowly. When Stephen had torn up his work in exasperation she had done nothing to start him off again. She had felt that she didn't know enough about writing novels. She saw now how little that mattered.

In just the same way she should have borne with him when he was late for meals, or irritable because some tiny thing had annoyed him. She ought never to have defended herself; that led to fruitless quarrels. She should have let him "talk big," and coaxed him back to good-humour.

"I see," she said. "I—I wish I'd met you before. I —always thought myself so helpless—beside my husband."

"And so you are, my dear, if you choose. If you're one of those as likes to feel your husband's strong and masterful, so much the better for you. As long as you get your own way I'm not denying that it's nice to think your man's a rock. Why, dearie, that's what all women want to think! It's Nature, and that's why we let our men master us on occasion. But they don't do it except by our consent, and never you believe it!"

"I don't think all men are so—weak and—and easily led, Mrs. Gabriel."

"Oh, some's easier than others, of course! There's times when a man's strong, and I'm not saying that a man's arms round you isn't a safe comfortable feeling. When something comes to frighten you, you'll run to your husband, and that's when he's top-dog. He's top-dog too when it comes to looking out a train in the A. B. C. That's a thing women don't understand; a man's in his element with a time-table."

Elizabeth laughed.

"Yes, that's so. One misses one's husband for those things. It's nice too—to feel that there's someone—behind you—to—to back you up, and—and take care of you."

"Urn!" said Mrs. Gabriel. "I've felt that way myself, of course. You go back to your husband, dearie, and remember that with all his faults he's necessary to you, same as you are to him. And don't fuss him, when he's not in the mood for it. That's an important thing to remember. Don't be for ever worriting him to change his wet boots or to come to bed at ten o'clock. He doesn't like it, and what's more he won't do it. Leave him alone; he likes to think he knows best what's good for him."

"But supposing it isn't good for him? I don't see how—"

"Never you mind. It's better he should take a chill and be laid up than that he should think you a nuisance. Once he takes to his bed you're top-dog again, because there's nothing so helpless and dependent as a man when he's ill. You've got it all your own way then, and he'll do any mortal thing you tell him."

"Will he? My husband—never was ill."

"More's the pity, then. When a man's ill, you feel old enough to be his mother. Once you feel that way, everything's all right. You go back, my dear, and give up expecting too much. You'll find you've got much more than you thought."

Elizabeth slipped down from the table.

"He may not want me. But if he does—I will go back."

*

Elizabeth told no one of her return to London, but on the day after her arrival she went at last to see Mrs. Ramsay.

She was taken to the drawing-room; Mrs. Ramsay got up quickly, and seemed to hesitate. It was Thomas who bounded forward and made much of Elizabeth. That relieved the tension; Mrs. Ramsay came forward.

"How dear of Thomas! Isn't he getting fat? I'm so glad you've come, Elizabeth."

Elizabeth took her hand.

"Mater—I beg your pardon! Mrs. Ramsay, if you can't bear to—to speak to me—I'll—I'll go. I know how you must feel." That cost her something, but it had to be said.

"My dear, I'd rather have 'Mater,' please. Come and sit down."

Elizabeth was pushed to the sofa; she sank on to it and began to stroke Thomas, mechanically. Mrs. Ramsay drew her chair nearer to the fire, and waited.

It was difficult to know how to begin; Elizabeth plunged headlong.

"Mater—does—does Stephen—still want me?"

"Yes, Elizabeth."

She looked up; Mrs. Ramsay saw how drawn were her eyes.

"That's—true? I—I want the truth, please."

"Oh, my darling!" Mrs. Ramsay cried, "Does he want you? If you could but see him!"

Elizabeth's mouth twisted; she bent over the dog.

"Thanks, mater. I'm—sorry. I'm a lot—older than I was, and—I think—a little wiser. N-not very much, perhaps, but enough to see—how wrong I've been, and—and how foolish. So—so I thought—I'd come and—ask you —whether Stephen still—wanted me, and—and whether I ought to—to write to him."

Mrs. Ramsay got out of her chair and came to sit beside Elizabeth on the sofa.

"Yes, dear, write to him. He's in England, at Queen's Halt."

"You—really think—he'll—come?"

"Good gracious me, yes! He'll probably exceed the speed-limit, and be taken to prison. You'll have to go to him then. How romantic! Or isn't one put in prison for scorching? No, I think you just have to pay a fine. What a pity!"

Elizabeth tried to laugh, only Mater's madness made her want to cry. It sounded so familiar, and, somehow, so precious. The laugh trembled into a sob. Mrs. Ramsay took her hand.

"Yes, darling, I know. Just tell me one thing:—Do you love him?"

There was a pause; there must be no evasions of half-truths now. Elizabeth looked up.

"No, mater. Not—as I ought to love him."

Mrs. Ramsay's heart cried, Poor Stephen, poor Stephen! but her lips said, "You'll learn, Elizabeth. Only—tell him."

"Yes, mater. I—I must do that. He may not want me —when he knows. But I—I haven't ever been fair to him—and I've realised at last—what I owe to him—and I'm—prepared to—to fulfill my—share of the—the contract. Thank you for—for helping me."

"My dear, I haven't done a thing," Mrs. Ramsay said. "Ring the bell, and we'll have tea. Then I shall have done something."

"I—I ought not to stay. I only came to—"

"Darling, I shall burst into tears if you go. I'm feeling horribly lumpy, goodness knows why. Don't cry, Elizabeth. It would be so awful if Mary came with the tea and found us melting on my new carpet. I should like you to kiss me, if you don't mind."

Chapter Twenty-Seven

Elizabeth spent nearly all one day trying to write to Stephen. Each successive letter seemed more impossible than the last, and was destroyed. She could not on paper tell him all that must be told; it was too bald, and her manner of writing too stiff. She longed for his facile pen, her own seemed halting and despicable. She could not in a letter offer to return to him; all that must be spoken. In the end she wrote only a short note, asking him to come and see her that they might discuss the future. Even that was unsatisfactory, but after some hesitation she dispatched it, feeling that she could do no better.

She was unprepared for his promptness in responding. She expected him to write, suggesting a day for their meeting, yet when she reflected, afterwards, she knew that his instant coming was more in keeping with his character. She sat at the window of her room on the following afternoon, and soon after three o'clock saw the familiar yellow car drive to the house and stop there.

She rose, breathless. Stephen switched off the engine in the way she knew so well, stepped from the cab and went quickly to the front door, with never a glance upward, to the window.

Elizabeth heard the vigorous peal of the bell somewhere in the basement, and of instinct flew to the mirror. Nervous hands patted her hair into soft curves over her ears; she turned, and stood as though on tiptoe, watching the door. A pulse throbbed in her throat, and her fingers twined themselves tensely together. She felt that of her own free will she had courted the worst ordeal of her life; panic threatened to overcome her; if escape had been possible she would have fled from the approaching interview. It was not possible. She had to brace herself to meet it, frightened, desperately embarrassed, and icily cold from head to foot.

There was heavy breathing on the stairs, a murmur of voices; she heard Mrs. Cotton say how the stairs ketched her in the wind, her having a weak heart and that. A deeper voice, that sent the blood rushing to Elizabeth's face, answered. Then the knock fell on the door.

Elizabeth tried to say come in, but could not. Mrs. Cotton came without invitation, and in a voice which breathed rampant curiosity, said,

"Here's your 'usband, ma'am. Mr. Ramsay."

Elizabeth managed to speak.

"Thank you."

Mrs. Cotton held the door for Stephen to pass through, then, reluctantly, shut it. Stephen came in with his clean stride and stopped just inside the door, facing Elizabeth.

In that brief moment, when both stood wretchedly tongue-tied, Elizabeth saw the sprinkling of grey in the hair above Stephen's temples, and the tiny lines about his eyes. He was pale, and his lips were shut tight in a way she knew well. Foolishly, she noticed that he was wearing a suit that she had not seen before.

Stephen broke the silence, holding out muddied hands. He spoke with unnatural matter-of-factness, in jerks that betrayed his embarrassment.

"I—beg your pardon, Elizabeth, but—a tire burst. Can I—wash? I'm—so sorry."

She thought, What a queer way for our interview to begin! but some of her fright left her, and she stepped forward.

"Yes, of course. I—I quite understand. C-come into my bedroom."

"Thanks." He waited for her to go first, and then followed her in. She remembered how uncomfortable Wendell had made her feel; it seemed perfectly natural for Stephen to be here. Yet once she had not thought so. She picked up the water-jug; Stephen took it from her.

"Don't bother, dear." He poured water into the basin, and began to wash his hands. She saw that they were unsteady, and grew calmer. She held the towel ready for him to use; in silence he dried his hands. Then they went back into the other room, and Elizabeth stammered,

"S-sit down, won't you? I—you'll—er—stay to tea— with me?"

Gravely he answered.

"It rather depends—on what you're going to say to me, Elizabeth. Your letter—didn't tell me much."

"I—there's a great deal—I must say. I—I am trying—but it's difficult. There's—there's so much, you see."

"Do I—make it difficult for you?" he asked gently.

"No. I—I expect it's my own stupidity." She smiled wanly. "I'm not so stupid as I was, Stephen. I—I couldn't be, could I?"

He did not answer. She stared into the fire, and tried to steady her voice.

"I—I want to tell you, Stephen, that—if you still want me—I'll come back to you."

He made a quick movement, as though to take her hand; she could not meet his eyes, but she knew that they were alight and eager.

"You'll come back? You— What—do you mean, Elizabeth?"

She swallowed hard; the colour tinged her cheeks again.

"I mean—of course—as your—wife," she said, almost inaudibly.

He was leaning forward, his eyes on her face.

"I—still don't understand. Elizabeth —" he paused, then almost harshly said, "Do you love me?"

Her head sank lower.

"No, Stephen. I'm—not—cheating, you see."

He rose, and went to the window, hands deep in his pockets. How well she knew that quick nervous step, and the furrow between his brows!

"Why do you offer to come back then?" he demanded, over his shoulder.

"There are—so many reasons. I—I think the biggest one—the best one—is that I've realised at last that—it's my duty to—to return to you—if you want me." She looked wistfully across the room towards him. He said nothing. With an effort she continued. "I—want to—explain—a little. I—you see, when you—married me I was so awfully—young and—and foolish—and uncontrolled. I—wasn't ready, and—and I wasn't wise enough to see that—having married you—I'd got to—fulfill my share of our—bargain. You—you were very kind to me, Stephen. Very patient. I didn't appreciate that at the time. I've learned to—just lately, thinking it over. It wasn't—your fault—that things went wrong between us. It was mine. Only—I hadn't really had—a fair start. I—I hadn't ever faced the—realities of life. I—cheated, just as you said. That—wasn't all my fault, either. It—it was how I was brought up. I'm—not excusing myself, only—trying—to explain." Again she paused, and still he said nothing. "You—you were quite right—to let me go. I've done a lot of—thinking during these months. I wasn't fair to you before. I—I shirked what was my duty. I—won't do that again—if—if you'll take me back." That was what she had made up her mind to say; it hadn't been so very difficult after all.

231

Stephen swung round to face her.

"You mean you'll come back to me because you conceive it to be your duty. Because you're sorry for me. Yes, out of pity. Do you think—do you think I could—take you— like that?"

She raised her eyes to his face; sadness lay in them, and it hurt him to see it there.

"I—was afraid—you might not—want me," she said simply.

"Want you!" He flung out his hand, then swiftly thrust it back into his pocket. "God, if you but knew!"

She was unutterably relieved; everything seemed blank and awful while she thought he would not take her back.

"It's not duty only," she said. "All these months— the loneliness—I—I can't live by myself any longer. I *can't*! I—once said I hated you. It wasn't true, Stephen. I—don't love you—not as I should love you, but I miss you—when you're not with me, and for my own sake I—I want to come back. But—but if you don't want me, say so! Please say so!"

"I want you so much that—" he checked himself. He began to pace restlessly up and down the room. From the sofa Elizabeth watched him and knew, now that her fate was uncertain, that she must go back to him. Hardly daring to breathe, she waited, wondering what would become of her if he refused to take her home. He came to a halt before her, and his voice when he spoke was hard with suppressed feeling.

"Look at me. Yes. I thought so. You're frightened, Elizabeth. Frightened—of me! Frightened lest I should agree to your terms. Aren't you?"

The words came rapped out sternly, but they did not alarm Elizabeth. She was thinking, How nice to hear him call me Elizabeth! I must always have hated Charles's "Betty," I suppose.

"No, Stephen. I'm not frightened. Not—as you think."

The hardness went out of him; he knelt, and she thought that she heard him sigh. He laid a firm, reassuring hand over her fingers, and held them tightly.

"Oh, my darling, my darling!" he said huskily, just as he might have said it a year ago. His head went down, his lips touched her sleeve. "I know—and I'm—grateful. You needn't be frightened; I love you too much to accept your terms. If you come back to me it will be platonically. There shall never be anything more than—friendship between us, until you wish it. Perhaps—that way—you'll learn to care. You'll only learn—to hate me—the other way."

Something within her chest seemed to swell and grow warm; she had thought this man a monster. Her fingers moved under his and clasped them.

"That would be cheating still, Stephen. Not—fair."

"No, sweetheart, because I know where I stand. We've wiped out the old bargain and made a new one. Mine are the only terms on which I'll take you home."

She looked at him in wonderment. Shyly she said.

"Can—you—bear those—terms?"

He was surprised; for her to have said that showed that she had changed indeed.

"I must, 'Lisbeth. I don't pretend—that it'll be easy, but I can't live—without you. I've—I've been through hell and I'll be content—with just your—companionship. I can do nothing without you. I—" The words choked in his throat. Again he kissed her wrist.

"You make me *ashamed*," she said, very low. "I—oh, you make me ashamed."

"There's no need for you to be that, my darling. When you've—dreaded final—separation—as I've dreaded it— this compact seems—a great deal. More than I expected. Only—think it over, 'Lisbeth, out of fairness to yourself. It wasn't only the—physical part that upset you. It was everything. You couldn't stand things I did and said; I got on your nerves. Won't that happen again, however hard I try to prevent it?"

There was a rush of tears to her eyes.

"Ah, don't, Stephen! I've learned better ways, truly I have! Living alone has taught me—so much! I'll be thankful for anything now—not criticising or letting myself be intolerant over the tiny details that don't matter. You see, I've discovered that they don't. I'm not saying this—out of impulse; I've thought and thought, and I know what I'm about this time. I've—had my eyes—thoroughly opened."

"Then come, Elizabeth," he said. "My—beautiful Elizabeth!"

There was more yet to be told; she would not shirk that task.

"Let me get up, Stephen. There's something else. You've—got to—hear it."

He rose at once, and it seemed to her that the haggard look crept back into his face. She came tremblingly to her feet, and stared resolutely up at him.

"About—Charles," she said, with an effort.

The lids closed over his eyes for an instant; she saw him square his shoulders, in readiness for a blow.

"You may not want me—I—you probably heard—things. People—talked. I let—him make—love to me. I—it was wrong, wicked—only I was—so lonely, and—and I thought that he was nice—and—"

He took a swift step towards her, brow lowering, eyes dark with suspicious anger.

"What did he do to you? Tell me, Elizabeth! Tell me at once! What did he do?"

The savagery in his voice sent a thrill through her.

"Oh, no, Stephen! Nothing! I—oh, you didn't think he was—was—my lover?"

"No!"

She drew a deep breath of relief.

"He wasn't, Stephen. But—he—might have been. That's what I must tell you. If he hadn't shown—himself to me—as he was—I might have gone away with him. I don't know. It never got further than a—vulgar flirtation, but I—I let him take me out, and—and all sorts of things. Horrid things. I let him make love to me. I—I *wanted* him to. Do—do you still want me—now that—you know?"

She thought he was going to take her in his arms, but he only put his hands on her shoulders.

"Could you doubt me, 'Lisbeth? As if that would count!"

She bowed her head.

"I didn't—know. I—I beg your pardon."

There was a little silence. When Stephen spoke again it was lightly; she knew that Wendell, all thought of him, had been swept from their lives.

"The Halt is waiting for you, 'Lisbeth. When will you come?"

"As soon as you like, Stephen."

"My darling, that's now. Can you manage it?"

"lean, yes. But I haven't seen Father or Aunt yet. I think I ought to tell them first. It doesn't matter, of course, but they'd be hurt if I didn't. And—I'd like to see Mater, too. She's been—wonderful to me."

"To-morrow then? After lunch?"

"Yes, I could be ready by then, if I pack now. Only what about Mrs. Cotton, Stephen? Won't she object?"

"Who the devil's Mrs. Cotton?" he demanded.

She laughed.

"My landlady. She's so awful, Stephen! She calls me 'pore dear.' At least, she did when I had 'flu."

"You've had 'flu again?" lie said quickly. "Here? Who looked after you?"

"No one. Mrs. Cotton."

"But, my darling!" Stephen exclaimed in concern. "Where was your aunt?"

"Away. I didn't want her. I was all right."

"All right! I ought never to have let you live alone! You're not fit to take care of yourself, 'Lisbeth."

"No, I don't think I am. I never know what to do in hotels, or things like that. That reminds me, won't Mrs. Cotton want a week's notice?"

"Not if I pay her the full week. Never mind about that; I'll attend to it. All you have to do is to pack your things, and see your people. You can leave everything else to me."

"Oh, I think I'd better—"

"*Everything* else to me," Stephen repeated firmly.

A man's got to feel good and masterful, or he's only half a man, had said Mrs. Gabriel. Elizabeth smiled a little. "Very well, Stephen! Thank you."

Chapter Twenty-Eight

When Stephen came to fetch Elizabeth next day he asked her whether she would rather go to Paris than to Queen's Halt.

"Darling, I've been thinking about it, and I wonder whether you'd like to go abroad instead of into the country? You didn't like the Halt in the winter, did you? So if you'd prefer—"

"But I shouldn't, Stephen. Thank you very much. I want to go back to the Halt. I *need* it."

His eyes brightened.

"Sure?"

"Quite sure. Quite ready too."

"Oh, splendid, Elizabeth! You saw your people?"

"Yes. They were glad, I think. Auntie cried. I don't know why."

"My dear, your aunt—" He stopped, remembering that she would brook no criticism of her relatives.

"I know," Elizabeth said. "She always does. Say what you like, Stephen. You must. Anything that comes into your head."

He stared at her.

"You wouldn't like it if I did, Elizabeth."

"No, perhaps not, at first. But I'm going to get used to it. I've—I've come to the conclusion that reticence— is rather dangerous. We'll be quite frank with each other now. I'm learning a lot, aren't I? Unlearning a lot too. I've got into the way of thinking quite honestly to myself. One does if one's alone. Oh, Mrs. Cotton thinks you're a real gentleman! She said so!"

"How flattering!" he said. "Are you going to bid her a fond farewell now? Shall I lend you my handkerchief?"

"Oh, I shan't cry as much as that!" she smiled.

They came home in the twilight and drove up the avenue to the house under damp trees, and over rotting leaves. Lights gleamed in the windows; somewhere a dog barked, not a challenge, but a welcome. Elizabeth saw the wolfhound bound out to meet them, and Flo, the cocker, and a great gladness rose in her throat. Dumbly she alighted, and stood still, looking about her, marvelling that everything should be still untroubled here, and the same. The flower-beds gleamed wet and dark; through the dusk she saw chrysanthemums, golden and red and white; at her feet were pale Christmas roses; behind her stood the house glowing warm from many lights, protective, she thought, her home.

Stephen's hand on her arm; his voice in her ear:

"My dear?"

"It is beautiful," she said. "Even in winter. Why didn't I see that before?"

"I don't know, 'Lisbeth. Perhaps you hadn't learned to see."

"All my life," Elizabeth said slowly, "I've been blind. A fool. Just a fool. Oh . . . Nana!"

Nana came out of the open door. She waited a moment, then quietly she said,

"Good evening, madam. This is a great day for the Halt."

Elizabeth stepped forward, and held out her hand.

"It's a great day for me, Nana. A fresh start."

"That's good, madam. We've missed you."

Jerry, the Airedale, came racing round the corner of the house to throw himself upon Elizabeth; Stephen let go the wolf-hound's collar, and Elizabeth, laughing, dishevelled, was lost under the violent welcome of the dogs.

Dinner in the panelled dining-room that evening was rather a silent meal, but across the table Stephen could see Elizabeth's eyes shining in content.

Candles, orange shaded, cast a warm light over the polished table; the silver sparkled, and the glass; a great bowl of hothouse carnations stood in the middle of the table, trailing asparagus fern about it. A carnation was tucked into Elizabeth's napkin; she fastened it in her dress, and smiled her thanks to Stephen.

"After lodging-houses this—" her gesture embraced all the room—"is very comforting." Her eyes twinkled. "I'm looking forward to my own bed to-night. At Mrs. Cotton's I had to arrange myself amongst the bumps."

"Poor 'Lisbeth!" Stephen said. "You shall stay in bed all day."

"Oh, no!" she said. "I shall get up very early and go and see the ducks. Oh, and Stephen!—could I have a cow one day?"

"A cow?" he asked, puzzled. "What for?"

"For fun. Two cows. One might be lonely. I've been staying on a farm, and I learned to milk them. I'd like a pig, too, please. Yes, and a pet lamb. Or would the dogs kill it?"

"We can teach them to leave it alone," he said, with twitching lips. Then his amusement got the better of him. "Oh, Elizabeth, you funny kid! Are you going to start a farm?"

"We'll see," she said profoundly. "If I did, we'd have to have more land. I don't think the neighbours would approve, would they?"

"Do we care?" he asked.

She considered.

"You don't," she said. "I—well, do I?"

"A bit. You'll learn to send them to the devil, same as I do."

"I wonder?" Elizabeth said.

She awoke next morning early, and lay for some time revelling in her surroundings. She was dressed and downstairs long before Stephen had moved. He came down to find her with her hands full of winter daisies, flushed and bright-eyed. He did not kiss her, although he knew she would have permitted it, but laid his hands on her shoulders, and huskily said,

"The utter bliss—to see you here!"

She blushed, and bent her head over the flowers.

"Aren't they beautiful, Stephen?"

"And you," he said.

"Also the smell of the coffee," Elizabeth remarked. "Let's have breakfast now; I'm famishing."

Over breakfast he said carelessly,

"You know Nina's going to be married next month?"

"No! Good gracious, I thought— Whom to?"

"Young Hemingway. They sail for India in January. Hemingway thinks everything Nina does is perfect. Even that extraordinary novel. Do you remember it?"

Of course she remembered. How she had hated it, and the endless discussions concerning it. Now she laughed, and nodded.

"Yes. She would read it to you. It was awfully silly, you know. I didn't know much about it at the time, but now I realise that no girl would have said the sort of things Jasmine said when Horace asked her to go away with him. By the way, Stephen, what are you writing now? I loved 'Caraway Seeds.'"

"Really?" he said eagerly.

"Yes. I didn't appreciate it at first, but I've read it three times now. What about the new book?"

He shrugged despairingly.

"It wouldn't come. It will now that I've got you again."

"Isn't any of it written?"

"Oh, a page or two."

She leaned forward.

"Give them to me to-day, will you, Stephen?"

"What for?" he asked. "They're no good."

"Never mind. I want them."

"All right, but what's the idea?"

She smiled mysteriously.

"You'll see. I'm going to present you with a sample."

He was thoroughly intrigued.

"Sample of what?"

"Don't be so inquisitive. I'll show you when it's done."

He shook his head.

"I wish I knew what you were getting at," he said.

After breakfast Elizabeth went to Nana's room, and stayed there for along time, talking. At the end of their conversation they shook hands, and Nana said,

"It will be quite different this time, madam, if we can work together." Then she spoke in her usual tone, and said sharply, "And I hope to goodness you're not thinking of walking to the village in those thin shoes, madam.

You'll catch your death of cold if you do."

Elizabeth knew then that Nana had accepted her at last. She changed her shoes, and, armed with a basket, went with the dogs into the village.

The sight of Lady Ribblemere emerging from the butcher's shop, sent the blood racing to her cheeks. Her first impulse was to turn and run away; she conquered it, and went on, head held high.

"Dear me, if it is not Mrs. Ramsay!" exclaimed Lady Ribblemere. "I had no idea you were back. And where have you been all this time, I wonder? There were some very strange stories afloat, but I paid very little heed to them. I always think rumours so untrustworthy."

Elizabeth looked her full in the face.

"Stephen and I have been living apart," she said clearly. "So I expect the rumours you heard were true."

Lady Ribblemere became uncomfortable, and somewhat flustered.

"Living apart, my dear! I hope that is all over now? Such a dreadful thing! Ah, I see you have the dogs with you! I do not think I have ever seen so large a dog as Hector. I hope you will have no fights. I always think a dog-fight such a terrible thing. And how is Stephen?"

"He's quite well, thank you."

"What a merciful thing! And his dear mother? I have not seen her for quite an age."

"She's well too. All the family is flourishing."

Evidently Lady Ribblemere was disappointed at having her solicitous enquiries cut short, for after a moment's indecision she turned away, and said vaguely,

"Well, I must be trotting off. I will come and call on you again one day next week and we will have another little talk."

In the grocer's shop Elizabeth walked straight into the Vicar's wife, who exclaimed loudly, and stepped back to inspect her.

"Good gracious, I thought you were in town!" she said, in piercing tones. "Mrs. Trelawney saw you there with some man. So you and Mr. Ramsay haven't separated after all? What an extraordinary thing!"

"That we haven't separated?" Elizabeth asked, seething with inward indignation.

Mrs. Edmondston gave vent to a shrill laugh.

"What queer things you do say, dear Mrs. Ramsay! No, really, I'm so delighted to find that all is well with you. One heard such strange rumours. How glad the Vicar will be when I tell him! He was most upset when he heard that one of his flock had gone astray. He always thinks of the people here as his flock. Such a charming idea, isn't it?

He will be overjoyed. He is so conscientious, you know. But I suppose I should not say that, being his wife. Perhaps you and he will have a little talk one day. He is so sympathetic."

Elizabeth smiled coldly, but said nothing. When she returned to the Halt she found Stephen in the library, writing. Remembering how she had annoyed him before by creeping about for fear of disturbing him, she went boldly in, and proceeded to let fly.

"I am to have a talk with the dear Vicar, because he's so sympathetic, and I am one of his flock. And isn't it an extraordinary thing that we haven't separated after all? The dear Vicar was so upset."

Stephen put down his pen.

"Shall I go and knock his teeth down his throat? Blasted impertinence! Elizabeth, you look such a darling when you're angry."

She laughed.

"It wasn't the Vicar. He wouldn't have said such things; he's nice. It was his—his—I can't think of a bad enough word—his abominable, beastly, inquisitive pig of a wife."

"Why didn't you throw a bloater at her?" asked Stephen, seeing them in her basket.

"Oh, what an awful idea!" cried Elizabeth, bubbling over. "Fancy her astonishment." Then she thought that she would make fun of Lady Ribblemere too, to make Stephen laugh.

He did laugh; he said she was a wonderful mimic. She went away thinking, How easy it is! Why didn't I do all this before?

She went to him proudly that evening, and laid a typewritten copy of the beginning of his manuscript before him. He stared at it, and then at her.

"What—who?" He picked the sheet up. "'Lisbeth, you didn't do this, surely?"

"Yes, I did," she said. "That's the sample. Will you take me on?"

He jumped up.

"My darling, how wonderful of you! When did you learn?"

"Months ago. Mr. Hengist gave me a Remington. I've been taking in typing."

That didn't please Stephen. His chin went up aggressively.

"What for?"

"Oh—amusement!" she said, watching him.

"Were you paid for it?"

"Of course I was."

He looked down at her sternly; she thought, He's being masterful.

"You needed the money?"

"Y-es."

"So sooner than touch mine you—took in typing!"

"I'm very sorry," she said meekly. "I don't see why you should mind, though."

"Oh, Elizabeth, of course I mind! It—it galls me horribly!"

She hung her head, but contrived still to watch his face.

"Well, I won't do it any more if you'd rather I didn't," she said dutifully.

"Certainly you will do no more," Stephen said severely. "I know now why you look so run down and tired."

She suppressed a smile.

"That was 'flu, Stephen."

"Due to pounding away at a typewriter," he said.

"But Stephen, can't I do your typing?" she asked. "I was looking forward to that so much."

"No, darling," Stephen answered firmly. "It's not fit for you."

Elizabeth was beginning to enjoy herself; this was an interesting game. She tried the effect of a sigh, quite a small one.

"I thought—it would give me such an interest in your work," she murmured. "But perhaps I don't type well enough?"

"It's not that a bit!" he said quickly. "You type beautifully! How ever you could unravel my writing beats me!"

She went closer to him.

"I loved doing it, Stephen. If I promise not to tire myself, won't you let me?"

He was weakening, she could see that. He looked at her uncertainly.

"You'd get so sick of it, 'Lisbeth."

"I'll stop if I do. But I like typing."

"Well, if I let you, it must only be my stuff. I won't have you slaving over other people's work."

"Oh no, Stephen, of course not!"

"I'll let you do it as long as you don't overtire yourself," Stephen said, with the air of one making a great concession.

"Thank you, Stephen," Elizabeth said demurely.

That incident, trivial though it was, seemed to make a difference to her. She had discovered how to manage Stephen; she was secretly elated; she had been wily, and had gained her point.

Stephen was late for lunch next day. His worried apology touched her; almost she felt maternal. She said, It doesn't matter, and for the first time in her life really felt that it didn't.

Stephen's attitude puzzled her. There was very little of the lover in his demeanour, except sometimes when he looked at her. The expression in his eyes then made her drop her own quickly; it disturbed her, because it told her so much. In his manner was sometimes constraint, but mostly he preserved an attitude of protective friendliness. Never once did he attempt an embrace or refer to their unnatural existence, but she knew that it was in his mind, that he was watching her, and waiting.

Her part was difficult to play. She felt that all the time she was behaving in a manner not her own, and it was a strain on her. Yet it was becoming more easy, bit by bit, made easy, no doubt, by the guard he set upon his temper and his frank tongue.

But his temper could not always be controlled. Hard at work on his novel he would grow tired and irritable and snappy. In the old days Elizabeth would have shown her hurt and her indignation; now she remembered the words of Mrs. Gabriel, and tried to be patient.

He lost a sheaf of papers containing notes for his book. That was everybody's fault but his own. He upset his drawers in search of the notes, and when Elizabeth came in, greeted her in a tone of rampant exasperation.

"Ah!" he said. His tone said, Here is the culprit! "There seems to be a conspiracy in this house to hide my papers! Good Lord, I should think I've told you often enough that I won't have anything in this room disturbed! It's really disgraceful!"

Elizabeth opened her mouth to retort. This was rank injustice; she wanted to defend herself. Then she remembered Mrs. Gabriel, and managed to smile.

"What have you lost, Stephen? I don't think I've touched anything of yours. Can I help to find it?"

"My notes," he growled, more quietly. "I really do think you might tell the servants to leave my room alone."

"I will," she promised. "Have you looked in that chest in the corner?"

"My dear girl, is it likely I should put them in there?" Stephen demanded.

"You might have done it in an absent-minded moment," she said. Now that the first flash of anger had subsided she was beginning to find this game interesting too. It was rather fun taming the fury of an unreasonable man-creature; it made you feel so old and Machiavellian.

Stephen ransacked another drawer.

"Chest indeed! The last place in the world where I should put them! Really, this is enough to put one off for a week."

Elizabeth went to the chest and tried the lid.

"It's locked!" Stephen snapped.

"Do open it!" she coaxed. "I shan't feel satisfied until I've looked inside."

"If anyone looks it 'll be me," Stephen said disagreeably. "I don't want all my papers in a havoc."

In the face of the muddle he himself had made in his efforts to find the missing notes, this was more unreasonable than ever. Elizabeth choked down another retort.

"All right. You come and look. Do, Stephen!"

He came unwillingly, and unlocked the chest.

"It's perfectly ridiculous," he said. "I shouldn't be such a fool as to forget that I put them here. You seem to have a very poor opinion of my— Oh!" He lifted the notes out of the chest and scowled mightily.

Wonderfully innocent, Elizabeth said,

"Perhaps one of the maids did it. I'll speak to them about it."

Stephen looked around at her sharply; she maintained an air of guileless gravity. Stephen's lips quivered; a twinkle came into his eyes; he began to laugh. Elizabeth laughed too, and at last Stephen said,

"Oh, 'Lisbeth, I am a bad-tempered swine! I'm awfully sorry."

Elizabeth thought, How right Mrs. Gabriel was! What a fool I used to be!

Chapter Twenty-Nine

A month slipped by; Stephen said that it was time they thought about Christmas. What would Elizabeth like to do? Elizabeth did not know; she would do what Stephen wanted. They stayed at this deadlock until a rambling letter came from Mrs. Ramsay, inviting them to spend Christmas with her, if they had nothing better to do.

"Oh, let's do that!" Elizabeth said. "I want to see Mater again."

She feared Cynthia's presence at the flat, but Cynthia had gone with Anthony to his parents, in Norfolk. She was relieved out of all proportion.

"Darling," said Mrs. Ramsay, "I've asked ever so many people to dinner, but I can't remember who, or how many. Isn't it trying? Stephen, whom do you suppose I asked?"

"Colonel Lambert and Bertha Tarrant," Stephen said promptly.

"So I did," Mrs. Ramsay agreed. "Oh, and Mr. and Mrs. Fletcher. Elizabeth,

Thomas nearly seized the turkey this morning. Wasn't it awful? You're in disgrace, aren't you, my angel?"

Thomas grinned widely and flattened his ears.

The party was a merry one, and Mrs. Ramsay more than usually amusing. The Tyrells were present, wilder than ever, and to Elizabeth just as incomprehensible. She thought them mad, and sometimes improper, but Stephen's eyes twinkled at her across the table, and she was able to tolerate the Tyrells. Stephen understood her feelings; that was a bond between them which made things easier to bear.

After Christmas they returned to the Halt, and this time it was Elizabeth who chafed to he in the country again. As soon as Stephen completed a chapter of his hook she typed it, and gradually her interest in the work grew till it was almost as if the book were her own.

Quite unconsciously she was helping him. She went to him once with a sheet of his manuscript, and pointed out a word.

"Stephen, is that 'crude' or 'coarse'?"

He looked at it, then at her.

"'Crude.'" he said slowly, thinking.

"Oh!" Elizabeth frowned a little, and turned away. Stephen's voice followed her.

"It ought to be 'coarse.' Of course it ought. Thanks for pointing it out, 'Lisbeth."

"'Crude' doesn't seem to be quite the word you want," she said apologetically.

"Not a bit. Change it, will you?"

The characters in the book became alive to her. She remembered the impatience she had felt when Stephen and Nina had talked of Norman as though he were a personal friend. She had learned to talk in just the same way about Colin Cardew, the impossible detective whose adventures she had typed out on paper. Miss Arden had thought it silly; Elizabeth saw now that it wasn't silly at all, but quite natural.

It was she who first spoke of Stephen's book in this fashion; he was careful never to speak of it, for fear of boring her.

"When's Frances coming back from Egypt?" she asked, one day at lunch.

Surprise and gratification leaped into Stephen's eyes.

"Oh, do you miss her?"

"Yes, quite. I'm fond of Frances."

"I'll bring her back at once," Stephen said. "What do you think of Davison?"

Her eyes fell; she toyed with her glass.

"Oh—I don't care about him much."

"Untrue to life?"

"No." Of impulse she added, "Too true. I—I recognise Charles."

"If that's so, 'Lisbeth, it happened without my knowing it. He isn't meant to be Charles."

"I'm glad he isn't," Elizabeth said simply.

Lady Ribblemere came to see her one afternoon, and made a determined effort to break into the library. Elizabeth managed to keep her out for some time, but before she took her departure Lady Ribblemere insisted on seeing Stephen.

"He—he hates to be disturbed when he's at work," Elizabeth said, thinking how rude it sounded. "I—simply daren't—let you in!"

Lady Ribblemere tapped her playfully upon the arm with her lorgnettes.

"What a stern guardian! I've known dear Stephen since he was a baby, my dear. I always think that makes such a difference. I shall certainly not disturb him, but I do not think he will mind seeing such an old friend for a few minutes."

With a quaking heart Elizabeth followed her to the library.

The first thing Stephen saw was Lady Ribblemere's massive person. Then, over her ladyship's shoulder he caught sight of Elizabeth's face, which said plainly, I'm very sorry, and I know you hate it, but I couldn't help it.

If Elizabeth had looked as though she thought he ought to like Lady Ribblemere's invasion he would have been furious, just as he had been on the occasion of Lady Ribblemere's first call. But Elizabeth looked horrified, and rather frightened. That amused him, and he smiled.

When Lady Ribblemere had gone (she stayed for half-an-hour), Elizabeth said, in a hurry,

"I tried and tried, Stephen, but she would come. I'm awfully sorry!"

"I know, darling. She's damnably determined. Thank God she doesn't inflict herself upon us often!"

Elizabeth heaved a sigh of relief; Stephen heard it.

"Were you afraid of an outburst from me, 'Lisbeth?"

"Oh, no!" she said quickly. "Of course not!"

A shadow crossed his face. With studied lightness, he said,

"That's an 'horrible story, 'Lisbeth. You were."

His smile made it less hard for her to be frank.

"Yes, I suppose I was."

The shadow disappeared; Stephen went to her. She thought he was going to kiss her, and instinctively she drew back. In an instant she had recovered herself, but it was too late. Stephen returned to his desk. Elizabeth had a fleeting glimpse of his face; the sternness about his mouth, his tight-shut lips and sad eyes made her ashamed and miserable. She rose, and out of pity went to him. He looked up, and blushing, she kissed him lightly, on his forehead.

A hand took her wrist firmly; Stephen looked into her eyes.

"Elizabeth—was that—love—or—just—duty?"

She could not answer him in words. After a moment he released her.

"I see. Don't—do it again, dear. There's a limit to what I can stand. I'd rather have—nothing—than—your loveless kisses."

"I'm sorry," she whispered.

He tried to sound cheerful.

"We won't try to force it, 'Lisbeth, will we?"

Mr. Hengist came to stay with them. Elizabeth drove to the station to meet him in her pony-trap, a gift from Stephen.

"Hullo!" he grunted. "You look Father different from when last I saw you, young lady."

"Was I an awful wreck?" she smiled.

248

"A miserable, skinny little fool," he said honestly.

Elizabeth laughed.

"If you're going to be rude I shan't drive you home in my beautiful trap," she threatened. "Stephen gave it me. Isn't it lovely? The pony's name is Timothy, warranted not to shy or bolt."

"I'm glad of that," Mr. Hengist said, climbing into the trap. "I'm not so young as I was."

"Oh, but he does!" Elizabeth said. "He's perfectly dreadful, but I don't think he means to be naughty. Anyway, he's a darling. Wasn't it nice of Stephen to give him to me?"

"Very. You're more lucky than you know."

She looked at him gravely.

"No, Mr. Hengist."

"No? Glad to hear it then."

"I haven't lived in a Baker Street lodging-house for nearly a year without learning to appreciate—things like this."

"Excellent," said Mr. Hengist. He then remarked, "I like your husband."

"Yes, so do I," Elizabeth said calmly.

Stephen was awaiting them in the garden, with the tea. He shook hands with Mr. Hengist very warmly.

"I didn't come to meet you because I knew Elizabeth wanted to show off in the pony-trap," he explained. "Besides which I was horribly busy."

Elizabeth could not choke the feeling that it was rude of Stephen to have said that. Mr. Hengist evidently didn't think so, but he, like Stephen, had a different standard of politeness.

He and Stephen played golf next morning, but in the afternoon when Stephen was at work, he came and sat beside Elizabeth under the elm-tree, and smoked.

For some time Elizabeth watched him in silence; then at last she said.

"Do begin, Mr. Hengist! I know you're going to talk."

He turned his head and surveyed her in some surprise.

"That," he said, "sounds most unlike you."

"Yes, that's why I said it," Elizabeth answered naively.

"Well, it'll do for my text," he remarked, and settled himself deeper in his chair.

Elizabeth put down her needlework.

"So far so good," Mr. Hengist said. "During the past year, my child, though you may not know it, you've been shedding the skin of hypocrisy. No, longer than that. Correctly speaking, the shedding process began with your marriage."

Elizabeth looked at him wide-eyed.

"When you were quite a small kid," Mr. Hengist went on, "you were Elizabeth pure and simple. After that you became Elizabeth-Anne. Do you see what I mean?"

"Yes, but I don't know that I—"

"Probably not. What I want to know before I go any further is, Are you going to snub me if I say things detrimental to your aunt's character?"

"Oh, I never snub—"

"That is Elizabeth-Anne," said Mr. Hengist, to a cloud above him.

She had to laugh.

"No, I'm not going to snub you."

"Thanks, Elizabeth. Your aunt is a reactionary. She belongs to a dead age, only she refused to see that it was dead, but instead tried to carry it on in the shape of yourself. No doubt she was actuated by the best of motives. Unfortunately she has a narrow mind, and you a pliant disposition. If, as a child, you had stuck to your own character your aunt would to-day be a very different woman. A strong-willed niece would have made her move along with the times. As it was, hers was the mastermind, and your character had to mould itself to hers. With women one must be top-dog and the other underdog. I discovered that quite early in life. Rather interesting. Are you listening to me?"

"Yes. I never heard anything like it before."

"All the more reason to listen carefully and afterwards digest it. I'd got to the point where your character, through weakness—we'll call it pliancy—got moulded into your aunt's character. I watched it happening with a good deal of regret, and some interest. What you've always lacked is moral courage. Sooner than brave the storm your own ideas would raise, you covered-them up and pretended to think as your aunt thought. Whatever she wanted you to think, you thought; whatever she wanted you to like, you liked. That is to say, you pretended to. Your aunt managed to convince you that it was wrong to have your own opinions, so you started on a double pretence. You pretended to your aunt, and you pretended to yourself. That's when you became Elizabeth-Anne. People like your father enthused about your sweet disposition, and tractableness. People like me, who are always rude, thought you insufferable. Well, the pretence became a habit, so much so that Elizabeth got thoroughly smothered until not even yourself knew that she was there. But she was. Asleep, I daresay." He paused, but Elizabeth made no remark. "Then you met Stephen. I'm going to hit hard now, Elizabeth, I'm afraid. You pretend to be in love with Stephen because he was a celebrity, and because you thought how jolly it would be to get married and be independent. That was Elizabeth stirring underneath Elizabeth-Anne. You didn't love him. You got caught by glamour—and ignorance. You married him, and your father and aunt were sentimental about it and thoroughly pleased. Next you discovered that marriage wasn't quite such an idyll as you imagined it was going to be. You were badly handicapped by the fact that you didn't love your husband. Elizabeth-Anne, being still on top, you tried hard to think you did love him, instead of facing the truth quietly and seeing what could be done about it. All this time, Elizabeth was slowly waking up. When you left Stephen you'd left off pretending for a time. I'm not going into the question of whether it was right or wrong to leave him. I only know that it was sincere. Well, you agreed to part, and then you began your life alone. I watched you. It was interesting. At first I thought you'd go home to your people. You didn't, and I realised that Elizabeth was more awake than I'd guessed. You began to get fed up with your aunt. That was rather a severe blow to Elizabeth-Anne. However, it didn't kill her. You made a fool of yourself over Wendell. You see the hand of Elizabeth-Anne? You evidently had a row with Wendell, and Elizabeth climbed uppermost again. It was Elizabeth-Anne who married Stephen, my child, but it was Elizabeth who parted from him, and who returned to him. And now it's a fight between the two. You're trying to be Elizabeth, but you can't help feeling that you ought to be Elizabeth-Anne. See?"

Elizabeth drew a long breath.

"I'm—beginning to. You—don't know how hard it is."

"No, I don't suppose I do. When you learn to love your husband it won't be hard."

"Shall I—ever?" she asked, a pathetic catch in her voice.

Mr. Hengist took his pipe out of his mouth.

"Why not?" he said.

"I don't know," Elizabeth answered helplessly.

"If I were you," said Mr. Hengist severely, "I should set about it as quickly as possible. Nothing will be natural to you in your life together until you do. Then it'll all be natural."

"I wish I could," she sighed.

"That's a step in the right direction anyway," grunted Mr. Hengist.

Chapter Thirty

It was surprising how amicably they were living together. At times it was a strain; occasionally Elizabeth-Anne gained the ascendancy over Elizabeth. On Stephen's side great forbearance was necessary, and greater patience. How big a strain that was, only he knew. There were days when the sight of Elizabeth almost hurt him; then he would go out for a tramp over the fields, alone, fighting himself.

His book failed to please him. He wrote and rewrote, fell into exasperation and tore up a month's work. Elizabeth saw him do it and was horrified. He threw the rent sheets into the fire. It was on the tip of her tongue to exclaim that it would make the hearth dirty and untidy. She remembered Mr. Hengist's words, and said severely to herself, Be quiet, Elizabeth-Anne. The hearth didn't matter; what did matter was Stephen's anger at his own failure.

Sympathy for him drove out annoyance. She was not sure what she could say: whether he would rather she paid no heed.

"So much for that!" Stephen snapped.

This, thought Elizabeth, is where I have to pick him up and start him off again.

"How much have you destroyed?" she asked.

"Six chapters. The rest can follow them for all I care."

She wrinkled her brow.

"Oh . . . from where Frances comes back to Southampton. Don't tear up any more, Stephen."

"It's all rotten," he said moodily.

"No, it isn't. I don't know anything about the style, but it's an interesting story. What are you going to do with Frances now?"

"Drown her."

She laughed.

"No, don't! I love Frances."

"Well, she's hopeless as soon as she comes back to England."

"Leave her in Egypt then," she suggested practically.

He sat down. He liked to discuss his book, especially with Elizabeth who knew it almost by heart.

"How can I leave her in Egypt? She's going to marry Derrick."

"Can't he go out there? If I were in love with a girl I wouldn't stay in England when she was abroad."

"Yes, but don't forget that he's too damned proud to ask her to marry him."

Elizabeth was silent for a moment.

"Stephen, I don't believe he would be."

"You— Don't you?" He was interested, and leaned forward in his chair.

"If he was so awfully in love with her—and knew that she loved him, it wouldn't matter about her money. Make him get some work to do and go out to her."

"Instead of my original idea of making her do the wooing?"

"Yes. Why not? I've read books where the rich girl makes the penniless man marry her, but I've never read one where it was the other way round."

Stephen sat still for a while, pondering it. Then he got up.

"I say, 'Lisbeth, that's rather a fine notion! I believe I can make something out of it. Thanks awfully for helping! I think I'll just sketch out a scheme now." He went back to his desk, and presently his pen began to move, faster and faster.

Elizabeth curled herself up on the sofa and smiled secretly. She watched Stephen's profile with tenderness in her eyes. She thought, I may not know much about writing a book, but I'm beginning to know a lot about this Man-thing of mine. It gave her a delightful sense of power. It was wonderful that anyone so big and strong could be so helpless and easily influenced.

Her glance travelled to Stephen's straight shoulders. She was glad they were not rounded from much writing; she would hate him to stoop.

She relaxed into the downy cushions behind her, and started to read. She had long since given up the habit of being unnaturally quiet while Stephen wrote. She had become so used to the scratch of his pen that she paid very little heed to it. He did not seem to mind if she coughed, or made up the fire, so she did both, whenever she felt inclined.

Presently one of the maids came in with the tea. Elizabeth made it herself, and she chinked the cups suggestively. She had discovered that if she called Stephen away from his work he hated it, just as he hated her to bring tea to his desk. But if she said nothing, but started to pour out he was sure to leave his writing and come to the fireside.

He did it to-day. The cloud had gone from his brow, and his eyes were smiling and bright. He sat down on a low stool and began to eat buttered toast from the dish in the hearth. He always ate it like that, promiscuously, and he always put his cup and saucer down on the floor beside him. Elizabeth, from thinking it unseemly, had grown to like the habit. She would never sit on the floor herself, and she would never eat lumps of sugar as Stephen did, out of the bowl, but she found it comfortable when he did so. It seemed cosy and intimate.

"Darling, it was a wonderful idea of yours! I'm getting on splendidly now."

"Do hurry up and let me have some to read," she said, elated at her success.

He looked eagerly up at her.

"Do you really want it, 'Lisbeth?"

"I shouldn't say so if I didn't."

"Yes, you would," he retorted audaciously, but smiled as he said it.

It was an understanding smile; instead of being hurt she returned it.

"That's a mean attack," she said. "Haven't I been frank with you?"

"You have, darling, and I apologise. Last night you said if I was going to cross out things and write squiggles on top you wouldn't read another word."

"Yes, and I meant it, too. Don't let the butter ooze on to the carpet, for goodness' sake!"

"Sorry. Did it?"

"No, but I was afraid it might."

"Oh, I see. Prevention's better than cure. Did I tell you I had a letter from Cynthia this morning?"

"No. Anything interesting?"

"She's had laryngitis and Anthony wants to take her away."

"Poor thing! Where are they going?"

"Nowhere, because their nurse is away on a holiday and there's no one to look after Christopher. Rotten luck, isn't it?"

Slowly Elizabeth put her cup down. She glanced down at Stephen.

"Do you think—I mean, would Cynthia mind—if we offered to take Christopher?"

"We—? I say, that's an idea! You're full of them today, 'Lisbeth. Wouldn't it be a bore for you, though?"

"I'd love to take care of Christopher. Only—Cynthia might not like it. I—I hardly like to offer . . ."

Bewilderment was in Stephen's face.

"Why not? Why should Cynthia mind?"

She flushed.

"She—doesn't like me. Oh, Stephen, you know! Because of our

separation—and—and Charles—and all that."

"And what has any of that got to do with Cynthia?" Stephen asked dangerously.

"I knew by her face—when she saw—Charles with me— what she thought."

"If she thought anything filthy she can go to hell and take her thoughts with her," Stephen said calmly.

"Well, really, Stephen!" Elizabeth expostulated.

"Whatever she thought she doesn't think now. That's a bit involved. Anyway, she knows Wendell wasn't your lover. You wouldn't be here if he had been."

She looked at him curiously.

"Wouldn't you—have taken me back?"

He stared into the fire; his profile was hard all at once, and stern.

"I don't know. I— Don't let's talk of such a thing, 'Lisbeth. It makes me feel ill."

Woman-like she pressed the point.

"No, but would you, Stephen?"

"What, be ill? Probably."

"Don't be so tiresome! Would you have taken me back?"

He knelt suddenly, and took her hands in his.

"It would have been an awful pill for me to swallow, 'Lisbeth, but—yes, I'd have taken you. I—couldn't have helped myself. When I came to you—that day—I was prepared—even for that."

"Oh—Stephen!"

He kissed her hands quickly.

"I didn't believe it, darling, I swear that! It was just—a possibility. Don't let's speak of it. What about Christopher?"

Her hands lay in his. An awed look was in her eyes.

"You—must love me—very much—to have been able to—come to me—thinking that."

"I didn't think it."

"You were afraid, though. I see now. I—I wish I were more—worthy of your love, Stephen."

He bent his head.

"You're worthy of much more. Don't let it—worry you, darling. You've given me more than I hoped for."

"I think it's time I did let things worry me," she said slowly. "I give you—nothing. It's you who give—all the time."

"You give all that you can. Don't be unhappy, my dearest."

"I ought to be unhappy. I hate myself. I hate Elizabeth-Anne."

He looked up.

"How much?"

She had not meant to mention Elizabeth-Anne; it had slipped out before she noticed it. She had to explain.

Stephen laughed.

"Just like Mr. Hengist! Now I shall know what to say to you when you reprimand me for being late for breakfast."

"What will you say?" she smiled.

"I shall say, Shut up, Elizabeth-Anne."

"That ought to cure me," she nodded. "About Christopher ..."

"Ring Cynthia up and put the plan before her."

"Oh, I can't! I— You do it!"

"Not going to. It's your job. Don't be silly, 'Lisbeth. Cyn'll jump at it."

"I'm not so sure."

"Well, I am." He jumped up and went to the telephone. Elizabeth heard him ask for Cynthia's number.

Presently the bell rang; Stephen unhooked the receiver. Evidently Cynthia herself had answered the call.

" Hullo, that you, Cyn? . . . Sorry about your illness. Sorry for you, I mean. Must be a relief for poor old Anthony to have your voice reduced to a whisper . . . What? ... I said it must be a rel— Oh, indeed? Nice way ter talk to your elders and betters . . . What? . . . What? ... I didn't say I was a plural. Elder and better, then. Glad you recognise the fact. Look here, Elizabeth wants to speak to you! . . . Yes, *Elizabeth*. . . . Hold on, will you?" He turned.

"Come on, old girl."

Reluctantly she took the receiver from him.

"Oh—how do you do, Cynthia?" she said, rather shakily. Cynthia's cracked voice reached her.

"Hullo, how are you?"

"I'm all right, thanks. I'm so sorry you've been ill. I—i wondered whether—you'd let—let me take care of— of Christopher for you—while you and Anthony go away. I—I would so love to—if—if you'd trust him—to me."

There was a short pause.

"That's extraordinarily nice of you, Elizabeth," Cynthia said. "Do you mean it?"

"Yes, oh yes! But I thought perhaps you'd— rather not?"

"Well, of course you haven't had much experience with small boys," Cynthia replied deliberately. "Still, I don't see that I need worry."

"I—didn't mean that—exactly."

"Didn't you? Look here—you can't, but no matter— If I send him are you sure he won't tire you out? He's fairly rampageous, you know."

"Of course he won't. And Nana will know what to do if anything happens, won't she? When shall I come to fetch him?"

"Anthony wants to bear me off on Friday. Would Thursday suit you?"

"Yes, any day. It's—nice of you to let me have him, Cynthia."

"I don't quite see it. The niceness seems to be on your side. I'll thank you properly when you come to fetch Christopher."

"Please, don't!" Elizabeth said. "Would you like to speak to Stephen again?"

"Not a bit, thanks. Till Thursday, then."

"Yes. Goodbye."

"Short and sweet," Stephen remarked. "I gather we are to fetch the Cherubic One on Thursday?"

"How clever of you!" she said, dimpling. "Stephen, won't it be fun?"

"We shall see," he said. "Rather strenuous fun if I know anything about Christopher."

"I don't mind that," she answered.

Christopher celebrated the first evening of his visit by howling lustily for "Marmar." Nana exhorted him in vain; Elizabeth's blendishments increased his tears. Stephen appeared upon the scene, and there fell a slight lull. Christopher sat up.

"Look here, my worthy nephew, how do you suppose I am to work when you kick up this unholy din? What's the matter?"

"Don't ask him that, for heaven's sake!" Elizabeth said hastily.

"Want *Marmar*!" sobbed Christopher.

"Oh, Lord!" Stephen said ruefully.

"Pick him up!" demanded Christopher, who generally referred to himself in the third person.

Stephen obeyed.

"Anything else I can do for you, my lord?"

"Take him downstairs," Christopher advised him.

"What do you think?" Stephen asked.

"I *think* he ought to stay in bed," Elizabeth answered, "but perhaps it would be more peaceful if he came down to the library for a bit."

So Christopher was carried downstairs, and regaled with three chocolates and the story of the Three Bears. He then fell asleep, and was cautiously conveyed up to bed. Having proved himself to have very much the master-mind he proceeded, during the rest of his visit, to rule his hosts with a rod of iron. The only person who could withstand him was Nana. With considerable sagacity Christopher attached himself to his uncle and aunt, and spent his time in riotous living. His chief joy was to accompany Elizabeth in the pony-trap when she went shopping, and to hold the reins. On one of these expeditions he was introduced to Lady Ribblemere, and when she bent to embrace him, backed quickly, and requested her to go away.

"I–I think it's because you have a large hat on," Elizabeth said, in excuse for his behaviour. "He–he doesn't like them."

"He does," Christopher said firmly.

"Aren't you going to give me a nice kiss, dear?" Lady Ribblemere coaxed him.

Christopher shook his head violently.

"Kiss Hector," he said, and nearly fell out of the trap in his efforts to clasp the wolf-hound round the neck.

"Dear me, he is a very sturdy little fellow," Lady Ribblemere said. "What are you going to be when you're grown up, Christopher?"

Christopher considered the point at length.

"Engine-driver," he said presently. "Ta-ta!" He waved his hand inexorably, and requested Timothy to Gee-up.

When his summary dismissal of Lady Ribblemere was reported, between giggles, to his uncle, Stephen tossed him up in his arms and told him that he showed great discrimination. Christopher grasped his coat collar and struggled for words.

"He had—a wide on the pony!" he informed Stephen. "Auntie held him on."

Stephen reflected that Auntie had never been so gay as now, when she was in such demand. It was a surprise to him when she romped with Christopher; all self-consciousness left her; again and again rippling laughter came, so that he laid down his pen to watch her, and to listen. Or he would be drawn into the game, much to Christopher's delight, and would impersonate an engine, or a pony, mostly of the runaway order, for his nephew's amusement.

Nana unearthed aged picture-books from one of the box-rooms, and these Christopher perused, with the aid of his hosts. He sat upon the floor with his aunt on one side and his uncle on the other, and the book open on his lap. One fat finger pressed hard upon a luridly coloured cow.

"Moo-cow."

His hearers applauded nobly. A catechism followed.

"What's his name?"

"Jeremiah," Stephen said.

"Oh! What's he doing?"

"Chewing the cud."

"Don't be so feeble," laughed Elizabeth.

"Well, you tell him."

"Not at all. I'm not a novelist."

"He's *eating*," Christopher said.

"That's what I said," Stephen pointed out.

"Didn't!" Christopher said scornfully. He turned to Elizabeth. You tell me 'about him."

So Elizabeth related a long story concerning the cow, punctuated by comments and stern questions from the auditor. Ribald suggestions came from Stephen, and a remark that the story would make fine melodrama.

Elizabeth ran dry at last, and ended the tale. Christopher digested it in silence, and looked so seraphic that Elizabeth hugged him and cried:

"Oh you noble angel!"

Over his head she met Stephen's eyes, and grew rather paler as she read the thought in them. She put Christopher down. Did Stephen want a son so badly? Their eyes held for a moment, her's wide with dawning realization. It was Stephan who looked away first, and who flushed, not Elizabeth.

"What is you staring at uncle for?" demanded Christopher, displeased at Elizabeth's sudden neglect of himself.

"Was I, Darling," she said, bending over him.

Stephan rose.

"I must get on with my work," he said, rather strained, and went out of them room.

Anthony and Cleopatra came at the end of the month to claim their offspring. Christopher welcomed them jubilantly, and in a state of wild excitement tried, in one sentence, to tell his mother all that he had done.

The Ruthvens stayed over the weekend, and the faithless Christopher had no further use for his aunt and uncle. He proceeded to tell Cynthia of Auntie's unheard of stupidity in various minor details.

"Marmar, when Auntie barfed him she didn't put a towel in the airwing cupboard!" he said in a shocked voice. "An' she didn't put his socks on afore his vest!"

"My son this is awful," Cynthia said solemnly. "I hope you told her how to do it properly."

"He did," Elizabeth said, grimacing.

"Most conscientiously," Stephen nodded. "Even my way of telling well-worn stories was hopelessly wrong."

"I shall miss him awfully," Elizabeth sighed.

Cynthia looked up for an instant, but said nothing.

Chapter Thirty-One

In March Elizabeth came hurrying into the library one morning in a state of great agitation.

"Stephen, what am I to do? They're trying to rope me into the Mothers' Union or something. Meetings and blankets and horrible coal tickets!"

"Who's trying to rope you in?"

"Lady Ribblemere, and Mrs. Edmondston, and Mrs. Fraser. I don't want to, Stephen!"

"Well, don't," he said coolly.

"Yes, but everybody seems to belong to the Union, or whatever it is."

"All the more reason for keeping out of it."

"But I don't know how to keep out of it without being rude! They all urge me to join and help my fellow-creatures. I don't want to."

"My darling, there's no earthly reason why you should. You're much too young. Say I won't hear of it."

"They wouldn't believe me. And it seems too rude and disobliging to refuse."

Stephen pointed an accusing finger.

"Elizabeth-Anne, depart!"

"I don't see that I'm being Elizabeth-Anne-ish at all. Lady Ribblemere's an awful bore, but she's been very nice to me, and I don't want to seem churlish. Besides, what'll they think of me?"

"Most of 'em will wish they'd been courageous enough to stand out too."

"Do you suppose they will?" Elizabeth said dubiously. She looked out into the garden, and the sight of the daffodils nodding beneath the window seemed to make her more indignant. "The idea of wanting me to go to meetings in a stuffy hall when the flowers are all coming up, and my speckled hen's eggs nearly due to hatch out!"

"Disgraceful!" Stephen agreed, controlling his quivering lip.

"I shan't join."

"No, don't."

Elizabeth's pet lamb appeared on the lawn.

"The angel! I don't care what they think! They haven't got a lamb to look after. Oh, it's eating the hyacinth buds!" She ran out to coax the lamb away from the flower-beds. To Lady Ribblemere, who called to ask her for the last time to join the committee, she extended a polite but firm refusal. She surprised Lady Ribblemere, but she surprised herself more.

She thought how delighted Mr. Hengist would be if he could hear. Elizabeth-Anne was dying, slowly but surely.

She had made new friends in the neighbourhood, young wives like herself, and Mr. Trelawney. To him she went for advice about her garden. He gave it willingly, and tried hard to make her familiar with botanical terms. Mindful of her first error with him she smiled prettily, and said,

"It's no good, Mr. Trelawney. When you say, I should put some Bachelor's Buttons on the south bed, I know where I am, but when you say _Ranunculus_ something-or-other, I'm absolutely at sea."

"It is astonishing how ignorant people are of the most ordinary terms," he said severely.

But he was a great help in the garden, because he knew when you had to plant out your boxes of seeds, and where would be the best place to grow sweet-peas, and that if you moved the peonies they wouldn't flower till a year afterwards.

What with the garden and the lamb and the broods of fluffy chickens, Elizabeth's time was fully and happily occupied. So that when Stephen went to London on business she elected to remain at the Halt.

He was away for a week, and she missed him unutterably. She missed the smell of tobacco in the house, the litter of papers in the library, the litter of

Instead of the Thorn

ties and shirts in his room. Meals without him were depressing and lonely; the evenings seemed interminable. She realised with a start that she wanted Stephen. Much as she loved the Halt, it was a prison without him. A dozen times in the day she wanted Stephen's help, or wanted to tell him something that had happened when she was in the village.

She began to count the days to his return, quite unconsciously. Then, on the last morning, a telegram came to say that he could not get back until three days later.

A wave of bitter disappointment swept over her. Until the telegram came she had not known how much she was looking forward to Stephen's return. She felt ill-used and miserable; none of her preparations were of any use now; there would be no cosy talk over the fire that evening.

Then suddenly she thought, Why am I so disappointed? Why do I feel as though I'd like to go to bed and cry?

In all her life she had known nothing to equal this strange sensation; she brooded over it, wide-eyed, twisting her fingers. She thought about Stephen, all the mannerisms that were his, everything he did or said. She looked at his empty chair by the desk, and a little, wondering smile came.

During the days that followed the smile was often on her lips. She had the look of one who hugs some delectable secret.

The day of Stephen's homecoming dawned at last. Elizabeth spent a long time over the arrangement of the dinner-menu. She put fresh flowers in all the rooms, and just before tea changed her frock.

The car purred to the front-door; Elizabeth heard it, and became very busy with the tea-cosy. Stephen's voice was raised in the hall.

"'Lisbeth!"

She went to him, flushed and shy, adorable, and stood temptingly before him. His arms went out, and fell again to his sides.

"Darling—it's damned good to see you again," he said huskily.

She smiled up at him, and waited. Stephen looked at her, then squared his shoulders.

"Am I—in time for tea?" he jerked out.

"It's just ready," Elizabeth said.

They went to the library, and he sat down at Elizabeth's feet, just as usual. For some time he did not say anything. Elizabeth touched his shoulder.

"New tie," she remarked.

"Yes. Rather nice, isn't it? I brought you some chocolates, 'Lisbeth, and—and this, if you'll have it." Anxiously he watched her open the little velvet case.

"Oh, Stephen, what a beautiful bracelet! Thank you very, very much!" She held out her hand. "Put it on, please. I'd like you to."

He did so; she saw that his fingers trembled slightly.

"Glad you like it, 'Lisbeth." His lips brushed her wrist. "Any news?"

"Heaps. Tell me yours first."

"It would bore you. Purely business."

"It wouldn't bore me," Elizabeth said. "Please tell!"

"Well, the biggest and best piece of news is that I've signed a contract with an American firm of publishers. For the new book."

"Stephen, how wonderful! Who are they?"

"Crosby, Thompson Company." He went into details. "And, 'Lisbeth, I'm going to have a shot at dramatising 'Caraway Seeds.' Think it could be done?"

She was almost as excited as he was; her eyes shone; she clapped her hands.

"What fun! Of course it could be done! As soon as you've absolutely finished the new book, let's go and see lots of plays and take notes about stage-craft. Isn't Mater pleased?"

"Thrilled to the core. She sent her love, by the way, and said that she was coming to pay us a visit soon. Now let me have your news."

"It won't sound much after yours. But prepare yourself for a tragedy. Two of the ducklings are dead."

"Not Samuel?" he said.

"No, thank goodness. Samuel is as perky as ever. I don't know what went wrong with the others, and all Nana said was, Ah, well!"

"How unfeeling!"

"Wasn't it? The other piece of news is that Maisie Fletcher has a baby-boy.

Mr. Fletcher's as proud as a peacock about it."

"Oh!" Stephen said. Then, rather drearily, he said, "Lucky chap."

Elizabeth's eyes were veiled by her lashes.

"Flo's going rather lame. She picked up a thorn, and it was rather deeply embedded. I managed to get it out, though, didn't I, Flo my darling?"

Stephen stroked the dog's silky head absent-mindedly There fell a silence. The maid came to clear the tea away, and Elizabeth picked up her work-bag.

The days slipped by; it seemed to Stephen that Elizabeth had subtly changed. Again and again he was struck by an intangible something in her attitude, and would stare at her, puzzled. It was almost as though she were coquetting with him, only that was hardly possible. She had never done it; he did not think it was in her nature. But whether she was coquetting or not, the change in her made it doubly hard for him to preserve his friendly calm towards her. One moment she was aloof, the next tantalizingly near. Nothing could have been sweeter than her treatment of him when, for two days, he was suffering from neuralgia. She hovered about with eau-de-cologne, and she was always ready to shake up the cushions. She wore a strange smile, too, so tiny that he wondered whether it really was a smile. It fascinated him, but his arms ached to hold her.

She was thinking, This is when he's helpless and docile, dependent on me. I like it.

She was gentle with him, and sympathetic, and she allowed no one to make a noise in the room. He lay on the sofa, eyes closed, frowning, and from time to time she went to him, to sprinkle more eau-de-cologne on a handkerchief. Once, because she could not resist it, she stroked back an errant strand of hair. Stephen's eyes flew open. She allowed her hand to rest for a moment near his head, then she went back to her chair, conscious that he was watching her.

Then Mrs. Ramsay came to stay with them, bringing Thomas, and after three days spoke tentatively to Elizabeth.

"Darling, how are things with you? Is it easier yet?"

Elizabeth would not look at her.

"Yes, mater. Much."

"Can I be officious, please? Does Stephen get on your nerves still?"

Elizabeth shook her head. Stephen had stayed in bed one day when he had had neuralgia, and he had not shaved. Elizabeth had hardly noticed it. That showed her how she had changed.

"I'm so glad, because he's such a dear thing," Mrs. Ramsay said. "So very human. Thomas is chasing the lamb again. How bad of him; Elizabeth, I want you and Stephen to be happy. Tell me when you are."

She did not allude to the subject again during her visit, but when she left the Halt, Elizabeth of her own accord put her arms about her, and whispered,

"Mater, I do love you."

Mrs. Ramsay laughed, and kissed her.

"I hoped you would, darling. Madness and all?"

"That is the part I love."

"Then you're a new Elizabeth, my dear, because I used to horrify you dreadfully."

"What were you and Mater whispering about?" Stephen asked, when his mother was gone.

"That's our secret," Elizabeth answered mysteriously.

"I don't think I altogether approve of you and Mater having secrets," he said solemnly.

Elizabeth laughed and went away to pick flowers for the drawing-room. It struck him that there was invitation in her backward glance, but he could not be sure.

Meanwhile his novel grew quickly, and as quickly was typed. Having found that her first, nervous criticisms were received favourably, Elizabeth grew bolder, and had many suggestions to make. On one occasion they came near to quarrelling, and she had to put a check on her tongue. She criticised adversely, forgetting that Stephen was sensitive about his work. When the argument became acrimonious and she saw that he was really angry she began to eat her words, very cunningly, until at last she had smoothed Stephen's ruffled temper and made him docile again, and repentant. Then he thought over all that she had said, lectured her severely, and went away to rewrite the few pages she had not liked. She was careful not to let him see her triumph.

In May Miss Arden wrote to beg Elizabeth to come and see her soon. Elizabeth did not want to go at all, but she replied that she would love to come to the Boltons for a week if Aunt Anne would have her. It was not Elizabeth-Anne who wrote that letter, but herself, in the spirit of coquetry that had come to her.

She told Stephen of the invitation, and demurely asked, Can I go?

Stephen sat up very straight in his chair; through her lashes she watched a blank look come into his face.

"But, 'Lisbeth, when I asked you to come to town with me last month, you refused!"

"I feel different now, you see," she explained. "I'd like to see Auntie and Father again. Besides the chicks were too young to be left last month."

"Damn the chickens!" Stephen growled.

Elizabeth played with her wedding-ring.

"I won't go if you'd—if you'd rather I stayed. If—if you—want me."

He squared his shoulders; the frown went out of his eyes.

"No. Of course you must go if you feel you'd like to. Only—how long will it be, Elizabeth?"

"Not more than a week," she assured him.

"Not *more*—! Yes, of course. I—I hope you'll enjoy yourself, darling."

She rose, looking strangely down at him. She was near to stamping her foot at his density.

"When do you depart?" Stephen asked, with studied coolness.

"The day after to-morrow," Elizabeth replied.

There was a pause.

"I see. You might look the Mater up while you're in town. Not unless you want to, of course."

"Sometimes," Elizabeth said breathlessly, "I'd—I'd like to hit you!"

He got up, slowly.

"What have I done? Why are you fed up with me? I didn't know that I'd—"

268

"You haven't done anything," Elizabeth answered:. "You don't."

He was puzzled and anxious.

"Don't? Elizabeth, what is it? Please tell me! What's the matter?"

She gave a funny little laugh that was also a sob.

"You—you silly old thing, Stephen! Nothing's the matter. Nothing at all!"

He took a. step towards her, but she turned quickly and fled.

Ten minutes later, from her bedroom window, she saw him stride away across the fields, with his hands deep in the pockets of his old shooting jacket and his head bare to the spring breezes.

She watched him go, the dogs leaping about him, and her heart swelled with pride of his fine shoulders and great height, and the even swing of his walk. She blew him a kiss from the tips of her fingers. He was hers; her man, clever and stupid, strong and so weak.

"Stephen!" she said softly. "I love you, I love you!"

But she went away on Thursday to stay with her father.

Chapter Thirty-Two

"Oh, my darling!" Miss Arden sighed. "After all these months. I've so longed to have you with me again!"

Elizabeth was touched. She slipped her arm about Miss Arden and hugged her slightly.

"I'm sorry, auntie, but I couldn't come before. You and Father must come down to the Halt this summer when the roses are in bloom. You will, won't you?"

"Oh, my dear, of course! Elizabeth, you're fatter!"

"She is looking the picture of health," Lawrence said complacently.

"I've never seen you so well-covered!" exclaimed Miss Arden, stepping back to survey her niece. "Never!"

"It comes of associating so much with the lady in Stephen's new book," laughed Elizabeth. "Stephen informs the world in three places that she's deep-bosomed. Isn't it an awful expression? I'm growing like her."

"Elizabeth *dear*! And—and how is—Stephen?"

269

Elizabeth went to the looking-glass and removed her hat.

"Rather peevish. He doesn't like being left alone, poor old thing."

"My dear Elizabeth, surely you must have known that our invitation included him?" Lawrence said.

"Oh yes, father! I just—didn't want him. How is Mr. Hengist?"

Miss Arden compressed her lips.

"Very well, I believe. That man is never ill. He is coming to dine with us to-night, I am sorry to say. I should have liked to have you to myself, but your father had already invited him. I hope you don't mind, Elizabeth?"

"Of course I don't. Mr. Hengist is my oldest friend. I *want* to see him."

"In that case, it's all right then," Miss Arden said, in a voice that told Elizabeth that it was not all right at all, but all wrong.

She longed to see Mr. Hengist; she put on a wispy black evening frock for his benefit, having found that in most men's eyes black found favour. She spent much time in the arrangement of her hair and when at last she was ready looked keenly at her reflection in the mirror.

"I've matured," she thought. "I used to be pretty. I'm more than that now. I'm different. I'm Elizabeth-pure-and-simple."

She went down to the drawing-room and stood for a moment against the white door, smiling. Mr. Hengist, rising, thought that her great eyes were like stars. She looked older, but infinitely more beautiful.

She came forward.

"By Jove!" thought Mr. Hengist. "She's suddenly grown into a woman. She's got poise at last! Poise and assurance."

"I'm so sorry if I've kept everyone waiting," Elizabeth said. "Mr. Hengist, I am so very, very glad to see you."

He kissed her, and patted her shoulder.

"My dear child," he said gruffly. "Yes, and yes, and yes."

She laughed up at him.

"Is it yes, Mr. Hengist?"

"It looks like it," he answered.

"Aha! You see, I've got a new name for myself." Her eyes danced; he thought her transfigured.

"Well, what is it, rogue?"

"Elizabeth-pure-and-simple."

"That's excellent," he said. "What chased the lady away?"

She shook her head.

"I shan't tell you."

Mr. Hengist looked at her.

"I believe I know," he said.

"What on earth are you talking about?" Miss Arden asked. "Come along in to dinner. ..."

"And how," said Mr. Hengist, shaking out his table-napkin, "is the *magnum opus?*"

"Ah yes!" Lawrence interjected. "The great book! Does it progress?"

"Fast," Elizabeth answered. "It's had some ups and downs, but I think all is plain sailing now."

"Quite an inspired writer," Lawrence said meditatively.

Elizabeth thought of the many times she had had to encourage Stephen to go on with the book, and had discussed it with him, and had coaxed away his fits of dissatisfaction. She smiled to herself.

Mr. Hengist was watching her.

"Does he need much inspiration, Elizabeth?"

"Sometimes," she nodded.

"I don't quite follow you," Lawrence said. No one offered to enlighten him, so he changed the subject, and asked Mr. Hengist how he thought Elizabeth was looking.

"Buxom," Mr. Hengist replied promptly, and there was an outcry. When it had subsided, he said, "All right, I retract. Is Stephen anywhere in the offing, or are you alone, child?"

"I'm alone. I've come up to see Auntie and Father, and to do some shopping. I—just thought I'd leave Stephen behind." Her dimples peeped out.

"Will you have time for anything else?" Mr. Hengist asked.

"It depends on what it is," she answered.

"Come and dine with me and go to a theatre afterwards."

"I'd love to. When, please!"

"When you like. What about Saturday?"

"I will. Thank you very much."

She went to tea with Mrs. Ramsay, the next day, and was welcomed with open arms. Cynthia came in the middle of tea, and although she was not very cordial she did not say anything unkind, nor did she sneer to her mother when Elizabeth had gone.

"Cynny, she's blossomed forth."

"Urn! Well?"

"Darling, I'm feeling incurably sentimental. She's in love with Stephen."

Cynthia threw the end of her cigarette into the fire.

"Is she really? Why has she left him at the Halt then?"

"I think she's flirting with him," smiled Mrs. Ramsay. "Trying to make him come part of the way to meet her."

"What if he doesn't? He may not understand."

"Then," said Mrs. Ramsay, "I believe she'll go all the way. Probably in a rush."

"Not she."

"She will, Cyn, she will. I think I want to cry. I'm— I'm thinking of the awful strained look in Stephen's eyes."

Cynthia put out her hand quickly, and laid it over one of Mrs. Ramsay's.

"If what you say is true, mater; it'll go."

"Well, young lady," said Mr. Hengist, "you're very gay. How's Elizabeth-Anne?"

"Dead," said Elizabeth, sparkling. "The funeral took place last month."

"Oh? Why then, exactly?"

Elizabeth looked at him across the table for one fleeting instant.

"She died, you see, when I discovered that I was in love with my husband."

"I thought as much," Mr. Hengist said placidly. "Pardon my rudeness, but does Stephen know?"

She shook her head.

"He—he—it's rather difficult to make him understand."

"I don't think I'm qualified to give advice," said Mr. Hengist.

"Oh, no! This is my own little game. I just thought you'd like to know. I found it all out in a flash, and— everything changed, as you said it would. And I—want to thank you—for all that you've done for me—and to tell you—"

"Beyond giving you a typewriter—" began Mr. Hengist more gruffly than ever.

"And the good advice. Oh, you know, Mr. Hengist! I was ungrateful and stupid at the time. I'm awfully grateful now. You did me more good than anybody."

"That'll do!" Mr. Hengist said loudly. "That'll _do_, Elizabeth!"

Chapter Thirty-Three

Stephen was on the station-platform, eagerly scanning each carriage as it passed him. He had sprung forward before Elizabeth could open the door, and had swung it open for her.

"Oh—'Lisbeth!"

She gave him her hands; he thought she looked radiant, and there was that in her smile which made the blood race madly through his veins. They walked down the platform together. Elizabeth's arm was in his; she squeezed it slightly, and said,

"Are you glad I'm back, Stephen?"

"That's—a silly question," he said. "You've enjoyed yourself?"

"Yes. Fairly. I—missed you rather." She was overcome with shyness. "And—and everything," she added hurriedly.

They got into the waiting car.

"Yes —exactly," Stephen said. "Did you see the Mater?"

"I did."

He looked down.

"More secrets?"

"Not—so very secret," she said. She snuggled down in the car, and looked with contented eyes about her: at the tender green of spring, the grey shadows cast by overhanging trees, and the winding road ahead, dusty, and mottled with the sunlight filtering through the leaves above. "It's good to be home again," she said.

"It's good to hear you—call it home," he answered. "To me it hasn't been home—all the week."

Her head touched his sleeve, caressingly. Then her voice changed.

"My dear, you're wearing the coat I put aside to give to the gardener."

He lifted one hand from the wheel, and looked sheepishly down at the rough tweed.

"Am I?" he said.

"You know you are. It's a horrible old coat, Stephen."

"Well, but I like it. We can't both of us wear new clothes on the same day."

She tilted her head.

"You like it?"

He did not look at the hat, but at her.

"Rather! You look—" He broke off and put the car along faster.

"What do I look, Stephen?"

"Beautiful," he said curtly.

She resisted the temptation to lay her cheek against his shoulder. She thought, He makes it very difficult. He won't help me, not one atom.

"The book, Stephen? How is it?"

"I've done very little more," he confessed. "I—I missed your presence in the room." He sighed. "I'm a discontented dog, Elizabeth."

She was silent, waiting.

"The roses are coming on well, aren't they?" Stephen said.

The car slowed down and stopped before the porch.

"Very," Elizabeth said dismally. "Oh, Hector, you dear thing, don't lick my nose!"

She went up to her room and was a long time over her unpacking. When she came down for tea she had changed her frock to one of lilac silk which she knew became her better than any other she possessed. Stephen's eyes lit up when he saw her, but all he said was, "Tea's ready, Lisbeth."

She sat down on the sofa; he sank on to his usual footstool and remarked that she was doing her hair a different way.

"Do you like it?" she asked.

"Very much. It suits you. How were your people?"

"Father had a bit of a. cold, but otherwise they were all right. I saw Mr. Hengist once or twice. He took me to see 'The Butterfly.'"

"Oh, was it any good?"

"Y-es, I think it was a clever play. I never like the ultra-modern stuff, you know. Oh, Sarah's engaged to be married!"

"No, really? Do we know the man?"

"No. I've only seen his photograph. Not fearfully prepossessing. Rather pudgy-faced."

"Perhaps he has a good heart," Stephen grinned. "By the way, I had a letter from Caryll yesterday. He asked me to remember him very particularly to you, and to say that he looked forward to seeing you again as soon as possible."

Elizabeth's face lit up.

"Oh, did he say that? How awfully nice of him!"

Stephen set his cup down.

"I scent an intrigue. Out with it!"

Pain came into her eyes.

"Don't, Stephen! Not—not even in fun. I—I can't bear it."

He was on his knees beside her in an instant, an arm protectively about her waist.

"My darling, I never meant to hurt you! I'm awfully sorry, 'Lisbeth. Of course I didn't think there was anything in it."

She let her weight rest against his arm; even she inclined her body slightly towards him. He let her go, and went back to his seat. For a time she could not speak for very disappointment, but presently she said,

"You see, I met Mr. Cary one day when—when I was with Charles. He—he said one or two things to me that— made me feel—ashamed and—very small."

"Oh, did he? D'you mind repeating just what he said?" Stephen demanded grimly.

"Dear, I can't remember. He was most polite, but— cold. It wasn't what he said that made me ashamed. It was his manner. Can I ask him down here some day?"

"I don't know. Not if he was anything approaching rude to you."

"He wasn't. Don't be so silly, Stephen. I shouldn't want to ask him if he had been rude. You've got a hole in your sock."

"I don't mind. Oh, Elizabeth, I . . ."

"Yes?" she said softly.

"Nothing. Did Mater send any messages?"

"Crowds. You aren't to overwork, you're not to let me overwork, you mustn't use the word 'jejune' in your books more than twice, and—"

"Do I run the word to death?" he asked quickly.

"I haven't noticed it. Mater says it makes her feel tired."

On those lines went the conversation; Elizabeth ached to feel Stephen's arms about her, yet could not summon up the courage to tell him. In this new pain, filled with this devastating want; she realized his feelings during the past year. She could not in silence bear her pain for long; he would bear his until of her own free will she gave herself to him. Her love for him was growing bigger and still stronger, but there was her instinct, and the training of a life-time to be overcome before she could bring herself to say to him, Take me; I am yours. If he would break the oath he had sworn to her, never to speak of love until she asked him, how gladly would she go to him. It seemed that he could not understand her new attitude, and would not follow the lead she gave him. He thought, perhaps, that she meant nothing by her little inviting actions. When she tilted her face upwards, standing close, very close, to him, he would not take the offered kiss. Did he think that she offered it out of friendship or compassion? He should be able to read all that was in her mind, and to see that in her glance was not friendship, but love. Yet this obtuseness, this obstinacy, even while it disappointed her, made her love him the more, tenderly and in pity for his blindness. Mrs. Gabriel had said that men didn't understand. Elizabeth saw now that when you loved,

276

this lack of perception no longer made you angry, but awoke all the mother that was in you, and made you feel how infinitely wiser you were, even though your husband was more clever than you.

In a thousand little ways she wooed him, audacious and shy, terrified lest he should see at last, miserable when he did not. When he called her to come and read some paragraph of his book, she would rest her hand on his shoulder, and bend over him so that her hair brushed his cheek and her breast touched his arm. She could feel the stiffening of his muscles, sometimes hear a quick intake of breath. All her instincts urged flight, but she stayed, hoping. His level voice cast down her hopes every time; she was back at the beginning again, bruised and sad, but still indomitable.

It did more to kill the prude in her than all else through which she had passed. With a tiny smile she reflected that she was not behaving like a "nice" girl at all, but like a minx. Then she thought, I'm not a girl, but a wife. Anything that I do with Stephen is right. Even when I try to vamp him. That made her laugh, for there was nothing of the vamp in her, and she knew it.

Once Stephen grasped her shoulders and said stormily,

"You drive me mad! What is this queer elusive air of yours?"

She shivered, and was still under his hands. The grip loosened.

"Sorry, 'Lisbeth. Forgetting myself."

She tried to say the words that were in her heart. They would not be spoken; she could only run from the room, furious with herself, and with him.

The book was nearing its end. When it is finished, Elizabeth thought, I will tell him.

But she hoped that he would see before that. Curled on the sofa in the evening, a rose-shaded light behind her, she watched Stephen at work, and could almost find it in her to be jealous of the woman in his book who occupied his thoughts. Time wore on, and in the hall the old grandfather clock struck midnight, but she would not go up to bed. Stephen would send her there if he remembered her presence, but he was absorbed in his writing; he had forgotten time and her.

Instead of the Thorn

An hour later he pushed the work away and stretched mightily, yawning. He rose, and saw Elizabeth, fast asleep among the silken cushions, her hair a little ruffled, and one hand lying palm upwards upon her lap. He stood very still, looking down upon her, drinking in her beauty till his hands clenched hard at his sides, and his mouth went awry at the pain of it.

Gently he slipped his arms under her; she stirred but did not awake; her cheek lay now against his shoulder, rosy in sleep; she was in his arms, yielding and sweet.

He carried her out into the beamed hall, where shadows lay, mysterious and soft, and up the shallow stairs to the floor above. He would not let himself look into her face, but set his teeth against the leaping flame within him, and went on.

On the bend of the stair she sighed, and opened drowsy eyes. He stopped and spoke quietly to her.

"It's all right, 'Lisbeth. I'm carrying you up to bed, you naughty babe."

But she had not been startled, or afraid; he expected a struggle, perhaps shrinking. Sleepily she said,

"Thank you, Stephen! How comfy!"

He thought she was only half awake, which accounted for this trust. He would not take advantage of her unconscious pliancy. Swiftly he went on.

Elizabeth nestled a little closer, looking up into his set face. Her hand tucked itself into his coat.

"Aren't I very heavy?" she murmured.

"No."

He crossed the landing and put her down, just inside her room.

"Good night, my darling," he said huskily, and went quickly out.

She was left standing by her bed, gazing blankly at the shut door. Like a child she rubbed her eyes, and her mouth drooped.

The stairs creaked; Stephen had gone down again. Listlessly she began to undress, and because she was tired and wanted his arms about her still, one or two big tears welled over her eyelids and rolled unheeded down her cheeks.

She thought, If only he would come back! I shouldn't be frightened; it's when he isn't here that I'm frightened.

Presently she heard him run up the stairs and go into his dressing-room. She stood by her dressing-table, fidgeting with the handle of her brush, blinded by tears. Then, obeying an impulse which would not be gainsaid, she stumbled to the door between their rooms, and knocked on it.

"Come in!" Stephen's voice was surprised.

She managed to open the door, and stood drooping upon the threshold. Stephen was in his shirt-sleeves, staring at her. He saw the tears, and was at her side in an instant.

"My darling!" Consternation sounded in his voice, and throbbing anxiety. "'Lisbeth, what is it?"

Words crowded in her throat, but would not be said; another big tear rolled down her cheek, and a little, lonely sob came.

Stephen drew her gently into the room, his arm comfortingly about her.

"Sweetheart, what is it? Why are you crying? I—I can't bear to see you— Have I done something to upset you? Tell me, dearest! Please tell me!"

Into his shoulder she said, between sobs,

"I've—t-tried to—sh-show you—but you w-won't see!"

"Tried to show me what, precious? You poor little thing, what is it?"

She wanted him to see for himself. She sank closer to him and buried her face in his shirt. He stiffened, and said hoarsely,

"'Lisbeth—I can't— You'd better go— I won't answer for myself if you—"

"I don't want—to go."

Almost roughly he pushed her from him, and held her so, at arm's length.

"Elizabeth, what are you saying? I'm—I can't bear much more. What is it that you want?"

So she would have to say it after all; it was a tiresome thing, his honour.

"I—want—you," she whispered.

The hands fell from her shoulders; Stephen made her look full into his eyes.

"Do you know what you've said?" he asked, unnaturally calm. "Do you—mean it—or is it just—"

Her eyes were dark, and bright with tears; she put up her little hands and grasped his shirt. Almost she shook him.

"Oh, can't you see, can't you see?" she cried, quivering. "Haven't I—shown you, my dear? I w-want you so much that it's tearing me in two! I want you! Won't you —*take* me?"

His arms were tight about her at last, crushing her against himself, his lips were on her hair, for her face was hidden again. She clung to him, laughing and crying, and heard his voice above her, broken and strange.

"Oh, my darling, my darling, my darling!"

Her hands went up to his neck; she turned her face upward, and he saw her lips expectant.

"I want—another honeymoon," she said softly. "I— love—you." She pulled his head down, and his kisses fell on her eager lips.

www.ingramcontent.com/pod-product-compliance
Lightning Source LLC
Chambersburg PA
CBHW021516240626
47154CB00002B/657